ONCE THERE WAS A WAY

A BREAKPOINT NOVEL

BRYCE ZABEL

DIVERSIONBOOKS

Also by Bryce Zabel

Surrounded by Enemies: What if Kennedy Survived Dallas?

*A.D. After Disclosure: When the Government Finally
Reveals the Truth About Alien Contact* (with Richard Dolan)

Diversion Books
A Division of Diversion Publishing Corp.
443 Park Avenue South, Suite 1008
New York, New York 10016
www.DiversionBooks.com

For more information, email info@diversionbooks.com

First Diversion Books edition December 2017.
Paperback ISBN: 978-1-68230-321-4
eBook ISBN: 978-1-68230-320-7

LSIDB/1710

As always, for Jackie, with all my loving.

INTRODUCTION

Imagine an alternative reality—it's easy if you try.

Back in June 10, 1976, I was a brand-new reporter at KZEL-FM, a counter-culture radio station in Eugene, Oregon. For the first time, Paul McCartney was touring America with his new band, Wings, when my program director came to what we called the "News Cave" to see me. "I just got a phone call," he said. "If it's going to happen, it's going to happen tonight."

"It" was the much-discussed, always out-of-reach Beatles reunion. I was given a show ticket, told to get in my 1965 Ford Mustang and start driving immediately to Seattle, about six hours away.

The entire ride up I could feel the very atoms of my being vibrating with anticipation to see John, Paul, George, and Ringo back on stage as the Beatles. As it turned out, the Beatles didn't get back together that night up at the Seattle Kingdome when sixty-seven thousand fans showed up, eclipsing the live audience record of the Fab Four. Instead, McCartney gave his audience a riveting run-through of Wings music but played less than a half dozen Beatles songs late in the show. I had seen a Beatle play live, and it was amazing beyond belief, yet there was still disappointment on the way out to the parking lot. Such is the power of the Beatles and the desire of fans to see them together.

Half a lifetime later, this attraction remains the greatest "What if?" in rock music history, even though Lennon's murder and Harrison's cancer and decades of time have removed any possibility at all of it ever happening. Still, the mind and the heart want what they want.

What if John Lennon, Paul McCartney, George Harrison, and Richard Starkey had actually worked it out at the end of the 1960s and kept making music as the Beatles for a few more years? Or longer? Or just kept going like their contemporaries, the Rolling Stones?

Once There Was a Way is the answer. Or at least one answer. You may say I'm a dreamer, but I'm not the only one.

Bryce Zabel
December 5, 2017
Los Angeles

"No one's more surprised than I am that the Beatles made it. Maybe Yoko."

—John Lennon

"Play, quit, repeat. That's been the secret."

—Paul McCartney

"Spiritual wisdom means not wasting the gifts of the Universe, even if it's the three of them."

—George Harrison

"We all quit. We just never all quit for good at the same time."

—Ringo Starr

From interviews with Rockstar *editor, Booth Hill.*

FROM THE EDITOR OF
ROCKSTAR MAGAZINE

Americans of a certain age still remember vividly how inevitable it once was that the world's greatest rock group would break up. The four youthful Moptops who seemed like best friends had become four angry men who acted like mortal enemies. From 1968 to 1971, virtually everyone knew the Beatles would be finished sooner than later.

And yet they were not. Somehow history broke in another direction. As a consequence, John Lennon, Paul McCartney, George Harrison, and Richard Starkey aged in place on performance stages and recording studios, playing a part in our lives from the moment they came to America in 1964, over fifty years ago.

From 1968 through 1975, the years of maximum danger, the Beatles, always on the edge of dissolution, still continued to produce a creative output of outrageously honest poetry, tuneful rock operas, and passionate tributes to a higher power. They took long vacations from each other, yes, but still found their way back home time and again.

If the Beatles had disbanded in 1970, they would still be fiercely remembered today, and they might even be far more mythic and legendary. By staying together through thick and thin, they convinced us that they would always be there for us. While we never took them for granted, we began to see them as part of our current musical landscape. Not a bad thing.

To source our facts, *Rockstar* has drawn from its own archives a great deal, and, in particular, we have revisited virtually all of the classic sit-down interviews our magazine has conducted with the Beatles over the course of the band's years together. We also put three of our youngest and most expressive journalists on the job—Coleman Birdwell, LeAnne Falby, and Emmer Hoffman— and told them to talk to everyone again. None of this trio was even alive when the Beatles nearly broke up in 1969. They have spent the better part of a year talking to spouses, children, friends, collaborators, enemies, competitors, and fans of the Beatles, and they have merged it into a fresh perspective.

The truth that they have reported here is universal. The Beatles were not destined to break apart or stay together. They made a choice to look beyond the slights, the disagreements, and their individual desires. They chose to remain the Beatles. This is how they did it.

Booth Hill
Editor, *Rockstar*

CHAPTER ONE

A DOLL'S HOUSE (1968)

THEY BLEW HIS MIND OUT IN A BAR

In May 1968, Paul McCartney and John Lennon traveled together to New York City to tell the world that Apple Corps Ltd. was the new company behind the Beatles. The *New York Post* headline proclaimed "Beatles Pitch Apple in the Big Apple."

McCartney and Lennon labored through multiple press briefings and interviews to explain why they had done it. McCartney took the position that it was a natural extension of the brand, a way to control their own destinies. "The Beatles are more than records," he explained. "We're a bit of everything these days, aren't we? We have to watch out for ourselves."

The reality was that Apple had been conceived as a tax dodge shortly after the death of their manager, Brian Epstein, in the late summer of 1967. Truly on their own then, the Beatles had received sobering news that over £4MM would need to be paid in taxes by the Beatles unless the money was used for business purposes. It was simple survival math since corporate tax rates were far lower than those for individuals. Under the new arrangement worked out by lawyers and accountants, each Beatle would own 5 percent of a company known as "Beatles and Co." and Apple—owned collectively by all four Beatles—would own the other 80 percent.

This line of reasoning played out as far too mercenary and boring for John Lennon, who chose to cast the entire decision as primarily a creative one. "It's so people who want to make a record or a film, you know, don't have to go on their knees in an office, begging for a break. They can just come to us and sit in one of our chairs if they want."

There was pushback everywhere to this idea that, inspired by capitalism, Apple could be embraced by its owners as a counter-culture answer to capitalism, opening its doors and its cash reserves to strangers while almost simultaneously trying to extend its brand to everything from clothing to technology. It was clearly a risky affair, given that the primary talent of the Beatles, up to that point, was making music.

At a St. Regis Hotel press conference, American journalists seemed as skeptical as their English brethren that these drug-taking leftist musicians could manage a real-world business. Worse than the skepticism, however, was the palpable lack of interest. Most reporters seemed uninterested in the new venture but fixated on the idea that the behavior and the music of the Beatles were alienating them from their fans.

Only a few days into the New York visit, after some back-and-forth with the press, both Lennon and McCartney found their moods darkening. Playing businessmen was supposed to be fun. Otherwise, what was the point?

On Tuesday, May 14, the two Beatles were scheduled to appear on *The Tonight Show Starring Johnny Carson*, where eleven million viewers could hear their pitch. When Apple publicist Derek Taylor broke the news to them on Monday that Johnny was unavailable the next night and that they would be appearing with substitute host and former baseball player Joe Garagiola, John had had enough.

"Fuck that," he said. "Let's just go home."

With twenty-four hours' notice, the celebrated team of Lennon and McCartney sent their regrets to the bookers of *The Tonight Show*. A miserable staffer, Craig Tennis, was sent to the hotel where John and Paul were staying to plead for them to reconsider. According to Tennis, Mister Carson was performing in Gaithersburg, Maryland, outside of Washington, D.C. It was something that was booked long before they ever knew that John and Paul were coming to America. Tennis explained that his boss "feels strongly that you need to be at the studio as was negotiated."

John Lennon gave Tennis the middle finger. "Negotiate this."

Paul, ever the perfect host, sent the staffer away with this message: "You just tell them back at the show that we always wanted to meet Johnny, you know. King of Late Night, they say he is, don't they? So maybe next time we can do it. No hard feelings."

Johnny Carson, not a fan of guests dictating terms to him or his show, still knew history when it called, and while he had made his peace with Garagiola getting this big one, he would be damned if he was going to lose two Beatles as guests at the height of their popularity. Carson knew this was a "get" that would be good for both him and his show and might introduce him to a younger audience. He sent back the flustered Tennis with only one condition: Carson would come back if Lennon and McCartney agreed to do the entire show and promised to sing at least one song.

Fortunately for the NBC-TV network, Carson's stipulation gave the two Beatles a chance to get away from the irritating interviews with stodgy reporters and change the subject a bit. They had shown their dominance again the past November with a number one single featuring McCartney's "Hello, Goodbye" on the A-side and Lennon's "I Am the Walrus" on the B-side. John had never been happy with that, thinking that his song was the superior choice. Paul, having won that battle when producer George Martin sided with him, saw a chance to throw a peace offering to his partner.

"Let's do it, John. You sing 'Walrus' and we'll blow his mind."

As a result, on that Tuesday, Johnny Carson canceled a gig at the last minute, returning to New York City. And John Lennon and Paul McCartney got in a limo, smoked a joint, and cruised over to Rockefeller Center in Midtown Manhattan, where *The Tonight Show* was broadcast from NBC Studio 6B.

Although the show felt live, it was actually taped hours earlier than it aired, at 7 p.m. Mayor John V. Lindsay, a Republican, and half his staff were there. Simon and Garfunkel tried to attend, but imposters had taken their tickets and they were turned away at the door at the last minute. The two Beatles had to be smuggled in through an underground tunnel to avoid a possible public incident.

The show began with Carson asking a block of getting-to-know-you questions focused on why rock stars adored by millions of available women would want to start balancing spreadsheets. Lennon and McCartney described the state of Apple to Carson before the commercial break. Soon Carson and the two Beatles were reminiscing about their 1964 arrival at Kennedy airport and the appearance on *The Ed Sullivan Show*. Lennon was as clever as his reputation made him out to be and McCartney was cheeky enough that every comment seemed to come with a wink. Carson seemed engaged and informed. McMahon chortled at everyone's jokes.

It was good television, and the show was only half over.

What Johnny Carson didn't know was how the two men sitting side by side on his couch were at a crossroads in their friendship. They were soldiering on with this trip to America, but back home they had been drifting apart for over a year or more. Carson saw them as close friends and pressed them for the secret of their friendship. He pointed out that he and Ed McMahon socialized together outside the show all the time. They'd had coffee just last week.

"Oh, we're great friends like that, we are," assured Paul.

Lennon did not miss a beat. "Although coffee's not exactly our drug of choice."

The audience held its breath to see how this confession from the long-haired Lennon would play with the straight-arrow Carson. The host timed it perfectly. "Of course not," he deadpanned. "Coming from England, you probably favor a strong cup of tea."

Another break, and then the magic came. Johnny asked them to play a song. Both Paul and John knew what a big deal it was. If they performed, it would be the first time they'd played before an audience of any kind whatsoever since they ceased touring in 1966.

"Well, you see, Johnny," Paul deflected, as if it hadn't already been discussed and decided, "it seems we've forgotten our guitars."

Doc Severinsen fixed that with a couple of instruments the band had procured in anticipation of the two Beatles playing on the show. In return, John reached behind the couch and presented Johnny with a tambourine. "We're not used to playing by ourselves. It's better when we have a quartet, you know?" He then turned to Ed. "Just sing along with the words that you know."

John began to pick out the opening chords to "I Am the Walrus."

"What does that mean," asked Johnny. "Why are you the Walrus?"

"We're all the Walrus," said John. "Maybe the Walrus was Paul."

"Johnny could be the Walrus," suggested Paul helpfully.

"No, no," the host said, waving them off. "The tambourine is all I can handle."

"It's just a word," John said, continuing to play. "It could be an Apple. We rather fancy that word now."

With that, John, Paul, Johnny, and Ed launched into a shockingly good but stripped-down version of "I Am the Walrus," complete with accompaniment from *The Tonight Show* band. Only this version banished the word "Walrus" in favor of "I Am the Apple."

As it ended, the audience gave the performance a standing ovation. Pumped up by the reception, it was John who suggested spontaneously that they do another. "Let's do the A-side," he said to Paul. "I wrote down your words, just in case." John produced a folded piece of paper with the lyrics written in his distinctive handwriting. "Your words" is how he had phrased it, not "our words." It was one of the first public acknowledgments that the unity implied by the Lennon-McCartney brand was part spin. The reality was clearly different.

John and Paul then delighted *The Tonight Show* audience with an acoustic version of "Hello, Goodbye" that they managed to turn into a Lennon-McCartney song instead of a McCartney solo.

PAUL: *"You say yes…"*

JOHN: *"I say no…"*

PAUL: *"You say stop…"*

JOHN: *"And I say go, go, go…"*

PAUL/JOHN: *"Oh, no… You say goodbye and I say hello…"*

As the broadcast came to an end, Johnny asked John and Paul if they were working on a new album. Not yet, they said, but both talked about all the new material they'd written while away in India. Ed McMahon wanted to know what they would call it.

"Well, we might call it *A Doll's House*, couldn't we? Or anything else that we might imagine," said Lennon. "Because it'd still be a Beatles album no matter what we call it." It was the same argument he made for changing "Walrus" to "Apple" in the song lyrics. Names were just labels and labels were not reality.

After the show, at Carson's suggestion, Carson, McMahon, Lennon, and McCartney went to *The Tonight Show* host's favorite watering hole, Danny's Hideaway. There, Carson and McMahon introduced the two Beatles to their favorite drinks—vodka sours and J&B scotch and water.

Years later, Ed McMahon would still describe the night as "fraught with danger." By that, Carson's sidekick meant that it soon became obvious to him that the famed Lennon and McCartney partnership showed distinct signs of having run its course. "These two brilliant young men had been placed under such pressure in extreme circumstances over the past five years that they were about to explode," he said. "They needed to push back against something and, particularly for John, that was Paul."

McMahon saw his own partner, Johnny Carson, wink at him before he turned to Lennon and McCartney and raised the first of several glasses. "A toast," said Carson, "to showing up."

Showing up, Carson and McMahon explained to Lennon and McCartney, meant that friends turned up for friends even when it was not convenient or fun or even appreciated. That's what Johnny and Ed had done for each other over the years. They joked that with all the marriages they had each been through, showing up to each other's respective weddings was the ultimate test of their commitment to their friendship.

What started out as an arduous return to New York for Lennon and McCartney had turned into a blast. McCartney never tired of talking about the night, always making himself the audience, and not the star, of the experience. The sixty-eight-year-old did so again for the 2010 edition of *Rockstar*:

> [Paul] "It was magic times magic. The two Johns—John and Johnny—just hit it off, and Ed and I were the two Macks—McCartney and McMahon. Ed seemed like he'd always been happy being Johnny's number two, but he could see that would never do for me. He told me to show up for myself but to also show up for John and that John would always act like it pissed him off, and that I should ignore all this and show up anyway."

Because of the delay in the show's time, John, Paul, Johnny, and Ed were all safely at their table in Danny's Hideaway when *The Tonight Show* aired. These two great partnerships watched the episode in the bar, with staff and other customers buzzing at the outer fringes of the action.

Over the evening, the men all signed autographs, took photos with Danny for the Hideaway Wall of Fame, and generally caroused like they were old friends. "We blew his mind out in a bar," quipped Lennon to Apple's new managing director Neil Aspinall the very next day. The two Johns and the two Macks stayed out until 2:30 a.m.

As the show aired in different time zones across the country, the reviews came to Johnny from a special phone that Danny had installed for his regular celebrity guests. Everyone who saw the show loved it. What the seventy minutes (the broadcast minus commercials) showed was John and Paul having a great time with Johnny and Ed. It was that rare piece of television—an authentic party in progress, unstilted and impromptu, full of high spirits and camaraderie.

One can only imagine how different the atmosphere might

have been had John Lennon and Paul McCartney spent their air time with Joe Garagiola and his scheduled guest that night, Tallulah Bankhead. Rather than being a positive mood lifter in the lives of Lennon and McCartney, the experience could have been remembered as the ultimate downer.

NBC had a policy of recycling the videotapes of their shows, and it is possible that this convergence of celebrities might have been lost to history. Carson writer Dick Cavett, however, realized immediately that this show was different and afterward made certain that the tape was put on a special shelf and saved. The Sunday after the Beatles returned to England, NBC aired the episode in primetime as an edited one-hour special, replacing a repeat of *The High Chaparral*. It won the time slot against *Mission: Impossible* on CBS and *The Sunday Night Movie* on ABC. The edited version did not include John's comment about their drug use.

The success of the Lennon and McCartney appearance made it clear that Apple Corps, no matter how idealistically conceived, needed a product to sell. Not that there was anything wrong with other musicians being signed, like Jackie Lomax or Mary Hopkin, but the product the world was interested in was the Beatles.

As the American audience watched John and Paul pitch the Apple story, the bottom line seemed to be that the Beatles were now going to use their influence and wealth to help young people reach their artistic dreams without the usual limitations to artistic freedom that they, themselves, had labored under.

That night on NBC television, the Beatles laid down their marker for the world. They were putting their own money on a dream to end artistic suppression and tyranny. And if straights from another generation did not dig it, then so be it. They were not asking for anyone's permission anyway.

"You sound like a couple of dreamers," said Carson as he thanked them for a great show.

"We're not the only ones," replied Lennon and then made a face to the audience.

THE CALL OF THE SHIRE

Before their trip to New York, the Beatles had done something that seemed oddly dangerous given their sudden founding of Apple Corps. They ran away and tried to forget about it.

In February, all four of the musicians and their respective wives and girlfriends packed their bags and left for Rishikesh, a place in northern India that overlooked the Ganges at the foothills of the Himalayas. They went to attend an advanced Transcendental Meditation training session at the ashram of Maharishi Mahesh Yogi, whom the Beatles had first met the year before at a retreat in Wales, only to have Brian Epstein's death cut short their introduction.

Although this more extensive retreat was George Harrison's idea, it seemed to make sense for everyone else in a cosmic 1960s search-for-enlightenment way. Off they went over halfway around the world with so much to consider and sort out amongst them-selves—only to spend their days trying to clear their minds and let their thoughts float upstream.

Destined to be one of the most prolific periods in the creative history of the Beatles, the majority of the songs they composed on the retreat appeared on the *A Doll's House* album. Two appeared on the *Everest* album, and others continued to be considered for other albums for years to come. Often, at night, John, Paul, George, and now even Ringo sat outside under the stars working on new compositions while their significant others gathered together in one of their rooms, often talking about the challenge of being a life partner to a Beatle. None of the women present, however, would make the final cut. Every single partner who took the trip with their Beatle—Cynthia Lennon, Jane Asher, Pattie Boyd, and Maureen Starkey—would be eventually replaced.

No one was facing that reality as squarely as Cynthia Lennon. Her husband had been continuing his dalliance with the highly educated alternative artist Yoko Ono, who had become a regular fixture in the Beatles universe. Even while in Rishikesh, Lennon would walk down to the local post office every morning to see if he had received a telegram from Ono. On almost every day, she had sent him something.

John and Cynthia had been set up at the ashram with a private room where they could share a four-poster bed. This lasted only two weeks before John asked to sleep in a separate room, noting that he could only meditate when he was alone.

It was during these meditative sessions, however, that John Lennon's agile and active mind, fueled by over two years of heavy psychoactive drugs, simply would not shut itself off. While Lennon was not opposed to ignoring group issues in the hopes that they would go away or meditating like George Harrison and the Maharishi expected him to, songs would come to him often, and he would try to either fight them off or postpone them, only to surrender and write them down, or pick up his guitar and let them form under his fingers. This was, he told himself, his form of meditation, and anyone who thought it made him a shortsighted, narrow-minded hypocrite could just go to hell.

From a small but growing corner of Lennon's mind came the insistent reminder that Brian Epstein had gotten the Beatles to sign a three-picture deal with United Artists back in 1964, and they had delivered only two: *A Hard Day's Night* and *Help!* The upcoming animated *Yellow Submarine* had been one of Epstein's last negotiations on their behalf, but it existed in a netherworld with lawyers for both UA and Apple arguing whether it counted or not. Given that they had appeared in only one scene in the animated film, the band would likely need to go before camera in a whole movie to satisfy the letter of the legal obligation.

Their 1967 BBC television film special *Magical Mystery Tour* did not count either, as it was neither a full-length film nor a United Artists project. Even worse, it was a bomb in a business that demands hits above all else, having debuted to nearly universal critical derision in the English press. The project had been all Paul McCartney's doing from the get-go, and while Lennon enjoyed watching what he saw as his overreaching partner stub his toe, it also meant that the group to which they both belonged needed a hit more than ever. Maybe even a hit with a more conventional foundation—like a screenplay and a professional director.

It was at this moment that John Lennon's mind turned to the Shire.

Packing at the last minute back in London, John had tossed well-worn childhood copies of both *The Hobbit* and *The Lord of the Rings* into his travel belongings. He had never entirely gotten them out of his mind, and now United Artists, the company releasing *Yellow Submarine*, had put them front and center again.

At that very moment, UA producers Sam Gelfman and Gabe Katza were in the second year of negotiations with author J.R.R. Tolkien to obtain the rights to *The Lord of the Rings*. First published in 1954, John had read a borrowed copy of the book when he was fourteen and had told the friend who had loaned him the paperback that he had lost it. It was that very copy that made the journey from England to India.

Executives at United Artists had made approaches to the Beatles about whether or not they might be interested should the film company successfully conclude the negotiations to option the property. The blend of fantasy, myth, and conflict had struck a chord in the '50s among everyone from scholars to school kids, and, now in the late '60s, the fans included a whole new counter-culture audience. The head of Apple Films, Denis O'Dell, also felt that this arrangement was the perfect alignment between the Beatles and the kind of material that would appeal to their fans.

John had responded positively and fast to the idea. The trick, said the executives, was that Tolkien was no Beatles fan, owing to a loud garage band in the cul-de-sac where he lived on Oxford's Sandfield Road. He complained about "young men who are evidently aiming to turn themselves into a Beatle Group." As for their practice sessions, Tolkien felt "the noise is indescribable."

Knowing the author's bias, all concluded that the matter would have to be hush-hush until UA had the rights locked up and things could move ahead in a more open fashion. The producers and the studio pushed the project into the fast lane, expediting a fifty-page contract that gave Tolkien £100,000 for his rights (or a mere 1/40th of the tax burden that caused the Beatles to form Apple).

Now sitting in the ashram, John Lennon meditated about how *The Lord of the Rings* could become a dream project that would elevate the group from Paul McCartney's pitiable *Magical Mystery Tour*. In John's vision, he would play Gollum, the Hobbit who had been corrupted by the ring and destined to exist in a netherworld of ugliness. He saw Paul taking on the primary character of the plucky and optimistic Frodo, with Ringo playing his warmhearted sidekick, Samwise Gamgee. George, the spirit warrior of the Beatles, would get the same respect in the film, playing the wizard Gandalf.

In other words, each Beatle would play the character in the book with which they (and their fans) were most likely to identify. The fact that the plot revolved around a ring, as did their second film, *Help!*, was ignored.

• • •

Rishikesh, India, did not convey its blessings on all the Beatles equally. Ringo Starr and his wife, Maureen, left after two weeks, and Paul McCartney and his new fiancée Jane Asher left two weeks after that. They were eventually followed several weeks later by John and Cynthia Lennon, along with George Harrison and his wife Pattie Boyd, after it was suspected that the Maharishi had been hitting on female guests, including actress Mia Farrow, for reasons more carnal than what he preached.

When they had all returned from India, they discovered that in their absence, the English press had been hurling torrents of abuse at them for their dalliance with the Maharishi. They had become front-page fodder, and not in a good way.

As if to illustrate that the Beatles umbrella could provide shade to a wide diversity of material, EMI released the last Beatles single ever to debut under that label (with Paul's roots-rocker "Lady

Madonna" on the A-side and George's spiritually ascendant "The Inner Light" on the B-side) immediately upon the group's return to England.

Apple press officer Derek Taylor had endured the past months with a certain British stoicism, but even that had its limits. Harrison's B-side convinced all the skeptics that they were correct—the Beatles were losing their bearings. Everything Taylor knew about journalism and public relations assured him of one thing: the Beatles simply had to change the subject. He reached out to contacts at MGM and convinced them to let John, Paul, George, and Ringo become the highest profile party crashers in film history.

In late March, Taylor wrote a desperate telegram to all the Beatles who remained in India and asked them to please come home immediately. He wanted them to see a movie.

Because of that outreach, on April 2, the Beatles attended the film premiere of Stanley Kubrick's long-awaited *2001: A Space Odyssey*. This allowed them to be seen not so much in the clutches of a high-pitched foreigner, the Maharishi, but walking a red carpet in London, in their finest mod garb, with beautiful women on their arms.

Taylor was correct in his assessment of the situation. The next day, all the papers, especially the tabloid press, had images of the Beatles and accompanying stories that seemed to suggest that their fling with the Indian guru was as much a publicity stunt as anything. Clearly, as seen in these pictures, the Boys of Britain had come home. Even John Lennon arrived with his wife Cynthia, making this the last public appearance they would ever make together, given his new romance with Ono.

That night, however, the most affecting images on the screen were those from the film itself. John couldn't believe his eyes. "How does a man make a movie like that without taking acid?" he asked more than once at the after-party.

Paul, George, and Ringo, inspired by the mind-blowing nature of the film and its psychedelic ending, began to agree with

John that a Kubrick-Beatles collaboration over *The Lord of the Rings* could be just what they needed to recover from the disastrous *Magical Mystery Tour.*

"Ah, well, we just got confused with our little film," said Paul, trying to be diplomatic and funny as always. "Maybe the audience is supposed to be stoned and not the director."

That same week, the Beatles dispatched the management team at Apple to arrange a meeting with Stanley Kubrick just three days later. "When Mr. Lennon called, I was prepared to say no to this," he told the Apple team. "I have so many other things on my plate."

Indeed, at the time, Kubrick had been deeply immersed in his next project, the screen adaptation of *A Clockwork Orange* by Anthony Burgess. He loved the book, to be sure, but he had run into some self-inflicted mental roadblocks in the process. He was tired, frustrated, and stuck. In contrast, the potential adaptation of *The Lord of the Rings* seemed more straightforward at the script stage, as the director was convinced that the main challenge would only be a matter of deciding what to leave out.

"I do think I might just be able to pull this off," concluded Kubrick. "I'm probably the only director alive who could." He told his representatives to work out a deal with United Artists.

With that, the notorious perfectionist began work on a screenplay. When Eastman and Klein later attempted to set a meeting between the director and all four of the Beatles, the request was turned down. "Mr. Kubrick feels that it would be better for him to see the film based on the underlying material rather than the actors who might play the characters," said his assistant in response. The idea that in Kubrick's mind the casting had a changeable quality created a measure of unease in the Apple offices but was not conveyed to the Beatles themselves.

As it turned out, the news of this possible collaboration between the Beatles and director Stanley Kubrick had leaked by the summer when *Yellow Submarine* had its own world premiere on July 17 at the London Pavilion in Piccadilly Circus. Again, all four Beatles and their ladies attended, and it was another mass demonstration of Beatlemania for those who had forgotten its impact. It was notable to Beatles historians, however, that John had substituted Yoko Ono on his arm for his soon-to-be ex-wife, Cynthia.

While press curiosity about *The Lord of the Rings* project could have stolen some of the thunder from the Beatles' own film, it had the opposite effect. Everyone stood in awe of the bravura filmmaking of *2001: A Space Odyssey* and now everyone loved the mind-blowing creativity of the animated color cartoon fantasy *Yellow Submarine*. It was destined to turn into an unqualified hit on its own, cementing the myth of the Beatles as psychedelic geniuses. It was both safe and childlike on the one hand, while remaining boldly counter-culture and subversive.

The two films from Kubrick and the Beatles created a convergence of cool at a time when the news of the past months had been horrible, concerned first with the death of Martin Luther King Jr., then that of Robert Kennedy. The very idea of blending Kubrick with the Beatles struck a public nerve and provided a needed distraction, the same way Beatlemania had helped pass depression over JFK's assassination.

George lingered on the red carpet to talk publicly about the project. He enthusiastically told the press that the film would feature full stereo sound, Cinerama, and a fantastic story. He even saw *The Lord of the Rings* as having the potential to bring the group together. "We've got to a point where we can see each other quite clearly. And by allowing each other to be each other, we can become the Beatles again. Even if we have to put on little Hobbity ears to do it."

When asked if he agreed, John shrugged. "He's a grand old wizard, George is. I'm just a smelly old Sméagol, living on cave fish. What would I know?"

Living in a Doll's House

What all the Beatles understood was that a film of such complexity as *The Lord of the Rings* could take years to reach the market. They turned their attention to something more achievable—a new, original album from the Beatles. Paul was the most enthusiastic to do so. He loved the Beatles and he loved recording with the group. John was resigned to the work, and he did have a number of new songs under his belt which he thought were all ready to record. Even he, at this point, was not really seriously entertaining a life beyond the band.

So from May through September, the four men worked at Abbey Road Studios on the recording of their first double album, *A Doll's House*. It was also the first Beatles album that didn't try to sugarcoat the reality of the fractured band. Instead, it gloried in the fact that they were almost mythically soldiering on as if marching through the mountains during a blizzard.

Even when they were all in the same studio, George, John, Paul, and Ringo were often working in different rooms. No one involved in the sessions could see what was really happening: a collection of individuals seemed to be pursuing their own ambitions—the antithesis of a cohesive band.

The title was Lennon's idea, borrowed from the 1879 Henrik Ibsen play about marriage inequality. John may have been channeling some idealized statement Yoko Ono had made by leaving her husband Tony Cox for him. The dissolution of his own marriage with Cynthia Lennon was hardly the stuff of heroism.

Everyone else who heard the actual words felt that it must have been more wry commentary by the band about themselves. Having lived through Beatlemania, the Beatles still felt like they were living in a doll's house where *they* were the dolls.

The title probably wouldn't have stuck around much longer had it not been for the red carpet walk at the *Yellow Submarine* premiere.

As he often did while living in the moment, John had tossed off *A Doll's House* as the title of the new Beatles album. The news bounced quickly around the world, even one where the internet was still a long way off. "The Beatles have a new album," said every disc jockey on every station. "It's going to be called *A Doll's House*."

"That," said Paul later, "was it. We didn't want to disappoint anyone."

One band was disappointed, however—an alternative UK band called Family. The group had an album due out in July that was to be called *Music in a Doll's House*. But if they released it with that title now, it would look as though they were trying to jump on the bandwagon with the Beatles.

Even so, the entirety of Family protested to Apple's leader, Neil Aspinall, who knew a member of the band through a mutual friend. Aspinall made them sign a release of all lifetime rights to any title remotely resembling *A Doll's House* for the tidy sum of £5000. He told the Beatles that Family had volunteered to back off because they were fans. Aspinall only confessed the truth about the payment to McCartney some two months after *A Doll's House* had been released, and only then after a newspaper reporter asked Derek Taylor about it.

Paul, more than all the others, had taken the challenge of Apple seriously. He had worked tirelessly with designer Gene Mahon and, at the end of the process, a shiny green Granny Smith apple against a black background became the symbol of the new company.

Apple relocated to new, roomier offices at 3 Savile Row in the next to last week of July. Complete with bright green carpets, the idealistic company was now open for business. In addition to publicly welcoming struggling artists, Apple had taken out ads encouraging those with good ideas for music, film, or other forms of art to write them up and send them over. An avalanche of submissions was being carted into the building every day.

[Ringo] "It wasn't just the mailmen who came like clockwork. There were days where Apple looked like the bargain basement at Harrod's. Hippies, street people, underground artists—they all started hanging around like they owned the place. They all thought we'd see their brilliance and start showering them with cash. This might not have been the best idea that John and Paul had ever had."

The company released its first two singles on August 26: "Hey Jude/Revolution" by the Beatles and "Those Were the Days/Turn, Turn, Turn" by new artist Mary Hopkin. The company soon followed with singles by both Jackie Lomax and the Black Dyke Mills Band, two artists lucky enough to be among the first to be signed by Apple. There were many others to come, with names like the Iveys, Doris Troy, Bill (later, Billy) Preston, Bamboo, Contact, the Pebbles, and the Modern Jazz Quartet. The roster also included the folksy American musician James Taylor. It was expected that this was only the beginning.

While the company was changing, so, too, were the four men who stood at its top as equal partners.

No one knew better than his fellow bandmates that John Lennon was a man undergoing radical transformation. They had seen firsthand that Rishikesh, rather than mellowing John out, had seemed to make him angrier. Plus, Lennon and Ono were using heroin now, and John seemed equally addicted to both his new girlfriend and to the drug itself.

In a year that had already seen assassinations, police riots, and the probable election of Richard Nixon, Lennon was becoming more politically outspoken as well. He not only felt the continuing escalation of the Vietnam War to be wrong, but also felt it impossible to forgive the entire system that had let it happen in the first place.

Lennon embraced the times with the new Beatles single's B-side—a fast, angry version of "Revolution." Clearly, the same man who told the world that all they needed was love had now found himself wrestling with the thornier issues of political struggle. When it came to destruction, he tried to split the difference—the lyrics of his song asked to be counted "out," then to be counted "in." That equivocation was coupled with the assurance that "*it's gonna be all right.*"

The album also featured a slower, bluesier version of "Revolution." Ironically, the ubiquitous song made Lennon—the most politically extreme of all the Beatles—a target of disappointment and anger from radicals worldwide, who now began to question his commitment to seeking a new world. Those same radicals had yet another controversial prism through which they could view the Beatles—as capitalists with something to sell: themselves.

Like the "Hello, Goodbye/I Am the Walrus" split, this new discord also made Lennon suspicious that he was in danger of being eclipsed by what he saw as the overly commercial instincts of his partner.

On August 22, Ringo cracked under all the friction in the recording sessions and quit the band, convinced that they all thought he was not playing well enough and that the others didn't really like him. He took his wife and family to Sardinia to escape the pressure he was feeling.

John, Paul, and George felt his absence immediately. All three of them tried to add drums to Paul's rocker "Back in the U.S.S.R." and failed miserably. They begged Ringo to return by both phone and telegram and, when he did after a two-week exile, he found his drum set decorated with flowers.

The artwork for the album cover was eventually done by Scottish artist John Patrick Byrne, who portrayed the four Beatles in a jungle-like setting. If the album's artwork was intended to compete with the colorful and provocative *Sgt. Pepper's Lonely Hearts Club Band* cover, it could only be judged as a runner-up. It was also completely at odds with the album title. A jungle is not a doll's house. It remains a testament to the chaos emerging at Apple that no one seemed to notice, or if they did, no one cared. The cover just emerged.

The greatest friction in the band came over Lennon's eight-minute plus version of experimental sound called "Revolution 9." The sound collage began its life as an extended ending to the album version of "Revolution." Lennon, working with his new love Yoko Ono, had taken the discarded coda, buried it underneath overdubbed vocals and speech, tape loops, and random sound effects, and had reversed the music. This sonic stew was then distorted further by using just about any audio effect that the equipment could create. "It's a painting," said Lennon, "of pure revolution in a society that's blowing itself apart." Through it all was Lennon's drone voice repeating "*Number nine, number nine, number nine.*"

It was not the first time that the Beatles had experimented this way. Just a year earlier, McCartney had made his own avant-garde recording titled "Carnival of Light." Though it amused him to make it, he immediately deposited it in the EMI vaults and left it there. While Paul was interested in experimentation, he still instinctively knew this material was not for public consumption.

Lennon, in contrast, felt no such prohibition. He was adamant that the "song" be included on the double album. This left everyone at Apple—particularly George Martin and Paul McCartney—aghast that such a non-commercial deviation be included on a Beatles album.

Illustrative of a dynamic that would plague the Beatles in the years ahead, both George Harrison and Ringo Starr felt that "Revolution 9" should not be on the album, but neither of them wanted to confront the increasingly volatile Lennon. They left that to McCartney, the one voice that Lennon was least inclined to hear and accept.

McCartney soldiered forward, arguing with his creative partner against using the track on *A Doll's House*. Ultimately, however, all four Beatles were drawn into the ugly debate. Ringo tried to lighten the mood, pointing out that the best part of featuring the song would be that it would "make my singing sound better than ever."

In the end, Paul, George, and Ringo threatened to outvote John on "Revolution 9." Such a three-to-one vote would have broken their previous unanimous agreements. "So now the three of you are telling me what's art and what's not," accused Lennon. "Have you listened to some of the shit you've put on this album yourselves?"

Paul thought about it overnight. More than the others, it was he who had a keen sense of John's personality. He could see his partner moving toward Yoko and away from himself. This new dynamic could, he thought, end the band completely, something he was loath to see happen.

In the studio the next day, almost as an afterthought, McCartney turned to Lennon. "Listen, John, since you feel so strongly about it and all, if you really want it on the album, I suppose that's where it's got to go." Nothing more was said, and they continued to work on overdubs for other songs.

The day after, it was Lennon's turn. He arrived at the studio early, which was unusual for him, and laid down a track for a new song he called "What's the New Mary Jane." After he played it for the others, he shrugged. "Put this in instead. I'll use Number Nine with Yoko."

He was talking about the *Unfinished Music No. 1: Two Virgins* album he and his new love were making. Already experimental in a decidedly non-Beatles way, "Revolution 9" fit right in with material that fans were likely to find inexplicable anyway. In actual fact, the other Beatles felt that "What's the New Mary Jane" was only incrementally less musical, but it did open up another opportunity.

As it turned out, it took more than "What's the New Mary Jane" to replace the lengthy "Revolution 9" and fill out the album's final side. Paul's new hit single "Hey Jude" had to be added as well, a decision that outside observers and fans would all agree made the album, particularly the side where "Revolution 9" was set to be included, a great deal more listenable. Traditionally, the Beatles did not like to include singles on albums, but "Hey Jude" was considered such a winner that they made the exception. For the album, they mixed a version that was two minutes shorter than the lengthy single version, defying the album tradition that singles were short and album versions could be longer.

In the end, John stood resolute that his song had to be included, and Paul caved. Paul's acquiescence gave John room for magnanimity. A sonic disaster had been averted, or, as George Martin noted, "I can sleep again without hearing that strangeness rumbling about in my head."

In September 1968, having tasted the relaxed vibe of a television performance on *The Tonight Show*, John and Paul wanted to give their bandmates a chance to experience it for themselves. The Beatles appeared on the popular *The David Frost Show* and played their now monster hit "Hey Jude" before a live audience. It was also, everyone agreed, a great promotion for the release of *A Doll's House*.

Even so, signs of stress were clear to those who would see them. On November 1, George Harrison became the first Beatle to release a solo album (also the first from Apple Records), the soundtrack to the 1968 film *Wonderwall*. The songs were mostly instrumental pieces that promoted Indian classical music and introduced instruments little known in the West, like the shehnai, sarod, and santoor. A little of this instrumentation had gone a long way in previous Beatle offerings, and now Harrison was putting forth something that felt spiritual and mystical but not commercial or melodic.

Lennon wasn't far behind. Just ten days later, Apple was compelled to release *Two Virgins*, Lennon's own solo effort (with Yoko). Ever more frustrated by his role with the Beatles, Lennon, with Ono, wanted the chance to explore avant-garde film, art, and now, music. The album's experimental sound had originally been the result of an all-night session between John and Yoko in John's home studio at Kenwood and had ended in the morning with their first lovemaking. The only piece that did not originate from that seminal night was "Revolution 9," now included since its banishment from the *A Doll's House* album.

Lennon and Ono's insistence that the album feature, as its cover, a nude photo of the new lovers who were hardly, despite the title, two virgins, caused an uproar within Apple and among fans. Using an automatic camera, they had posed for the photos while Lennon's wife Cynthia was conveniently on vacation in Greece. By the time she returned, Lennon's new relationship with Ono was established fact, and his marriage was essentially doomed.

Neither *Unfinished Music No. 1: Two Virgins* nor *Wonderwall Music* sold many copies. Both albums, in fact, perplexed and alienated a fair share of Beatles fans. Both albums suffered mightily in comparison to the first double album from the Beatles, *A Doll's House*, released on November 22, 1968, the five-year anniversary of the death of President Kennedy.

A Doll's House was an instant hit, and the fact that it cost so much more than a normal album turned out to be no impediment to sales at all. Every fan had to own it.

Although today the double album is seen as an unchallenged success, when it was released, there were naysayers. *Rockstar*'s own music critic, David Swanson, found it a sad harbinger of breakup, adding: "The Beatles aren't the Beatles anymore. They are now exactly the sum of their parts, and it shows."

THE BUS TO LIVERPOOL

George spent the 1968 holidays in Woodstock, New York, with his friend Bob Dylan. Earlier, while he was in Los Angeles, producing tracks for Jackie Lomax's debut LP, he had met a number of Hells Angels. Now, on December 4, he sent the following telegram to Apple headquarters:

> "Hells Angels will be in London within the next week, on the way to straighten out Czechoslovakia. I have heard they may try to make full use of Apple's facilities. They may look as though they are going to do you in but are very straight and do good things, so don't fear them or up-tight them. Try to assist them without neglecting your Apple business and without letting them take control of Savile Row."

Richard DiLello, the self-proclaimed "House Hippie" at Apple, was dispatched to procure copies of journalist Hunter S. Thompson's *Hell's Angels: The Strange and Terrible Saga of the Outlaw Motorcycle Gangs*. The books were brought into Apple to help the staff and the Beatles understand their new guests and to calm everyone's nerves. In actual fact, Thompson's searing nonfiction novel about the nearly two years he spent living and working among the notorious bikers frightened every single person far beyond what they would have felt had they remained ignorant. The section where Thompson suffers a brutal beatdown by gang members was particularly unnerving.

Before anyone could act on this sense of impending dread, two gleaming Harley-Davidson motorcycles arrived at the airport, requiring Apple to shell out £250 of shipping costs to get them through customs.

Paul and Linda McCartney, accompanied by their children, were working in the Apple studios on a Christmas song, when two Hells Angels bikers, Billy Tumbleweed and Frisco Pete, along with another sixteen stoned California freaks—all part of the "Pleasure Crew"—showed up at Apple. The Angels had brought the infamous writer and hippie Ken Kesey along for this ride, too. Everyone seemed to be wearing headbands, ripped Levis, boots, cowboy hats, you name it. The halls of Apple reeked of patchouli oil, sweaty leather, and marijuana—all joined together in a single potent fragrance.

Upon seeing the Pleasure Crew descend onto Apple, Paul left Linda and the kids in the recording studio, telling them to stay put.

Suddenly, with George missing in action, Paul and the Apple employees were faced with the insane chaos of Hells Angels gang members roaming the hallways, crashing on the sofas, and eating the food. DiLello called it "the mescaline icing on the hashish cake."

Paul called John. "Our kindhearted young George has bollixed it up good this time," he informed him. "We've got to get his friends out of here."

John agreed and had an idea, a way to turn a past defeat into a present victory.

Two hours later, the wildly painted bus that had been used for the *Magical Mystery Tour* film pulled up in front of Apple. Inside were Ringo and Maureen, and John and Yoko. Mal Evans, the driver, had pulled the bus out of storage at John's request.

Peter Brown arranged for the song to be played inside Apple

over loudspeakers: "*Roll up, roll up, for the Mystery Tour*." It was explained to the entire Pleasure Crew that the Beatles had prepared the bus to give their guests a tour of London and Liverpool.

Ken Kesey would write about what happened next for *Esquire*. Kesey found himself chronicling his adventure with the Beatles in the same way that Tom Wolfe has written about his adventures with Kesey and the Merry Pranksters in 1968's nonfiction novel sensation *The Electric Kool-Aid Acid Test*:

> "The Hells Angels and the Pleasure Crew were just tourists looking for a ride on the streets of London. They filed onto that bus missing only a Nikon hanging around their necks. It was everything that Magical Mystery Tour wasn't. Authentic, dangerous, and actual fun. The whole crew, guided by three honest-to-God Beatles and their women, took off for Liverpool with an escort of two-wheeled marvels, front and back, in the heart of London's West End. Monkey bars, chrome work, erotic curves to the gas tanks, and outsized twin exhaust pipes. Passers-by stopped and gawked, sure that whatever they were seeing would never pass that way again. The Beasts sitting on their Beauties were out of place and out of time."

Kesey's poetry aside, the Pleasure Crew found the day's adventure to be a combo *Acid Test/Mystery Tour*. John, Paul, Ringo, and their wives led the interlopers from Apple to Liverpool, a four-hour drive. There they showed them the sites—where they grew up, their schools, even docks where Hells Angels had no guarantee of being the toughest on the street.

By nightfall, while the Pleasure Crew was busy drinking to excess in the celebrated Cavern Club, all three Beatles and their spouses, plus Ken Kesey, were hustled outside to a waiting van and driven back to London. When the night was over, Mal Evans explained to Billy Tumbleweed and Frisco Pete that the Beatles wanted the Pleasure Crew to enjoy touring Britain on Apple's account for the next week, that they were not to return to the offices, and that Evans himself would be their driver. Just to make sure that there were no hard feelings that would lead to trouble, Peter Brown hired twenty London soccer toughs to stand guard at Apple for the next week in case the Pleasure Crew returned, but they never did.

"For the moment, these bearded men seemed no different from the rockers who had run across London in *A Hard Day's Night*," Kesey concluded in his *Esquire* article, marveling at the sheer fun he had witnessed. "They disposed of a threat, but did so in that cheeky way that made the world love the Beatles, even when they misbehaved. To see John, Paul, and Ringo escaping a pack of motorcycle outlaws and making it look like a week of entertainment was to know that if the band could have more days like this, the Beatles actually could play forever."

It was a grand, chaotic affair unfolding at a time when everyone should have been focused on *A Doll's House* rising meteorically to the number one chart position in the United States. Instead, everyone's attention was occupied by the party crashers who had to be gaslighted into riding in a massive prop for a failed film. Still, the plan worked. Mal Evans received a bonus payment of £1,000 for his skill as a chaperone.

The three Beatles who were a part of the manic bus trip wrote George Harrison a telegram the following day: "*We have finished hosting the Hells Angels,*" it read, "*and gotten some good press out of it. Apple secured. Happy Xmas.*"

Part metaphor and part nightmare, the arrival of the Hells Angels made clear to all who saw it that Apple Records, in existence less than a year, was already in serious trouble. No business could tolerate such danger, excess, and incompetence, and yet there it was. It would have to be fixed or else. Nothing less than the survival of the Beatles was at stake.

CHAPTER TWO

EVEREST (1969)

ROUNDHOUSE PUNCH

Recording sessions for a proposed *The Lord of the Rings* soundtrack started in January under a cloud of negativity. John Lennon had given an on-the-record interview to the British pop weekly *Disc and Music Echo* and was far too off-the-cuff, remarking, "We need these itty-bitty Hobbits to save us, don't we, because without 'em, the Beatles will be bankrupt soon, the way that Apple's being run into the ground."

Lennon was his usual indiscreet and hyperbolic self in choosing those words and that timing, but he was not wrong. There was a whiff of desperation regarding producing a soundtrack album for a movie yet to go before the cameras. And with over 150 people now working at Apple, including an astrologer named Caleb who also served as a fortune-teller for the staff, the company did look like an undisciplined mess.

Apple had been lumbering along under the direction of ex-Beatle road manager and now managing director Neil Aspinall. Working closely with Aspinall was the late Brian Epstein's personal assistant Peter Brown, who had continued on as social coordinator to the Beatles. New to the team was PR man Derek Taylor, whose office was always stocked with potent marijuana and fine whiskey.

Bright and attentive as the trio could be, running a company of Apple's magnitude and complexity was not in the direct wheelhouse of any of the men, and they were the first to admit it. No one was up to the job, especially given that the job had never been defined.

What all three men agreed upon was that having the Beatles on the docket encouraged new artists that they, too, could be wrapped up in the magic by joining Apple. There had already been good signings, such as James Taylor and Mary Hopkin, and others, like David Bowie and Fleetwood Mac, were becoming a possibility.

A newly formed group—Crosby, Stills & Nash—had just arrived in London to audition for Apple Records. George was favorably impressed, but John dismissed their sound as "twee nonsense" that was no better than elevator music. Paul argued that it was smart to sign a group whose members came from the Byrds, Buffalo Springfield, and the Hollies. With the band departing for the airport to sign contracts with Atlantic Records, Lennon relented in his opposition, and CSN signed their contracts in the classic Belmond Cadogan lobby at the last possible moment.

The biggest part of CSN's attraction to Apple was, of course, being on the same label as the Beatles. And so John, Paul, George, and Ringo dutifully reported to Twickenham Film Studios to begin work on the soundtrack for *The Lord of the Rings*. The idea was to lay down a single album side's worth of songs (the other would be scored by George Martin as he had done for *Yellow Submarine*) and the entire session would be filmed by documentarian Michael Lindsay-Hogg to accompany the final movie.

There were plenty of solid reasons to record the soundtrack at Twickenham, and getting away from the madness at Apple was among them. But recording there also had its distinct disadvantages.

The space was gargantuan, not intimate like Abbey Road or even like the new studios under construction over at Apple. Several camera crews were constantly filming there, putting the Beatles and their process on public display. The lights turned the entire space into a hot box within hours.

They started work under difficult conditions. The Beatles, with the exception of Paul, liked to come in late and keep going until the sun came up. Now they came to work first thing in the morning and, thanks to the union regulations of the camera crew, knocked off at bankers' hours.

All of this might have been taken in stride if the Beatles' relationships with each other had not already fractured. Even after their high-spirited caper to deport the Hells Angels from Apple, the Lennon and McCartney relationship had resumed its previous dysfunction. Meanwhile, Harrison chafed at his second-tier status, while Starkey wanted only to live again in the harmony of the band's earlier days.

Their frustrations boiled over into open revolt against the studio that was paying for the sessions. The Beatles began by angrily rejecting a request from United Artists that all four of them appear in costumes as their characters. With that idea soundly refused, UA had cardboard cutouts made and shipped to England to make the background more colorful. Staring at themselves in Hobbit gear did nothing to improve the moods of the musicians.

> [Ringo] "We'd made fun of this kind of business with the Pepper album, having the Moptop versions of us on the cover. But that was making fun of the past and this was the future making fun of us. We all thought we looked silly. Plus, our heads were too small. This was probably the first time any of us had said that about John and Paul, you know."

Through it all, there was the divisive influence of Yoko Ono's presence and John's silent arrogance about it. Yoko had been on hand for *A Doll's House* the year before, but now Paul, George, and Ringo felt it had gotten completely out of hand.

The Beatles could have tried to establish some kind of artistic understanding with Yoko, but John routinely acted to prevent this. He seemed to fear that she could somehow be taken from him when, in reality, the others simply wanted her to not attend sessions, to respect their work methods as their own wives and girlfriends had always done. Now she was a fifth presence, one that wore a continual face of boredom and apathy. And that presence was the only one that mattered to John. His vote had been hijacked.

Yet there they were, day after day, forced together for the cameras that recorded their increasingly sour moods toward each other. To anyone watching only the video, it would seem like they hated working on *The Lord of the Rings*, when, in fact, it was the one part of the experience they all supported.

Inflamed over what he saw as Yoko's constant negative judgment, George ended up in an actual physical fight with John and left the band as Ringo had done the summer before.

> [George] "I knew that the girls we all had were part of the Beatles scene now. None of them were Beatles, though, but in John's mind Yoko had all the rights and privileges. She told me how to play my guitar one time too many, I suppose. Anyway, John pushed me so I pushed him back. He was so high I know I could have hurt him so I left instead. Then I realized I had nowhere to go so I came back."

In reality, George came back because he sensed the soundtrack sessions were his opportunity to step out of the shadow cast by Paul and John. He showed up with the most material, much of it spiritually tinged and able to fit the constraints of a fantasy film project, including the songs "All Things Must Pass," "What Is Life," "Beware of Darkness," and a re-working of "Let It Down" that now referred to the ring itself, newly re-titled as "Put It On."

Even in this disaster area, however, there were seeds of salvation for the group. The Beatles' relaxing and showing off for the cameras by playing songs that would never make it on *The Lord of the Rings* soundtrack generated a historic creative output far too valuable to waste. Many of the songs that didn't make the film soundtrack appeared on future albums put out by either the individual artists or the group as a whole.

Through the highs and more abundant lows, the cameras rolled, capturing the insults, staredowns, silent treatments, and walkouts. They continued to roll on January 11, and they recorded the most dramatic moment in the entire documentary when Stanley Kubrick dropped in unexpectedly at Twickenham Film Studios.

A secretary working for Kubrick had given him Lennon and Ono's *Two Virgins* album, featuring the frontal nudity of both John and Yoko, a few days prior. Remaining open-minded, the director tried to listen to it and found it "gave me a major headache." The brain pounding he experienced from the recordings, however, was not as bad as the one he was getting from his battle with the screenplay he could not seem to tame. He said that he had come to realize how immense the project was in terms of story, locations, extras, and battles. He thought it would take too much time, particularly with "an untested talent pool."

Paul tried to buck up Kubrick by assuring him that director Richard Lester felt they'd all held their own on *A Hard Day's Night* and *Help!* "That wasn't exactly Shakespeare now, was it?" mocked Kubrick.

This, of course, was the wrong thing to say to a group whose leader, John Lennon, had risen from the streets of Liverpool and done so by never backing down from a fight. "You're afraid," he said to the director. "You don't think you can pull it off." Kubrick assured him that he certainly could pull it off if he felt like it. "Prove it," said Lennon. "Show us your screenplay."

"I'll do no such thing," said Kubrick.

Ringo suggested that maybe they should all retire to the pub a few blocks away and talk it out. They could leave all these camera crews at Twickenham to film themselves filming themselves.

Kubrick didn't want to have a pint with the Beatles and said so directly. He had no desire to strike up a friendship, he said—his primary concern was that as a director, he was losing confidence in the impact their casting would have on his project.

Before the contemplated dissolution could happen, however, those same cameras recorded that George, who said not a single word in the encounter, looked ready to abandon his spiritual principles and come off his chair to kick Stanley Kubrick's ass. "You can't fucking fire the Beatles," he told him.

"I'm very sorry this hasn't worked out," said the uncomfortable filmmaker, who then quickly took his leave.

As the door closed, John Lennon pronounced his verdict. "Bloody hell!" was all he said before setting to work, kicking over all the cardboard posters and characters. He dragged them into a pile in the center of the room and proceeded to urinate on the whole lot of them, even as the cameras continued to roll.

The next day, January 12, the four Beatles convened at Ringo's house to make a plan. Incensed at their situation, they all agreed that Stanley Kubrick had made fools of them for prematurely recording songs for an album that would never be. As it was, this "enemy of my enemy" anger was enough to cause all four men to behave for the briefest moment as they had at the band's beginning, when they felt it was them trying to prove themselves to the world. Kubrick's betrayal had given them someone to be mad at besides themselves, or each other.

The easiest decision of the day was to stop the sessions for *The Lord of the Rings* literally in their tracks and to leave the soulless ambience of Twickenham at once, never to return. They elected to move to the recently constructed studio in the basement of Apple's plush headquarters at 3 Savile Row in London's West End, even though none of them had yet laid eyes on it.

They determined to continue filming the documentary, paying for it out of Apple's pocket instead of UA's. Now, instead of showing how the soundtrack for *The Lord of the Rings* was made, the film would provide a final burial to that dream and showcase the beginning of another one. Before the warm embers from the fireplace around which the studio had been built, the Beatles began work on a stripped-down roots rock and roll album to be known as *Get Back*.

They would, as John put it, "stick our finger up Kubrick's ass and watch him jump to the fuckin' Moon." Apple PR man Taylor later spun that sentiment into, "The Beatles and Mister K have suffered from creative differences and all have agreed to move on to other world-changing ideas."

"We've been misinterpreted in film before," Paul said to the press days later, choosing not to give voice to the band's active participation in the misinterpretation, "so we've all just decided to get back to doing what we do best, to be a rock and roll band."

Paul had gotten what he most wanted: everyone was on the same team making an album together. To celebrate, the marijuana came out, and then Paul pushed just a bit harder. He suggested that the ultimate ending to the documentary and the process of making the album be a live performance of the album in its entirety.

This inspired much loose talk of performing before both Houses of Parliament or on an ocean liner or even in front of the pyramids, but every option seemed like too much trouble. McCartney, trying to keep the balloon of optimism inflated, suggested trying north London's famous Roundhouse, an engine room of creative expression and home to an increasing number of British rock performances.

Showing up unexpectedly at a London venue to play would create a legend, said Ringo. "And besides that, it'll support local bands because they can always leak out a rumor that the Beatles may turn up."

As John and George resisted even the local one-off, everyone agreed that if the songs were ready when the time came, they would embrace the Roundhouse concept. But first, they had an album to create.

The Beatles rang up Alexis Mardas and told him to get the Apple studios up and running. Mardas, also known as "Magic Alex," was considered to be the mad genius of Apple. A Greek national in his mid-twenties, he was always coming up with pie-in-the-sky ideas, like phones that could recognize your voice, a force field around a home as a security system, and even a functioning flying saucer. None of these, however, had ever come to fruition, although he was on the Apple payroll to the tune of £6,000 a month and during his tenure was thought to have spent over £300,000 on his various projects.

In any case, Mardas had claimed over a year earlier that he

could build a groundbreaking studio that would easily eclipse the antiquated 4-track they were used to at EMI's Abbey Road. He said he could make a 72-track tape machine and mixing console where each track, incredibly, would also have its own speaker.

When the Beatles showed up to inspect the new facilities, they were shocked by what they saw. There was no 72-track tape deck, no soundproofing, no intercom, and not even a patch bay to run the wiring between the control room and the sixteen speakers that Mardas had fixed haphazardly to the walls. The only new piece of sound equipment present was a crude mixing console which Mardas had built and which looked like bits of wood and an old oscilloscope that was to operate as a sound level meter. Harrison lost his cool immediately, calling the chaotic tableau "medieval."

Called in to render a second opinion, producer George Martin agreed with Harrison's assessment at first glance. He immediately set about borrowing two 4-track recorders from EMI. Longtime Beatles engineer Geoff Emerick was given the task of building and setting up a studio with portable equipment. Mardas was banished from the premises, relegated to his workshop at Apple Electronics in the Marylebone area of London. He was about to lose his job in the most spectacular way.

What the Beatles, Martin, and others closely involved with Apple did not yet know was that in building his self-perceived studio of the future, Magic Alex had knocked down a wall to create a more "open" space, a tactic he expected would be the best way to capture the sonic imagination of the Beatles. The problem was that Mardas, a man with no construction or architectural experience, had removed a load-bearing wall. No one at Apple understood the danger either and had simply deferred to his presumed expertise.

Three days later, George Martin, Geoff Emerick, several Apple employees, and a team from Abbey Road were hard at work removing all traces of Mardas's technological incompetence and replacing it with a functioning studio set-up. As they worked, they heard a terrible groan from above. Pieces of plaster began to crash from the ceiling. Within seconds, one of the Apple secretaries shouted down to them: "Get out!"

As the basement ceiling began to crumble, the floor above it lost its own structural integrity. It had been strained from the moment Mardas removed the wall two weeks earlier and had finally given way to physics. When ignored, gravity will slowly exert its sway, and it always wins.

Mercifully, a grand creaking roar caused everyone to flee the studio. The twelve-by-sixteen-foot hole that appeared sent wood, plaster, desks, chairs, tables, and Apple's green carpet from the office above to the basement below. A water pipe was broken during the descent, making everything that much worse.

When the damage was assessed later, it was obvious that the destruction had crushed the Abbey Road equipment on loan, several of the Beatles' prime guitars, and a piano. Also destroyed was any lingering image Apple had previously maintained of functioning as a legitimate business. The collapse served as a metaphor for the company's own implosion.

Given the fact that the last year ended with Hells Angels roaming the halls and was quickly followed by the Beatles being fired off a picture by Stanley Kubrick, the disintegration of Apple was not a good sign. The London papers gave it brutal front page treatment, with the *Daily Mirror* proclaiming, "Apple Rotten to the Corp!"

There was, briefly, the feeling that since Twickenham and Savile Row had turned out so badly, it would be best to just give up entirely. Support for carrying on came from an unlikely source: George Harrison.

"I don't want to do this any more than the rest of you," he said, "but we've got the material, so let's just go finish it up."

With that, the Beatles returned to EMI's Abbey Road, Studio Two, the third location they had recorded so far on their return-to-roots album, *Get Back*. This final location was familiar and comfortable, the place where most of the recorded output of the Beatles was laid down over the years.

The bandmates were well aware that despite the overwhelming commercial success of *A Doll's House*, fans and critics alike were beginning to notice that the Beatles were now playing as each other's session men more than as fellow band members. John Lennon, perhaps urged on by Yoko, was speaking more and more openly about his tenuous new relationship with Paul McCartney.

"It's no secret Paul wants to run the show, is it?" Lennon had asked a reporter for London's *Melody Maker* magazine. "The whole 'leader-of-the-band' trip. Ask him. He'll tell you."

"John is the only leader of Beatles there can be," chimed in Yoko. "And there can be no Beatles without John."

McCartney fumed when he read such talk printed in the music trades. Especially irritating was the fact that Yoko, even now, could not seem to bring herself to call the group by its proper name with the definite article—*the* Beatles, not just Beatles. McCartney also felt Lennon knew better than anyone on the planet what the truth was: Paul first stepped in because he was more organized and a harder worker, then because John was tripping out on acid, regularly. Then came Yoko, and then "JohnandYoko" started doing everything together, including heroin, something they began shortly after Yoko suffered her first miscarriage in November of 1968.

Even as the rehearsals for the new album continued, there was a palpable sense of anxiety over what to do about Apple. In an effort to shore up Apple's artist roster, John, Yoko, Ringo, and Maureen caught a performance of emerging artist Elton John at a small London venue where they could slip in and out without too much fuss. Elton was preparing to record his first album, *Empty Sky*, and was trying out material. Years before, the talented songwriter had worked in the office of early Beatles music publisher Dick James when the Beatles sent in their demos, creating a musical relationship between the artists of which most people were unaware.

Afterwards, the two Beatles and their wives visited the new artist backstage. John was effusive about Elton's performance. "You've fucking got it," he declared.

Suddenly, John Lennon's resistance to playing the material from *Get Back* before a live audience dissolved. He had seen with his own eyes how Elton John had commanded concertgoers, and he knew the Beatles could do the same. A plan was hatched to use the influence of the Beatles to book Elton John into the Roundhouse.

On April 7, then, Elton John performed five songs and took an unexpected break. "We're going to take a few minutes to rearrange the stage, if you don't mind," he told the audience. "But I promise the wait will be worth it."

When the lights came back on thirty minutes later, the lucky audience found themselves watching history as the Beatles played their first fully live concert performance since 1966. The performance at the Roundhouse turned out to be both a surprise and a success, meant to cap the documentary that had started so sourly with the confrontation with Stanley Kubrick. The *Get Back—Live at the Roundhouse* album is culled from both the work sessions and the April 7 performance.

The film documentary includes one powerful and unexpected moment. One young man, a house painter named David Morehouse, had angrily left the venue that night when Elton John left the stage. The next day, when he heard that he had missed out on seeing the Beatles, Morehouse went to the Hornsey Lane Bridge that connects the Highgate and Crouch End areas of London and prepared to jump.

As a crowd gathered, the breaking news coverage emphasized Morehouse's despondency over missing the Beatles, which attracted the attention of Linda Eastman. Soon she and Paul were in their car being waved through the police line. The documentary crew had been alerted and were filming at a respectful distance when Paul got out of the car and walked up to Morehouse, who was standing precariously on the edge of the bridge.

"The Beatles have been having a rough go of it, ourselves," he told the stunned house painter, who nearly passed out and fell off the bridge. "We need all the fans we can get these days."

Less than ten minutes after McCartney had gotten out of the

car, he and David Morehouse walked up to the documentary crew together and told them all about their little chat.

"Don't everybody start going to the bridges now," McCartney said with his best poker face, straight to camera. "We're all quite busy, you know, and there'd be no guarantee that you'd get a Beatle."

Derek Taylor was on the scene by this point and shoved one of his local reporters forward to ask the question, "When will your *Get Back* album come out?" Paul took the opportunity to act high-minded while simultaneously promoting for the Beatles.

> [Paul] "This isn't the moment to be talking about such things. But it's not just an album anyway, it's a concert, an album and a film, all three of them as live as live can be. Call up Apple if you want to talk about it, but right now, let's give this man a chance to get home."

With that, McCartney signed an autograph on the arm of Morehouse's girlfriend, Anne Thompson. He waved at reporters and then he got back in the car with Linda and they motored off through the crowd.

UNDER NEW MANAGEMENT

The lack of a new manager for Apple had risen to a high priority for all parties involved. Everyone finally began to search in earnest for someone who could take control of Apple and fix it. There was even talk of finding a "simple bank manager and a simple solicitor" under the guise that it was only accounting discipline that needed to be imposed—but the dream of simplicity never materialized. Everyone knew that whomever they chose needed to have both experience and guts.

Lists were compiled and meetings scheduled. Individual Beatles were involved in some of the outreach, but so were Neil Aspinall and Peter Brown.

During this period, candidates included Lord Poole, chairman of Lazard's Bank; Lord Goodman, lawyer to the prime minister; Cecil King, newspaper baron; and Ronan O'Rahilly, the visionary founder of the first pirate radio station, Radio Caroline. The Beatles, Aspinall, and Brown also discussed Tony Defries, the manager of David Bowie; Albert Grossman, the manager of Bob Dylan; and Peter Grant, the manager of Led Zeppelin. And the name of Lord Richard Beeching kept coming up. He was the man who was widely credited with saving Great Britain's railroad system. He had done it by being ruthlessly efficient about expenditures and notably non-sentimental about failing lines that cost more than they brought in. He was not always liked, but he *was* respected.

McCartney met him first. Beeching was not particularly interested in taking over the management of the stumbling Apple Corps. Still, he felt the Beatles were a matter of national pride, not unlike the country's trains, and if he could help save them, he felt the country would be better for it. At the same time, he also knew that a desperate private company like Apple would likely pay a savior a significant sum.

Paul suggested that John take a meeting with Beeching. Lennon, to put it charitably, did not have as much respect for Beeching as his partner did. "He looks like a Dickens character and smells like it, too," was his post-meeting analysis.

Paul, desperate to find someone sooner than later, suggested the names of the buttoned-down entertainment attorney Lee Eastman, nearly 60, and his son John Eastman for the job of saving the group's finances. The Eastmans had the distinction of being Linda's family and Paul's soon-to-be father-in-law and brother-in-law. Paul saw this familial connection as a way to avoid being fleeced by outsiders who didn't care about the Beatles personally.

John, George, and Ringo were highly skeptical of Paul's plea to bring in his in-laws, saying that such an arrangement would hardly guarantee neutrality and fairness among the band's individual members.

While others considered and vetted and mused, John Lennon

acted. On January 30, 1969, John and Yoko met with Allen Klein, the manager of the Rolling Stones, a tough-talking New Yorker who won their immediate affection. He knew what songs John had written for the Beatles, and he could recite the lyrics from memory.

The next day, John and Yoko announced to Apple, and thus to the other Beatles, that they would now be represented by Klein. The others could do what they wanted to do, but John would introduce them to Klein, and they could make their own decision.

Soon the Beatles split into camps, or, more accurately, one camp and one individual. John convinced both George and Ringo to side with him to bring in Klein, arguing that he knew the music business inside out and, based on what Mick Jagger had said, was enough of a right bastard to bring royalties into line with their true worth.

The vote was about to go three-to-one when Lennon was reminded by Starkey that the Beatles refused to invoke plain "majority rule" on him when it came to "Revolution 9." They had backed away then, preferring to keep the unanimous decision policy intact within the band. The question now was, on a matter of this importance, could they do any less?

There was no hope that Lennon or McCartney would change positions and switch over to supporting the other man's nominee. If they were going to stick with unanimous decision making, they would need to find a mutually agreeable candidate. This seemed impossible.

The group decided that the management search would continue but, in the interim, John, George, and Ringo would go with Allen Klein, and Paul would stick with Lee and John Eastman. No one, not even Klein or the Eastmans, considered this to be a long-term solution.

SIGNIFICANT OTHERS

While John Lennon believed that he was the leader and Paul McCartney the follower, that belief had more to do with emotion than fact. One of the starkest examples concerns the wedding of McCartney to Linda Eastman, followed just a single week later by the wedding of Lennon to Yoko Ono. Both weddings came immediately on the heels of Paul leaving his longtime girlfriend Jane Asher and John leaving his wife Cynthia, each man shedding a long, meaningful relationship for something new and exciting.

On March 12, 1969, Paul McCartney married Linda Eastman. He'd been increasingly taken with the confident New York photographer, to the point where they had become inseparable. Their bond could scarcely be considered less than the one John Lennon shared with Yoko Ono, though *paulandlinda* had not had the same impact as *johnandyoko,* with its intercultural overtones.

The event invoked classic Beatlemania: girls waited outside, cried at Paul's new unavailability, and mobbed the newlyweds when they emerged from the civil ceremony.

The marriages of Paul McCartney and John Lennon had transcended the realm of typical celebrity buzz to become an iconic watershed event. Under the guise of "showing up" for each other, John and Yoko staged the ultimate performance art when they crashed the civil ceremony marriage of Paul to Linda. John and Yoko insisted it was a spur-of-the-moment decision:

> [John] "Paul and me weren't talking, you know? The whole Hobbit madness made it shit for all of us. When I heard he was getting married, I wasn't going to go. The last thing I wanted to do was pretend things were all lovely when they weren't."

> [Yoko] "Paul and Linda didn't invite us. We knew that she was always intimidated by me. But then Paul was always intimidated by John."

> [John] "It just hit me, about an hour before. We were in London, and we'd just got these white outfits back from the cleaners, and we just put them on. Looked like we belonged on the cake. So we just drove on over."

The arrival of the Lennons surprised the soon-to-be

McCartneys, who were already inside the building where the ceremony would take place. Paul and Linda heard the not-un-familiar screams of the fans outside and went to the window to wave to them. The fans, however, were too distracted to see them because of the arrival of John and Yoko in a psychedelic painted Mercedes-Benz.

"What is he doing?" asked Linda.

Paul, whose first instinct was anger upon seeing that his partner had upstaged him at his own wedding, had to smile. John Lennon was being outrageous by simply showing up. Clever boy he is, thought McCartney.

Paul would get the chance to return the favor just one week later, when John married Yoko—only Paul had to come back from his own honeymoon and fly to the island Gibraltar near Spain in order to do so. It had all been quietly arranged by their over-whelmed manager, Peter Brown. "Linda informed me that I'd be getting her and Paul to the Lennon wedding or she'd cut my balls off," he said. "It had to be a secret, too, because they'd never told her they were coming to hers."

Lennon would never officially admit to being inspired by McCartney's own nuptials, but it would be a very long shot indeed if that were not the case, given the time proximity. In truth, McCartney's wedding had fired up his own competitive spirit. Like brothers fighting to get recognized, John determined to marry Yoko as soon as possible. It came together in less than a week.

> [John] "We both got very emotional about the actual marriage ceremony. We're both quite cynical, hard people, but very soft as well. Everyone's a bit both ways. And it was very romantic. Or it was, until he turned up."

Lennon was hardly in a charitable mood when his newly married business partner showed up at his wedding with his own new bride. "Now Paul, why have you two gone and done such a thing?" When it came to him as the recipient of a visit, John had no appetite for the concept of showing up.

Shortly after the wedding, John and Yoko flew off to Paris and began a new run of social activism after their Gibraltar elopement that included the now classic "Bed-In" for Peace masterstroke. It was a two-for-one deal for John: he got to upstage McCartney's nuptials and turn "Peace" into a product that he could use his celebrity to help market.

When eccentric cartoonist Al Capp attacked John for the "filth" of the *Two Virgins* album and even took a shot at Yoko, it was McCartney who came to their defense from his almost-working farm in Scotland. "This guy is slagging off Yoko—and that's one thing you don't do," reminded Paul who, by some accounts, had done the same. "You don't slag off someone's woman—that's tribal time, isn't it?"

George and Ringo missed both weddings. Since the respective marrying parties had issued no invitations to either and since the wisdom of Ed McMahon had not been directed at them, *showing up* was impossible. George professed to be relieved of the obligation.

> [George] "I'd put my heart into the *Lord* soundtrack, and when it fell apart, it felt like my work was being rejected, and me along with it. I just went back home and started gardening. I planted and chanted for days at a time. I didn't want to see them any more than they probably wanted to see me, if you want to know the truth."

Ringo was another matter. He liked being a Beatle and, since he was not in competition with either John or Paul for creative control of the group, he could afford to like them personally as well.

> [Ringo] "It's cool now that it went down the way it did, I suppose. They each got married the same week. No one told me. But they went to each other's wedding. Oh, well, I thought, what should I expect? Nobody hires a wedding drummer."

In the aftermath of the weddings, John and Paul actually converged on Abbey Studios (without George or Ringo) to record a single about their wedding experiences. The A-side was Lennon's "The Ballad of John and Yoko" and the B-side was McCartney's "Two of Us," which he claimed was about his relationship with Linda. There was give-and-take musically between the two men, and a bit of fun, according to the men themselves.

The leaders of the Beatles now each had someone more important in their lives than their professional partners.

• • •

In late June, the *Everest* sessions were set to begin in earnest at Abbey Road Studios. It was a curious time—each of the four musicians now believed that this could easily be the last album they would ever make together as a group.

Maybe that's why the squabbling of *A Doll's House* and *Get Back* was replaced by a sense of purpose on *Everest*. They were simply devoted to the idea of making one last great album and going out in style.

All four men brought in material but, for the moment, they also all agreed to work on as many of their other bandmates' songs as possible.

When Yoko Ono began showing up to every one of the sessions, Paul decided that Linda should do the same. The two women were developing a relationship known these days as "frenemies."

In the same way that *Sgt. Pepper's Lonely Hearts Club Band* had been a concept album with the band posing as another band, a new concept informed and organized *Everest*. One side would be the great music that the public had come to expect from the Beatles. The other would be a collection of song fragments fused into a "suite" that was one single musical experience, an idea that Paul thought was keen and John thought was weird. Harrison watched as an observer:

[George] "I had no real opinion, other than I just wanted my songs on the record, you know, because I knew how strong they were. But when I heard that John was opposed to the idea of the suite or whatever because it was too weird, well, coming from him, I thought we ought to try it. I took a bit of pleasure in driving him mad because he'd certainly done it to me a few times."

McCartney was alone and in a troubled mood in Abbey Road Studios that first weekend in July. The Rolling Stones had just held a free concert for a quarter of a million fans in Hyde Park. They had been introduced as "The greatest rock and roll band in the world!" and had debuted their new song "Honky Tonk Women." Paul hated that Jagger's band seemed so at home on the stage. It was all he wanted for the Beatles.

These thoughts consumed him until he heard the news called in from Scotland. John had been holidaying in the Scottish Highlands with Yoko, her daughter, Kyoko, and his son Julian. Now there was a hospital on the line, saying that all four of them had been taken there after a bad car accident. Paul heard the news, rang up Linda at their home, and told her to pack for Scotland.

Lennon was a notoriously bad driver. Shortsighted and inexperienced, he hadn't even gotten his license until he was twenty-four. Still, he decided to drive the 700-odd miles to where John's relatives lived near Edinburgh. Les Antony, a chauffeur for the Beatles, had offered to drive them, but John and Yoko were determined to have a back-to-basics experience without all the usual rock star affectations.

Squinting into the distance, John saw another car coming at him on a very narrow Highland road, near the Kyle of Tongue. The other driver was a German tourist, equally ignorant of the rules of the road, and the two of them were on a collision course. John swerved his white Austin Maxi out of the other car's path.

The Lennon vehicle soon was out of control and took a hard landing in a ditch where John and Yoko, in the front seat, received the full impact. Soon an ambulance arrived from nearby Wick to ferry all four of the Lennons and Onos forty miles south to Lawson Memorial Hospital in Golspie.

Both John and Yoko needed facial stitches. During this procedure, doctors were told that Yoko was in the early stages of pregnancy. She was immediately rushed to another wing to be looked at by doctors with neonatal experience, particularly important given her miscarriage the year before.

John insisted that he and Yoko be given beds side by side, but that broke the hospital's rule of separate wards for men and women, which the hospital administrators insisted must be adhered to. They assured him they would look into it even as they gave the Beatle a strong sedative so that he could sleep.

Unexpectedly, when John woke up in his room, it was Paul who was sitting there watching him. "Here's Johnny!" were the first words John Lennon heard spoken to him.

Paul assured him that everything was under control. He had Linda watching Yoko, and both of the kids were with a private nanny who had just been hired.

"Why bother?" John was honestly perplexed.

"You saved me from the Hells Angels," said Paul with a shrug. "Least I could do."

As the hours drifted by, John defended his relationship with Yoko. "She's my thing now," he explained. "You all need to understand that."

Paul said that he did. In fact, he pointed out, he and John had traveled a similar path. In the beginning, in Liverpool and in Hamburg and the other small venues, there had always been the new girl every night, if they ever wanted one. No strings attached. "A real shagfest, it was," agreed John.

"I love Linda just as much as you love Yoko, you know," Paul told his partner.

After the small talk died out, Paul brought up a piece of band business. There was going to be a concert in the Woodstock area of New York State. Nearly half a million people would be in the audience for three days of rock and roll. Of course the organizers wanted the Beatles.

"You wait until I'm weak and sickly with no resistance at all and then you try to pull us back out onto some stage in Woodfuck, New York?" asked Lennon.

McCartney shrugged. "That's about the size of it, mate." He tried his best attempt at reverse psychology. "You're right. It's better to just play it safe."

"You see? You're doing it."

"George and Richie said they'd do it, if you were healthy enough."

"George said he would play at Woodstock?"

"Bob Dylan has a place up there. Says it's nice."

"On one condition. We have to play 'Give Peace a Chance' and 'Cold Turkey.'"

Paul would have negotiated the terms except that John had fallen asleep, heavily medicated as he was, during the conversation.

After watching him for another hour, Paul went out into the hallways and chatted with Dr. David Milne. He assured the doctor that he well understood the reason why the hospital frowned upon men and women sharing a room, but he explained that John and Yoko were so close that it would naturally speed up their recoveries.

Milne, by this time, knew very well who his patients were. The tiny cottage hospital was already playing host to a media circus of reporters and TV crews that had snatched up every spare B&B in the area.

"Maybe I can get them to behave for you," offered Paul. "Let's make everybody happy."

With that, Paul went outside to meet with reporters and fans. He gave journalists the perfect sound bite: "This is what happens when you let John Lennon behind the wheel." After some friendly Q and A, he played an acoustic version of "Two of Us" on a guitar thrust before him by a fan and dedicated it to John and Yoko's speedy recovery.

Inside, Milne had asked for volunteers to move John next to

Yoko in the maternity ward. All the hospital staff wanted to help. The move was accomplished in record time, and John agreed to sign autographs if everyone else at the hospital agreed to no photos because both he and Yoko had suffered facial cuts.

Once John and Yoko were side by side, it was "as if Linda and I'd disappeared or were invisible," said Paul. The McCartneys then took their leave, having spent just a few short hours on their mission of mercy.

Even so, they had shown up, making it one of the greatest respects that can be paid to a partnership or a friendship, and, as a consequence, the Beatles were going to play Woodstock.

BY THE TIME THEY GOT TO WOODSTOCK

By late July, John Lennon was back in the studio where the *Everest* recordings were in session at Abbey Road. Yoko was there, too, in a bed that the couple had moved in so she could rest and take it easy on her back. She did so for three days and then declared that the recording sessions were giving her a headache and that she would feel better back at their home. John said he would stay with her, but she insisted that he continue his work.

With Ono departed, there were moments of cohesion between Lennon and McCartney, particularly as they worked to fit together fragments of different songs. By the end of the month, they had their rough draft of the song medley that ran from "You Never Give Me Your Money" through "The End."

In just two weeks, the Woodstock Music and Art Fair would be underway in New York, and the band still had not decided as a group if they were really going to play. The incentive was that Woodstock was expected to be the largest rock concert of all time, scheduled to last for "three days of peace and love" and attract up to a quarter-million music lovers. If they didn't go, Apple would be represented by the new group they'd signed, Crosby, Stills & Nash.

This, apparently, bothered John Lennon so much that he decided that the only band to represent Apple would be the Beatles.

> [John] "I was out of my mind, of course. CSN was a great band, like we were a great band. I guess they were the competition that got my out-of-size ego to say yes. Once we were committed though, I mean, we'd played before five hundred people at the Roundhouse, and this was going to be five hundred thousand. And we had nothing prepared for a live show. We had two weeks. Paul'd put it in our heads, in that way he has, and we were sunk."

Allen Klein was informed that the Beatles would be playing between eight and twelve songs, a mix of released material and some new songs they had written this year but not as yet recorded. He also managed to keep CSN on the schedule, despite Lennon's wishes.

The Beatles set to work rehearsing in the Abbey Road Studios. Engineers recorded everything, and much of it has been released over the years. The focus, however, was on the performance. It was an excruciating timeline for a concert where expectations could not be higher.

> [Paul] "John was freaking out for about three days, I seem to remember. Then he came in one day, very intense, we'd seen that look before, and he says, 'If we bail, we fail.' The thing is, John Lennon had not seemed like the leader of the Beatles or anything for years by this point, but he did then. I just saluted him and said, 'Permission to come aboard.'"

Even George thought Woodstock was a good idea because his mentor, Ravi Shankar, was scheduled to play on the first day. Ringo's primary concern was that they should bring their own food and not trust what was being served in the August sun in upstate New York. The only thing that George and Ringo wouldn't do, they told Klein privately, was get on a stage with Yoko Ono. It was either a Beatles performance or it was not, but Ono was not a member of the band.

Klein, no fool, never passed these thoughts about Ono on to Lennon. Instead he told him, "John, I know you'll be worried about Yoko, knowing that she'll need to stay here in London and not travel, for her own safety. But I want to give you my absolute word that she will be taken care of round the clock."

Up to that point, John had assumed that Yoko would go with him. Now he was being complimented for his concern over leaving her behind and given assurance that Apple had his back over her care.

"Don't think this is going to fix the Beatles," Lennon told Klein. "I can't just keep playing on and on telling myself that it's the last time, and then there's another last time, and the madness never ends. It has to stop sometime."

After sharing a joint together to think on it more clearly, the two men agreed that the band would end after the concert and after the new album. Klein agreed to this scenario, buying time for Lennon to change his mind.

Festival organizer John Roberts and Apple agreed the appearance of the Beatles should be a secret until they actually showed up on stage, the same way it had gone down in London at the Roundhouse. Roberts agreed because the concert was a guaranteed sellout, and logistics were already overwhelmed.

The Beatles disembarked without incident at New York's JFK International Airport on Saturday, August 16, the second to last day of the concert. Personnel from nearby Stewart Air Force Base were available to assist in getting the Beatles in and out of the concert venue. Sullivan County, where the concert was taking place, had already declared a state of emergency.

That same morning, New York Governor Nelson Rockefeller ordered ten thousand New York Army National Guard troops to the festival.

"The situation is too volatile, and it's an unacceptable risk to the health and safety of the band," argued Peter Brown. He strongly urged everyone to get back on a plane and return to England.

If the imminent presence of troops wasn't enough trouble, the concert was also hopelessly behind schedule. Woodstock had swelled to nearly five hundred thousand-plus concertgoers, who became, in and of themselves, a giant counter-culture rumor mill, churned by the chaos of bad weather, overcrowding, poor sanitary conditions, too many drugs, and not enough sleep.

The Beatles arrived at Max Yasgur's farm by a helicopter which dropped and swayed because of the turbulence, just as the approaching thunderstorm stopped the concert in its tracks. Joe Cocker played his last song, a cover of "With a Little Help from My Friends," and then the stage went dark, and the heavens fell in buckets.

Cocker's song choice seemed to confirm the rumors about the Beatles' surprise appearance. Over half of the audience stood in the rain and mud and waited. When the Beatles were finally brought in by the airmen of Stewart AFB, fans threw things at them, thinking they were part of the dreaded National Guard response. The group was transferred into hastily acquired panel trucks from a local bakery.

It became obvious there was not nearly enough security to protect them from the crowd. When the Beatles had to exit their vehicles, unruly fans pushed over a cyclone fence and nearly crushed the Beatles to death with their affection. Not since Beatlemania had the threat of trampling been so real.

The raging thunderstorm had created a power outage that roadies were working mightily to overcome. One man, Jason Andreason, suffered an electrocution that nearly killed him.

It was at that point that Nelson Rockefeller's contingent of National Guard troops actually showed up in force. Their uniforms and guns set off the crowd as it had never been set off during the previous two days. It was one thing to stand in line for three hours for an overflowing portable toilet, but it was something else entirely to see a police presence rolling up.

Backstage, it was clear to the Beatles and their entourage that this was turning into the closest call the band had experienced since an airport stand-off with the Philippine government during Beatlemania.

The four Beatles huddled together to determine what to do. Safety was already compromised, but now that the crowd was getting angry and belligerent toward the distant troops, the chance to escape was looking more and more time-critical.

"If we don't get up there and play," said McCartney, "this crowd will tear us apart."

"They'll tear us apart either way," said Lennon, his eyes flashing.

"If we're going to make a run for it, we should probably get moving," said Ringo, lighting a cigarette. "Or stay. Either way a dying man gets one last smoke."

George, as described by stagehands, had closed his eyes for what seemed like a minute while his bandmates argued. Ringo held up a finger to quiet them. "Careful, boys, we don't want to wake him."

When George opened his eyes again, he spoke as if it was glaringly simple, an answer in front of them the entire time: "The way out is the way in. Play on."

Harrison's line is now a legendary part of rock and roll history. In 1998, the Nike shoe company licensed this phrase for its re-branding campaign from "Just Do It" to "Play On."

The Beatles took the stage at 3:57 p.m. as the clouds began to clear, and some ten thousand National Guard troops fanned out around the crowd. The internal debate that had swirled about for days as to whether they would begin with a McCartney or a Lennon song was solved by circumstance in favor of a Harrison song, in particular, "Here Comes the Sun," which they had learned how to play only in the last month.

At the end of the song, Lennon addressed the crowd:

[John] "That's a song by George that'll be on our next album. Some of you may have noticed that more people have just shown up here, some music fans that the State of New York has given a day pass in order to join us. This next song's for them."

With that, the Beatles broke into "Come Together" from the *Get Back* album, followed by "Lucy in the Sky with Diamonds," "Let It Be," and "All You Need Is Love."

While the band had prepared only these songs for performance, they were informed between songs that the promoters were in conversation with the governor's office in hopes that Rockefeller would pull the National Guard troops back beyond the venue to the outside perimeter. If the Beatles would only keep playing, the crowd would focus on them and then once the deal is concluded, the band could make the announcement. It was a way to avoid violence.

After playing some jam-session quality versions of "Back in the U.S.S.R.," "While My Guitar Gently Weeps," and "Glass Onion," the band could pass on the good news.

[John] "We've just been told that the National Guard has enjoyed the concert very much, and have agreed to start heading home. We want them to remember their visit, so we thought we'd sing them out of here. You know the words."

With that, the Beatles launched into Lennon's "Give Peace a Chance," a song everyone knew the lyrics to. The performance became a sing-along as troops began a more or less orderly withdrawal through the mud, setting up perimeters at the Yasgur property lines.

This, of course, left the Beatles with one big problem. Now that they were done playing, they, too, wanted to make a strategic retreat. Only now all the concertgoers knew that any rumors they might have heard about the Beatles were true.

In the end, subterfuge won the day. Allen Klein, who had come with them on a mission he told people was worth risking his life for, put together a matching team of hippies with approximately the same hairstyles and beard growth as each of the individual

Beatles. Then he had John, Paul, George, and Ringo swap clothes with them.

> [Ringo] "It was straight out of one of our movies. George
> ended up with pants that were too big and almost fell off him.
> I ended up with pants that were too tight, but that was okay.
> It made me feel I was back in Liverpool starting my career."

The imposters left with an impressive security guard, heads down, and did a feint to the left. With crowd dynamics at work, the four Beatles, their entourage, and a better security detail went out to the right.

Once they were safely back at New York's JFK, Lennon minced no words. "I shat my pants. Fortunately, they weren't mine to shat upon, and all is well again."

As it turns out, the four stoned hippies who swapped clothes with the Beatles made it out alive, too. There were tense moments when the crowd discovered that they were not the Fab Four but just average guys like themselves. Scott Colosimo, one of the four decoys, summed up his experience: "I wish I hadn't been on acid when I agreed to do it," he said. "I didn't even know what was happening, and when I woke up in the mud the next day, I was naked. People knew I was wearing George's clothes, and I guess they just helped themselves."

Woodstock remains, to this day, not only a seminal cultural turning point for rock music but yet another redefining moment for the band. Not only were the Beatles the biggest attraction in the world, but they had performed under extremely dangerous circumstances. Their legend was not growing smaller with time, but larger.

Today it's impossible to think of Woodstock without remembering the Beatles on that stage, helping the counter-culture say goodbye to the 1960s.

CLIMBING EVEREST

When the Beatles returned to England, they met with reporters at Heathrow. John opened with, "We're all glad to be alive. Love to Yoko."

"We're all going to take a few days, but not too many," Paul said, "because we have an album to finish called *Everest*, and we'll be getting back to Abbey Road to work on it." When asked what the Himalayan mountain had to do with anything, he said, "Because you have to nearly kill yourself to get there, man, and, when you do, you can barely breathe." It was a dark snapshot of his own mind.

Ringo was eager to get back to work. "Playing drums all day may be the only way to calm me down," he said, lighting one cigarette off his last one.

George spoke little, primarily serving to confirm exactly what he had said to his bandmates before they took the stage: "The way out is the way in." Asked to explain it further, he answered the reporter testily, "You know exactly what it means. It means what it means."

The usual witty banter of the Beatles was in short supply this day. They answered questions for just six minutes before John walked out. Soon he and Yoko were reunited at their new Lennon estate at Tittenhurst Park at Sunninghill, Berkshire. The Lennons then went to bed in their early-Georgian country house, refused all calls, and emerged four days later. Both of them went to the Abbey Road studio together, and the conflict the band felt toward Yoko's presence resumed to the level it had been a month earlier with one difference.

> [Yoko] "I could have stopped John from going to Woodstock with them. Since what happened, I wish I had. But they knew I gave John to them for what they wanted, but now they had to give us something back that we wanted."

The sessions went on, with Yoko often knitting quietly in

the studio, occasionally giving John a note about what the band was doing. Linda McCartney actually dropped by twice and the women—both newlyweds—talked about something else they had in common. They weren't going to let the Beatles play in public again unless security was elevated dramatically.

"We called John and Paul out of a session and told them they were taking us to lunch," said Linda to her biographer before her death in 1998. "We explained that we weren't okay with what had just happened, and we weren't going to sleep with them anymore until they fixed the situation."

The next day, Apple's Allen Klein signed a contract with the security consultants he'd worked with while managing the Rolling Stones.

The actual recording sessions for *Everest* continued to be marked by a certain civility between the participants. After the final music was on tape, they all returned to Lennon's Tittenhurst estate to shoot the album cover. They dutifully posed in a variety of locations, standing in weeds, outside of buildings, and in the beautiful garden area.

They even posed for an alternate cover that was created by a team of set designers and was built to display John, Paul, George, and Ringo against a photo backdrop of the peak of Mount Everest. For this version, they posed in cold-weather gear and mocked planting the Union Jack in the snow.

After the photos had been taken, Lennon presented a catered lunch with food for everyone from George's favorite Indian restaurant, including selections from a special non-spicy menu for Ringo's stomach problems.

It was just a month since Woodstock, and they were celebrating the imminent release of their most ambitious album yet. Klein had shown up for the lunch with signature copies of the new deal he'd struck with Capitol Records that let the Beatles determine the ways in which their music could be manufactured and sold.

The contracts were signed, and the party was breaking up. "Just one more thing before you go," said John.

"It was the way he said 'just one more thing,'" said George. "I knew what he was going to say before the words got out of his mouth."

"I think we're all daft, talking about the rules for playing on stage again, and it's not just Woodstock," said John. "It's playing at all. I'm done, boys. I want a divorce, and this seems as good a time as any to do it."

Klein immediately said that it was the worst possible time. The people who had just put so many more dollars in their pockets with the new contract would not be happy to hear that the band had signed and then broken up the same day.

"It's always the worst time for you, Allen."

"Except that this time, it really is."

John was only too happy to enumerate his complaints: He wanted to spend all his time with Yoko. He thought Paul wanted to run the band and he was ready to let him, finally. Neither Allen Klein nor John Eastman could measure up to Brian Epstein. He found himself caring more about politics than music anyway.

To each complaint, there was an answer, usually one that Paul was forced to put forward. It was not either-or, he said. John could spend time with Yoko like he had been doing for nearly two years now and still record with the Beatles.

"I don't want to record with the Beatles, Paul," said John. "It's been a romp and a half for longer than we all thought and now we've all got to let it go, don't you see?"

Paul—gung ho, pro-band, believer in Beatles Forever—did not see. "This was your dream, John," he shouted, jabbing his finger forward. "It wasn't easy then and it's not easy now. But nothing else in your life is ever going to touch this."

"Thank God for that," said John.

John and Paul went at it, sending words spewing out of their mouths that they couldn't possibly want anyone to remember. George could go either way, he said, and delivered that message with the surly attitude he had been wearing since the Kubrick disaster. Ringo said it wasn't his call, given the givens, so he had no opinion. If they wanted to play, he would bring his sticks.

The solution for the moment was to grant John Lennon the reality that he so wanted others to ratify—that he was no longer in the Beatles. In exchange, Lennon agreed that for the moment, the demise of the group would remain a secret until the timing was better.

• • •

When *Everest* was released on September 26, 1969, fans immediately declared the album a masterpiece and bought it in record numbers. Ironically, the cover used neither the band's conventional rock group photos that were taken in the gardens of the Lennon estate, nor the ones that they posed for in front of the Mount Everest backdrop with the fake snow.

Instead, the album cover featured all four of the Beatles walking briskly, legs outstretched as if in choreography, to the Woodstock stage area. Despite the seriousness of the moment, Paul McCartney appears to be laughing at something that John Lennon has said to him.

Whatever the source of the magic, the picture leaves an indelible impression. The fact that it was taken at Woodstock and, therefore, had nothing to do with the album whose cover it graced was simply ignored. It demanded to be used.

"John told us to step lively," Paul explained later about his smile. "He said we wanted to look good marching off to our executions. It was quite absurd."

John was about to place a new absurdity in the Beatles equation. Within mere days of the release of *Everest*, he had recorded another controversial single, this one about his struggle with heroin addiction.

Lennon, never one for halfway measures, decided to quit heroin all at once. He would go cold turkey, stop using, and ride out the storm. When he came out the other side, he did exactly what a great artist who has experienced a monumental life event might be expected to do. He wrote a song about it. Fresh off his rejection of the Beatles as a viable group, he recorded the song with Eric Clapton and Klauss Voorman, with only Ringo representing the band.

"Cold Turkey" was more of a Beatles song than "Revolution 9," but it made the heroin-inspired "Happiness Is a Warm Gun" feel like pop music by comparison. This one went beyond the personal pain of addiction and into the sheer agony of withdrawal.

Lennon was proud of the song. He was ready to release it as a solo with Ono's "Don't Worry Kyoko" on the B-side and planned to give the credit to his Plastic Ono Band concept. The problem, of course, was that doing so would make the current split that much more public.

Hearing about the brewing impasse from their respective Beatles, Allen Klein and John Eastman realized they would have to speak to each other and work something out. The only problem was that Klein and Eastman were no longer speaking to each other. Paul back-channeled to Lord Beeching, the man who had come closest to being named the leader of Apple earlier in the year, and asked him to introduce himself into the situation as a necessary "layer of separation."

At a hastily arranged meeting of the Beatles and their representatives, Lord Beeching was presented as a consultant who had been brought in by Klein and Eastman to review the overall financial condition of Apple and, of course, the group itself.

> [Lord Beeching] "While the solo ambitions of each member of the Beatles should be respected long-term, for the immediate future and the viability of your company, you simply cannot let that division in your ranks be visible as you seek to instill solvency and discipline to Apple Corps. The Beatles must remain the priority of this company if your goal is to save the company, on this we cannot compromise."

Lennon stared at Beeching for the entire monologue and,

when it was finished, innocently asked, "Who are you again?" Lennon felt he was being ganged up on, and he complained to Klein, loudly.

Beeching told everyone that the question was greater than what should happen with "Cold Turkey." He believed that any singles that came out should be released as Beatles records, no matter who wrote them or recorded on them. Although this was clearly directed at John, Beeching took aim at Paul as well.

He demanded that all songs written by a Beatle be recorded by the Beatles. Paul's current work on "Goodbye" for Mary Hopkin had given her an international hit. The same was true for "Step Inside Love," which had been a hit the year before for British singer Cilla Black, and "World Without Love" back in 1964, which had been a number one hit for Peter and Gordon. Most recently there was "Come and Get It," written by McCartney, slated to be recorded by Apple's Scottish protégés, Badfinger, and used in *The Magic Christian* film. That, Beeching said, needed to be reversed immediately. He demanded the song be placed on the next Beatles album.

Beeching slammed his palms on the fine wood conference table.

> [Lord Beeching] "These are bad business decisions. They must stop. Apple artists should not require the Beatles working for them as songwriters. They do need a company that operates as a professional business, and allows them to pursue their artistic ambitions and seek financial reward for them. They deserve that, and nothing more."

"I was prepared to walk out because they were obviously there to kill 'Cold Turkey,' but then Old Man Beechfinger started yelling at Paul more than me," said Lennon. "I started to like him a lot more, honestly." Beeching did leave room for an exception to the rule, which allowed a member of the Beatles and another artist to perform a kind of music that was clearly not the music of the Beatles. This was aimed to not only give Lennon the wiggle room to continue to record and produce avant-garde material with his wife but also to let Harrison do an Indian sitar album if he wished. As for "Cold Turkey," the song could easily exist in the Beatles catalog, and that's where it belonged, even if it was about drugs.

"You think you can all just ignore what I told you out at my house and I'll forget about it," Lennon told the room. "I'll agree, for now, you buggers, but the day is coming."

The agreement that Lennon signed on was simply that "Cold Turkey" would be released as a Beatles song on the A-side. Yoko's song was moved from the B-side and placed on the Lennon-Ono experimental *Wedding Album*, a similar solution to the "Revolution 9" impasse. McCartney was not eager to contribute a B-side to a piece that was about heroin withdrawal, so he stepped aside, opening the way for Harrison to get a song of his that had been passed over in the *Everest* sessions to take the spot. His "All Things Must Pass" would be the flip side, both musically and spiritually to Lennon's painful lament.

Though Lennon's open-mindedness on the subject of tolerating the Beatles a while longer was something that Paul, George, and Ringo did not expect, it did not come as a surprise to Allen Klein. He knew how shaky his number one client was, and he was doing something about it.

Klein heard the news out of Hollywood first. It seemed that United Artists was exploring an animated *Yellow Submarine*-style film for *The Lord of the Rings*. Based on signed contracts, UA had the right to do this irrespective of the Beatles' cooperation.

Not wanting to see the Beatles re-cast as cartoon characters, Klein reached out to UA to begin high-stakes negotiations between Kubrick, United Artists, and Apple to discuss whether an agreement could be reached to complete the live-action film version of *The Lord of the Rings*.

Given that Kubrick and Lennon had spent the better part of 1969 ridiculing each other to anyone who would listen, this was surprising news to Lennon, who couldn't understand why Kubrick would change his mind and why he should care if the director did.

"You and Kubrick have gotten great publicity out of your

fight," said Klein. "Now two world-class pricks are coming together to make the movie of the century. I can sell that." Only Allen Klein could have gotten away with calling John Lennon such a name, but he knew how Lennon thought.

Both John and Paul were mired in controversy as 1969 ended—John, for his full-frontal nudity on *Two Virgins*, his acknowledgment of drug addiction, and the return of his MBE medal, and Paul, for literally having to defend his life after an American disc jockey started a rumor that convinced fans that "Paul is dead." Among the proof offered was the fact that McCartney was the only one smiling in the *Everest* cover photo, which could only mean he was laughing in the graveyard.

"I'd been looking for a sign, a way to keep the Beatles alive," McCartney said to *Look* magazine. "Having people out there saying I was already dead feels like a bit more than I was expecting."

At Christmas time, John and Yoko planned to finish up their Bed-In year with a shocking billboard campaign, featuring giant white spaces in Times Square and London and eight other global hot spots. The signs would read, "War Is Over! If You Want It. Happy Christmas from John and Yoko."

Trying his own strategy to keep John in the band, Paul suggested to the Eastmans that Apple should pay for the campaign and that the signs might even be funded by the Beatles. John reacted to this news as if Paul was trying to steal his grand idea. It was Yoko, however, who showed him what the campaign cost might be and actually suggested that this time Paul just might be right. John signed off on the idea.

"If John thinks war can be ended just by changing your mind and thinking differently," Paul said to Ringo, "then maybe he'll change his mind about the band."

Ringo considered this over a cigarette before offering his opinion. "Don't count on it," he concluded. "Wars are simple things. The Beatles have real issues."

CHAPTER THREE

AND THE BAND PLAYS ON (1970)

NO PART HARMONY

As 1970 dawned, everyone knew that whether the group survived or not was up to the capricious moods of John Lennon more than anything else. These days, he seemed to feel as if the Beatles were no more real than an LSD experience after you've crashed, slept it off, and started a new day with a jolt of strong coffee.

Lennon and Ono had stayed in Denmark over the holidays to be with Yoko's daughter, Kyoko. It was here, in Aalborg, that Lennon and Ono announced plans to shave off most of their shoulder-length hair, pledging to auction the shorn locks for a charitable cause.

On the other side of the world, in America, the ploy was noticed by Bernardine Dohrn, the radical Weather Underground leader, and her boyfriend William Ayers. As busy revolutionaries, they filed the memory away and went about their work supervising bomb-making and writing manifestos. Their attention would haunt John Lennon in years to come.

In the present, however, Lennon's publicity stunt was in clear violation of contracts that stated *The Lord of the Rings* would require all four Beatles to be on the set in early March with "no significant changes to their current appearances." Even so, Lennon mailed director Stanley Kubrick a lock of his hair with a doodle inscribed *"sorry, luv, johnandyoko."*

Kubrick immediately sent the lock of hair to Apple offices with his own handwritten note:

> Please advise your client, Mr. Lennon, that he will need to submit to the shears once again, as I have now determined, based on his current actions, that the role of Gollum will need to be played with a bald head. Best wishes, Stanley Kubrick.

Not that John Lennon cared much about contracts of any kind. He and Ono had recently performed at the Toronto Rock and Roll Revival, singing several new songs, even though, technically, under the current Beatles operating agreement, playing outside the group was not allowed. Lennon didn't ask for permission then, nor was it granted.

• • •

George Harrison had been on a recent creative tear, touring with Eric Clapton and Delaney & Bonnie, basking in the creative equality he felt was so missing in his experience with the Beatles. If Lennon went ahead with his Plastic Ono Band solo project, Harrison reasoned, then he would pull together all his songs that had been rejected by Lennon-McCartney into his own solitary declaration of independence to be called *What Is Life*. While his mind was still technically open to new Beatles collaborations, he knew that if the solo years arrived, then he would be out of the gates with new material as fast as any of them.

Even Ringo was working on an album called *Sentimental Journey*, a collection of standards so square that he hoped they might actually be hip. Mostly, having been bitten hard by the film bug after his appearance in *The Magic Christian*, he was looking for a path to more screen work since the buzz on *The Lord of the Rings* was already huge. Ringo found himself in negotiations with B-movie producer Russ Meyer to appear in his next film, *Beyond the Valley of the Dolls,* and while he'd at first jumped at the opportunity, he soon had agents telling him he could do better.

Paul McCartney was still at his home at St. John's Wood, where he had reluctantly started his own solo album just before Christmas. He'd always wanted the Beatles to succeed more than the others had and was now determined not to be the only one standing empty-handed musically if this was truly the end. McCartney, the Beatle most likely to go commercial and add the producer's extras, wasn't even playing with a band. His concept involved doing everything himself, including the drums, with just minor assistance from Linda.

Still hanging over all this activity was the critical decision about how to properly run Apple. The manager's job was not exactly Allen Klein's, nor did it belong to either of the Eastmans. The differences had been papered over and the group had lumbered on. Yet if Apple was to be truly righted, it wouldn't happen with only solo albums and emerging artists.

Everyone knew that success had a name, and that name was the Beatles.

• • •

As if to force the issue, John Lennon awoke on the morning of January 27 with the song "Instant Karma!" in his head and made plans to record it the same day. As it happened, Phil Spector, the legendary American producer known for his signature Wall of Sound technique, was in town, looking for work after his self-imposed retirement in 1966. That same night, the Lennons and Spector converged on London's Abbey Road Studios, along with George Harrison representing the Beatles, Billy Preston, and Klaus Voormann. George Martin was not asked to attend.

Lennon's goal with "Instant Karma!" was to write, record, and release it within a period of mere days, making it one of the fastest released songs in pop music history. He intended it to be a Plastic Ono Band song, not a Beatles song.

The concept had emerged during the Denmark vacation when the Lennons were introduced to the idea that the eternal Buddhist law of cause and effect could be instantly achieved and not spread out over a lifetime. For the always impatient Lennon, it meant, for good or ill, your actions could catch up with you overnight.

When he played the rough song for Allen Klein, hoping it would help explain his vision of a John Lennon solo single, Klein explained back that John needed to play by the rules currently in effect until they were not in effect anymore. Translated, this meant that if "Instant Karma!" was to be released as a single, it still needed to be a Beatles single, and the writing credit would still have to be in favor of Lennon-McCartney.

"You asked me to wait, and I have, but when is that over?" asked John. "I'm paying you to represent me, so fucking represent me, Allen."

"John did it the Beatles way over 'Revolution 9' and 'Cold Turkey,'" Ono reminded Klein.

Klein had no choice but to agree that the time was at hand for a real sit-down to determine the fate of the band. He would set it up as soon as everyone returned from the film shoot in Ireland, nearly six months in the future.

Stranded in Middle-Earth

The *Woodstock* documentary and its accompanying soundtrack were released while the Beatles were freezing on the set of *The Lord of the Rings* in a harsh Irish winter.

Copies were messengered from London to their hotel, one for each Beatle. Each of them and their wives, girlfriends, and family members, plus the associated Apple polishers, all piled into the pub. The room had a turntable and a sound system that was only modestly bad, and cranked up, the distortion actually sounded edgy. Crew members, hotel staff, and patrons were all forced to stand outside the closed door, listening. The only outsider allowed to attend was the bartender, Innis Magruder.

Every member of the group still harbored mixed feelings about the Woodstock performance, or "debacle," as Lennon dubbed it. The experience produced an adrenaline-inducing surge they had never felt before, yet all four would go on to describe the events of that day as the most terrifying they had ever endured in their entire lives.

That day in the pub they played the entire album from start to finish in the order it was built. Everyone talked back and forth through much of it, and pints were downed in the process. When it came to the side devoted to the Beatles, however, no one spoke.

It was a miracle set, however. Not only had the Beatles survived, literally, their encounter with their fans on Max Yasgur's farm, but they were all so amped up from the experience that their playing maintained an urgency and power that surprised everyone.

At the end, Ringo lit another cigarette and broke the ice. "Too bad Apple doesn't have a bigger piece of that one."

Apple did not distribute the Woodstock project. Until the last minute, it was unclear whether Apple would allow the performance by the Beatles to be included in either the film documentary or the soundtrack. A deal was struck after concert promoters threatened to sue the Beatles for using the iconic image from Woodstock for their own *Everest* album.

• • •

During the long winter and spring of 1970, the members of the Beatles were writing songs but most often keeping them to themselves. The leadership at Apple Records, feeling desperate for a new product and cash flow, kept a wary eye on this dynamic.

The public had a voracious appetite for any product from the Beatles. Allen Klein wanted new songs, but he would settle for what he could get.

With the help of Neil Aspinall, Klein began relentlessly

dissecting the Beatles catalog for songs that hadn't made the cut in past sessions and remained unreleased but recorded. He also inventoried all the singles. It had been standard method for Apple not to release singles on albums ("Let It Be" being the exception on *A Doll's House*), making the buyer pay twice for a song. But if they could all be collected and combined with a handful of unreleased new songs, that could provide a lot of value for fans.

Klein's intense commercial assessment of product practically guaranteed that *The Beatles Again* would be an album with no cohesive theme in content or production legacy. It was simply a packaging by him and Aspinall, a "cleaning up" of the catalog as it were, a chance for fans to own all the songs on thirty-three LP albums and not just forty-five RPM records.

Even so, it was a Beatles album. It was even one that John Lennon had to love, or at least not completely hate, because it included his "Cold Turkey," now formally embraced into the canon of the Beatles. And Yoko approved of the inclusion of "The Ballad of John and Yoko."

George liked the fact that he got three songs for the first time. Ringo did not place a song but, as always, made his point with humor. "There's so many incredible songs of mine to choose from, who can really blame them? It's impossible to pick just one."

Lord Beeching loved *The Beatles Again*, too, even though he never took to the music himself. He felt victorious that the recording of "Goodbye," a song that had been designated for Apple artist Mary Hopkin, had been pulled back into the Beatles universe through some behind-the-scenes politics.

So, for a thrown-together pile of yesterday, it remained a tasty meal. The album was still the dominant form of music for almost all Beatles fans. They wanted these singles on an album they could enjoy without having to change records. Even the fans seemed happy.

The question, then, was whether a brand-new album by the Beatles would suffer the same analysis. Would it sound like a set of tracks that had no relation to each other, like the Lennon-inspired anarchy of *A Doll's House*? Or would it sound like the magical McCartney-fueled polish of *Everest*?

• • •

Late in 1969, the script for *The Lord of the Rings* had been greenlit by United Artists, which was something of a formality given the famed director had been working on pre-production since the year before, and then some. Making it official, however, meant that the Beatles had an obligation to perform, a stipulation they'd agreed to almost two years prior when they affixed four individual signatures to a contract.

Soon messengers arrived at Apple Records with copies of production schedules detailing the scenes each Beatle would be in and on what days, and on and on. Work started the next month.

"At that point, I was only interested in one thing," said John. "How much of my life did they want?"

As it turned out, the production requested four entire months of their lives, with the option to call them back for shoots of up to three weeks. Because the four characters never all appeared in the same scene, there was individual time off planned into the schedule, and Lennon received more of it than any of the others.

Kubrick had decided on the gear he would take into battle—a Mitchell BNC camera and a pair of ultra-rare Carl Zeiss prime lenses. They had been created for NASA to use in the Apollo space program and were modified especially for the director to create a painterly and cinematic Middle-earth.

The war he intended to wage was in the service of one mission—to shoot *The Lord of the Rings* in natural light. His soldiers included the Beatles, and he openly questioned their readiness for the task ahead. Still, he thought, he could bend them to his will if he had to. To make his human actors appear to scale as the Dwarves, he decided to have oversized settings and giant props, meaning that there would be arguably way more special effects than were used in *2001: A Space Odyssey*.

What the four Beatles didn't know at this moment was that J.R.R. Tolkien had balked strongly at their casting and demanded that the production be stopped. In an act of supreme and unheralded irony, Kubrick got on a plane bound for Los Angeles to meet with UA executives late in 1969 and told them he had come around on the Beatles.

"I do not personally like these young men, nor do I listen to their music," he stated. "But I know they have something special to give as artists, and it will be a cultural loss if we do not make this statement on film this year."

Tolkien was then told that the contract he signed would be honored, but that contract did not give the author creative rights over the film version of his books. The studio made the decision to give that authority to Stanley Kubrick, said the lawyers, and Kubrick had exercised his authority properly in the casting of the Beatles.

Tolkien, 78, let the matter go, knowing that at his age he might not be alive for another attempt at the material's adaptation and secretly breathing a sigh of relief that it would be a live-action film and not an animated one. His rationality paid off. The pre-production screenplay began with a character known as "The Author," who sat in a book-lined study. The part was offered to Tolkien himself, and he accepted.

It was against this backdrop that the Beatles reported in the winter of 1970 to the freezing Irish countryside.

The production took over Ireland's Ardmore Studios and fanned out across surrounding County Wicklow, with a couple of side trips to the highlands of central Ireland. Kubrick had set an army of carpenters and set designers to work, and when the Beatles and their families arrived, they were able to walk through a model of Middle-earth as big as a Hollywood studio. Annamoe, a small hamlet some thirty-two kilometers south of Dublin, became the base camp for the production and for the Beatles. The Glendalough Hotel was ground zero.

Overall, the Beatles had arrived in poor spirits, miserable

about being forced together by a signed contract with UA for a project that they wished they could abandon.

> [George] "I don't know if they'll admit it even now but we were all scared to death. Kubrick was the most intimidating man I've ever met. And I knew Allen Klein."

When they were on set, they would just often as not ignore each other. If the breaks were long enough, they would return to their individual trailer to work on songs and hang out with their wives and families when they visited the set.

Over the next five months, the Beatles would be together often, each trying to satisfy their collective commitment to the production of a movie that grew more complex with every passing day. Yoko was the only one of the wives to have shown up on the first day and remained at John's side the entire time. When he was on set, so was she, often seen sitting quietly in a director's chair. She spoke to John often but rarely to anyone else.

Soon, Linda McCartney joined Paul, along with their children, Heather and Mary. Linda tended to stay near the hotel as her base camp and was rarely seen on the set. "I know nobody really needs me there," explained Linda to the locals in town, "and I see Paul every day as it is when he comes home."

Eventually, both Maureen Starkey and Pattie Harrison turned up as well. Over the five months, the spouses came to know each other "too well," as the joke went. Sides were chosen; first, Maureen and Pattie against Linda or against Yoko. In time, this led to an awkward alliance between Yoko and Linda, who both felt that they were each more special than the others, mirroring the feelings their husbands had to their own bandmates.

At first, the antagonism the Beatles felt for each other did become visible, both on set and at the nearby Glendalough Hotel, a smallish accommodation that was thoroughly unprepared to host the film crew and the Beatles at the same time. As the days turned to weeks and then to months, however, some of the bandmates were working together by virtue of proximity, usually involving George as the catalyst. Slowly and steadily, the work allowed them to hate each other less by aiming their tired and negative feelings at the man who never let them forget that he was in charge: Stanley Kubrick.

Kubrick felt that the Beatles, John and George in particular, were not professional enough, not committed enough to the movie. George was quiet in his defiance, while John was another matter entirely. The problem was that each represented an iconic *Lord of the Rings* character. There was no cutting any of them from the film.

George was cast perfectly, most people agreed, as Gandalf, a characterization that allowed him to stand on a height-conveying apple box in each dialogue scene. Apple had their own branded apple boxes made up and sent over during the production. Both Harrison and Kubrick agreed they were too cheesy to use, and the boxes were given away to fans who plagued the production from the first day. Within a year, they could fetch a price of over $1,000 each.

John was often vocal, quick with a put-down or an ironic dismissal, or stoned and, on occasion, drunk and belligerent. On the other hand, he was playing Gollum, another inspired piece of casting. He had even submitted to a near head shave. "Near" because the director had the hairdresser cut Lennon's hair in such a way that it seemed to be falling out as if from a terrible affliction.

"I'm just being a method actor, I am," explained John to Kubrick on one particularly trying day. "I can't just turn on and off being a complete arse like it's a switch. You have to get your head in the game."

Kubrick tolerated Paul as an inconvenience to be overcome in his filmmaking process but drew the line at letting Paul shadow him to "pick up a few directorial tricks and such." Playing Frodo made Paul the most important of Kubrick's untested actors, and the director knew his performance would either hold the movie together or launch it into space. He was dedicated to suppressing

Paul's overt charms and replacing them with a more brooding Hobbit attitude that he described as "happy-go-lucky meets the end of the world."

Ringo was dismissed as "just an actor," a statement that Ringo agreed with. In this context, the drummer knew from his other non-Beatles film experiences that it was best to put everything you could aside and think about the job at hand. Ringo took the role of Samwise Gamgee quite seriously and went so far as to have an acting coach flown in.

The production ground on. Kubrick was as precise and tyrannical as his reputation and had a very clear image of what he wanted, down to storyboard and planned shots. Ringo, while professing his desire only to act, was also on the set most days, obviously watching.

> [Ringo] "He would take lenses and a viewfinder and get on the set with the actors, us or whoever, and maybe a grip with some tape. We'd have to go through the scene ten, fifteen, twenty, thirty times while he looked at every possibility with every lens and figured out his first shot. Then everything grew out of that first shot, including you. Exhausting, man."

While Kubrick's reputation as a control freak was huge in the industry, the truth as experienced by the Beatles was different. They saw a filmmaker who seemed to be always trying things out and experimenting. Often, Kubrick would ask the Beatles to improvise a scene or a line of dialogue, and if something interesting came out of it, he would push it even further.

By far the most unexpected by-product of the filming of *The Lord of the Rings* was the chance encounter between Lennon's father, Freddie Lennon (and his wife, Pauline), and Paul's father, Jim McCartney (and his wife, Angie).

It began with the arrival of Lennon's father, a man by whom John had been cruelly abandoned as a child and never involved with after. According to the son, "Now he's just showing up with his hand out."

Suddenly, Freddie and Pauline had a room at the Glendalough Hotel, courtesy of the production team. They hoped that by helping out Lennon with his family, he would be more compliant to their needs. "They should have barred him at the door if that's what they wanted," John shouted when he heard the news.

Over breakfast, Freddie and Pauline ran into Paul and Linda, who were sleeping in because of Paul's late call that day. Paul told Freddie about his own father, James, and what a fine musician he still was. Freddie, known for playing the trumpet and singing, said that they should get together and that he just knew they would hit it off.

McCartney mentioned this to his own father in a call later that day. Two days after that, James and Angie McCartney had a room at the Glendalough Hotel, courtesy of the production team. Whether this was a typical Paul quid pro quo or an act of wonderful empathy mattered not to John, who destroyed his own hotel room in a rage.

That afternoon, James McCartney and Freddie Lennon shared a pint in the bar at the Glendalough, a fine dark wood affair with darts and pool and a piano. When Paul and John returned from a long day of shooting in bad weather, they found their fathers singing tunes with some local Irish around the out-of-tune piano. The next night, Paul joined them. The day after that, the production had a tuner show up to set the piano back to health.

John could not quite make peace with this turn of events. He raged to Yoko against Freddie, and the fact that he couldn't throw him out without everyone hating him. He asked Yoko to do the deed and she refused. They decided that the only thing they could control was their own exit.

Under the evolving plan, John would strike a deal with Kubrick that he would stay three more weeks if the director would ban all family members from the set, providing a pretext to dismiss Freddie. It was at that point in the conversation that the phone rang. Kubrick's assistant was on the line, wondering ever so politely if John would be available to meet with Mr. Kubrick the next morning. Yoko ascribed this convergence to John's emerging psychic powers. In her mind, her husband had literally willed Kubrick into calling him by imagining the conversation.

Whether true or not, it was fact that three months into the production, Kubrick was ready to fire Lennon for insubordinate behavior, a charge that might have stuck better in the army than on a film set. The conversation took place during a scene break at 9:17 a.m. (so precise was the director that he noted the time in his diary), a time that Lennon felt was too early, although Kubrick had been on set for well over three hours at this point.

"I told him that he was a disruptive influence on the set," explained Kubrick to his biographer. "The fact that he had such a strong leadership personality but was so unwilling to work for the greater good meant that he had to go."

Stanley Kubrick told John Lennon that there were essentially two choices: either he could be fired and sued for damages to the production or he could drop the attitude long enough for the production to shoot a succession of three critical scenes. If Lennon played ball, then he could be on his way in ten days.

"We've got a deal then," John told his exacting director.

The next day, John tried to bid farewell to Freddie Lennon but ended up yelling threats so loudly at his father that the hotel staff wrote them down and gave them to Freddie in case he needed their testimony for a future legal case. Still, John Lennon got what he wanted—his father was on the next bus out, and, soon after, John and Yoko were in a limo on the way to Dublin, and a flight to Los Angeles.

MAKES ME WANT TO SCREAM

While killing time on the set in the early days of the production, John read *The Primal Scream* by California therapist Dr. Arthur Janov. He believed nearly all neurotic behavior could be traced to traumas endured in childhood. Given the scars inflicted upon

Lennon by his own parents, he hoped that he had found the cure he'd always been looking for.

Janov's therapy took the patient back to childhood to confront the pain by screaming it out, like a newborn just emerged from the womb. Lennon's troubled past began at age six when he was forced to choose between his separated parents. He selected his mother and then was abandoned by her anyway. And, of course, recent memory included screaming his pain at Freddie, then fleeing the film set.

As a direct result of primal therapy, Lennon's newest songs were exposed and vulnerable, presenting him as an angry rebel, a devoted soul mate, and even a questing artist trying to free himself from the shackles of Beatledom.

"As it turned out, I knew I had to find a way to express my feelings. I could scream or I could write songs or both," declared Lennon. "What seemed impossible was writing songs to be performed by the Beatles for even one minute longer."

Seeing his patient's torment, Janov confronted Lennon about his feelings toward the Beatles. He felt that John was not in a good place to make such a significant decision as to whether or not he was leaving the group for good. He should not break something that important until he had finished therapy. "These men, and they were all clearly men by this point, had gone through a special experience together," said Janov. "In my view, it was possible that the most meaningful way for John Lennon to cope with his feelings was to share them with his bandmates and the world."

Lennon commiserated about how Janov was making him feel "all wishy-washy" about the Beatles to one of the few men who could understand his feelings—Ringo Starr. The drummer had come to Los Angeles for more film auditions now that there was buzz over his performance in the Beatles-Kubrick collaboration.

Ringo read John the highlights of an interview Stanley Kubrick had just granted *Daily Variety*: "Asked about how the Beatles had turned out as actors, particularly John Lennon, Stanley Kubrick replied, 'Better than expected.'"

"Story of my life," concluded Lennon. "Let's hear it for low expectations."

The two men briefly discussed the group's future. It was simple, said Ringo. If the Beatles existed, then they needed to make an album. As strictly a business matter, *Everest* had been their best-selling album ever, and the soundtrack from *The Lord of the Rings* would hardly count as a full album to fans any more than *Yellow Submarine* did. If the Beatles did not exist, however, then they probably needed to break the bad news to the fans. Which way, he wondered, did John want to go?

There was some pressure to decide. Along with the *Daily Variety*, Ringo also had a copy of the month's *Rolling Stone* article that asked, "What Now Beatles?" That month, even our own *Rockstar* succumbed to doubt with the cover story "Are the Beatles Dead?"

Not creatively, they weren't. In the same way that the adventure in Rishikesh had generated its share of songs that the band recorded in their *A Doll's House* album, the time spent in Ireland making *The Lord of the Rings* had birthed a backlog of material from all four musicians. It would have to find an outlet as Beatles material, solo material, or a combination, but it wasn't going to remain unrecorded forever.

THE GRAND BARGAIN

Apple was still hemorrhaging money due to its pervading ethic of idealistic hippie chaos, expressed on the most petty level by rampant employee theft. It was so bad that several company cars had gone missing and were completely unaccounted for. Already the Apple Boutique clothing store had shuttered, and other divisions were looking like candidates for similar treatment. Apple Records was the only viable division, and with all the business troubles, even that designation seemed tentative.

The management situation remained unresolved, allowed to

continue as such by deferred decisions and indirect lines of communication and authority. Informally on retainer as a consultant, Lord Beeching had been coordinating between Allen Klein, on financial and accounting issues, and Lee and John Eastman, on legal and contractual issues. Yoko acted as a buffer for John, and Paul acted on his own behalf, with George and Ringo reporting to Klein. The arrangement was fraying nerves all around.

The Eastmans subscribed to the theory that being a part of the Beatles team was better than losing a fight and ending up in exile. What else could they do? What else could be done?

In a 1974 *Playboy* interview, Klein said, "Did I like this Rube Goldberg set-up? Of course not. Was I going to let it screw me out of the Beatles? No fucking way. I said yes so I could be around the next time the pieces had to be picked up."

• • •

Shortly before filming began on *The Lord of the Rings*, George Harrison took possession of his new property, the infamous Friar Park estate. The former residence of eccentric lawyer Sir Frank Crisp, it featured a massive garden system that included caves, grottoes, underground passages, a multitude of gnomes, and even a huge Alpine rock garden resembling the Matterhorn. The garden was in disrepair, but the home itself, a 120-room Victorian neo-Gothic mansion in Henley-on-Thames, was in even worse shape. A collection of cottages dotted the grounds, and most were equally in need of repair.

Yet the run-down Friar Park became the scene of perhaps the most important two days in the life of the Beatles as a rock group. After principal photography on *The Lord of the Rings* wrapped in Ireland on May 17, George was eager to spend some time at his home, which he had seen only in passing for the past four months. He and his wife Pattie strolled the grounds and the residence and realized that it would cost huge amounts of time and money to bring the property up to its full potential.

Pattie noticed that George was smiling. "We need to throw a party," he explained. "Our friends can't make it much worse, can they?"

With Peter Brown's help, the Harrisons produced an invite and list for a get-together that would begin on Friday night, May 29, and continue over the weekend, May 30 and 31. With more rooms than most hotels, even out-of-towners and expats could find a place to bed down. Furniture was rented and arrived in large trucks over the next week.

All three of Harrison's bandmates were going to be in London at that time for a Friday morning business meeting with Apple management. After they all agreed to come by George's at some point over the weekend, the meeting was moved to Friar Park and scheduled for Sunday afternoon. To this day, no one takes credit for the dubious idea to place a business meeting after a blowout party, but no one seems to have objected to its casual fusion, either.

Suddenly, however, what was being called "Weekend at George's" morphed into an event exponentially larger than its origin. George had visualized a dozen people when he first thought of bringing a group together to celebrate the fact that he and Pattie had moved into Friar Park. That group hadn't even included the other Beatles. Now, suddenly, it seemed like everybody was coming, and the guest list kept expanding.

Everyone working for Apple had been invited, and no one wanted to miss it. Allen Klein, Lee Eastman, John Eastman, Peter Brown, George Martin, Neil Aspinall, Mal Evans, and Derek Taylor. At least a dozen others. Many showed up with a family member or a plus-one for rock history.

Each Beatle was bringing a spouse, so Pattie Harrison was tasked with welcoming Yoko Ono, Maureen Starkey, and Linda McCartney to the house. She called each one of them to personally invite them and had rooms designated for each Beatle with decorations selected by the women in their lives.

Word spread throughout the music community. Elton John, Billy Preston, Eric Clapton, Mick Jagger, Keith Moon, Harry

Nilsson, Mary Hopkin, and James Taylor all said they'd drop by. Music producer Phil Spector heard about it and even though he had no plans to be in London, he told everyone that he was going to be in town on business and would definitely come by to see the place. Producer Glyn Johns would be there, and so, too, would Peter Sellers, Ringo's new actor friend from *The Magic Christian*.

Meanwhile, with the scale inflating by the moment, Harrison reached out not to Stanley Kubrick (whom he was not inviting) but to some of the key grips and other crew members he had met while filming *The Lord of the Rings*. Before long he had electricians laying soccer field quantities of electrical cable, powering temporary lights on the grounds and in most of the main meeting rooms inside. Several carpenters were on the job almost immediately, beefing up floors and walls as needed, while craft services swarmed the unique, wonderful, and horribly run-down kitchen.

Three large tents were rented and placed on the property in case it rained (which was likely), or in case leaky ceilings forced everyone outside (which was considered nearly as likely). Mostly the tents were there to accommodate any last-minute entertainment or to serve the food if the kitchen was deemed unusable.

Originally, the weekend had been pitched to potential attendees as an opportunity to enjoy some debauchery among friends, a kind of group urban camping adventure where guests could celebrate the relief of wrapping up their grueling film experience. That is certainly how the Beatles themselves viewed the gathering. To this day, however, no one is certain who first had the notion that people should show up to support George, Ringo, Paul, and John in working it out and keeping the Beatles alive. Nonetheless, the solidarity concept circulated rapidly.

"It might be better for the Stones if the Beatles left the scene," admitted Mick Jagger, "but they push us, and we can't be as good as we want to be without them. So, being selfish bastards as we are, we want them around."

George Harrison's Friar Park estate, in such sad disrepair, became the central nexus where the fate of the world's greatest rock band was likely to be decided. The venue seemed to embody the spirit of the group at the time—something once great and majestic, now falling apart, with secrets hidden in shadows.

On Friday night, the guests began to arrive. The Harrisons had hired Richard Eagleton, a professional planner, to coordinate with Apple and their friends. Eagleton had planned four Apple events over the past two years. Even Eagleton had to admit that this one had the potential to be epic, whether epically good or epically bad.

Eagleton had a list, four assistants, and four beefy security guys who bounced for local clubs. Everyone getting paid for their work had already passed the discretion test and could be counted on to keep quiet.

When Neil Aspinall arrived several hours early, it was decided that since George and Pattie were in the Manor (as they called it) and thus unavailable to be with the other Beatles, the Lennon, McCartney, and Starkey parties would be hosted in the individual cottages. This allowed all the Beatles and their spouses to either socialize or spend private time together and offered them the greatest respect for their privacy. Furthermore, they could feel free to come and go at different and overlapping junctures.

The only problem was that the cottages could be hard to find, especially in the dark, and George had no map to offer, so new was he to his own property. On the first night, John Lennon led Yoko Ono in the wrong direction, and the two of them wandered the grounds in a large circle for hours.

At the point when they were nearly ready to sleep in one of the caves they had stumbled onto, they ran into the McCartneys making what the Americans called "s'mores" with their daughter Heather and their baby, Mary. John and Paul had not seen each other since a mid-March argument in a torrential Irish rainstorm.

McCartney's parting words were, "Nice chatting with you, Sir Winston. Send us a post from the colonies."

Now, months later, in the glimmering outdoor fire pit outside their cottage, Linda offered to make something for their guests to eat, but Yoko begged off for them, saying they were suffering from jet lag and primal scream therapy.

"What do you scream about?" asked Paul. "If you don't mind me asking."

"We scream about all the fucking idiots who have thrown shit at us all our lives. You ought to know something about that." Lennon was spoiling for a fight.

McCartney looked over at his wife and kids. "Lin, baby, why don't you take the kids inside and put 'em in bed?" Linda understood it would be better for her children not to watch whatever might be next. In they went.

Not happy about being described as just another obstruction to John's brilliance, Paul hit back. "You're spending too much time inside your own head, John," he said and then turning to Yoko he added, "And you're not helping him."

"I'm the only one who is," Yoko replied.

With that, John and Yoko stormed off to find their own cottage. The enraged Paul followed them and was soon joined by Linda, who had put the kids down for the night.

By this point, the passion and profanity of the shouted attacks had attracted the attention of others who were at the party, including Apple "House Hippie" (formally, Client Liaison Officer) Richard DiLello, who was close to all the Beatles and their wives, plus the Apple Polishers, that inner circle of agents, managers, and others who worked for and with the company. DiLello had heard from enough of them that the potential breakup of the Beatles would be an event of such high magnitude that it should be documented, if possible.

DiLello had talked to documentary director Michael Lindsay-Hogg that very afternoon. Lindsay-Hogg, the man who documented the entire Kubrick-Beatles confrontation at Twickenham, was still working on a short promotional film to support *The Lord of the Rings* when it was released, and the confrontation was the centerpiece, including Lennon in Middle-earth costume relieving himself on the cardboard cutouts of the band members.

DiLello found Lindsay-Hogg unpacking his gear in the Manor and told him to grab his camera and some film. Together, the men ran across the property.

They set up the camera far enough away that neither the Lennons nor the McCartneys were aware of their presence. The microphone was a top-of-the-line directional style, and it managed to pick up the greatest open mic audio in pop culture history. It began:

> [John] "Your petty little lives aren't making you happy, man. Not that I personally give a fuck if you are or if you aren't. It's just an observation."

> [Paul] "Being a Beatle doesn't make your life petty. Thinking that it does, that's what does that."

As the battle raged, the documentarian snagged clean audio of John Lennon and Yoko Ono unleashing primal scream therapy at Paul McCartney and Linda McCartney, who managed to rage quite primally back at them.

For over an hour, the McCartneys and the Lennon-Onos stood among the trees of Friar Park, under a near full moon, screaming and cursing at each other. Eventually, having lost their voices, both couples retreated to their respective cottages.

"I said to Yoko after that, 'Well, now you see what I'm dealing with,'" said John with a shrug. "We wanted to leave then, but we were quite fucking exhausted, we were, so we crashed in the little fucking Hobbit cottage that George was so proud of and dreamed about ways that Paul could die for real this time."

McCartney was more stoic. "These people in Los Angeles just blew John's mind with their primal bip-bop or whatever you want to call it. I don't know if telling John Lennon that it's a good thing to yell at people is great advice, but they never asked my opinion."

By Saturday noon, nearly three dozen people were on the property. "Part couples retreat and part primal scream therapy" is how PR man Derek Taylor put it for members of the press who were, for the most part, excluded from the party on the basis of the band's need for privacy.

When *Rockstar*'s own Booth Hill found out about the weekend, he confronted Derek Taylor, who demanded as a condition of attending that he write directly and for attribution only if all four of the Beatles allowed it. Both Hill and Taylor knew that this was both impractical and unenforceable but pretended otherwise, feeling that if the event turned out to be a significant one in the life of the band, a trained journalist should be there to observe it.

To great fanfare, Mick Jagger showed up shortly after noon with a giraffe that he had rented from a traveling zoo. Jagger arrived by limo, drinking champagne, while the truck with the giraffe followed behind. He'd been wearing a pith helmet, but it fit so loose that he quickly lost it.

That afternoon, Jagger, whose band, the Rolling Stones, was no longer represented by Allen Klein, told Lennon frankly that McCartney was smart in wanting to hire his entertainment lawyer father-in-law Lee Eastman to manage the Beatles. "Oh, bugger off" was Lennon's reply.

By this time, an informal jam session had begun on the makeshift stage and continued on into the night. At one point, more people were playing instruments or singing on the stage than were actually in the audience.

That same night, Lennon and Klein tangled verbally in a drunken exchange. By the next morning, John realized Paul's, and now Jagger's, disdain for Klein was probably justified, although he remained staunchly opposed to Eastman. "I'm not asking Paul to sign off on my mother-in-law's hairdresser to comb his hair, and he shouldn't ask me to sign off on his father-in-law to watch my money," said John.

• • •

The official business meeting of the Beatles was scheduled for

Sunday after lunch in the dining hall of the Manor, around a grand table that was capable of serving thirty people.

"The vibe I got was that everything was going to be on the table," said Neil Aspinall, looking back in an '80s-era interview with *Rockstar*. "Considering the size of that table, it meant anything goes."

Richard DiLello and Mal Evans were set up at the entrance door. Their hand-scrawled list included all four of the Beatles, their spouses, Apple Management, Allen Klein, Lee and John Eastman, and Lord Beeching. Everyone else had to be evaluated before entering. One person who actually came in from the kitchen and took up position without permission was *Rockstar*'s Booth Hill.

Lord Beeching called the session to order. He noted that he was appearing for the second time in the capacity of a consultant, and that while he was happy to do so, it would also be the last time he would take on such a tenuous role. He addressed his first remarks to the Beatles themselves.

> [Lord Beeching] "You have created something extraordinary, and despite any negative emotions you may be feeling at this moment, you have every right to take pride in your accomplishment. Only the four of you can decide whether or not you should continue. It is our goal here today to give you the facts you need to assist you in your decision. Our first and only real order of business is you."

Beeching asked all the Beatles to postpone plans for their solo albums. He then asked them to blend their work on one more joint Beatles release in order to buy Apple time to set the house in order out of the glare of the media's spotlight. There were the fine points of implementing a new royalty deal to be worked out, and Apple needed to come at them from a position of strength.

Klein ventured his opinion that "Kubrick's damn movie" and all the powerful and rich people behind it would take an extremely dim view of the Beatles breaking up before they could help market the project. "These are Hollywood money people. They want the

Beatles, but they won't be afraid to sue us, and they have a lot of legal talent on their team."

Eastman ventured his rather cautious analysis of the contracts that had been signed with United Artists. While the contract was ambiguous on this point, he also felt that if the Beatles were not an active group during the film's release, UA would potentially seek damages.

The bleak assessment triggered immediate bickering. John accused Paul of setting up the entire weekend in some pathetic attempt to postpone the inevitable. "You should have just come to us, Paul, and we could have settled it among ourselves. We *have* settled it among ourselves. I have, anyway."

"Good for you, John," Paul said, "but the rest of us should be able to leave with our money, not without it." He noted that George, not he, had planned the party, and sat down with a huff.

The team eventually called a break so that John Eastman could meet with McCartney and Klein could meet with Lennon and Ono. Eastman and Klein told Harrison and Starkey that they were welcome to be a part of either discussion. They both alternated sitting in with the two groups and found themselves not liking Klein as much as John did and not liking the Eastmans as much as Paul did. However, both George and Ringo had one highly unexpected revelation—they both found Lord Beeching to be, as George expressed it, "highly tolerable."

After this had gone on for an hour, Ringo poured himself a stiff cognac from George's bar, placed the glass down, and started banging out a rhythm with his bare hands on the wood table. As people stopped talking and started listening, he wrapped up his percussive display with a flourish, took a drink, and said, "Let's hammer out this Grand Bargain then."

• • •

That's all that *Rockstar* can say with certainty. Booth Hill, the only journalist in the room, had been trying to appear as invisible as possible in the corner, but, despite his strong protests, was evicted when Lord Beeching learned that he was a reporter.

What we know from later interviews is that the tension in the room had not dissipated when they returned to full session. As Beeching began, Yoko whispered in John's ear. Eventually, Beeching's voice trailed off as all eyes fixed on the Lennons, waiting for Yoko to finish. Everyone knew that her opinion would likely settle the argument for John.

Finally, John leaned back in his chair and sighed. "What's it look like to be a Beatle for another year? Or five years?" he asked the men and women at the table. "That's what we want to know. Show us that, and maybe we'll dance on your string a while longer."

For the next two hours, Lennon stubbornly fought the room in a pitched battle to secure his artistic freedom to abandon the Beatles altogether. The pushback was strong. Not yet.

When they took their next break, however, Lennon sang a different tune. As he and Ono went outside to smoke, they ran into Mick Jagger, who asked how it was going.

"Looks like you may get your ass kicked by us a while longer, Mick," answered Lennon.

After three and a half hours of more discussion, everyone went home or back to their rooms and cottages on the Friar Park estate. Most party guests had already gone, but a few stragglers had stayed outside, smoking and drinking in the tents, curious to see how it would turn out.

The truth is that most of the participants in the Grand Bargain negotiations left that night or the next morning with slightly different memories of what exactly had been agreed to. Fortunately, John Eastman had a strong constitution and superior penmanship. He sat in the middle of Harrison's long, imposing table, and he filled two yellow legal pads with notes. They included details of the agreement, doodles that were bad impressions of John Lennon's artwork, and some dead-on observations about the relative strengths and weaknesses of the people he shared the table with.

Beatles scholars have gone through these legal pads at length.

Their favorite notation involves Eastman's description of the relationship between Lord Beeching and Allen Klein.

"*Barking Klein dog so far up Beeching's ass,*" wrote Eastman in block letters, "*that he can see light coming from the hole in his head.*"

Eastman took his legal pads and his son's near-photographic memory and translated them into a private memo from the offices of Lee Eastman. The memo has been quoted at length among historical documents but, given its usefulness in the central purpose of this article, we present it here in full.

• • •

TO: Lord Richard Beeching, Allen Klein
FROM: Lee Eastman, John Eastman
DATE: June 23, 1970
SUBJECT: The Beatles - Conference Notes

This is a summary of our understanding of the elements of agreement reached in the sessions held at Friar Park Estate over the weekend of June 19 to June 21. It has been constructed from our contemporaneous notes and follow-up conversations with several of the participants, notably yourselves.

Please do submit your questions, clarifications, and additions, and this office will release a revised version. A summary of this weekend's discussion and agreement now follows:

APPLE MANAGEMENT

The company will formalize its current corporate management structure. Lord Richard Beeching will assume authority for the company, effective immediately. Allen Klein will maintain responsibility for Management and Marketing functions. This office, and specifically Lee and John Eastman, both individually and collectively, will provide all Legal services. In matters where Klein or Eastman are in disagreement, the matter will be referred to Beeching for a final decision. Current Apple employees will be reevaluated by this management team, acting in concert to implement the decisions.

APPLE/BEATLES UNDERSTANDING

The Beatles agree to promote the upcoming *Lord of the Rings* film and soundtrack as a unified band in all their public pronouncements through a period of at least three months after the film's public release.

The Beatles agree on an annual basis to provide Apple with at least one original studio recorded album and one studio recorded single with an A-side and a B-side. Live performance albums are not included in this understanding.

Solo albums are not to be encouraged and should not affect the delivery in a timely manner of a yearly Beatles album.

The rules of the Lennon/McCartney songwriting credit will be changed. If the song is primarily a John Lennon song, the credit will be "Lennon/McCartney." If the song is primarily a Paul McCartney song, the credit will be "McCartney/Lennon." If the song has significant creative input from both, the credit will be "Lennon/McCartney."

INTERNAL BAND ISSUES

Each member of the Beatles spoke at length about their vision of the band's future, should they continue on together into the 1970s.

Paul McCartney states that he would like the Beatles to play live as a band and to even consider touring again, albeit with smaller venues. He cites the Roundhouse performance as a prime example. McCartney expects other band members to bring more energy to future recording sessions, although he did believe they were moving in the right direction with the recent *Everest* album.

John Lennon states that his sole attachment to the Beatles is that its financial success allows him to support more causes dedicated to social change. He will be contributing political material to all future albums and does not expect this material to be blocked by the others. He believes that the Beatles and Apple itself should align on the side of the protest movement in the Vietnam War debate.

George Harrison states that he expects to operate with creative equality to both McCartney and Lennon in all future albums. He is reticent to tour and play large crowds, citing the unfortunate events that occurred in upper New York state in the summer of 1969 at the so-called "Woodstock Concert."

Richard Starkey states that he is looking for a more stable band environment. He expects his three bandmates to accept their responsibility in making that happen.

There appears to be deep and genuine disagreement about the role of wives and girlfriends as they relate to the creative process. However, the Beatles state that they will work this out between themselves and that our assistance is not needed.

First brought up by Harrison but strongly endorsed by Lennon is the belief that there should be at least six months out of every year where they have no obligations whatsoever to the Beatles. They believe that all recording, marketing, and/or touring duties can be confined to a six-month period. They agree that a decision on the dates will be made by mutual agreement and our assistance is not needed unless asked for.

SUMMARY

The significant legal changes appear to be:

1) the management clarification,

2) the agreement by the Beatles to remain an operating group through the release of the current *Lord of the Rings* film,

3) and their agreement to supply Apple with a minimum yearly album and single, ideally for a period of five years.

We believe a brief memo, from Lord Beeching, stating these three developments and expectations should be sent to John Lennon, Paul McCartney, George Harrison, and Richard Starkey. With your sign-off, we will draft one for signature.

As Harrison, Lennon, McCartney, and Starkey all wish their

internal band dynamics to be an oral agreement held between them, there will be no need of signature copies and we will prepare none on those issues.

On the subject of the actual agreement between ourselves, however, a formal signature agreement will be available next week.

(Dictated/LVE)

• • •

So, there it was, laid out in a lawyer's dispassionate language. The so-called Grand Bargain.

It was a fragile peace, the equivalent of a temporary halting of the bombing raids that were then taking place over North Vietnam. Would it last? No one knew.

London music journalist Ray Connolly talked to Lennon shortly after the Weekend at George's and asked him about the process. "We all said some things we needed to say," said Lennon. "You have to be good and trashed sometimes to give peace a chance. World should take a fuckin' lesson now, you know?"

HOUSE BAND ON THE TITANIC

As it was, Paul McCartney gave each of his bandmates a week and, when he had heard from none of them, decided to ring them up himself.

He called Ringo first. The Apple studio was available next Tuesday for recording. "See you then," said Ringo. He liked being a Beatle—it was an all-access pass to a world that the solo Ringo could never inhabit, and he wasn't keen to start over.

Armed with his 2–0 status, Paul called George next. He laughed bitterly when he heard Paul's summons. "I wondered how long you'd give us." But George could hardly be the one to pull his support now, given that he had allowed his own home to produce the Grand Bargain.

That left only John. Paul found himself sitting at his dining room table looking at a phone that he could not bring himself to use to call Lennon. So he called George back and told him that he would have to be the one to call John.

> [Paul] "If I'd rung him, it's anybody's guess, isn't it then? But with George, it felt more business-like because John already knew that George would just as soon call it a day and go home, but that he'd bought into the whole rationale. That there must be a Beatles because Apple needs cash."

George made the call. "Hello, John."

"Oh, God no," said John. "Paul's gotten you to do this."

Invoking Paul's name made the conversation seem a bit less onerous to John and George alike, who talked briefly with one another to sort out the details. Tuesday morning, George suggested, looked good.

"I'll be in by four in the afternoon," said John, and then he hung up.

"I showed up at noon the first day," remembers Ringo. "Paul came by at one, George dropped in at two, and John made an appearance with Yoko at three, which we took as a good sign, as it was an hour earlier than when he said he would be there."

Each one of them had been preparing an album to release if the Beatles broke up, and Paul and George were well along in that regard, followed by Ringo and John. This meant that they all brought in songs to demo for the group.

What they found out, almost immediately, was that all of them had already cross-pollinated many of their creative thoughts during those long months they spent in Ireland trying to survive under Kubrick's heel. There were George songs he did with John, Paul songs he did with Ringo, a few with just Paul, and several George songs; even Paul and John songs that had riffs from one to other conveyed through George acting as a third party.

As the sheer amount of material became apparent, they briefly considered doing another double album in the style of *A Doll's House*. After some discussion, they came to the mutual agreement that they would prune what they had to a single album.

Still, the Grand Bargain had left one huge controversy unspoken and unresolved. Who, besides the Beatles themselves, should be allowed in a recording session?

To the irritation of three-fourths of the Beatles, Yoko Ono was back in the studio, as she had been for *Everest*, and *A Doll's House* before that.

> [Yoko] "John and I wanted to be together all the time so why shouldn't we? I knew how they felt about me but we knew that the only way Beatles could be saved was when they accept me."

> [John] "After *Everest*, I was done. I'd held it all in, been all nice and spicy, but I was on my best behavior because it was finally over. But now everyone says it has to go on or we're all going to be broke, you know. We figured if I couldn't get out right away, at least Yoko could come in so it wouldn't be so horrible."

There it was. It was John's decision that Yoko was going to be there for every single moment of this new album, whatever it ended up being called. Paul, George, and Ringo would just have to deal with it.

What John and Yoko didn't know was that Linda had made friends with the wives of the other Beatles during the film production of *The Lord of the Rings*. The women had even come to jokingly call themselves "The Club," an exclusive group where only women who were romantically involved with a Beatle were allowed to join. There were four of them in total, one woman for every man: Maureen Starkey, Pattie Boyd, Linda McCartney, and Yoko Ono.

The four members had never spent time with one another on their own terms, which seemed a shame, so they set a lunch at the

Cork and Bottle. Ono would only agree to go on a day when John was not in the studio with the Beatles, which meant that every other woman going to lunch had to pay the price of not being with their own Beatle on a day off.

Linda, Yoko, Pattie, and Maureen had all witnessed some bad behavior from their respective Beatles at the Weekend at George's. The behavior, and the issues behind it, was deemed too potentially explosive a topic for a friendly lunch. Better to concentrate on the present.

What the women had in common in the here and now was that their husbands were working men, for the moment, and were involved with the new album project. It soon became obvious what divided them: Yoko thought that it was her job to go be with John, while the other women thought it was their job to respect the fact that their husbands needed to have private space as a band.

The Beatles had discussed setting aside one day a week where the spouses could come in, or if not one day, then special hours, but Yoko wasn't interested in any change. "John wants me to be with him." It was as simple as that for her.

Linda smiled. "That's really wonderful," she told Yoko. "So I'll be seeing you tomorrow then."

Linda explained that it just wouldn't do for her to be seen as less supportive of her own husband. If Yoko was going every day, then she would step up her own game. Whether she would come every day or not remained to be seen.

"I'll come on the days you can't," pitched in Maureen.

"If everybody's doing this, then I am, too," said Pattie.

For a while, Yoko came and stayed all day, as she'd been doing previously. Every day that Yoko came in, however, at least one of the wives did the same.

Their husbands appeared to be doing their level best to just get through the sessions. Yet each session produced the inevitable artistic and personal tension that set the women on edge. It was clear that John didn't like having the other wives in the session any more than his bandmates liked having Yoko around. It was a stand-off where everyone was uncomfortable and obligated, and no one knew how to stop it.

A day came, however, where Yoko never showed up at the studio. Called at home, Yoko claimed to have had her fill of the Beatles anyway. "I'm writing an album of my own," she said, "and I didn't want Beatles to take my good ideas." Paul always claimed that Yoko was kidding when she said that, but Linda maintained that she was dead honest.

As they had first done with the *A Doll's House* album, each of the four arguing Beatles relegated the other three members into sidemen for his own work. They were the best supporting musicians that anyone could ask for, and even while sulking, fighting, and arguing, their tracks were always a cut above anyone else's.

• • •

The force truly keeping the Beatles together was the group's specific gravity, the undeniable, ineradicable impact they had had on contemporary music and culture. At the end of the day, everyone knew that it might be good therapy for the Beatles to bitch about being Beatles, but nothing they would ever do after this chapter closed could possibly be this significant.

So they kept at it. They made another great album by each bringing in their new music and picking the best fourteen songs. Then they made sure that every song had at least two of them playing on it.

In the final mix of *And the Band Plays On*, McCartney got five songs (ranging from the evocative "Every Night" to the bouncy "That Would Be Something"), Lennon grabbed another five ("Instant Karma!" to "Mother"), Harrison got three, led by the power-hit "My Sweet Lord," and Ringo placed one barn-burner in "It Don't Come Easy" (also co-written by Harrison). To some critics, the sides sounded less organic than *Everest*, but there was no question that it added up to a Beatles album.

During interviews supporting the release of *And the Band*

Plays On, Paul McCartney sounded the most gung-ho of all the Beatles. "I think we're all reasonably talented blokes," Paul said, smiling, "and we might make a go of it on our own, but together we add up to just that little bit more that makes something special. Be a shame to spoil all that." In other words, two plus two equaled five, a fact the increasingly confident McCartney understood.

Harrison said, "We've got unity through diversity," and people seemed to accept that.

The album was originally called *Back from the Brink* (John's title). In his mind, the Beatles had been sinking, and he toyed briefly with the idea of calling the record *Deck Chairs* and using images of the *Titanic* on the cover. In the end, then, *And the Band Plays On* became a compromise—it worked on Paul's level to mean "joyfully soldiering on through a crisis," while to John it signified "dithering away the last meaningless moment of existence."

Released in September 1970, *And the Band Plays On* became the third most successful Beatles album of all time, behind only *Sgt. Pepper's Lonely Hearts Club Band* and *Everest*. The album's cover art was a call-back to *Yellow Submarine*—the sub was black instead of yellow and appeared to be sinking to the bottom of the cover.

Lennon was actually the most pleased of all the Beatles by this work. His "More Doll, Less Mountain" analysis received great coverage in the music press. He explained that the album abandoned some of the pop polish of *Everest* in favor of a return to the creative anarchy of *A Doll's House*. *Rockstar's* Bill Friedlander said in his review:

> "The Beatles as we once knew them are gone. Dead and buried beneath competition, jealousy, and too much of a good thing. But the Beatles as we hear them now have their own power. This is a group of young men who will all soon be in their thirties, men who are married and have children, men who have fought addiction, and men who have chased transcendence. Their voices are not so much blended today as they are heightened."

The album is notable for another addition. Michael Lindsay-Hogg, with Richard DiLello's assistance, provided the sensational primal scream tapes recorded during the Weekend at George's. The recording is of a marginal quality, but it makes an appearance on Side Two of the *And the Band Plays On* album, between "Working Class Hero" and "The Back Seat of My Car." In the bridge, Lennon seems to be screaming "Fucking Asshole" and McCartney seems to be screaming back "Bloody Junkie," although no one would ever confirm either the phrases or the authorship.

Its family-friendly work environment notwithstanding, *And the Band Plays On* did not work its magic on all listeners. One, in particular, was Elvis Presley, who had never quite warmed to the Fab Four knocking him from his perch back in 1964. On December 21, 1970, in a bizarre tête-à-tête with President Nixon, Elvis offered to work as a special agent for the Feds and described some of the activities of the four British citizens as being "very anti-American." The entertainer particularly singled out the "loud-mouthed Lennon."

Nixon had a phonograph in the Oval Office. A copy of *And the Band Plays On* was placed on the turntable by Elvis Presley, who cued it up to "Working Class Hero."

"He says some things on this record, Mr. President. Things that, if I'd said them, my mama would have washed out my mouth with soap."

The two men saw eye to eye on the potential for further disruption that these arrogant British musicians could bring to America. The president called them "outside agitators," and the King did not disagree.

Nixon had never listened to anything by these musicians, preferring more refined music. Indeed, Nixon was an accomplished pianist who played for guests in the White House. After cringing through half of Lennon's complaint about how the working class was getting screwed, the two adjourned to the East Room, where Nixon played Christmas carols for the staff, whom he encouraged to sing along with the already-crooning Elvis.

While Nixon and Elvis conferred during this holiday season, Paul McCartney and John Lennon couldn't even bring themselves to exchange Christmas presents, despite their long-standing tradition of doing so. They spoke to each other most often through others, with Paul trying not to incite John in the studio and vice versa. In actual fact, and with only two exceptions, they didn't play on each other's songs.

1970 came to an end with a New Year's Eve party thrown by Ringo at Ronnie Scott's Club in London, complete with a celebrity jam session that included Eric Clapton, Maurice Gibb, Charlie Watts, and Klaus Voorman. Ringo had invited John, Paul, and George, yet none attended.

"We'd all had more to do with each other in 1970 than we wanted," said Ringo. "We all needed to party with some new people."

The Beatles had played together and kept everyone happy, but they jolly well did not have to be happy about it themselves.

CHAPTER FOUR

SAVILE ROW (1971)

SHOOTOUT AT SAVILE ROW

1971 could have easily turned into the year that the Beatles broke apart for good. Instead, it became their most successful year ever, even eclipsing the explosive first year of Beatlemania in 1964.

Despite or because of the incredible pressure all four musicians were feeling, the group managed to turn 1971 into a year that changed the music industry forever and changed the culture even more.

Over a twelve-month period, they created a trilogy of events that, to this day, continues to define the legend of the Beatles. Ever on the brink of self-destruction, they still recorded the top album, starred in the most successful movie, and performed in a groundbreaking concert. All told, the Beatles' collective endeavors amounted to one studio concept album and two soundtracks, each fantastically different and diverse, admired by critics and embraced by fans.

The Beatles would accomplish all of this nearly by accident.

• • •

On January 9, 1971, the sitcom *All in the Family* introduced Americans to the squabbling family of Archie Bunker. While his wife, Edith, was comically clueless, the conflict between Archie and his son-in-law, Meathead, was dramatically compelling since they were two men who saw the world from completely different points of view. They were both stubborn and strong-willed, and neither of them was inclined to retreat from a fight.

The same could be said of John Lennon and Paul McCartney.

Even as the friction between the fictitious Archie and Meathead turned the CBS television series into an instant hit, the real-life acrimony between the flesh-and-blood Lennon and McCartney was playing out far more dangerously in London.

Fans by now knew full well there was discord in the House of Beatles. The deteriorating dynamic was visible firsthand in the film documentary *Get Back*. Lennon and McCartney, in particular, had served up healthy doses of human drama with their almost-weekly sparring in the music trades. In fact, for most observers, the only question remaining was how four guys who had been in that headspace then could be now functioning effectively as a group.

Lord Beeching had been hired because of his experience of making trains run on time, and he continued to believe that Apple could be made to heel the same way the British train system had. Juggling each of the four Beatles individually was a terrible task that was complicated even further by the direct input from Allen Klein and the tag team of Lee and John Eastman. Even so, pink slips, personally signed by Lord Richard Beeching, were going out at Apple at a regular clip, and morale was sagging even as the financial bottom line began to tick up noticeably.

Lord Beeching drew only one line in the sand. The Beatles must honor their agreement to suppress their growing inner dissent around the upcoming release of *The Lord of the Rings* film and soundtrack.

Though they'd agreed to it just a half year ago, the so-called Grand Bargain was being tested daily. During a promotional interview for *The Lord of the Rings*, Lennon still could not stop himself from analyzing matters in a way that seemed to imply that, in his mind, the Beatles were finished. Speaking from his own impressive estate at Tittenhurst Park, he free-associated his emerging thoughts:

[John] "It's just one too many is what it is. *Everest* should have been the last album, but then we got talked into one more. *And the Band Plays On* is not a great album, it's a convenient album. If this is the future of the Beatles, it's got to end. But the whole Ring-Thing Dream-Team, we're all just happy to get it out there and out of our own heads. Giving it to the world, and moving on. That's about the size of that."

1970 had been, as Lennon also suggested in that interview, a hard year to be a Beatle, and 1971 looked to be more of the same. Tensions were as high as ever between all four men, and it wasn't just a grudge match between John and Paul. George, who had been instrumental in brokering the deal with his bandmates, now privately confessed he felt he had made a huge mistake. Only Ringo was prepared to go along, no matter what it was the others decided.

[Ringo] "I didn't see it as if it was my decision to make, actually. I liked *And the Band Plays On*, and it was a considerably better album than I would have made by my lonesome, so to speak. It was not a good dynamic for me. Instead of Paul and John just working it out between them, they added George to the argument. And, yes, I know I was the first one to leave the group back during *A Doll's House*, which is part of the reason I just stay out of it now."

Indeed, during the first months of 1971, all of the Beatles were giving interviews that held out the possibility that the group had recorded its last album together with *And the Band Plays On*, which critics considered placing somewhere between *Get Back* and the exalted *Everest* in terms of quality.

After the better part of a year of steady construction, the re-built Apple Records entrance lobby and the new basement retreat of the Apple recording studio were set to open together at Apple Corps headquarters at 3 Savile Row. The disaster of the original studio, designed by Magic Alex Mardas, the con man of

Apple Electronics, could only be forgotten when new songs were being recorded in a state-of-the-art studio worthy of the Beatles.

Unlike the Mardas disaster, this newly designed dream studio featured some standard items, like a working patch bay and a talkback system between the studio and the control room. It also had working central heating and soundproofing. This version now included its own natural echo chamber and a wide range of recording and mastering facilities and could turn out mono, stereo, and quadrophonic master tapes and vinyl discs. It was meant to rival EMI's Abbey Road, and it did.

The redesign and rebuilding of the basement to accommodate proper recording facilities had been overseen by former EMI engineer Geoff Emerick. Originally scheduled to take eighteen months at an estimated cost of $1.5 million, construction was instead completed in half the time for twice the money, so urgent was Apple's need to put on a new face.

The studio needed to become a second home for Apple Records artists. Klein, in particular, had insisted that the Beatles get in there and show the youngsters how it was done.

> [Allen Klein] "We had good bands, don't get me wrong. But Elton John was on tour, just starting to break, actually. And Crosby, Stills, Nash & Young were such an American band that having them record in London would have seemed wrong. None of the other acts we had signed had their stature, let alone that of the Beatles."

Allen Klein called Lennon, Harrison, and Starkey while Lee Eastman called his son-in-law McCartney. Everyone was on the same page. For the good of Apple, the Beatles had to start making new music at Savile Row.

The McCartneys threw the entire family in a van and drove nearly six hundred miles to London from their home at the Mull of Kintyre in Scotland. "When we heard about it," said Linda, "Paul's eyes lit up like it was Christmas and he'd just gotten a new toy. He needed to go play, so we did."

"Everything I was playing around with in Scotland was cool, but very minimal, very home fires burning, if that can be done with rock and roll," said McCartney. "The kids weren't in school for another two weeks, so we just got in the car and took off for London."

Paul got Geoff Emerick to give him a look at the studio as soon as he arrived in the city. On the spot, he decided to "give it a test run" and got Emerick to help him record a demo of a song that he called "Too Many People." The song was not supposed to be about John Lennon, Paul would always contend, but he made the connection apparent with a careless and provocative line added in the studio that day, "*Yoko took your lucky break and broke it in two*." It was a line he would replace later, he stated.

It was no lucky break for McCartney or for the Beatles that Lennon was sitting at home at Tittenhurst Park debating whether to finish the recording studio he had started building or to sell the whole place and move to America. He had been avoiding joining Harrison for final tweaking on the soundtrack for The *Lord of the Rings* because he was sure that his collaborator had gone off the deep end already and "soaked it all up in God juice," making it overly religious. Now, suddenly, there was a studio to visit where he "wouldn't have to talk about Hobbits or how they might sound and whether they chant."

Lennon went in to sample the new studio equipment two days after McCartney had come in. Informed that Paul had paid his own visit just forty-eight hours earlier, John wondered if he had recorded anything.

Lennon listened to "Too Many People" three times. The first time he seemed to like it until the Yoko line, which confused him enough to demand that Emerick stop the playback and start over. The second time every articulation seemed offensive, causing him to sum it all up with "Paul's a fucking little cunt." The third time he turned off the equipment himself and told Emerick, "I'll be back tomorrow." He left the room without another word.

The next day, John arrived and recorded his own demo with

the eye-raising title of "How Do You Sleep?" With lines like "*The only thing you done was yesterday*" and "*The sound you make is Muzak to my ears*" there was nothing subtle about the intended target.

Lennon was so proud of his response to "Too Many People" that he called up McCartney and forced Emerick to play the song for him over the phone. Lennon picked up the phone after the song was over. "You started the argument, and now it's finished," he barked into the receiver. Then he hung up.

Of course the argument was not over—it had only just begun. Paul and John had accidentally created the conditions for the release of the most controversial album in recording history, the now-famous *Savile Row*.

The news that McCartney and Lennon had each gone into the brand-new Savile Row studios separately to record demo songs attacking the other ricocheted through the offices of Apple. The more Geoff Emerick refused to let anyone hear the tapes, the more everyone talked about them and assumed the worst.

When Emerick told George Martin to explain how explosive he felt the material was, Martin went straight to Lord Beeching and let him know that if things were as described, the company could be in hot water again. The two older men had become friends over the past year, wary but honest with each other. Off they went to hear for themselves what all the fuss was about.

Under cross-examination, engineer Emerick confessed to Beeching and Martin that Allen Klein had beaten them both to the punch and had just had the songs played to him over the telephone. Even as they spoke, they learned from an Apple secretary that Klein had jumped on a plane to insert himself into the middle of whatever was to come next.

The songs were powerful, Emerick told Martin and Beeching, acknowledging that Lennon's attack on McCartney was the most personal one he had ever heard in songwriting. Then they all listened together. After the session was over, the room fell silent.

"I take it that this kind of behavior does not happen often in the world of modern music," said Lord Beeching.

"Do we know what use they intend to make of these demos?" asked Martin, hoping that John and Paul might just forget about them, as if they hadn't happened. Matters had drifted away like that in the past from time to time.

There was a brief discussion that if Lennon and McCartney pressed the case, they could release the songs as a single with two A-sides. Then they could do their best to ignore that single from a marketing perspective and let it quietly fade away. Yet it was obvious that could never work. The world had never ignored a single from the Beatles. The songs publicized themselves.

As it was, Beeching had a group meeting with the Beatles scheduled for the next week. Based on an actuarial account he had commissioned, he had once again been preparing a report on the state of Apple Corps to go along with his always dark assessment of the financial impact the group's dissolution would have.

Martin should attend, said Beeching. After the business discussion, he could talk to the Beatles straight ahead about the tiff that had broken out in the Savile Row recording studio. Except that Allen Klein was coming to town. Because he represented Lennon, Harrison, and Starkey, he would want to be in that meeting, too. And if the Eastmans, who watched out for McCartney, got wind of what was going on, they would insist on attending, as well.

While the Apple leadership dithered, the Beatles acted in a way that some might call precipitous.

First, George came over to see the new Savile Row facility from his Abbey Road session, where he was working on *The Lord of the Rings* soundtrack. While he was at Savile Row, he listened to what McCartney and Lennon had each laid down. Harrison got out his own guitar and recorded a demo of what would become his classic "Wah-Wah," which, he explained, is what he heard in his head when John and Paul were fighting, as they so often did these days.

Second, Ringo had a private conversation with each of his bandmates about what was going on, and the group reached a surprising consensus. They should keep doing what they were already doing: writing additional songs they felt inspired to create by the most recently recorded track. When they managed an album's worth of songs, that would be the ideal time to stop.

Lennon was immediately enthusiastic about such a radical creative concept. "Fuck, yes," he shouted. "Let's fucking do an album like that!"

This reaction elicited an equally strong "Fuck, no" from Paul. But John was like a dog with a bone. The irony, controversy, and in-your-face acknowledgment of the split between the two aligned perfectly with his current feelings about continuing the band.

Paul, a pragmatist at heart, decided to spin the decision to the group's advantage. "It's a concept album," he concluded. "Like *Sgt. Pepper* and *Everest*. It's a call and response."

There was a brief discussion that the album itself could be called *Call and Response*, but that idea was abandoned in place of the simple designation of where it was recorded—*Savile Row*. In 1969, the Beatles had toyed with calling *Everest* by the name of the studio in which it was recorded—*Abbey Road*—but stuck with their original idea. The actual studio was the organizing principle of the current album, however.

"*Savile Row*," said Lennon. "That's it, isn't it?"

The next week, the band presented their new concept to Beeching, Klein and Martin (present in person), and Eastman (present on the phone from New York). Ringo, between drags of his Marlboro cigarette, summed up their thinking as a fait accompli. "We don't know why particularly, but we just all like the idea."

Ringo had already been in the studio two days earlier. He contributed a work-in-progress called "Back Off Boogaloo," which sounded a lot like he was taking a shot at Paul. The new studios at Savile Row had four songs, and fingers were being pointed. Something primal was being tapped into here, and no one could be certain where the journey would take them.

"You're next," John said to Paul as he left Apple headquarters.

George Martin, initially a skeptic, found that the longer he thought about the concept of an album that unfolded with one song inspiring the next, the more he liked the idea. He could not argue with Klein's take that the rebuttal type method squeezed another album out of the group and demonstrated clearly that they need not be getting along to remain a musical force. Martin also felt that the energy behind this concept might turn out to be powerful and would certainly make for something musically unusual. More than that, though, he felt it might "let the boys blow off a bit of steam at each other." He knew that could not hurt.

By the end of the day, he had rung up all four of the Beatles and laid down his ground rules. He would only agree to produce the album, if, as per the Grand Bargain, at least two band members (preferably three, ideally all four) would work on every song. He would randomly select the order of the band members' contributions, supervise the individual sessions, and perform his customary producer duties that he had performed on all the previous Beatles albums.

Although he kept his opinions to himself, McCartney told Linda that he did not think too much of the idea of airing their dirty laundry for the world to see.

"Too late for that," she said. "Maybe you forgot about the *Get Back* film." Linda scored that point.

Paul mused that, of course, he could still revise "Too Many People" to lose the Yoko line. He was not so sure about Lennon's song, though. Its lyrics left very little doubt about its intended victim.

"You guys are about to write the strangest album in history," Linda concluded. "Everyone will have to listen to it at least once." McCartney didn't care. That was already the case with every Beatles album that had come before.

In any case, McCartney was designated next up by virtue of the original rotation, as well as Martin's direction. "I should think there's some unfinished business for you after John's contribution," the producer told his artist. "Maybe you want to take a shot at wrapping that up, perhaps in a way that opens the door for a new topic." A pivot might be just the ticket.

Paul wrote his rebuttal to the hurtful "How Do You Sleep?" in the form of a song called "Dear Friend." It was far less angry in tone, but resigned and sad, featuring lyrics such as, *"Dear Friend, what's the time? Is it really the borderline?"*

Lennon opted for the pivot. He could have come straight at McCartney as before, but his passion was spent. He had already begun to tell people that his song was just a song, and it only represented how he felt at the time that he wrote it.

This time, John Lennon went after what he loved, not what he hated. He named the song "Oh Yoko!" an unabashed love song for his wife, the great partner who had replaced Paul.

George Martin could have called in George or Ringo next, but he felt the inherent drama that was being played out. He went back to Paul.

Days later, after McCartney had been in the studio laying down the track for his response song, Martin listened to it with Lennon in the studio control room. It began with a soft little ditty McCartney labeled "The Lovely Linda." Lennon scoffed, "Christ, he's not even trying." The look on Martin's face was proof that he agreed.

At that point, McCartney blew their minds when "The Lovely Linda" transitioned into "Maybe I'm Amazed," a song that clearly belonged in the same league as "Let It Be" and "Hey Jude."

Lennon pushed up his glasses and leveled that look of his at Martin. "I'm not following that one. Put George back in."

Martin knew Lennon had a point. It was time to put Paul and John back on the bench and get the other players on the field.

Harrison started off Side Two by going spiritual with "Hear Me Lord." If John could profess his love to Yoko, and Paul his love to Linda, then George would profess his love to God almighty.

Lennon wanted back in after that one. He followed Harrison's religious theme with his scorcher "God" that ended with *"I don't believe in Beatles."*

McCartney took that thread of disunity and preached about the Beatles' lack of stability with "3 Legs." Still, he managed to convey his message in an oblique way by putting it to a jaunty tune. No real harm, no foul.

Starr was not eager to play this game any longer, but he also had something he wanted to say. He tossed in a musical trifle, "Early 1971," as his own lament about harmony lost in the band he still loved. He had written an earlier version called "Early 1970" that he'd never shared, and his feelings really hadn't changed all that much. Ringo just wanted to keep playing music with these guys and wished they could understand just how simple it could be.

Harrison blew past Starr's outreach and aimed his own song "Not Guilty" at his bandmates, with no references to God to obscure his meaning. Its pop and jazz vibe was dominated by electric piano and rough vocals, which conveyed a cool distance to his anger. Harrison was restrained in his irritation. It seemed like a great way to end the album.

For over a week, Apple staff, Beatles, and friends would drop in to the Savile Row studios, put on headphones, and listen to the entire album. Often, they would listen again. Despite the album's often incendiary vocals, the listeners' biggest knock against it was that it had not yet pulled all four members into its orbit—there wasn't a single song on which they all performed together.

George Martin knew he could turn *Savile Row* into a hit. He had ideas upon ideas after hearing it. "Strong stuff," he pronounced. "Full of anger, but not unwarranted."

• • •

While Martin toiled away and staffers speculated, Lennon turned up at McCartney's home on Cavendish Avenue near St. John's Wood on a Sunday morning, where he caught Paul wearing Linda's bathrobe. (He hadn't been able to find his own when the doorbell rang.)

"I've got one more you should hear," said John, letting himself in carrying his new custom acoustic guitar, a Yamaha given to him by Yoko.

Linda, wearing an available raincoat, handed Paul his robe and took back her own. This was all done in front of John, with no trace of self-consciousness. He and Paul and Linda had spent countless hours on the road together, of course, and Linda's attitude was that family was family, even when you're not getting along. "I'll make some breakfast," she said and headed off to the kitchen.

Paul and John hadn't spoken directly to each other for months. The lyrics in the songs each had recorded for the *Savile Row* album experiment were bitter toward the other. John acted like none of that happened, or mattered, and Paul was experienced enough in their friendship to just play along without comment.

After tuning up, John played a ragged version of a song that had, as its chorus, the line "*It's better to arrive.*" It was the line John had wryly spoken to his friend back in Scotland in the summer of 1969, in the aftermath of his car accident. Even so, the song still had bite to it.

Paul considered it. "It's good."

"No, it's not," said John. "It's shit. It needs something."

Paul agreed that, indeed, it could possibly use a bit of work and asked John carefully what he thought the missing ingredient might be. At that moment, Linda leaned back in. "These peppers are a lot hotter than I thought. If I put in some cheese to cool them off, will you two still eat them?"

Both Lennon and McCartney agreed that they would. As Linda disappeared again, Lennon shrugged. "I put the peppers in already. What have you got?"

McCartney smiled. It was a dig within a compliment. "You want a little cheese?"

McCartney had a thought. He, too, had a song fragment under his belt, a tune he called "Show Up" that was based on the advice Ed McMahon had given him years earlier. He explained that it was McMahon's advice he was following when he showed up at the hospital in the first place.

"Let's just not make it all maudlin. Nobody will believe that crap," said Lennon.

And that was it. The advice from Johnny Carson and Ed McMahon had transferred to Paul McCartney and John Lennon, at least for a song.

Two hours later, they had not only wolfed down a tasty omelet prepared by Linda, but they'd written their first music together in years. The song they composed was not sweet at all, but it wasn't angry, either. It was pragmatic; they had developed a process from all those years living, playing, and working together. "Show Up" had input from both men, beginning with a verse from Lennon, followed by a chorus from McCartney. The original chorus, "*Show up, it's so easy to do, show up, it could happen to you,*" was re-written to sub in a new final phrase "*makes it better for you.*"

The idea of showing up was not that it made things better for the other guy, but that it made things better for you. It was not a perfect solution, but, under the right circumstances, it could help.

Even though loyalty called for doing the work over at Apple's Savile Row studios, a local band was booked into them, and McCartney and Lennon were keen to capture the energy of the moment and record the song in the same day it was essentially written. They decided to work in the ramshackle garage set-up that Harrison had put together over at Friar Park but that looked decidedly working class. They called up George first and told him they were on the way. Then they called Ringo.

"You've got to come over to George's now," declared John. "This has to be done by midnight."

Paul thought this was probably a far too literal interpretation of wanting the song to be recorded that same day. On the other hand, he was loath to throw any obstacles in the path of John's enthusiasm.

By three in the afternoon, all four of the Beatles had convened in George's garage, along with Geoff Emerick. Two Apple employees were nabbed, each given a 16MM camera and told to shoot enough to make a short music film. Because the lighting was awful and everyone thought the Beatles would look like pasty vampires in the final cut, the decision was made by Paul to shoot the whole thing without directly filming the face of any of the band members. Even though the video's official name is "Show Up," many fans refer to it as the "Headless" video.

Even without heads, John, Paul, George, and Ringo seem to be into what they're doing. John takes the verse and Paul takes the chorus, George breaks free with two driving guitar solos, and Ringo pushes the beat strongly, along with Paul's bass line. In the film, a matchbook from Danny's Hideaway makes an appearance in an ashtray.

As it turned out, "Show Up" became the only song on the entire *Savile Row* LP to have all four Beatles playing on it. That it came to be the last song on Side Two of the album could actually be perceived as hopeful. The Beatles had expressed themselves, gotten it all out, and now were prepared to work together in harmony again.

That would be an optimistic way to look at it, except that after the group left the Harrison garage that next morning at nearly 2 a.m., it would be another two months before they spoke to each other. They wouldn't see one another in person until the next August. Recording "Show Up" turned out to be a one-of-a-kind event. Lennon and McCartney did not begin writing together again, nor did they end their feud. They simply found a way to articulate that feuding was now part of their process, and if the fans could not dig it, then that was their problem.

> [Paul] "We wrote it a little oblique, I guess, so we could both do the song and say it wasn't about us, really. Now people hear it and think it's about them and their own friend. That's what makes me think it's a good song."

• • •

Maybe Martin was right about the collective blowing off of steam, but the sessions to finish up the album had certainly gone much smoother than anyone had expected. True, except for "Show Up,"

McCartney did not play on a single Lennon tune, nor did Lennon play on one of McCartney's. Yet they were in the studio together from time to time, and no one was physically hurt.

The public seemed to love the story behind the story of *Savile Row*, and Apple's Derek Taylor enhanced it upon every telling. "It's brilliant, you know," he told anyone who dropped by Apple for a drink and a toke. "They're completely honest with each other, just like the brothers they are." When the music reporter from *The Guardian* pointed out that some brothers go years without speaking over perceived injustices, Taylor shrugged. "I can't tell you that you're wrong."

On the other hand, no one could doubt that these were songs written by men who had issues with each other. It was one thing to witness McCartney and Lennon slug it out in the music trades, but now Harrison and Starkey had gotten in on the act as well.

Rockstar gave *Savile Row* the cover treatment, using the stark black-and-white photos from the *Get Back—Live at the Roundhouse* album and rotating them so the band members' faces were turned away from each other. Over a third of the issue was devoted to dissecting the album's meaning. The magazine branded it "The Shootout at Apple Corral" to drive home the metaphor that Lennon and McCartney had assaulted each other with virtual guns on this thirty-three RPM firing range.

> [Rockstar] "Rhetorical bullets are flying in these songs, some are near misses, some are direct hits, and all of them carry with them the capacity to cause great injury. It's a dangerous, emotional album, full of raw power. The fact that it ends with a Lennon-McCartney tune is the kind of mystery that only the Beatles can serve up to their fans."

The imagery never really took off: Lennon and McCartney seemed more like dark assassins of the Beatles myth than gunslingers, even though the B-side felt less combative to most listeners. And there was the matter that both Harrison and Starr had participated in the stirring of the proverbial pot, contributing three and two songs, respectively.

Rockstar's Booth Hill tried to interview John and Paul together, but they refused. At that particular moment in their historical feud, it was still all they could do to get in the studio to make the music; they certainly were not going to go at it in front of a journalist, even one they knew personally.

Rolling Stone characterized the *Savile Row* album as one beginning with an "angry and mournful" state that ended with a meditation on friendship, after touring through spouses, religion, loneliness, and existential doubt.

In *Creem*'s article, Lennon said the album had to happen in order to "clear the air" and allow Paul and him to work together in the future. McCartney simply shrugged and said he accepted it was the price of keeping the band together and that he was willing to pay it.

Savile Row—the concept album—would sweep the Grammy Awards, a high compliment to a group in the middle of what appeared to be public therapy. The success of *Savile Row* was a surprise in itself, but no one could have predicted what was to come next. Incredibly, the Beatles were about to put something even bigger and more complex onto the world's cultural radar.

STANLEY KUBRICK PRESENTS J.R.R. TOLKIEN'S THE LORD OF THE RINGS STARRING THE BEATLES

Released on May 23, 1971, *Stanley Kubrick Presents J.R.R. Tolkien's The Lord of the Rings Starring The Beatles* was a film phenomenon, shattering records, inspiring mass repeat viewings, and vastly enhancing the value of anyone who touched it.

And the Beatles not only touched it, they embodied it.

Clearly, having what remains one of the longest film titles in cinematic history (nearly an entire Tweet by today's standards) provided no obstacle to the film's ability to gain momentum. The film's title came together when lawyers—representing United Artists, Kubrick, Apple, Tolkien, and representatives of the Screen Actors Guild, Directors Guild, and Writers Guild—joined up in Hollywood and ultimately, after much discussion, found the most value in placing everyone's name in the top credit.

United Artists had originally planned to call the film *The Lord of the Rings*. Stanley Kubrick then insisted as an incentive to signing his contract that he be given the possessive credit in all marketing. *Stanley Kubrick Presents The Lord of the Rings* is what the director wanted.

When Allen Klein heard about this, he instantly phoned Beeching and said that Apple should sue UA if they used that title without including the Beatles. UA knew the Beatles would either carry or kill the movie, so they agreed to call the film *Stanley Kubrick Presents The Lord of the Rings Starring The Beatles*. At the last minute, in a nod to the now raging popularity of *The Lord of the Rings* in its trilogy novel format, the title was finalized as *Stanley Kubrick Presents J.R.R. Tolkien's The Lord of the Rings Starring The Beatles*.

Today, regular film lovers refer to the movie as simply *The Lord of the Rings*. Serious fans, however, recite the entire name as if it were a mantra. At conventions, it's possible to hear lines like, "The set design on *Stanley Kubrick Presents J.R.R. Tolkien's The Lord of the Rings Starring The Beatles* is groundbreaking for its time." Others try to call it "SKPJRRTTLOTRSTB" or "Skip Jert Loter Stub," but those haven't really caught on, despite best efforts of some devotees.

In a way, *Stanley Kubrick Presents J.R.R. Tolkien's The Lord of the Rings Starring The Beatles* deserved any distinction bestowed on it in 1971. Whatever name you called it, the film blew away the competition the week it opened. The collaboration between Kubrick and the Beatles had a domestic gross that year of over $91MM, decisively edging out another United Artists film *Fiddler on the Roof* for the highest-grossing film of the year. It also had what Hollywood refers to as "legs," meaning that people wanted to see it again and again. In most cities of the United States, before the advent of home video, revival houses played it year-round. It has always drawn crowds and has sold to new audiences in VHS, DVD, Blu-ray, and now, streaming.

At the time, however, it was a bumpy promotional ride for the film. Kubrick publicly complained that he could have done more with better actors. Lennon responded that the Beatles felt the same way about the director they got stuck with.

In truth, both were right. The labyrinthine Kubrick screenplay, weighing in at 187 pages (120 pages was considered normal at the time) had 37 minutes removed from it in the UA cut that Kubrick ultimately signed off on. Several of the trims were done because the performance of one of the Beatles was considered to be "less in character than we would have liked." Others were done because Kubrick had attempted certain visual effects sequences that simply were not realized well enough to be shown.

Regardless of the behind-the-scenes drama, the film remains the Beatles' most beloved, primarily because it seems to transcend them. They are the stars, yes, but only as actors. The film itself became the star. The only other film that seems to have had the equal staying power is one that followed it in 1972: *The Godfather*.

Fans and filmgoers alike seemed happy with the film, and some were downright delirious about it. Only a small minority carped that the Beatles should have been doing something more important with their time than making some fantasy flick. Naysayers also pointed out that it was the second film the Beatles had made about a ring (the first being *Help!*)—only this time Paul got to wear the sacred jewelry instead of Ringo.

Critics were in the distinct minority, however. The film was nominated for an Oscar along with *The French Connection*, *Fiddler on the Roof*, *The Last Picture Show*, and *Nicholas and Alexandra*. All of the Beatles showed up for the ceremony, except for John Lennon, who did not want to see Stanley Kubrick and force a smile for reporters.

For many people, seeing the film is when the 1970s really started. For everyone else, it seems, that pivotal moment occurred when they first heard the film's soundtrack.

The soundtrack, like that of *Yellow Submarine* before it, was divided into two sides: one was devoted to music from the Beatles and the other to the George Martin soundtrack score. Fans consistently refer to the "Two Georges" in describing the soundtrack's creators.

The soundtrack's A-side was produced by George Harrison, who worked with the other Beatles to incorporate songs still left over from the ill-fated Twickenham Studio sessions. Many listeners remain adamant that it is George's own spirituality that translated so beautifully to the story behind *The Lord of the Rings* that it still, to this day, elevates the music to its iconic status.

MY FRIENDS CAME TO ME

Two days after the recording sessions on *Savile Row* ended, John Lennon and Yoko Ono packed up most of their worldly belongings and headed for New York City. It was the summer of 1971, and they were looking for Yoko's daughter, Kyoko, and felt they needed to be in the United States to fight a custody battle with Yoko's former husband Tony Cox, who had taken Kyoko to America back in 1969 to keep her from Lennon's influence.

More than that, however, they just wanted to be in America. Lennon famously compared New York City, the home base of the American empire, to Rome, where you need to be if you wanted to be in the middle of all the action.

Apple had made England the center of the Beatles empire, but the office had provided only stress for over a year now.

Lennon had his mind on the New World, literally. "America is where it's at," he said in December. "You know, I should have been born in New York, man, I should have been born in the Village! That's where I belong."

As they found themselves increasingly at home in the Big Apple, the Lennons moved beyond an interest in avant-garde music and art to immerse themselves in the radical political movements of the time. The day they arrived in New York, they were met by Jerry Rubin and Abbie Hoffman, leaders of the Youth International Party, a.k.a. the Yippies. "They almost grabbed me off the plane," Lennon recalled, "and the next minute, I'm involved."

They began to take part in rallies for political prisoners, as well as in demonstrations in support of the IRA and Attica prison riot victims. But for all the good they thought they were doing, there were still people who saw John Lennon, and his bandmates, as a threat—particularly after Lennon and Ono headlined the "Free John Sinclair" concert before fifteen thousand fans in Detroit, Michigan, on December 10.

Sinclair, a poet and former manager of MC5 (Motor City Five), had been sentenced to ten years in Michigan State Prison for marijuana possession. The week before the concert, Lennon had joined the bill. Ticket sales, which had been sluggish, went through the roof.

If that was to be expected, the state of Michigan's decision to set Sinclair free just days after the concert was astonishing. Lennon could not only move concert tickets. He could move state legislatures.

The night of the Sinclair rally, however, an undercover FBI agent was in the crowd, trying to blend in. He wrote down every word Lennon said and sang that night. This became page one in an FBI file that would ultimately be used against Lennon, and, by association, his bandmates.

Clearly, John and Yoko made no attempt to hide their beliefs. They even co-hosted *The Mike Douglas Show* for an entire week, booking radicals like Abbie Hoffman as guests. In New York City, the arrival of John and Yoko was being seen in radical and leftist circles as a once in a lifetime experience that was having the practical effect of bringing people together. But all this activity also drew increasing attention from the U.S. authorities, particularly men in high places within the Nixon Administration.

The Lennons were stirring other darker forces against themselves and, by association, the Beatles. Without knowing it, they had managed to get the attention of President Nixon's lawyer, John Dean.

• • •

While there was always the primal pull to break apart, the Beatles seemed to have an equally strong force keeping them together, one that continued to work in mysterious ways. In the early winter of 1971, this counterbalance was in full effect.

"*My friend came to me,*" started George Harrison in a note he sent first to Eric Clapton. The message went on to explain that he had heard terrible things from his friend Ravi Shankar about what was happening on the other side of the world, in the vulnerable and crumbling country known as Bangladesh. The place had been ravaged by both the war of liberation and a war of nature incited by the Bhola Cyclone and was facing an imminent refugee crisis.

After meditating on what could be done to effect change, Harrison came up with the idea of championing a charity concert that he would call *The Concert for Bangladesh*. Clapton thought the idea sounded like it just might work, although he pointed out that it had one large drawback: no one had ever done anything like this before.

"No one ever thought a rock band could make millions of teenage girls scream and faint, either," George answered. "Maybe we can harness all that madness into something good."

As the idea evolved in the back-and-forth between the two men, it became obvious that they'd have to take action no later than August, which was only seven months away. They would reach out to friends and put together an all-star lineup, and all the profits would be donated to the relief effort.

"Why don't you just do it with the Beatles?" asked Clapton.

George, having just made yet another angry album with John, Paul, and Ringo, had had his fill of the still-simmering tensions. He wanted to do this one on his own. He planned to issue only halfhearted invitations to his bandmates, hoping that they would be too busy or otherwise engaged to attend.

Clapton, to his unending credit, told his friend that was not acceptable. Clapton was a serious heroin addict at this point, and he feared that without the Beatles, Harrison might depend on him to get through the concert, a role he was not prepared to fill.

Clapton argued that asking the Beatles to play a set hardly prevented them from reaching out to other artists. With the Beatles on the roster, they might even be able to get Bob Dylan to play, something he hadn't done in years. While George was supposedly considering a more magnanimous approach to his own bandmates, Clapton send effusive telegrams under Harrison's name to John Lennon, Paul McCartney, and Ringo Starr.

"*Come on over for a set,*" the telegram read. "*We'll make it short and sweet like half of a Roundhouse, only in Madison Square Garden. You have to be here. I'm counting on you.*"

George was furious and threatened to expose Eric's insane meddling. But by the time he was entertaining that as an option, Eric had received return telegrams from the other three Beatles saying that they'd be there. John pointed out he could walk to the venue from his apartment. Paul, who would have to travel from his farm in Scotland, slipped into his telegram a proposed set list that generously included one more song for George than John and himself. Ringo received his invite at the exact moment he had signed the papers to buy John's home in Tittenhurst Park, after it had become clear that the Lennons, smitten with New York, had no immediate plans to return to England. On the phone with John, Ringo pointed out the irony: "I'm the one who wants to do the bit with Georgie, but I live half a world away, and you're the one who wants to get out of it but has no excuse."

"He knows I don't want to do this," said John, "but even I can't refuse to play so some starving kids can eat."

So, there it was. George had become a concert promoter and had just booked the biggest band in the entire world. It would be the height of craziness to turn down the opportunity. With the Beatles now involved, more money would go to Bangladesh and, after all, that was what the whole idea was about in the first place.

The power of the Beatles did, in fact, get Bob Dylan on the concert bill. Then they booked supporting musicians to fill out the roster, names like Leon Russell, Billy Preston, Badfinger, Klaus Voormann, Jim Keltner, and Jim Horn. Ravi Shankar would start off the night with the opening performance, as well as introduce the political aspect of the occasion.

They had an all-star concert. The date was set as August 1, 1971, at Madison Square Garden. The idea was to play an afternoon and evening concert that same day and edit the best version together for a film and a soundtrack.

First, Ravi Shankar performed for a half hour to polite fans who were crawling out of their skins with expectation. The Bengali musician was followed by George Harrison, who appeared with a collection of backing musicians to blow the house down with his new song "Bangladesh." Besides raising money for the good cause, the concert was also designed to raise consciousness for George Harrison by featuring some of his own classics, affording him the recognition he had often been denied in the Beatles.

Harrison followed with his hit "My Sweet Lord" and went spiritual with "Awaiting on You All." Then he stepped back, letting Billy Preston shine with "That's the Way God Planned It" and Leon Russell, with "Jumpin' Jack Flash/Youngblood." Everyone joined him for "While My Guitar Gently Weeps," the final song in his set.

Bob Dylan came next and did not disappoint. His choice of songs seemed to be brutally relevant in this new decade, particularly his politically infused version of "Blowin' in the Wind" and his apocalyptic "A Hard Rain's a-Gonna Fall."

At the end of Dylan's set, Harrison came on to stand side by side with Dylan and usher him offstage to thunderous applause.

Most of the people in the audience still could not believe that the best was yet to come.

The stage sat dark and silent for an eternal thirty seconds. As the shadowy visage of Ringo Starr appeared, taking his place behind the drums, the crowd came alive. When John Lennon, Paul McCartney, and George Harrison emerged from the wings seconds later, the crowd of twenty thousand exploded. As he tuned up, Paul yelled, "Hello, New York City!"

The screaming drowned out what Paul said next. Then something wholly unexpected happened. The entirety of Madison Square Garden fell into a hush, wanting to hear from the Beatles, not to drown them out.

John, stunned, looked over at his bandmates. "Now we have to say something important." He flashed a peace sign to the audience. "The last time we played in the U.S., up in Woodstock, we nearly got electrocuted in the rain," noted John. Then he pivoted to George, saying, "Thanks for getting us back to the city."

"He wanted to make sure you'd show up," said Paul.

"The Garden's only a cab ride for John," George explained to the crowd. "We all had to come here just to see him."

Ringo did a rim-shot off his drums. "What shall we play, boys?"

"It's John's hometown now," said Paul, nodding to John. "You pick."

Of course the song had already been picked. It was John's new one, "Instant Karma!"

The Beatles performed fourteen songs that night, almost an entire concert. Their own lineup included something for everyone. Starkey got to sing "It Don't Come Easy," while Harrison performed more of his songs like "Beware of Darkness" and "Something." McCartney scored big with "Back in the U.S.S.R.," "Get Back," and a little ditty he had once called "Bip Bop" that took on new words and meaning when the band rocked it up as "Stop War." It was the only time the song was ever performed.

At the end, everyone took the stage with the Beatles, including Dylan, Preston, and Russell, who joined George on "Here Comes the Sun." The encore song of the night was "All You Need Is Love," which segued into a group version of "Across the Universe."

In the end, *The Concert for Bangladesh* project broke ground as the first major rock and roll humanitarian relief effort. It made the Beatles seem relevant and compassionate. It even raised more money than expected, though whether or not that money ended up in the right pockets was dubious at best, a lapse that bothered George until the day he died.

That those two concerts were transcendent moments in rock has never been challenged. They spawned a concert film, as well as a three-record album soundtrack that made George a full Beatle in the minds of everyone who heard it, a matter that was not lost on his two feuding bandmates. He had proved that recording artists were more than just celebrities. They could be positive world citizens, too. They could put aside paychecks and egos long enough to help the suffering, a lesson that still resonates today.

John and Paul both knew that if the Beatles broke up, the legacy of their feud album and George's triumphant live album would haunt them forever. They decided to do better in 1972, making good on Paul's request and John's agreement that they would make at least one more album.

Another Year Over

What happened in 1971 cannot be minimized.

The Beatles, barely hanging on as a musical group, won the trifecta. They had created what would be recognized by the Grammy Awards as the "Album of the Year" with *Savile Row*. They had starred in and produced the soundtrack to the film of *The Lord of the Rings,* which would win the Oscar for Best Director and earn multiple nominations and wins for the Beatles in the next year's Academy Awards. They had reinvented the concert structure that had stolen their love of touring and turned it into something new. The success of *The Concert for Bangladesh*, a one-off charity concert, erased the sour feelings still lingering from Woodstock.

Album. Film. Concert. They broke the rules and the records in all three categories in the same year.

• • •

George Martin felt a sense of history about 1971 and thought that he should do something about it. Before he took his plan to John and Paul, however, he made sure that Beeching, Klein, and the Eastmans were on board.

He wondered if, given how intensely the year had begun, it might be possible to throw the world a bone of peace at Christmas. Martin went to John and Paul separately. "Do you feel that you've made your point now?" Upon reflection, both seemed to feel that they had done just that.

Would they consider going back to what had always worked before—Christmas? He asked both Lennon and McCartney to consider contributing a Christmas song to a seasonal single that would be two A-sides. He thought it would give people a breather after the emotion that had started the year. Besides, he reasoned, Christmas releases were something of a tradition in Beatlemania. In a bid to transcend his growing reputation as an angry political radical, Lennon immediately signed on, saying he wanted "to go balls out for Santa." He already had the song—"Happy Xmas (War Is Over)"—something he and Yoko had performed in a live concert setting almost two years ago. That it did not exactly transcend his "angry young radical" image was not something anyone at Apple felt compelled to point out.

McCartney had been toying with a song that he would later release on his own. That song was "Wonderful Christmastime," an entirely pleasant ditty that simply could not hold up to the power of Lennon's compelling peace tribute. He considered ducking this comparison altogether, believing that one Christmas classic per season was more than enough, even for the Beatles. Still, there was the reality that a new single needed a new song on each side.

"In the end, I just couldn't let myself take a pass," he confessed. "I felt I had to give it a go, but instead of competing with John, I just went off in an entirely new direction."

He had successfully turned the trifle "Bip Bop" into "Stop War" at *The Concert for Bangladesh*, and it had translated well on the album.

McCartney decided to go with a tune he had been working with already, "Smile Away," but twisted it into a Christmas configuration. He had tried recording the song, an up-tempo rocker with nonsense lyrics, during the 1970 *And the Band Plays On* sessions, but Harrison had made a snarky remark, seconded by Lennon, and Paul had sensed it just was not worth fighting for at the time.

McCartney now re-tooled the song with entirely new lyrics, changing the title from "Smile Away" to "Santaway." If Lennon's contribution was anthemic and powerful, McCartney's, with its truth-talking Bad Santa loose on the streets, was just plain fun.

> *"I was looking at the sky the other night*
> *Who did I meet?*
>
> *I met a man in red and white and I did say,*
> *'Man, I can smell your reindeer a mile away'*
>
> *Santaway, Santaway, Santaway, yeah Santaway."*

So it came to pass that the two songs were released just after Halloween. The single became a huge sensation, selling more and more as Thanksgiving came and went, and then even more as Christmas approached. Fans bought them up in unprecedented numbers, as did less avid listeners, and their love for the single did not stop until mid-January of the next year.

"Happy Xmas (War Is Over)" became the instant radio hit, dominating the airwaves. It was catchy, hopeful, and popular. Yet, even with the success of "Happy Xmas," McCartney's "Santaway" was not buried. Many fans loved it, and it, too, found its way into heavy radio rotation, played for years almost as frequently as Lennon's classic. In the end, these two recordings became the third best-selling single in the entire Beatles catalog.

The ultimate irony is that Lennon almost preferred McCartney's song to his own. His partner's entry was witty and observant but still in love with the holiday. "Santaway" took itself far less seriously than "Happy Xmas," something that bothered Lennon all his life, if his interview comments are to be believed.

"When Paul rocks out, there's nobody better," he admitted. Then he added, "To hell with him."

• • •

In 1964, the Beatles were at the forefront of the music world and inspired Beatlemania. Seven years later, the band and its members had radically changed, but they appeared to be as relevant and creatively vibrant as ever, and probably more so.

They had planned to leave each other. They wanted to leave each other. But their pledge to wait for the release of their new film had turned them into the greatest success story of the new decade.

CHAPTER FIVE

IMAGINE ANOTHER DAY (1972)

A NEW ONE JUST BEGUN

Early in the year, George Harrison found himself surrounded by reporters at one of his rare appearances at Apple. He was supposed to be supporting both the Beatles album and the upcoming Beatles film of *The Concert for Bangladesh*. While the concert had been a creative success, both the film and the album were hampered by technical issues, and legal entanglements were affecting the need to get money to the troubled country that spawned the concert in the first place.

Harrison, appearing gaunt, sounded as exhausted as he looked. "The biggest break in my career was getting into the Beatles," he told the men and women in the press. "These days it feels like the biggest break might be getting out of them."

Harrison had, in fact, put far more energy into *The Concert for Bangladesh* than any of his bandmates, and the exertions of the benefit had taken a toll. He was in need of recuperation and retreat, goals that proved elusive, given that, at home, he and his wife had become increasingly estranged.

As it turned out, however, it was more than Harrison's lack of energy and the continuing differences between the four Beatles that threatened the group's cohesion. It was also the perceived threat that they posed to President Richard Nixon's re-election effort.

As the year began, White House counsel John Dean began subscribing to underground newspapers to keep tabs on radical activities that might threaten the coming Republican National Convention, scheduled for Miami Beach in August. One quote got his attention:

> [New York Free Press] "There is something in the air to give the radical movement hope again after a tough two years. Here in New York City, many people think it started with the arrival of John Lennon and Yoko Ono. By keeping the Beatles together, rather than walking away from them as he might have wanted to do, he has kept them as a potent political force if he chooses to use them that way."

Dean was not the only Republican soldier paying attention. Just three weeks into the new year, presidential assistant for Congressional Relations William E. Timmons received a letter from conservative Senator Strom Thurmond with an attached memo prepared by the Senate Internal Security Subcommittee. The memo was shocking in that it directly targeted the most popular rock band on Earth for surveillance and harassment by agencies of the United States government.

• • •

MEMO FROM SENATE INTERNAL SUBCOMMITTEE STAFF

Re: The Beatles and the Radical Left
Date: January 23, 1972

John Lennon, Paul McCartney, George Harrison, and Richard Starkey are British citizens who collectively form the musical group known as "The Beatles." All have visited the United States for both personal and professional reasons beginning eight years ago. All of the members of the group are currently in the United States filming a motion picture. That production, known as *The Hot Rock*, features the band members portraying common criminals.

John Lennon, in particular, is the only member of the group currently attempting to stay in the United States as a permanent resident and is currently residing in New York City. He has claimed a date of birth of October 9, 1940, and he is presently married to a Japanese citizen, one Yoko Ono.

The December 12, 1971 issue of the *New York Times* shows that Lennon and his wife appeared at a December 11, 1971 rally held in Ann Arbor, Michigan, to protest the continuing imprisonment of John Sinclair, a radical poet. Although his Beatles group did not perform, he explained that "they are with us in spirit and may be coming back to America sooner than you imagine. Dump Nixon!"

Radical New Left leaders Rennie Davis, Jerry Rubin, Abbie Hoffman, and others have been observed in the New York City area with Lennon. According to a confidential source, they have devised a plan to hold rock concerts in various primary election states for the following purposes: to obtain access to college campuses; to stimulate eighteen-year-old registration; to press for legislation legalizing marijuana; to finance their activities; and to recruit protestors to come to Miami Beach during the Republican National Convention in August 1972. Several of these individuals are the same persons who were instrumental in disrupting the Democratic National Convention in Chicago in 1968.

This same source, whose information has proved reliable in the past, states that Davis and his cohorts intend to use John Lennon to influence his band, the Beatles, to promote the success of the rock festivals and rallies. The source feels this will pour tremendous amounts of money into the coffers of the New Left and can only inevitably lead to a clash between a controlled mob organized by this group and law enforcement officials in Miami Beach. This would tarnish the Republican party with the same brush that protestors used against Democrats back in 1968.

The source feels that if Lennon's current visa is terminated, and any application by McCartney, Harrison, and Starkey is refused, it would be a strategic counter-measure to these conditions. The source also noted the caution which must be taken with regard to the possible alienation of the so-called eighteen-year-old vote if Lennon is expelled from the country and his bandmates are refused entrance.

• • •

While the memo worked its way through the West Wing staff at the White House, President Nixon, a lifelong cold warrior, went to China on February 21, 1972, and talked to Communist leader Mao Zedong, who the United States had pretended for more than two decades did not exist. It was a delicious irony that John Lennon had already dissed the powerful world leader in "Revolution" when he sang, "*If you go carryin' pictures of Chairman Mao, you ain't gonna make it with anyone, anyhow.*"

In the eyes of the world, Nixon's visit to China was the beginning of a cold peace between the giants of the West and the East. Fans might be forgiven for wondering that if Nixon could go to China, what was stopping John, Paul, George, and Ringo from getting their own acts together and making more music?

As personal and sometimes heated as their differences were, neither Lennon nor McCartney had the emotional capital to continue an energetic feud. They both publicly walked back some of their earlier statements from the *Savile Row* period. John's explanation was the craziest: he had written "How Do You Sleep?" as much about himself as anyone else (meaning Paul). No one believed him, of course, but as far as "never minds" go, it was one of the boldest denials ever lodged with a straight face until the Trump Administration's Sean Spicer.

After Nixon's triumphant return from China, presidential assistant Timmons wrote to Senator Thurmond, informing him that "the Immigration and Naturalization Service has served notice on him (Lennon) that he is to leave the country no later than March 15. Additionally, Mr. McCartney, Mr. Harrison, and Mr. Starkey have all been put on the INS watch list, and any visa applications they file will receive enhanced scrutiny."

The Immigration and Naturalization Service then began moves to keep all the Beatles from the United States by deeming them to be "undesirables." John had a 1968 drug conviction from the UK. So, too, did McCartney and Harrison. That gave the INS an official reason for what was ultimately a political act.

While McCartney, Harrison, and Starkey, who were living outside of the United States, could all take their time to consider their relationship to the country, Lennon and Ono, who were living in New York, had to make a decision, and soon.

They committed to the fight by hiring successful immigration attorney Leon Wildes, a man who, incredibly, didn't know who his new client was, let alone that the Beatles were still the most famous band in the world.

The first thing that Wildes argued was that the Lennons needed to stay in the United States as long as they could continue to get court-ordered delays due to the appeals process. Lennon, who loved New York, was on board with the plan.

Wildes, however, also argued for Lennon to stay involved as a member of the Beatles because he would look better in the group than as some malcontent crazy renegade who could not get along with anyone.

"It's always one more thing before I can get out," complained Lennon. "First, I had to stay in the group for the fucking Hobbits, and now I have to stay in so Tricky Dicky can't throw me out of his Fourth Reich."

So the Beatles remained a group, but there was grave doubt about getting them in the same recording studio together. Lennon could not leave the United States, and his bandmates were being told not to push their luck by trying to overstay their current visas. For the moment, it was the government, not their own issues, that was keeping them apart.

• • •

On January 30, in the Bogside area of Derry, Northern Ireland,

British soldiers shot twenty-six unarmed civilians during a peaceful protest march. Thirteen people died that day, many while fleeing from the soldiers or trying to help the wounded. Other protesters were injured by rubber bullets or batons, and two were run down by army vehicles. The massacre became known as "Bloody Sunday."

As it happens, both Paul McCartney and John Lennon carry Irish roots in their lines of descent. Both men were moved to express their anger and explore their heritage in song. Lennon booked space at the Record Plant in New York, and McCartney headed for Abbey Road in London. Lennon cut two songs: "Sunday Bloody Sunday" about the incident itself and "The Luck of the Irish" about the Irish conflict in general. McCartney recorded his own political anthem: "Give Ireland Back to the Irish."

Even though they each were driven to song by the events, neither man knew about the other's work. It's not clear if they even thought of what they were doing as something that should involve the Beatles. John worked with Yoko on his songs, and Paul worked with Linda on his.

As had happened during the *Savile Row* sessions, the two recordings placed producer George Martin squarely in the middle of a negotiation.

> [George Martin] "All three of the songs were good in their own right. My first thought was that Yoko's and Linda's tracks should be plucked out of their respective tunes, and the Beatles should be tracked in their place. But, of course, that never happened."

Lennon dug his heels in first, insisting that Yoko was an integral part of the creative process for both of his songs. In a now familiar scenario, he wanted an immediate single pressed and released, and if the songs were too political for the Beatles to affix their name to them, so much the better. He was shocked to hear that Martin had received another song about the Irish Troubles from McCartney on the same day.

All three songs were circulated between the two men, their

spouses, the other Beatles, and the Apple management and creative teams. When McCartney heard about Lennon's insistence that Ono's tracks should remain, he insisted that his wife's tracks should remain as well and be expanded.

Both Harrison and Starkey were in London and informed Apple that they would play on the songs, or not—they were fine with either option. Both men were concerned that songs featuring contributions from Yoko and Linda could hardly be considered pure Beatles songs.

In the end, that may have been the single's saving grace. The songs felt timely and not entirely appropriate for the next Beatles album, which was due to be recorded in Los Angeles in the spring. By putting the songs out on a single, and only as a single, Lennon, McCartney, Harrison, and Starkey made it clear that the tracks were not technically a part of the Beatles canon. It was the same thinking that went into last year's Christmas single.

Lennon went to work to merge "The Luck of the Irish" into a single song that built into "Sunday Bloody Sunday." McCartney refined his "Give Ireland Back to the Irish." Both Harrison and Starkey came into the Savile Row studios to add their contributions. Lennon and McCartney had written a single together, but neither man had performed on the other's individual song.

While the song was being mixed, Derek Taylor spun out this release:

> [Derek Taylor] "The Beatles are citizens of England who have feelings like all citizens. John and Paul each independently felt it was time that people questioned what we were doing in Ireland. George and Ringo agree. So they have come together to raise these questions and to see if music might bring some peace to this troubled land. Plus, they like the songs, too."

With the songs completed and the press release ready to be triggered, both Paul and John received a call from Sir Joseph Lockwood, the chairman of EMI. He wanted them to know that EMI simply could not release this single because it was too inflammatory. Both of the Beatles told him essentially the same thing: they felt strongly about it, and it must be released.

"It will be banned, you know," said Lockwood.

The chairman was right. It turned out that it was banned by the BBC. This fate, however, was not entirely new to the Beatles, who had seen "I Am the Walrus," "Come Together," "A Day in the Life," "Lucy in the Sky with Diamonds," "Hi, Hi, Hi," and "The Ballad of John and Yoko" previously banned.

The single did reach number one on the charts in Ireland and Spain, but did not receive a U.S. release. Record executives there felt that Americans had enough troubles of their own with Vietnam, and, beyond that, the Ireland conflict was far too difficult for them to understand.

• • •

To counteract this evolving image of the Beatles as drug-taking undesirables and political fringe elements, Allen Klein brought a bold plan to Lord Beeching that would allow Apple to re-package these angry, edgy young men as the Moptops one last time.

> [Klein] "I thought, 'Who doesn't love a Greatest Hits album?' The Beatles had so many hits over the years that they could have the Greatest Hits album of all Greatest Hits albums. In fact, I thought, they could have two of them. And each one could be a double album."

Klein had a vision, and he pursued it with dogged determination. That vision had been triggered by the appearance of a bootleg version of Beatles hits, which was illegally taking profits from an unexploited public demand. If anyone should be taking profit, he reasoned, it ought to be Apple.

Klein briefed Beeching (whom he considered woefully ignorant of Beatles history) about album lengths. *A Doll's House* had been a two-record album, and rather than turning off fans by its price, it turned into a giant bestseller. *The Concert for Bangladesh* had done it again with three records and great sales of its own. Klein now proposed that the Beatles release two Greatest Hits albums, each with two LPs inside, for a total of four records.

He began to package a "Red" album and a "Blue" album, the former covering the early years of the band, and the latter covering the years leading up to the Grand Bargain. They would be *The Beatles/Red (1963–1966)* and *The Beatles/Blue (1967–1969)*.

The packaging was stunning. For the group's 1963 debut LP, *Please Please Me*, photographer Angus McBean took a distinctive color photograph of the group looking down over the stairwell inside EMI House, the company's London headquarters in Manchester Square.

In 1969, the Beatles asked McBean to re-create this shot. The contrast between the clean-cut young men framed in red on the first LP, and then the bearded, mustached hippies they had morphed into in the second LP, was striking.

Klein's first take on what came to be known as the "Double-Doubles" was to curate a representative chronological collection of Beatles hits and successes to cover the four sides, maintaining the image of the cohesive group.

As it turned out, however, Lennon, McCartney, and Harrison all complained and asked that the sides be divided in a way that allowed them to feature the songs that were predominantly theirs on a side dedicated to them alone. Starkey was the only voice to the contrary, feeling that he would not be able to fill two full sides with songs that related only to his work.

While many fans still could not tell a Lennon from a McCartney song in the *The Beatles Red* album, that was not the case for *The Beatles Blue*.

When the "Double-Double" albums were released, their very organization seemed to tell fans about the new Beatles. They still recorded as a group, but they were clearly four separate musicians. The albums gave each man his solo due, and every one of them could feel properly recognized for their own individual talents. Another compromise had lent itself to a positive spin.

While the Red and Blue albums kept the Beatles in the eyes of the world musically, they did nothing to actually move the band toward recording new material. That decision was still being postponed.

• • •

Hollywood continued to push the Beatles before the public eye whether they were really in the mood for it or not. In early 1972, before the Nixon Administration had told the INS to bar them at the door of America, they had come to the U.S. to shoot a new film, *The Hot Rock,* and to attend a round of awards shows in support of their last film, *The Lord of the Rings*.

To mention *The Hot Rock* today brings out the knives in debate among Beatles fans, as some see it as comedy just slightly beyond the complication factor of *Help!*, while others see it as a complete sellout. In 1971, when the papers were signed and the film greenlit for production, however, it was simply an acknowledgment by Hollywood that, coming from the success of *The Lord of the Rings*, the Beatles had earned the right to have big movie offers brought to them.

The mood in the Apple offices on Savile Row reflected resentment at the hammerlock UA had on the Beatles' earlier films. On the deal for *The Lord of the Rings*, UA had stuck with terms that had been agreed to back in the early days when the Beatles were not considered to be film stars. The film division wanted to continue those terms, even after this latest film became a critical and commercial hit.

With the Beatles free to make movies with anyone they chose, 20th Century Fox had come calling with *The Hot Rock*, the kind of ensemble project that seemed perfectly suited to the Beatles as they were coming from a hit and needed to get product to market quickly and efficiently.

As a caper-comedy, *The Hot Rock* had originally been developed to star Robert Redford and George Segal. Peter Yates was attached to direct from a screenplay by William Goldman, based on Donald E. Westlake's novel of the same name. The film would introduce Westlake's long-running John Dortmunder character. The story concerned a team of four men who steal a massive diamond from a museum and then have to break into prison to rescue the one team member who got caught and swallowed the diamond during the heist.

The studio asked screenwriter Goldman, who was coming off the success of his own original *Butch Cassidy and the Sundance Kid*, to revise his draft to accommodate the casting of the Beatles and their own quirky screen personas. In his classic book *Adventures in the Screen Trade*, he remembers his first reaction.

> [William Goldman] "I nearly walked off the project. I'd been hired to write the first draft because of my relationship with (Robert) Redford, now he's off the picture and John Fucking Lennon is playing a part that he had no business playing. Totally trying to punch above his weight class. The problem was I fucking loved John Fucking Lennon, so I shut up and re-wrote the script."

Goldman set out to revise his own script to play to the strengths of the Beatles. He even managed to create a credible reality where four British criminals could operate effectively in New York City. It was ironic to the extreme that in his new draft, John Lennon played a naturalized American citizen originally from the United Kingdom.

In the opening scene, Lennon's character, jewel thief Dortmunder, is released from the State Prison into the hands of his safecracker brother-in-law, Andy Kelp, played by Paul McCartney. Harrison got the part of the driver who handled the getaway car, which fit in with his own extracurricular interests in auto racing, and Ringo was the bomb maker who ends up needing to be broken out of prison, which caused Ringo to name himself "McGuffin."

Shot over thirty-seven days in February and March in New York City and its environs, screenwriter Goldman had been on the set for much of the production. In his book, he vividly remembers watching Yates direct the scene with Lennon's Dortmunder being released from prison to McCartney's Kelp. One of the actual prison guards, taking it all in, observed to Goldman about McCartney: "My wife said to me today that she would get down on her hands and knees and crawl through glass just for the chance to fuck him one time. One time."

Everyone associated with the film at this time knew that it was not going to win the awards *The Lord of the Rings* had but that the magic of the Beatles still might propel it to commercial success.

• • •

Although the production of the Stanley Kubrick version of *The Lord of the Rings* was now in the rearview mirror, its impact was still being felt during Hollywood's awards season in the first months of 1972. The film itself was nominated for Best Picture by the Academy Awards, the Golden Globes, and all the major guilds. Kubrick was nominated as a director across the board.

The acting was another matter. In the end, the group-think of Hollywood seemed to settle on Paul McCartney and Richard Starkey as the breakout stars.

George was considered an interesting but one-note wizard in his portrayal of Gandalf. Similarly, John was thought to be slightly over-the-top in his characterization of Gollum.

Paul and Ringo, however, seemed to touch a nerve as the likable duo of Frodo and Sam. Both were nominated by the Academy Awards and the Golden Globes, Paul in the Lead Actor categories and Ringo in the Supporting Actor categories. Both men won the Golden Globe for their work. Whether he did so out of jealousy is debatable, but John referred to the award as the "Golden Knob Job."

The 44th Academy Awards were presented April 10, 1972, at

the Dorothy Chandler Pavilion in Los Angeles. The ceremonies were presided over by Helen Hayes, Alan King, Sammy Davis Jr., and Jack Lemmon. For the first time in the history of the Awards, the nominees were shown on screen while being announced, an advance many observers attributed to the program's producers capitalizing on the chance to broadcast actual living, breathing Beatles in their seats.

It became something of a joke when, in category after category, the presenters were forced to pronounce the full official name of the film—*Stanley Kubrick Presents J.R.R. Tolkien's The Lord of the Rings Starring The Beatles.*

On Oscar night, the movie had nominations (and wins) in mostly all the technical categories and included nominations that were part of the official television broadcast, like Best Picture, Director, Cinematographer, Writer, Soundtrack, Song, Lead Actor, and Supporting Actor.

Early on, it became clear that the night was a battle between *The French Connection* and *The Lord of the Rings.* Kubrick himself won two Oscars, for Best Adapted Screenplay and Best Director.

The actor known as Richard Starkey won Best Supporting Actor in a category that included Ben Johnson, Jeff Bridges, and Roy Scheider. Paul McCartney, however, had to applaud politely for Gene Hackman, who took the Best Actor award. Even so, critics and audiences alike believed that McCartney had delivered his best performance ever on film and that appearing with Ringo by his side made him seem even more relatable.

As always, the evening came down to the battle for Best Picture. In 1972, the films nominated included *The French Connection, Fiddler on the Roof, The Last Picture Show,* and *Nicholas and Alexandra.* Jack Nicholson was the category presenter:

> [Jack Nicholson] "And the Oscar for Best Picture goes to… well, wouldn't you know it…*Stanley Kubrick Presents*…aw, what the hell, it goes to *The Lord of the Rings.*"

Kubrick had made it known that only producers should go on stage if the film won in the Best Picture category. That meant that Paul McCartney, Richard Starkey, George Harrison, and George Martin (John Lennon did not attend) were supposed to stay in their seats and politely smile. Both the telecast producers and the audience, however, had other ideas and practically propelled the three attending Beatles toward the stage.

In his speech, however, Stanley Kubrick never mentioned the Beatles, nor were they allowed to speak for themselves. On the way off the stage, Ringo approached the still hot mic and uttered the words that would become his trademark: "Peace and Love."

FEAR AND LOATHING IN AMERICA

As far as fans were concerned, John Lennon and Yoko Ono came to America because Lennon felt that the United States, and New York City, in particular, was the center of the universe for Planet Earth. After his years in the United Kingdom, he was ready to take up residence where the action was.

There was another reason, one that got less press coverage because he spoke about it less frequently, both to protect his wife's privacy and because it did nothing to increase his mythological status in the counter-culture. Lennon had come to America with his wife to look for Yoko's daughter, Kyoko. Ono's previous husband Tony Cox had gone into hiding with the girl, even though Yoko had been granted shared custody.

By now, Lennon's limited three-month stay granted by the Immigration and Naturalization Service had been regularly revoked and subsequently appealed. By 1972, he and Yoko were in a constant struggle to stay in the United States, and it was not going well. The Nixon Administration's perception that they were a threat made their daily lives unbearable. And they still had not found Kyoko in all this time.

As a result of the constant harassment from the INS and

the FBI, John and Yoko had actively inserted themselves into radical left American politics. They marched in support of Native American rights, met with the Black Panthers, wrote columns for leftist magazines, and attended anti-Vietnam protests. They were by no means trying to maintain a low profile.

As a consequence, the Nixon Administration had moved far beyond simply paying attention to the comings and goings of the Lennons. They worried that Lennon might motivate young people to vote against Nixon's re-election and that he'd have particular influence over the millions of voters, mainly Americans aged from eighteen to twenty, the ones who would vote for the first time in 1972.

The Nixon team was correct to worry. Lennon, having flirted openly and heavily with radical politics, saw 1972 as one last chance for the system to save itself. That meant that Richard Nixon had to be sent packing from the White House. Senator George McGovern from South Dakota was the first Democratic challenger who had come forward, but Lennon thought he was too nice, too unknown, too untested, and would be battered badly by the Nixon machine. He began looking more and more at Senator Edward Kennedy as the only politician who might get into the presidential race and take on Nixon.

Lennon's lawyer was also instrumental in his tilt toward the political center. He felt that it would be better for his client to be preaching democracy to eighteen-year-olds than revolution to the world. He encouraged Lennon to do whatever he thought was appropriate to show an interest in the mainstream American political process.

There was one thing John Lennon had learned in his time in America: when he telephoned someone, they usually took the call.

On January 17, Lennon called the Washington, D.C. office of Senator Kennedy and asked to speak to the senator directly. The staffer who answered thought it was a joke, and it was not until Lennon sang a bar from "Help!" that he was asked to hold the line. After a minute, he got his wish.

"This is Senator Kennedy."

Lennon introduced himself and said he wanted to talk about how Kennedy should enter the race and defeat Richard Nixon. Kennedy thanked him for his support but stated that Senator McGovern had an organization that was already built and he would be starting from scratch. "As you'll remember, my brother, Bobby, entered late in 1968, and many people thought he was an opportunist for taking on Senator McCarthy so late in the game."

"There's a big difference, Senator," explained Lennon. "This time the Kennedy in the race will have me on his side."

It was a cordial conversation but one that didn't change Kennedy's mind. He had his own stumbling blocks, namely the Chappaquiddick scandal from 1969 when he drove a car into a river and a young girl drowned. This was compounded by his own reputation as the lightest weight in the Kennedy brand. Having the endorsement of a drug-taking radical was not going to make his chances any better.

"Let me know if you change your mind," said Lennon as he hung up the receiver and turned to Yoko, who was eager to hear how the conversation had gone.

"He's thinking about it."

The irony was that Lennon was correct. Kennedy was under enormous pressure from the party to challenge Senator George McGovern before the primary voting started. Most of that pressure came from the politicos in the Democratic party who felt that Nixon could be beaten, but not by a back-bench peacenik senator from South Nowhere. They needed a big gun to take out Nixon. They needed a Kennedy.

Years after the 1972 election, Kennedy reflected on the Lennon call. "All my children and my nieces and nephews and all my staffers made me tell that story over and over and over. They were pretty sure that I was nothing special, but the thought of possibly meeting the Beatles made them push me as hard as they could to get in the race."

• • •

While there was much to squabble over, there was also the simple fact that all of the Beatles agreed that their legacy could not end with *Savile Row*. If they were to close down the band for real, they would have to do what they had done with *A Doll's House* and *Everest*. They needed to show critics and fans the musical power of the group and not the personal pain of its disintegration. This urge to end on a high note was where *Imagine Another Day* was born.

The biggest impediment to actually producing the album was logistics. Lennon was still locked into staying put in the United States on the advice of his own lawyer, while the rest of the Beatles were scattered. Paul preferred Scotland, George hungered for the tranquility of Friar Park, and Ringo preferred Monaco when he was not jet-setting about the rest of the world.

Yet all four of the Beatles had been in America to film *The Hot Rock* at the beginning of the year, and they had lingered to attend the Oscars and the Grammys. Even Nixon's INS could make no argument that they had not been well behaved. Applications for Paul, George, and Ringo were filed, and the INS granted them permission to return to America in the spring.

While Lord Beeching lamented not being able to properly monetize the assets of the Beatles by recording in England, the axis of Beatles music, because of John's legal woes, thus tilted from the United Kingdom to the United States.

Plans were made to record at LA's Record Plant for the month of May. What the Beatles team did not foresee at the time was how politics would supercharge those sessions.

In the battle for the Democratic nomination, Senator George McGovern, running as the anti-war candidate, had to defend his political left flank when Senator Edward Kennedy entered the race. Lennon always took credit for persuading the Massachusetts Senator, but Kennedy insisted to historian Theodore White that he had entered in spite of the Beatle's entreaty, not because of it.

McGovern's support withered away with a Kennedy in the

race, so powerful was the family pull. By March of 1972, McGovern had endorsed Kennedy in exchange for a promise that he would be named Secretary of State, only to have former vice president and now senator Hubert Humphrey jump back in the race and challenge Teddy from the political right.

At the exact same time that the Beatles were recording at the Record Plant in May, Kennedy found himself fighting a bitter struggle to earn the Democratic nomination over Humphrey, and the entire campaign seemed to be coming down to California. Kennedy and Humphrey staged a series of three debates, each within a few days of the other, in the final week of the California campaign.

The first debate came on May 28, just a week before the June 6 winner-take-all California primary election and its mother lode of 271 delegates. Lennon was far more taken with the primary duel than McCartney, Harrison, or Starkey, and broke up the session to watch the debate in the lobby of the recording studio, on a black-and-white television with a metal hanger for its antennae.

Seeing Humphrey come out swinging against Kennedy had one impact on the *Imagine Another Day* album in that it caused Lennon to revise his earlier "Gimme Some Truth," a song that first took form in 1969 but had never made it to any Beatles album since then. John was also inspired to push for the inclusion of "Power to the People," a song he had written a year earlier. John's passion for political change was at its peak, fueled by his perception that he was "Public Enemy #1" to the Nixon Administration.

The Beatles converged on the Record Plant studio in the early afternoon of June 4. Lennon had convinced them that they should all get there in time to do a little work before taking a break to watch the final Kennedy/Humphrey debate. By this point, even the dismissive Harrison had to admit that it all had turned quite dramatic. If Kennedy could win California, then the nomination was his. If he lost, then it seemed obvious that Humphrey would be the Democratic nominee for president, as he had been four years before, and would face President Nixon in a November election repeat of 1968 when they had run against each other. Even the apolitical McCartney could see the problem with that. "It's like watching a re-run of a show on the telly that you didn't much fancy the first time you saw it."

Lennon thought it was even more apocalyptic.

[John Lennon] "I thought Nixon was the Devil, I really did. But I didn't think anybody named Hubert could beat him, and this particular Hubert had already had his chance. But Teddy, you could see him doing it. His brothers were about the only other humans on the planet with the sizzle the Beatles had, and both of them were dead. The little brother was the best we could get, but it might just be enough. Of course, Yoko thought I was daft; she thought all politicians were phonies. I said, 'Of course, he's a phony, dear, but he's our phony.'"

What none of the Beatles knew that day as they worked on a McCartney tune called "Monkberry Moon Delight" was that legendary journalist Hunter S. Thompson was straddling his new Vincent Black Shadow motorcycle and heading at extreme speed in their direction. Writing for *Rolling Stone*, Thompson knew that if he could weave the Beatles into his narrative, editor Jann Wenner would eat it up.

Thompson was in town with all the other political reporters, but he had taken a side trip up to Ventura, where he had purchased what he described as a "genuinely hellish bike" with a top speed of 140 miles per hour. He was riding it in their direction in second gear, where he claimed the vibration nearly fused his wrist bones and the boiling oil from the bike turned his right foot completely black.

By the time he found his way to the Pacific Coast Highway, Thompson had also gobbled up a hit of LSD that he had gotten from some hardcores in a Ventura bike gang. He had both high speed and a mind-scrambling drug in his system, and he was having the time of his life.

It was in this pre-high buzz that he showed up at the Record Plant. No one knew he was coming. Not the engineers, nor the staff, and certainly not the Beatles. Yet there he was in the lobby, smoking a cigarette, twisting the black-and-white TV's hanger antennae, and shouting, "Tell Lennon and his boy toys that there's a real man here that needs to talk to him!"

Up until this point, the fact that the Beatles were in Los Angeles recording a new album had been kept a secret. Thompson said he had found out the way any good reporter would—he'd heard about it from someone in a bar and then bribed a police officer providing security for the Kennedy campaign with Dodger tickets and the name of a willing call girl in exchange for the actual location.

The other three Beatles had already had enough of McCartney's song and happily took a break to greet Thompson. George, in particular, needed to reassure himself that the fringe journalist and motorcyclist had not brought any Hells Angels with him.

"Hell, no," said Thompson. "They can't keep up with a Shadow." He explained that the days when he wrote about outlaw motorcycle gangs were long gone and that his new book was about this year's election. "It'll be better because politicians are even more venal than bikers."

Ringo wanted to know if he intended to put the Beatles in that book. "Only if I remember any of this," was Thompson's answer.

That was good enough for the Beatles, and they retired back into the studio with the demented journalist. By now, Thompson was starting to trip in a way that made him seem amiably incoherent when he demanded an encore of "Honey Pie" from the *A Doll's House* album.

Lennon looked like he was ready to murder his guest, who broke into a loud laugh. "I'm fucking with you! Play 'Glass Onion.'" The fact that he knew enough to pick a Lennon song won him an instant friend in John and a puzzled reaction from Paul.

Thompson offered to share some of his biker LSD with the band, none of whom had taken the drug in years. John had replaced it with heroin; Paul had returned to his old standby, marijuana; George was experimenting with cocaine; and Ringo's drug of choice was alcohol.

George pushed back immediately, reminding everyone that he had not taken that specific drug in years and was seeking the positive effects it sought to convey through spiritualism instead. In fact, none of the Beatles had dropped acid since before the *Everest* sessions. Besides, on the off chance that you were looking for someone to get high with, Hunter Thompson seemed risky.

It was Ringo, however, who shrugged at his friends and smiled. "Sounds like it could be fun, just this once," he said. "I mean, if we all do it together, like the old times."

Like the old times. In other words, everyone was going to be in or everyone was going to be out on this one.

Next up, Paul. "Old times. Why not?"

Lennon pushed back his glasses. "I'll do it, but I have to call Yoko first."

Then George. He was obviously the most conflicted. "Let's not make a habit of this, shall we?"

Now that the group-mind had spoken, each man received a dose contained in a small blue pill that Thompson called "Thunder Road."

They continued to play while waiting for the drug's effects to kick in. By this point, Thompson was scaling new heights of being stoned when he asked, "Wait, what day is this?"

Told by George that it was Sunday afternoon, Thompson stood up on the piano bench and announced in his trademark staccato style: "Today we all have to go into the rancid belly of the beast despite the ominous possibility that the speedy free-falling Super Bowl swagger of the evil bastards and their underdog trip will be the lowest goddamn jerk-off perpetrated on the drunken lapdogs they have let loose on the people of California."

The Beatles, only partially accountable by the impending rush of their own acid trips, would later admit they had not the faintest idea what the so-called gonzo journalist was talking about. But Thompson had just realized that he had less than an hour to get from the Record Plant location on Sycamore Avenue in Hollywood to the ABC Television Studios on Prospect, a distance of about four and a half miles. Kennedy and Humphrey were due for their final debate, and Thompson was supposed to watch it live from the press room and write it up for a special edition of *Rolling Stone*.

Thompson said that he would get all the Beatles into the press room if they would get him to the studios. He no longer felt up to "taming the raging beast of the Black Shadow." As it turned out, there was a limo standing by for the Beatles that could be called into service.

Ringo wondered if the press room for a national political debate in the United States might be a party that was more than a little difficult to just crash. Wouldn't they need identification or some kind of press pass?

"Mother of God," declared Thompson. "You identify yourselves."

With that, the limo, driven by surprised driver José Escamilla-Santos, was called into service.

> [Hunter S. Thompson] "By the time I got into the limo, I saw four Beatles heads, but there was only one body that seemed recognizable, and it was wearing some kind of psychedelic tunic made out of tie-dyed blue jeans. I could taste the music coming out of their mouths by this time, some kind of fantastic, oozing mess of melody that made my own head feel like it had floated through the open roof and was escaping to the moon. And even when I tried to speak, to explain this unholy unhinging of my mind and body, all that came from my mouth was some kind of screech that sounded like koo-koo-ka-choo from the beak of a crow. This was before the full effect of the drug had kicked in and it made me nervous that perhaps this time I had actually gone too far."

In order to calm everyone down and make them presentable before the national press corps, Thompson advised a stiff drink or two of Wild Turkey straight bourbon whiskey, chased with a freshly cut grapefruit, two of which he had carried with him in his backpack during his harrowing motorcycle ride just a few hours earlier. Even though it may seem ludicrous on the face of it that Hunter Thompson and all four of the Beatles could arrive at a network studio to see a presidential debate while stoned on acid and reeking of whiskey, no one seemed to offer any resistance to the idea. And so off they went.

The limo with the Beatles and Hunter Thompson made it to ABC Television Studios with seven minutes to spare before the debate began. Thompson told the security team at the ABC gate that he was bringing the Beatles with him. Highly skeptical, they inspected the limo, only to have Paul McCartney tell them, "We've just come along for the ride, so to speak. Let's keep it our little secret."

As Thompson, Lennon, McCartney, Harrison, and Starkey entered the press room, it is fair to say that all eyes went from the monitors, where Kennedy and Humphrey could be seen sitting around a bright red rug, waiting to be questioned by Sam Donaldson for a special edition of "Issues and Answers," to the spectacle that now appeared before them. These were hardened reporters, the so-called "Boys on the Bus" of campaign journalism, and yet they all dropped what they were doing to gawk at John, Paul, George, and Ringo. Among those stopped in their tracks was David S. Broder of the *Washington Post*.

[David S. Broder] "You have to understand that we had followed these politicians around for so long that we could have delivered their own speeches for them without missing a beat. We had seen more of them than our own spouses for nearly six months. Speaking for myself, I had never met a Beatle. And yet, there they were. I shook John Lennon's hand and mumbled something about his immigration troubles, and he said, 'It's all pie in the sky to me. I'm afraid you'll have to speak English now.' I'm not sure what he meant exactly, but he sure made more of an impression than Hubert Humphrey, I'll tell you that."

The debate began minutes later, and the attention turned to the see-through glass that looked down on the studio floor. From a straight journalism point of view, it can only be said that the four Beatles seemed to be taking it all in stride, watching quietly, smoking cigarettes, and laughing at the oddest statements about tax policy and the like. Given the nature of it all, perhaps it is best to let Thompson's own words from his *Fear and Loathing: On the Campaign Trail '72* tell the story.

[Hunter S. Thompson] "This was madness in every direction. The Beatles were no longer Moptops if they ever were, but instead were bearded men with wild eyes that knew no good could come of this. They looked afraid, and they should have been, since the two white men sitting on the stage, lit up by red shag carpet that caused even the most advanced cameras to shimmer and jiggle, were the best that America could offer to a world choking on its own bile. When Humphrey spoke, flames poured from his throat like the hot, glowing fire that Uncle Sam had used to light up the Japs on Okinawa back in the day when America really could kick serious ass in the Eastern world, before the Viet Cong showed the world what a pussy we could be, even if we did have Agent Orange now. Kennedy could only smile, those white teeth beating back the heat, his eyes shifting, wondering if the next bullet out there in this goddamned hellish cartoon of a nation had his name on it. The Beatles, these British interlopers, were just as high as I was, only I knew we were doomed, but they were just seeing it for themselves and it tasted like curdled milk that had been swallowed quickly and spit out like vomit."

Whether or not this was a true summary of what the Beatles were feeling at that moment can be argued. What was true, according to at least a dozen accounts of reporters in the room, however, is that they lasted only fifteen minutes into a debate that went on for an hour and a half. By the time that consensus in the press pool awarded the victory to Kennedy on style points, the Beatles were long gone.

Before the night was over, the entire group, including limo driver Escamilla-Santos, was partying in LA's Laurel Canyon, at the home shared by Don Henley and Glenn Frey. Guests included David Crosby and Graham Nash of the Apple band Crosby, Stills, Nash & Young, Apple's Glyn Johns and Peter Asher, Lennon's good friend Harry Nilsson, and two women everyone seemed to know, Joni Mitchell and Linda Ronstadt.

> [David Crosby] "It was a scene, man, just a scene. I didn't want to be left out, you know, so I dropped acid, too. But I was so far behind them that by the time they were coming down the next morning, I was still flying high. George Harrison and I had a moment in the middle of the night when we both thought we could read each other's minds. Don't ask me what he was thinking, though, because I have no idea."

Lennon woke up the next morning in the home of Ronstadt. He had obviously slept with the emerging rock star and now remembered nothing about it. "If I'd known we were going to have sex," he said, "I'd have held off on the last drink."

"We only tried to," she said, correcting him.

"Should we try again?" he asked.

Ronstadt passed on the opportunity and instead fixed him a breakfast of bacon and eggs. Afterward, she drove him around Hollywood in her 1970 Buick Skylark before delivering him to the Record Plant. In what may have been a first, John Lennon was on time for a recording session that all three of his bandmates were late for.

In the years to come, all of the Beatles have denied most of these events happened, particularly the drug-taking, leaving the impression that Thompson made up or imagined the entire LSD angle after sharing dinner and some high-quality reefer with the group following a recording session. The other alternative, of course, is that Thompson's version of events was true, but the Beatles made a pact never to acknowledge it, hoping to avoid the debate that their new music was drug-inspired.

Whatever part is true or false, it seems clear that John, Paul, George, and Ringo created a new group memory out of the chaos with rebel journalist Thompson. "From what I remember," George has always maintained, "it was a bit like the old days, which we all thought we'd never see again."

MORE DOLL, LESS MOUNTAIN

After their 36-hour bender, the Beatles went back to the Record Plant to complete their next album. It's not surprising that, after a revelatory acid trip, each man now saw the endeavor through somewhat new eyes.

John Lennon wanted "More Doll, Less Mountain." By that, he simply meant that the group should embrace the musical anarchy from *A Doll's House* over the polish and precision of *Everest. And the Band Plays On* was not even part of the discussion in Lennon's mind. In an interview with *Rockstar* at the time of its release, he had called it "puerile."

Paul McCartney actually had a great deal of affection for the tuneful *And the Band Plays On* effort. In many ways, he viewed it as the perfect compromise between the raw 1968 double album and the 1969 studio sound. Still, McCartney saw the greatest value in keeping the Beatles together.

"I'm with John," McCartney told Harrison and Starkey. "It's every man for himself, and we back each other up whenever we need to."

This, of course, was the essence of the Grand Bargain's understanding: to put out one Beatles album each calendar year, no exceptions. The process itself did not have to be pretty. The work just needed to get done.

Harrison had gone almost entirely silent since the Thompson-inspired acid-fueled blur of the past few days. He had said nothing at all in the studio while Lennon and McCartney held forth.

"What do you say, George?" asked Ringo. "All good by you?"

Harrison peered over his sunglasses, which he had taken to wearing both outside *and* inside. "So long as I get my songs," is all he said.

Eighteen songs were worked up during the sessions, and when the album sides were laid out, fourteen made the cut, leaving the tally Lennon five, McCartney five, Harrison three, and Starkey one. But Ringo's was "Uncle Albert/Admiral Halsey" that had been written for him by Paul. In any case, McCartney had decided that whatever Lennon wanted on the album would be fine with him. He had seen that look in his partner's eyes before. He was looking for an excuse to bolt. Again.

Harrison obviously did not see things the same way. He was outraged that he had only three songs. Lennon shot back that Harrison had "hijacked" the soundtrack album for *The Lord of the Rings*, stacking it with his own material. This, of course, was so fundamentally true that even Harrison had to concede. In the end, Lennon backed down, shelving his jaunty "Crippled Inside" to make room for Harrison's "I Dig Love." McCartney and Lennon had their parity, Harrison had his dignity, and Starkey just did not care, happy to extend his streak of ocean-based songs that began with "Yellow Submarine" and "Octopus's Garden" by including the "Uncle Albert/Admiral Halsey" confection, which he cheerfully said "sounded like two songs anyway, the way Paul has written it."

The process itself was business-like. Since Lennon and McCartney had both insisted in the Grand Bargain that neither of the former writing partners should be able to veto the other's work, McCartney forced the inclusion of "Another Day" to answer Lennon for his unkind reference in "How Do You Sleep?" on the *Savile Row* album.

Even with this pettiness still in play, McCartney still knew Lennon's peace-dream "Imagine" was the foundational masterpiece of the album, destined to become a classic. Side One's beginning with "Imagine" was considered the bedrock that could not be moved. The question for weeks had been which song would follow it. When George Martin argued that "Another Day" should get the position, it was Lennon who quipped instantly that the album title needed to be *Imagine Another Day*. No one could come up with a better idea, and so it was that, despite tensions, *Imagine Another Day*, a cheeky title created by mashing up a Lennon tune with a McCartney tune, became another Beatles classic.

Coming from the widespread relief that the crisis of breaking up had been averted (at least temporarily), this record quickly became a personal favorite of many fans due to its strong collection of catchy hooks and emotion. Reviewers had a harder time with *Imagine Another Day*, many finding it at least as disparate as *A Doll's House* but without its energy and charm. *Rockstar*'s own Booth Hill found himself both impressed and disillusioned by it.

> [Booth Hill] "The album doesn't gel the way *Everest* did, but it also doesn't have the raw power of *A Doll's House*. It has been put together by a committee. Granted, that committee's most powerful members are the Beatles themselves, but they are bending and stretching their own material to fit the outcome of their own negotiations. The so-called Grand Bargain looks less grand than it ought to."

The album, based on the testimony of those who participated in it, was created with Paul McCartney working in one Record Plant studio and John Lennon working in another on the vast majority of days, with George Harrison and Ringo Starr each contributing to all the songs, but John to only one of Paul's, and Paul to just two of John's.

Whether the critics agreed, *Imagine Another Day* was still a huge success, breaking sales records and cementing the Beatles once again as the world's most popular rock band. While the album's popularity did not exactly consign *The Concert for Bangladesh* to record store nostalgia bins, it did erase any doubt that might have lingered among rock critics that the Beatles, together, were as good as it gets.

• • •

When the recordings for *Imagine Another Day* had finished, it had become more obvious than ever that Senator Kennedy would be the Democratic nominee. Kennedy had defeated Humphrey in California, but by a mere two points. Lennon shrugged off the closeness, calling it "two more points than absolutely necessary." He was right, given that California was a winner-take-all state when it came to delegate allotment.

Lennon was keen to fold the Beatles into a movement that would sweep the hated Nixon out of office once and for all.

"We can't even vote, John," reminded Ringo. "Not being American and all."

"Maybe we've done enough," said Paul. "We could all go home and take a bit of a vacation from it all."

"You can fucking go home. I can't leave this country or I never get back in. Nixon has to go." John had that look that they hadn't seen for a while. He was drug-free, at least for the moment, and he was fired up.

Lennon argued that because of the new album's political content, it should be rushed into a summer release. Even though the Apple marketing team would have liked more time, the general feeling was that a Beatles album always seemed to market itself anyway. *Imagine Another Day* was hurried into production and scheduled to come out July 8, two days before Democrats would nominate Kennedy to run against Nixon.

Many of the delegates to the Democratic convention plugged stereo components into the electric sockets of the hallways of the Miami Beach Convention Center and listened to the album over and over, drawing large crowds and turning the songs into the soundtrack for the event.

Inside the actual hall, spontaneous singing broke out prior to the nomination of Kennedy. Even though "Imagine" was considered the strongest song, the track of the hour was "Power to the People"—it fit the mood of the fight against Nixon, and, candidly, the words were much easier to remember.

While this sloganeering might have been a positive for

attracting the youth vote, the fact of the matter was that the newly empowered 18–21 crowd was not watching televised convention coverage. Most of them were out enjoying the summer, drinking beer, smoking pot, and having sex with their friends. It was their parents who were watching. And, for the older generation, there was something unsettling about these slogan songs and the fact that the men who wrote them were not even Americans.

The numbers for Kennedy still were not good. He prevailed at the convention, just barely, by a vote of 1523 delegates to 1459 for Humphrey. A Gallup poll conducted after the nomination was secured by Kennedy showed he was still behind the incumbent in the White House by a 48 percent to 39 percent margin.

Urged on by his friends in the radical left, Lennon made plans to stage a protest concert at the Republican National Convention, which was to take place in Miami, in the same convention center, just forty days later. The idea was to play a free outdoor concert for youthful protestors in Miami's Bayfront Park at the exact same time that Nixon was being nominated. It would steal away press coverage and present the alternative point of view. Lennon intended to perform "Ready Teddy" and asked McCartney to work up his "Teddy Boy" into versions that would promote the fortunes of Teddy Kennedy.

When the city of Miami refused the concert permit, stating that security would be impossible, the park was too small, and time was too short, TV viewers were spared the split-screen of the responsible leadership of Richard Nixon being validated on one side, and the chaotic, stoned hero worship of the Beatles on the other side.

The two songs, however, were recorded as solo efforts by Lennon on the A-side and McCartney on the B-side and released with profits to be donated to the Kennedy campaign. As it turned out, like the *Concert for Bangladesh* charity angle, by the time the money from the single was accounted for, the election was long over.

• • •

George Harrison was the most adamant Beatle about not performing any protest concert in Miami that summer. It wasn't about the politics—he saw Nixon as a warmonger as much as the others. Harrison opted out because in his mind, he had already given the Beatles more than enough of his time that year. He had made peace with the notion that he would put up with the nuisance the Beatles had become but vowed to only do so six months of each year. The other half of the year belonged to him.

Among the things that Harrison did to keep his mind off the Beatles in the off-season was to indulge his love of Formula One racing. He had followed it since he was twelve years old, when he saw Liverpool's first British Grand Prix. As the Beatles took over his life in the 1960s, he caught a few other races, mainly in Monte Carlo, where he often hung out with Ringo.

After the Grand Bargain had been reached, he began to do what many people do to hide their pain or discomfort—he bought things. For Harrison, it was cars. By 1972, when Lennon was talking about giving all his possessions away, George already had a Jaguar XK-E, Ferrari 365 GTC, and an Aston Martin DB4. In February, he'd crashed his Mercedes into a lamppost at ninety miles an hour, sending his wife Pattie Boyd flying into a windshield. She spent the next few weeks recovering from a concussion. George lost his license for that one, the second time he had it taken away for speeding.

> [George Harrison] "People think it's odd for me to care about fast cars. They think I'm too pious for that, but they're wrong. Cars can be meditative, even spiritual. When you drive a racing car to both its limits and yours, your senses are as keen as they ever will be. Heightening of the senses can happen in a car, or it can happen with a guitar. Besides, when I'm driving as fast as these cars can go, there's no time to think about Beatley things. If I think about what Paul did yesterday, or John did last week, I could get myself killed, you know?"

Immediately after the Beatles concluded production of

Imagine Another Day, Harrison returned to Britain and attended the British Grand Prix in Brands Hatch. He followed that by attending the German, Austrian, and Italian Grands Prix throughout the summer into the fall.

Meanwhile, Lennon and Ono had gone ahead and negotiated the purchase of an apartment in the Dakota, a gothic building situated on Manhattan's West Side overlooking Central Park. It was the same place that Roman Polanski had filmed *Rosemary's Baby*. Lennon and Ono hoped that the purchase would help show their commitment to living in the United States.

The FBI was still trying to come to grips with Lennon as an adversary. One information sheet the organization compiled listed his birth date wrong. Another showed a photo of a guy with long hair and granny glasses, thought to be Lennon. It was David Peel, one of Lennon's New York radical friends.

During this period, however, the FBI did initiate one of the strangest attempts to gather intelligence on John and Yoko. They reached out to Elvis Presley, the rock legend who had previously offered his help to Richard Nixon, and asked him to approach the Lennons, befriend them, and report back on their plans for illegal activities.

> [John Lennon] "My phone rings one day. At this point, we're suspicious of anything we hear because we know we're bugged. And this voice says, 'John, it's your old friend, Elvis Presley.' I thought it was a gag so I told him to bugger off and hung up. A minute later, some woman calls back, gives me a number in Memphis, Tennessee, says it's Elvis's number and tells me to call him. So, I did, and it was him. Can you believe it? He said he was coming to New York and wanted to know if I wanted to hang out. I said, sure, but Yoko's coming, too. He said no problem, that he was a big fan of hers. Of course, that's when I knew he was full of shit."

As it turned out, John and Yoko had become attached to a young reporter for WABC-TV's *Eyewitness News* named Geraldo

Rivera. He had been covering the Lennon immigration case, catching John for a sound bite on the courthouse steps more than a few times. Rivera had launched a charity crusade called "One to One," designed to improve living conditions for Staten Island children with special needs. Lennon and Ono had agreed to appear, along with Sha Na Na, Stevie Wonder, Roberta Flack, and a local New York group known as Elephant's Memory.

Elvis's arrival in the city, on August 29, coincided with the time of the concert, scheduled just one day later, a fact Lennon used to coerce Elvis into performing with him. The superstar was in the middle of his "comeback" period but had officially filed for divorce from his wife, Priscilla, just ten days earlier. He said he needed to get out of Graceland for a while because it was full of "too many memories."

Ironically, Presley had come to New York to sabotage a man he felt was a bad influence on young people because of his drug use at a time when he was heavily into drugs himself. Elvis was taking strong doses of barbiturates and had been doing so for years. He fell asleep on the couch in the Lennons' Dakota apartment. "I thought he was dead," said Ono. "I put my head on his chest to see if his heart was still beating."

It was. In the middle of the night, Presley regained consciousness, took some unidentified pills, and then woke up Lennon, demanding they rehearse a song. Lennon suggested "Hound Dog," and Presley argued for "Burning Love," his latest top ten chart hit. They agreed to double the anticipated output for the concert and perform them both. Presley taught Lennon the words and guitar licks for "Burning Love" while Ono made a second pot of coffee.

As had worked so successfully for *The Concert for Bangladesh*, two concerts took place that day—one in the afternoon, and another in the evening. Elvis was fine for the midday concert but was slurring his words badly by the next one. Lennon told the mixer to pot down Elvis's voice and bump his own up, and Lennon carried both tunes for an audience that never seemed to notice the difference.

By the time the concert was over, the Elvis Presley security team, led by Red West, had located the artist in the backstage men's room, bundled him away into a limousine, and warned Lennon that "if you talk about this, there's going to be trouble."

John felt it was one of the most uncomfortable moments of his life. "Seeing Elvis like that," he told Paul McCartney later, "it's enough to make you give up drugs for good."

Still, Apple was impressed enough that they later approached Elvis's label, RCA Records, about jointly releasing the "Hound Dog" and "Burning Love" songs as a single. RCA replied that they would consider it but would only share the proceeds 90/10, seeing as how the songs were Elvis songs. Apple was open to giving the matter some thought, but Elvis's manager, Colonel Tom Parker, vetoed the deal as soon as he heard about it.

As it turned out, Elvis did report back to his FBI handler, telling him of Lennon's ardent support for Senator Kennedy, which the FBI already knew. Nonetheless, this information worked its way up the chain of command, into the office of Chief of Staff Bob Haldeman, and, ultimately, into the Oval Office with President Richard Nixon. The White House team had been debating the Beatles all summer long, fearing this possibility of a protest concert, and, at the same time, ridiculing the political potency of these "degenerates" whose music was being lauded by the Democrats at their own convention.

In fact, President Nixon and Chief of Staff Haldeman had discussed the Beatles on the afternoon of June 20, 1972, and Nixon had ordered Haldeman to use the force of the FBI and the INS to "squash them like the bugs they are." At the moment, only the men in the meeting knew this, but that would soon change.

• • •

After Labor Day, when the presidential campaign began in earnest, John Lennon followed it in the *New York Times*, the *New York Daily News,* and the *New York Post*. He also watched the news on all the networks. During those two months, all three of his television sets were on night and day.

Ultimately, what he saw was not encouraging. The Committee to Re-Elect the President (CREEP) had gone after Kennedy with a vengeance. Nothing was off-limits. There were commercials about the Chappaquiddick scandal with haunting pictures of Mary Jo Kopechne, the woman who had died when Kennedy drove his car, with her in it, off Chappaquiddick's Dike Bridge in 1969. Kennedy got out alive, but Kopechne drowned.

The commercial that affected Lennon the most, however, came from the batch conceived by the Committee to Re-Elect the President to portray Senator Edward Kennedy, the brother of the beloved President John Kennedy, as nothing more than a radical left-wing extremist who was incompetent to serve as president.

The ad in question—"Acid, Amnesty, and Abortion"—had a tone of derisive mocking. "The Democrats say that Teddy Kennedy has a Triple-A rating with the ACLU. Maybe that's right. If by Triple-A, they mean Acid, Amnesty, and Abortion." The audio was paired with film images of marginalized protestors—young or black or women, or some combination of the three—who all looked angry and unpatriotic. It also included three particularly unflattering shots of the Beatles from photo shoots for their albums, one of which depicted Lennon flashing the peace sign at the Bangladesh concert.

Kennedy turned out to be not nearly as strong of a candidate as the Democrats had hoped—a fact that even John Lennon, one of the most staunch Kennedy supporters, was aware of. In a sit-down interview, Walter Cronkite asked Kennedy to respond to the ad and to the lifestyles of the Beatles who were portrayed in it. Kennedy's reply was incoherent and hurt his campaign badly.

[Senator Edward Kennedy] "Well, uh, let me just say this about this particular issue you raise. I think it is clear, uh, that I do not support, well, behavior that is…What I mean is that protest is part of the American, I understand that this group you refer to are British, but...The point behind this that I'm not for any of that, that you refer to. I hope this clarifies the issue."

Even so, the perception in the New York City where John Lennon and Yoko Ono lived was that Richard Nixon was so evil, so venal, so unacceptable, that Kennedy would win anyway, whether or not he was a good candidate. He had the right name, and with his brothers gone, it was his turn.

On election night, John and Yoko went to a party being held in the Soho home of their Yippie friend Jerry Rubin. They arrived early, when hope was still alive, and the party was cooking with the likes of Abbie Hoffman, Allen Ginsberg, and their comrades. As the returns filtered in at an agonizingly slow pace, it became more and more clear that Nixon was going to win in a potential landslide. Within a couple of hours, the party was turning into a wake.

"People like my music all right," Lennon told the party. "They just don't want to hear the message."

At about this time, Ringo showed up. John had invited him when he learned that he would be in New York seeing friends. When the Beatles drummer was told that Kennedy was going to lose, and big, he hailed a taxi to Jerry Rubin's, intent on cheering up John.

Cheering up, in this case, meant that the two men began to drink tequila shots as a game. Every time Nixon won another state, they would take a shot. The problem was that Nixon was winning a lot of states. It was becoming clear that tarnished by scandal and tarred by the Republican charges, Teddy was likely to lose decisively.

For the anti-war left—basically everyone at the party—it was a devastating result. Lennon took it personally, and he took it badly. He felt that all of his activism over the past few years had backfired.

The more bombed John got, the more he directed his paranoia and rage at the other guests, accusing several of working along with the FBI to sabotage his career and crush him creatively. He told his host, Rubin, to his face that all the wiretaps and the surveillance tails he, Yoko, Ringo, and the other Beatles had endured convinced him that his friend was actually a CIA agent. "You're nothing more than a cheap fraud who talks revolution, but you'll betray anybody to save your own skin."

"Really?" asked Rubin. "That's funny coming from the man who said 'you ain't gonna make it with anyone, anyhow.'"

As the staggering size of Kennedy's loss became clear and the party disintegrated further, Lennon made the one mistake that would haunt him for years. He began to flirt with one of Rubin's female roommates, Carol Realini, a woman that Abbie Hoffman himself had slept with, and he did it right in front of Yoko. After kissing Realini, he took her to an empty room, and, to Yoko's horror and to the amazement of the other guests, proceeded to have loud sex with her.

Having never warmed entirely to Yoko, even now, Ringo suddenly found himself sitting next to her and sharing her pain. "It was the only time I ever saw her break down in tears," he said later. "It was awful. I knew I had to do something."

Ringo gently placed his sunglasses on Yoko's face so she could hide behind them. He offered to take her home, but she demurred. Hammered as Lennon by this time, with no more good ideas, Ringo started drumming loudly with a pair of kitchen spoons and tried to lead the group in "Give Peace a Chance," hoping to drown out the lovemaking in the bedroom. As the sing-along fizzled, Lennon and Realini could still be heard.

Accounts differ, depending on who tells the story, but the predominant rumor was that Yoko nodded to Ringo and took his hand. Together the two of them left the party.

When Lennon finally emerged from the room and learned that Yoko had left with Ringo, he again became enraged. Fuming and unsteady, he went outside and hailed a cab.

When he got to the Dakota, he was greeted by Ringo, who was waiting in the lobby. "She's asleep now, John. She says she wants to be alone for a few days and that we should go drink ourselves to death some other place."

Only Ringo, his longtime friend, could have spoken this way to John. With anyone else, the interaction probably would have become a drunken fight. But John just shrugged. "I've fucked it up pretty good this time, huh?"

Ringo could only nod his agreement. "You've had better days."

With that, the two men headed to Ringo's suite in the Park Plaza and drank up all the liquor in the refrigerator, in a binge that would become a two-day bender.

Lennon could not break his TV habit, and so in Ringo's living room he watched as the news reported the depth of the disaster. Nixon won the Electoral College in a landslide of Rooseveltian proportions, garnering 472 votes to Kennedy's 65, with only 270 needed for victory. Kennedy won only his home state of Massachusetts, plus New York and Maryland. The popular vote was closer. Nixon received 42,168,710 votes to Kennedy's 34,173,122.

As the sun came up on the third day, Ringo found John eating room service, drinking coffee from a French press, and smoking his Gitanes cigarettes.

"The Beatles don't mean anything to me," he said. "Even if you all want to continue, it's my band, and I'm finished."

Ringo wondered out loud if John should be making such big decisions under the influence of a killer hangover.

"The dream is over, Richie. Better get used to it."

With that, John Lennon went back to the Dakota, his relationship with his wife at an all-time low, and told her that he was giving up on the Beatles and devoting himself exclusively to her.

In a later interview with *Rockstar*'s Booth Hill, Yoko Ono made her true feelings clear.

> [Yoko Ono] "John thought that saying what he said made
> everything right. How could it make what he had done to me
> right? I thought. But I was also afraid. I did not think I could

handle him all the time. I thought Beatles should do their share. John needs a lot of attention, you know."

For the next few months, under the flag of an uneasy truce with both Yoko and his bandmates, Lennon went into hiding at the Dakota apartment. When Paul McCartney called to console him about the election results, John hung up on him. When George Harrison called to see what plans he might have for future Beatles projects, John said, "Ask Ringo" and hung up on him, too.

Yoko was miserable, so much so that when Linda McCartney called her while in New York for a meeting, she agreed to do lunch to get out of the Dakota and away from John's mood. Candidly, Yoko had few female friends and had spent more time with Linda than almost anyone else. They may not have been close, longtime comrades, but they had something in common.

"The Beatles are just four men and we're sleeping with two of them," said Yoko, after they had finished an expensive Chianti. "What is it that *we* want?"

"I want the Beatles, even if they don't," answered Linda.

Yoko wasn't nearly as sure. It had already been three years since her husband had announced his intention to leave the group. Staying in obviously wasn't making him happy.

"Look, if you want to take care of John Lennon twenty-four hours a day every day, then you let him quit the Beatles," said Linda. "I give you two months."

Yoko could hardly argue the point, given that she was already being driven out of her mind by John's current mood and her anger at his election night infidelity.

"Well, if we let them break up, you know the two of us will get blamed," said Yoko as they ordered a second bottle.

CHAPTER SIX

BAND ON THE RUN (1973)

TO LIVE AND LET DIE

1971 had been a great year for the Beatles, with the trifecta of *Savile Row*, *The Lord of the Rings*, and *The Concert for Bangladesh*. In 1972, the band could claim *Imagine Another Day* as another classic studio album, in addition to earning the Academy Award for *The Lord of the Rings*. In stark contrast, 1973 was not looking good at all, particularly since John Lennon had again taken the position that the end had come for the group.

"There hasn't been a time in the last five years when John wasn't talking about quitting," McCartney told Australian journalist Lillian Roxon, who was writing her own drumbeat for doomsday for New York's *Sunday News*. What would happen if John finally did leave, she wanted to know. "I'll just tell everybody I quit first, and you can all write what you want."

Given that Lennon was speaking to no one, publicly or privately, McCartney's comment was the best the press could get. Articles continued to be written, as they had been since 1968, and the world showed no sign of tiring of the ongoing saga of John, Paul, George, and Ringo. Part of the Beatles' success was that, in an era before reality TV, they had become the genuine celebrities everyone thought they knew. Bad behavior made them that much more interesting and made their records that much more necessary to own. Even the public feud between John and Paul mesmerized fans worldwide and created some memorable music.

In the moment, their enmity could seem profoundly ruinous for the survival of the group, but later, they would each act like it was all a charade the public did not understand. Some fans bought into a theory that John and Paul were still staunch friends but had created this feud to spark further record sales.

> [Paul] "Next to everyone saying I was dead for a spell, I found this rumor that John and myself were just faking the whole thing to sell more albums to be a shocker. The things John said to me in public just devastated me, and yet there were people out there who just thought it was all an act. I decided it wouldn't hurt so much if I just played along. But, no, John and I, we never talked about it as any big strategy or anything."

No one knew more than Yoko Ono that the John Lennon everyone saw was the real thing, for better or for worse. Living with John's issues had become more and more challenging for Yoko, and the chill between the once inseparable lovers had only deepened.

Even in the best of times, Lennon could be difficult to live with, but the upcoming second inauguration of Richard Nixon and the crushing surveillance he had brought down on the Beatles as a result, plus the ever-present immigration case, had turned Lennon's world more sour than ever before.

> [John] "I'd leave the Dakota to go somewhere and there were men in cars watching us. If we'd get picked up by a driver, these men would follow us. They weren't even trying to hide it. They wanted us to know they were watching us. So I stopped going out."

For months, Yoko tried to ignore the three televisions at the Dakota apartment that were always on, as well as the fact that her husband's attention seemed perpetually focused on them and not her. John had been fascinated by a trio of breaking news stories in the past month—the final Apollo mission to the moon, the hard-to-accept ending of the Vietnam War, and the deepening of the Watergate scandal. He rarely spoke to Yoko about these events, but from time to time she would hear him talking on the phone to people whose identities she did not know.

On January 20, 1973, all three TV screens were broadcasting the same image: President Richard Nixon taking the oath of office for his second term. Lennon watched as long as he could, but when Nixon began to credit himself with "a new era of peace in the world," he switched off all the TVs, unable to listen to another minute of the man who was making his life so difficult.

"Well, that's that," he said to his wife. He went into the back room, closed the door, and began to tune his guitar.

• • •

Indeed, the election had unleashed Nixon's police state, and Watergate was in the process of making it uglier and more desperate than ever. Shortly after Nixon's inauguration, two of his top aides—G. Gordon Liddy and James McCord Jr.—were convicted for their roles in breaking into the Democratic National Committee headquarters. Rather than shutting down operations, Nixon's underlings were in full panic mode, trying to contain investigations that might point the finger of blame at the White House.

By now, all of the Beatles were also experiencing surveillance whenever they were in the United States and had come to believe they were being treated as "enemies of the state." No one knew this officially, of course, but the Beatles felt it. They knew things were not right. Even Paul, a continent away, felt its presence.

> [Paul] "The phone system in Scotland wasn't that good in the first place, but during the 1972 election, we started hearing the noises. Every call sounded like it was being recorded. We started making a joke out of it. We'd get on the phone and say, 'Hello there, Nixon people. We're going to have a little chat with some friends, so you'll probably want to turn on the tape recorders.' The thing is, I think they actually did."

On a visit to London, McCartney paid a visit to Harrison

at Friar Park. Naturally, the conversation turned to Lennon and what he was thinking and doing on his New York retreat. Paul and George wondered if there was anything they could do to help him out. Maybe there was a way for the Beatles to protest about their treatment by the American government and show their contempt for the re-election of Richard Nixon. Harrison's idea was that they should record their next official Beatles album in another country and tell the world that the group would not return to America until Richard Nixon was no longer president and the war in Vietnam had ended.

Paul and George rang up John in New York to talk about their idea but hit the familiar roadblock. "I've quit the Beatles for good this time, boys," said John over the telephone. He wondered why this was not obvious.

The dynamic remained the same. Lennon seemed always poised to tear the group apart, while McCartney was ready to change and bend any way of doing business if it kept the Beatles alive. Paul thought recording the next Beatles album in another country and protesting their return to America would force the band members to work in yet another completely new way if they were to continue to play together. He dangled the magic word in front of his partner. "It's *experimental.*"

"It's daft," Lennon replied. "I'm stuck in Nixon's Hell, if you haven't been paying attention. My lawyer says if I leave the country, I won't get back in."

It was a fair point. Both Paul and George had potential problems with drug run-ins of their own. George had a cannabis arrest on his record going back to March 1969, the one that had caused him to miss first Paul's and then John's wedding. Paul had an August 1972 arrest in Sweden over marijuana possession that had cost him only $2,000 but remained a part of a criminal record. Now, a year later, Scotland authorities had found marijuana plants on his property at the Mull of Kintyre. He had been convicted of illegal cultivation and fined £100.

The visas that got George and Paul into the country the year before had been granted with "special circumstance," namely the shooting of *The Hot Rock* film and their appearance at the Academy Awards. They might not get so lucky again.

"So you stay in the U.S., John," said George. "The rest of us will go someplace else."

McCartney thought that using EMI's many recording studios around the world might provide the inspiration necessary for the Beatles to produce yet another successful album. There was even a studio in Nigeria. "That should light up some sparks," he reasoned.

"When I said someplace else, I wasn't thinking of Africa," said George, shooting down his own trial balloon.

With the energy dissipating, McCartney suggested the idea of recording the next Beatles album with each band member in a different country altogether. He called this idea *A Band Apart*, based on *Bande à part*, the 1964 New Wave film directed by Jean-Luc Godard. The French title derived from the phrase *faire bande à part*, or "to do something apart from the group."

"We protest the war *and* all of us take a break from each other," summarized George.

"Tell me how that could work," demanded John. "How?"

As they argued the details, a framework emerged. Each Beatle would pick a corner of the world. With John entrenched in the United States, Paul would send his contributions in from Nigeria. Ringo could work from his home-away-from-home in Monaco, the gambling capital of Europe. George would go back to India. Each band member would record tracks of their songs, pass them around at a preliminary stage, keep some, lose others. Those tracks that made the cut would be recorded under the supervision of George Martin with an individual Beatle or multiple Beatles contributing, and then master tapes would be sent around to other Beatles for their contributions.

John said it sounded like too much work but that he would think about it. He then ended the call and went back to working on his solo album.

That left Paul and George to call George Martin to get his opinion. Years later, he offered it, unvarnished.

> [George Martin] "I thought it could never work. On the other hand, John and Paul were simply done with each other, again, at least temporarily. They needed space between them, and this might give them what they needed, and would keep it from becoming personal. Of course, for such a plan to have a chance, I'd have to take up residence at Savile Row, and commit Apple's substantial resources to the task. We'd literally have to will it into existence."

On the call, Martin stated in his usual reserve that he would do whatever the Beatles needed him to do. He thought it sounded nearly impossible. That, he concluded, also made it sound "interesting."

• • •

If the music empire of the Beatles was interesting and complicated, their film empire was chaotic. Hollywood was never quite sure what lessons to take from 1971's explosive hit *Stanley Kubrick Presents J.R.R. Tolkien's The Lord of the Rings Starring The Beatles*. The problem could be seen in the elongated title itself. Was it Tolkien's underlying material? Kubrick's boldly creative director's vision? Or the Beatles' huge fan base and their soundtrack music?

In truth, it was probably the alchemy of all of them. What can be said for certain, however, is that the film won awards, crushed the competition at the box office, and caused Hollywood to come knocking with offers at a time when the group members were not really committed to their musical life together, let alone their film life.

United Artists had lost their hold on the band by letting 20th Century Fox sign them to star in *The Hot Rock*, released in the United States on January 26. The film was supposed to premiere during Thanksgiving 1972, but arguments between lawyers for

United Artists, 20th Century Fox, and Apple made that date impossible to achieve as well.

Shot for a budget of nearly $7 million (attaching the Beatles had raised the budget by $2 million), the film went on to make $23 million at the box office in the year of its release. Because of its place in the Beatles' film canon, *The Hot Rock* has continued to earn money as each new technology, from VHS to LaserDisc to digital download, changes the market. Its one major distinction is that it's the only film all four Beatles appear in without contributing or performing a single song.

When *The Hot Rock* was released, however, the popular consensus was that it was only slightly better than *Help!* but inferior to *The Lord of the Rings*. The *New Yorker*'s Pauline Kael spoke for many when she put forth the notion that the film was simply a light confection and not a full meal.

> [Pauline Kael] "John Lennon is the straight-man leader of the band, I mean, gang, while Paul McCartney is a nervous lock picker who probably plays a mean bass guitar between jobs. This leaves the door open for George Harrison to deliver an unexpectedly comedic turn as a wild getaway driver and Richard Starkey, better known as Q in the Bond films, to appear here as a loopy bomb wizard. Would using the American actors have been a better movie? It seems unlikely. The sheer fun of seeing the Beatles in these roles turns this wisp of an idea into a charmingly spry little comedy that's well worth a watch."

Even with the split decision on the film, the Beatles were primed to take a break from their own cinematic universe. Production, they realized, took an enormous amount of time and commitment. That was fine when they were making their first movies and spending all their time together. Now they wanted to pursue their own personal lives and interests and record a single album per year as the Beatles to keep their company liquid and alive.

The exception to the Hollywood bug was Ringo, or, as he was

becoming known in films, Richard Starkey. Ringo was the only one who had created an acting career separate from the band, playing "Q," the Quartermaster of Research and Development, in the last James Bond film, *Diamonds Are Forever*.

Coming off a highly praised performance in the hit 1972 Christmas film *The Poseidon Adventure*, Ringo radiated Hollywood "heat." Originally cast by director Ronald Neame to play the part of Acres, the injured waiter, Ringo had been given the enhanced role of haberdasher James Martin at the insistence of producer Irwin Allen, who hoped to cash in on the success of Ringo's inclusion in the Bond franchise and his Supporting Actor Oscar in the Kubrick film that followed. In the musical chairs set in motion by this decision, Roddy McDowell got the Acres role, but Red Buttons was bumped, allowing Ringo to play the love-shy, health-conscious bachelor who survives the *Poseidon* disaster.

During the New Year's Eve party scene, Ringo holds hands with Jack Albertson and Shelly Winters and sings a rousing version of "Auld Lang Syne" before the water rushes in from the upended boat. It seemed almost metaphorical. Even if the ship that was the Beatles was taking on water and likely to go under eventually, Ringo would accept what was in store with plucky good spirits and be a survivor come what may.

With Starkey's film star on the ascent, the bonds of attachment between the Beatles and UA were still strong enough to cobble together a new deal for *Live and Let Die,* the next film in the James Bond franchise.

The film was to star a new actor in the Bond role: Roger Moore. He told producers Harry Saltzman and Albert Broccoli that he did not find Ringo particularly credible as a drummer, let alone a genius inventor, and that he wanted the role re-cast with Desmond Llewelyn, an actor whose work he was familiar with. As it turned out, Llewelyn was unavailable due to work in a TV series.

Not wanting to traffic in the truth, the producers informed Starkey that the role of Q was being cut from the franchise because they felt "too much was being made of the film's gadgets."

This might have been the end of the line for Starkey's block-buster franchise film career, had it not been for the fact that the producers approached Apple about the Beatles recording the theme song for the film. John was not much interested, but Paul jumped at the chance—especially because George Martin had been hired to provide the soundtrack score.

When he learned that Ringo would not reprise his role, Paul threatened to withhold work on the new song. "He was quite good in the last film," Paul told Broccoli. "If Ringo's not in this one, I couldn't really get my mind around a song. Nothing personal, you know." It was the same tactic that he had seen Lennon practice so successfully on Johnny Carson five years earlier.

The next day, the screenplay was re-written to include the Q character, and Ringo had a contract to play the part. As it happened, Paul had already composed a version of the soon-to-be classic "Live and Let Die," which he hadn't let on about to any of his bandmates. He also wrote a bonus song, a trifle of lightness called "Q-Ball," that was played out in the scene between Q and Bond. The theory was that a Beatles song might cement the decision of the producers to keep Ringo in the film.

> [Ringo] "When I heard what Paul had done for me, it made
> me feel like the old days, you know. We could always talk trash
> to each other back then, and we did, we really did, but we
> didn't like it when other people said something bad about one
> of us. John always said to me that Paul wouldn't really have
> walked away if they didn't keep me in the picture, but I think
> he's wrong."

"Q-Ball" reached number two in the United States for two weeks running. The song was released on the film's soundtrack album, but the Beatles retained the rights to include it on their next album, if there was a next album to include it on—although that never came to pass.

The film premiered at Odeon Leicester Square in London on July 6 with only McCartney, Starkey, and George Martin in attendance. Produced for about $8 million, *Live and Let Die* went on to earn over $160 million at the box office. What it was not, however, was a Beatles film. The absence of Lennon and Harrison, who had nothing to do with it, gave testament to its status as just a James Bond franchise movie that had a bit of Beatles dust sprinkled into it.

Apple management implored all of the Beatles to appear together in their next film to avoid this kind of brand confusion. Finding the right roles was not easy. When director Sidney Lumet sent the script for *Murder on the Orient Express* to Apple for all four of the Beatles to star in, everyone thought that it was no *Lord of the Rings* but that it might do.

LOST ASSHOLES

The big secret in John Lennon's life was that his relationship with Yoko Ono was even more tenuous than his relationship with the rest of the Beatles. He and Ono had moved into the Dakota apartment thinking that it was a physical manifestation of the profound love they had for each other. In reality, it quickly became a place where the two of them coexisted, more or less silently. Lennon seemed to tolerate this well enough, but Ono now felt at her wit's end.

Eventually, she came to the realization that if it had become impossible for them to live in the same space, the only solution was for one of them to move out. She believed it should be John, and she told him so, according to her 1994 *Rockstar* interview.

> [Yoko Ono] "I hoped by letting John stay in the Beatles that I would not have the whole burden of his neediness. By this time, I was glad he was still in his band because I felt less guilty when I asked him to leave me."

Yoko did more than let John stay in the Beatles. In actual fact, she began to encourage the others, under the radar, to fight to keep him involved and not let him slip away. This tactic involved meeting privately with Linda McCartney when she was in New York and encouraging Paul to drop by the Dakota to reach out, once again, to John.

> [Linda McCartney] "I know that no one can believe that Yoko Ono and Linda McCartney could have had anything to talk about. But we each had one thing in common—not the Beatles, per se—but men in our lives who needed an outlet outside of their marriages. The band gave them that, and it gave us some peace of mind."

In 1973, however, John was in a fighting mood with Yoko and most certainly with Paul. He remained noncommittal about the Beatles, continued to work on that solo album, and encouraged the other Beatles to do the same.

Yoko was not ready to divorce John, but she was ready for change. She asked him to leave her, but she refused to give up all the ties—co-activist, collaborator, wife—that bound him to her. She dispatched their secretary, May Pang, to go to Los Angeles with him to keep him out of trouble. Pang's job, incredibly, was not only to sleep with Yoko's husband (to keep him from straying too far afield) but to report back what she was seeing.

Next to New York City, Los Angeles was comfortable ground for Lennon. It was where the Beatles recorded their last album, *Imagine Another Day*. There was a vibrant music scene that boasted one significant plus for John: it did not include the Beatles. It was All-American.

> [John] "New York City and Los Angeles are basically the Sodom and Gomorrah of the United States. Each has its own attraction, I suppose, but both are great places where anything goes. My kind of places."

Lennon had two connections that he immediately got back in touch with when he returned to LA. The first was Beatles recording engineer Glyn Johns, who had introduced him to the Eagles when they had flown across the pond to record their self-titled *Eagles* album in 1972 at London's Olympic Studios. The other was Peter Asher, the brother of Paul's '60s girlfriend Jane Asher and the former head of Apple Records. Asher was then working as James Taylor's manager, and Taylor remained a superior Apple artist.

Both Johns and Asher had been taken in by the booming Laurel Canyon music scene, which included everyone from the Eagles to Joni Mitchell, from Frank Zappa to Linda Ronstadt, the female singer whom John had briefly met at a party the year before.

He set himself up in a small house in the Hollywood Hills of Laurel Canyon, where he and May Pang could live. The bills were sent to New York where Yoko Ono continued to pay them, not out of subservience but so she could keep an eye on him from afar.

Those bills and receipts, of course, could only tell part of the story. The rest of it Yoko got directly from Pang.

> [May Pang] "It was very confusing to me. I was only twenty-two years old and John and Yoko put me right in the middle of their marriage problems, and then she sent me off to the other side of the country with her husband. Here I was having sex with a Beatle, which was still every woman's dream, and then calling his wife to tell her about it. But he wasn't being loyal to me any more than he was to her."

Asher, a member in good standing of the music community for several years now, had just been hired to work on Ronstadt's latest solo album, *Don't Cry Now*, with musician John David Souther, as well as John Boylan, who had negotiated her contract with Asylum Records. She had chafed at what she saw as their sexist attitudes and had sought out Asher as someone willing to work with her as an equal.

Ronstadt was coming out of a period where competition, insecurity, bad romances, and a series of boyfriend-managers had her reeling. Asher became the first major producer Ronstadt had worked with without getting herself romantically involved with him. At least publicly, Asher believed that having a business-only relationship was the only path toward professional success with Ronstadt.

"It's harder to have objective conversations about someone's career when it's someone you sleep with," he told Lennon.

"That's how Yoko and I did it," Lennon responded. "Of course, if you ask Paul or George or Ringo, they'd probably take your point."

In fact, McCartney, who had a closer relationship with Asher than the other Beatles, had actually called his almost brother-in-law and asked him to set Lennon up with someone, preferably someone who was not Yoko's designated spy.

"I never thought that would be Linda Ronstadt," said McCartney, "but when I heard about it, I thought she might be a bit more pro-Beatles than Yoko, so I encouraged it from afar, you might say."

Besides having attempted drunken sex with Ronstadt the year before, Lennon was taken by the fact that she had just recorded her own version of "Good Night," the song he had written and Ringo had recorded for the *A Doll's House* album. He wanted to meet this woman again now that he was "on the rebound."

Despite Paul's urging and John's willingness, Asher considered talking Lennon out of this set-up but realized it might serve his goals perfectly. A personal relationship with Linda would create room for John to take, briefly, the non-professional role of a friend and advisor to Asher's client. With Ronstadt about to kick-start a huge career playing arena rock, the question was simple: Who better than a Beatle to talk candidly with her about touring, fame, and the lurking exploiters she would soon encounter daily? He hoped one of the pieces of advice that John could give her was to stick with Peter Asher.

[Linda Ronstadt] "Obviously John and I were not a match made in heaven. He was a different man when we hooked up in 1973. He felt like he was going to jail if Nixon had his way, and he felt like he was personally tearing apart the Beatles. Both of those things are probably true, by the way, but they made him more human, at least to me."

Ronstadt was clearly the diamond in the rough in rock music. There were few "girl singers" on the rock circuit at the time, and they were often relegated to no higher status than that of a groupie, a designation Ronstadt was keen to avoid. She imposed an enormous amount of pressure on herself to compete with "the boys" at every level but still did not want to sacrifice her femininity.

Lennon was enchanted by this woman, who was apparently just as tough as Yoko Ono. He did his research on Ronstadt, finding a 1969 interview in *Rockstar* where she noted how difficult it was being a single "chick singer" with an all-male backup band. Ronstadt found it nearly impossible to get a band of compatible backing musicians—it seemed as if all the qualified male musicians in Los Angeles were afraid of being labeled sidemen for a female singer.

Lennon provided the solution she was waiting to hear. "Fuck them all," he said. "I never treated Yoko as anything but an equal."

Ronstadt was quick with her comeback: "Everyone knew you were the star. I'm more like you." Indeed she was. What further attracted Linda Ronstadt to John Lennon was that, as a Beatle, he could sleep with practically anyone, buy almost anything, and that he really did not need her. After Ronstadt reached the conclusion that Lennon wasn't like all the others who wanted something from her, they became friends, and soon after that, friends with benefits.

Ronstadt, no stranger to the loneliness all traveling musicians experience on the road, was steeling herself for more of the same on her upcoming tour. Lennon told her, "People are always taking advantage of you and everybody that's interested in you has an angle. So what's your angle going to be?"

Lennon spent the majority of his time hanging out at Ronstadt's home and enjoying the company of her friends. Pang continued to live in the rental property, on call for whenever Lennon needed her to arrange details of his life. He did not, however, need her to sleep with him anymore, a fact that Pang painfully disclosed to Ono.

That part did not seem to bother Yoko. She knew that John could not maintain a real relationship with an American rock star for more than a short while. She *was* bothered greatly, however, by the revelation that her husband was entertaining thoughts of abandoning the immigration case (that bound them together) and moving back to Britain.

• • •

Ironically, while the world saw John as the wild card who could destroy the Beatles because of his inseparable relationship with Yoko, it was Paul who was finding his joy with his own mate. He and Linda were almost never seen apart these days, blending their personalities with one another as seamlessly as Yoko and John had done. Similarly infatuated with Linda, Paul had just written "My Love," a song that also spoke of his passion for his marriage. It would go on either the next Beatles album, or it would lead off his first solo album.

Together, the McCartneys were all about family. Linda had brought her daughter Heather into the marriage, and now they were making kids of their own. Paul and Linda raised their children in Scotland, but whenever they traveled (and they traveled often), they brought the entire brood along with them. When they were met by drivers at airports, Paul would always say, "You get a lot of McCartney for your money with us."

Ringo continued to have the most to do when he was not making music with the Beatles. Once it had become clear that Lennon and Ono were locked into their immigration battle for the long haul, he had bought John's house in Tittenhurst Park and moved his own family there. Although he still spent much time in Monaco and Los Angeles, the home became the new center of his life.

Lately, Ringo had even begun to frequent the recording facility

John had built there but hardly ever used. He was now working on two songs: a song called "Photograph" that George had co-written with him and a song called "I'm the Greatest" that John had given Ringo. Lennon could never have gotten away with singing the song himself, but with Ringo's charm it came across as a lost gem from the *Everest* sessions. As for "Photograph," everyone knew it was pure Ringo and destined for the same kind of hit status that fans and critics had given to "With a Little Help from My Friends."

George's marriage to Pattie Boyd had been getting worse and worse as his twin (and alternating) passions for cocaine and spirituality made her feel increasingly estranged. Their reality was complicated further by the fact that their mutual friend Eric Clapton was not only a regular visitor to Friar Park but also used his time there to try to talk Pattie into leaving George. Clapton was madly in love with his good friend's wife, and Pattie found it terribly difficult to resist Clapton's attentions.

None of this, however, could have been as threatening to the future of the Beatles as what George did next. He professed his love for Maureen Starkey in front of her husband and his longtime friend and bandmate, Ringo. Ringo had not been any more faithful to his own wife than George had been to his, but the expectation that their own wives were off-limits to each other had never been broken. The circle of dangerous liaisons was complete.

Soon, Ringo's marriage to Maureen would end, with George's separation from Pattie not far behind. But somehow, George Harrison and Richard Starkey managed to remain in the Beatles and make music together during these tumultuous months.

[George] "I suppose we could have said, 'Well, that's it, no more Beatles.' But the Beatles were hanging together on only a few months each year as it was. I think both Richie and myself felt like if anyone was going to break up the band, for real and for good, it would be Paul or John. Not us. We didn't need another guilt trip."

By September of 1973, tabloids and newspapers seemed to

have no clue about either George's marriage or Ringo's, but they continued to focus on the Lennon-Ono relationship. Both John and Yoko continued to portray it as one of the great love affairs in history. But as that image began to crumble, John Lennon, feeling he had nowhere to hide, became more withdrawn, and, with good reason, even more paranoid.

ENEMIES LIST

President Richard Nixon and his political lieutenants knew that the Beatles weren't being paranoid about being followed and having their phones tapped. Ever since his meeting with Elvis Presley and the warning from Strom Thurmond, the president had held his own paranoid grudge against John Lennon, Paul McCartney, George Harrison, and Richard Starkey. He had gone so far as to have them targeted by the FBI for surveillance and by the INS for deportation.

The Beatles, however, weren't Richard Nixon's biggest problem—not by a long shot. In the summer of 1973, the Nixon White House was falling apart, unraveling over the break-in at the Democratic National Committee headquarters by men working for the White House itself. As the constitutional crisis deepened over the cover-up orchestrated within White House walls, there was a steady drip of scandal.

Even so, no one had a real understanding that the world's most popular rock band had been targeted by the Administration. That changed in July, when former presidential lawyer John Dean, in testimony before the Senate Watergate Committee, confirmed the existence of a Nixon White House "Enemies List," which contained the names of all four of the Beatles.

> [Senator Ervin] "Mr. Dean, what are you saying here? That the president of the United States of America turned both the FBI and the INS loose on a rock band?"

[John Dean] "Yes, sir. He took the political activism of Mister Lennon quite seriously."

[Senator Ervin] "Why on Earth would he do that?"

[John Dean] "Because his own government was telling him that he should."

That was shocking enough, but Dean had more. He remembered a conversation that was supposed to have taken place between Nixon and his chief of staff, Bob Haldeman, on June 20, 1972, just three days after the break-in at the Democratic headquarters. The conversation reportedly turned to the plan for the Beatles to play a protest concert in Miami Beach during the upcoming Republican convention (although such a concert never took place).

That day's tape recording was among eight others subpoenaed by both the Senate Watergate Committee and Special Prosecutor Archibald Cox to confirm Dean's testimony. Initially, Nixon refused to turn them over, and the matter ultimately went to the Supreme Court the next year, and produced a ruling ordering Nixon to do as he was told. Before that, however, Nixon produced edited transcripts of the tapes.

This is the section that included references to the Beatles.

TRANSCRIPT OF A RECORDING OF
A MEETING BETWEEN THE PRESIDENT
AND H.R. HALDEMAN IN THE OVAL OFFICE
ON JUNE 23, 1972, FROM 10:04 TO 11:39 a.m.

PRESIDENT: They're coming at us from everywhere, Bob. This is not what we bargained for. Not by a long shot.
HALDEMAN: No, sir, Mr. President. It certainly is not.
PRESIDENT: You know it's exactly two months until our convention, down in Miami. Two months today.
HALDEMAN: [Unintelligible].
PRESIDENT: I'm not worried about the homosexuals. It's

those goddamn outside agitators that Elvis Presley warned
us about. I thought we told the INS to get them deported.

HALDEMAN: You're talking about the Beatles?

PRESIDENT: [Expletive deleted] leftists. We should squash
them like the bugs they say they are.

HALDEMAN: Well, the thing is that this Lennon, he's got a
fancy New York lawyer, and they're fighting it. Plus, the
others aren't here to deport, but we had to give them work
visas for a movie they were shooting.

NIXON: They're not even Americans.

HALDEMAN: They, uh, well, apparently, they're planning to
hold a concert of some kind in Miami at the same time the
convention will be nominating you.

PRESIDENT: [Expletive Deleted]

HALDEMAN: How do you want us to play it?

PRESIDENT: Tough as nails. That's the way the Left plays it
and that's the way we're sure as hell going to play it. Tell
Gray to get the FBI on it.

HALDEMAN: Of course. To do what, exactly?

PRESIDENT: To make them sweat. Put the heat on them.

HALDEMAN: Okay.

PRESIDENT: [Expletive Deleted] [Inaudible]

The conversation continued, but the long and the short of it
was that Nixon explicitly instructed his chief of staff to have the
FBI continue its targeting of the Beatles as left-wing radicals and
to use the INS to stop them from getting into the United States in
the first place.

Nixon ordered the illegal use of government agencies to target
and harass the Beatles simply because they intended to participate
in the expression of free speech at a U.S. political convention,
organized by American citizens who would publicize their message. Still, the Beatles were not American citizens, and their civil
liberties fell in a gray area.

This transcript and the subsequent audiotape evidence were
eventually included in the Abuse of Power and Obstruction of

Justice articles that led to Nixon's impeachment by the U.S. House of Representatives.

By mid-summer 1973, when John Dean was delivering his explosive testimony about the Beatles having notched places for themselves on Richard Nixon's "Enemies List," the reality was that the band was hardly functional. By this point, all four of its members were working on solo work, more or less acknowledging that the group would end with no fanfare whatsoever, unless something drastic happened to change the situation.

The dirty little secret of 1973 turned out to be that Richard Nixon, who by his own account loathed the Beatles, was the force that kept them together a bit longer.

Like the rest of America, John Lennon was finding it impossible to ignore the summer's televised Watergate hearings. He watched them from start to finish on either the modest color TV set in Linda Ronstadt's home or on all three televisions in the home he was supposed to be sharing with May Pang. On the day in question, he was watching TV with Harry Nilsson and a bottle of vodka when he heard his own name uttered by the man who had been the lawyer to the president of the United States of America.

"I fucking told you!" he screamed. While many would be terrified to be on anyone's "enemies list," let alone the president's, Lennon saw it as vindication. He was not paranoid. Nixon really did have it in for him.

"All the Beatles are on the list," corrected Nilsson.

"But they got on because of me!" To John Lennon, this was as much a badge of distinction as it was something to fear.

As soon as Dean's testimony for the day ended, Lennon picked up his guitar and went to work on "Enemies List," a song that is now universally acknowledged to be in the lineage with "Power to the People," "Give Peace a Chance," and "Gimme Some Truth" and considered by some to be the best of all four.

The next morning, Lennon called his attorney Leon Wildes and played him the song. Wildes did not know much about rock music, but he knew that what had just happened on TV, combined with this song his client had just played him, had the power to change the legal situation—whether for better or worse, Wildes couldn't be sure.

As it turned out, Wildes's advice inspired the first Lennon-McCartney songwriting credit since "Show Up."

> [John] "I wanted to write it myself. But Leon said that if I wrote it with Paul, it would prove that I was a working musician in a band that was being illegally harassed by the Nixon Administration. That way Nixon and his criminals wouldn't be able to use it to portray only me as anti-American. I would have ignored old Leon, I think, except that I thought Paul could put some melody in to go along with my all my piss and vinegar."

> [Paul] "Even John knew that if you're going to write a song that gives the finger to the president of the United States, it better be a good one."

The process that created this classic Beatles protest song was enormously time-intensive and confusing. First, John sent his original take to George Martin, who made some notes and sent it to Paul, who recorded his own version. Martin made some more notes. Paul and John got on the phone together to hammer out the differences, and the conversation became so heated that had they actually been in the same room together, they might have come to blows. In telling the tale, even today, both men remember hanging up on the other first. In the end, the matter got dumped back on Martin, who managed to cobble a coherent track together and bring both George and Ringo into the studio to add their own parts.

Somehow, though, it worked. "Enemies List" is on anyone's list of protest songs to this day, right up there with Dylan's "Blowin' in the Wind" and Guthrie's "This Land Is Your Land." Its passion transcends the time and circumstances that gave birth to it, and it now plays as an attack on corrupt leadership that devotes its energies to its survival rather than helping the people it is supposed to serve.

Not to mention that it kick-started one of the most storied Beatles albums of their entire time together.

IF WE EVER GET OUT OF HERE

Complicated as it was to make, within ten days Apple had a hot new song that was highly relevant to everyone, and, miraculously, had all four Beatles playing on it with a Lennon-McCartney writing credit. The problem was getting it to market. Even if the Beatles started work on a new album immediately, it would be months before anyone could buy it.

"I'm just the drummer," said Ringo, "but even I know we have to get this into record stores before Nixon gets out of Washington."

All four Beatles agreed to release "Enemies List" as the A-side on a single and get it out ASAP. The one remaining question was what to put on the other side. The only other song recently produced under the Beatles banner was "Live and Let Die." It was due to be released on the film's soundtrack album on July 2, a mere four days after John Dean concluded his Senate testimony.

Lawyers called lawyers, and a deal was struck that would allow the song to be included on a new single from the Beatles. The writing credit on the film's soundtrack version was given solely to McCartney, but that would be changed for the single to McCartney-Lennon, to balance out the Lennon-McCartney credit on the A-side.

With egos assuaged and the Senate Watergate Committee still in session, the "Enemies List/Live and Let Die" single hit the stores. It received massive airplay on FM stations and gave anti-Nixon partisans something to do to show their disapproval—they could buy a Beatles record. As a bonus, they got a hit song from the new James Bond film.

With another hit single, there was renewed energy from the

Beatles to make a full album. Once again Leon Wildes, the man who did not even know who John Lennon was when he accepted him as a client, altered the course of rock history. He explained his thinking to the *Princeton Law Review* years later:

> [Leon Wildes] "I became convinced that the Dean testimony changed everything. Nixon was not only on the run, but anything bad that happened to John Lennon or any of the Beatles was the kind of publicity that the Administration didn't need and could no longer afford. I decided against caution, and to roll the dice instead. I told John to leave the country and make that album with the Beatles, but to make sure Yoko stayed in New York. Then, when he tried to return, if the government tried to stop him, we would have the additional argument that they were preventing a husband and wife from being together."

Of course, the husband and wife team of John Lennon and Yoko Ono were not currently together, a detail that was simply ignored in the legal thinking. They had a valid marriage certificate going back to 1969. To all interested parties, so long as they showed up at court together, they would look like they *were* together, and that was enough.

On a more practical level, the band had yet to address the major detail of where to record this new album. Beeching was strongly in favor of the Beatles returning to Savile Row to record, as were George Martin, Allen Klein, and Lee Eastman—Savile Row was certainly the more controllable environment, they reasoned. McCartney, however, was still in favor of recording at an EMI studio in another country, feeling that the exotic locale would energize the songs. "Just get me out of the U.S. for a while so I can go back," Lennon responded.

In the end, McCartney got his way, mostly because he had the strongest convictions, and no one else seemed to care as passionately for any alternative. As a result, after receiving a list of all of EMI's international recording studios, John, Paul, George, Ringo,

George Martin, Allen Klein, and Lee Eastman selected the one in Lagos, Nigeria.

There was no opportunity in those days for someone to perform the quick Google search that would have swept away the band's vision of this exotic location, in which they would sunbathe by day and record music at night. The reality on the ground was that conditions in Nigeria were tense and difficult. The country had only just emerged from a civil war in 1970 and was now being run by a corrupt military government. August also marked the tail end of the West African coast's monsoon season, when heat and humidity peak. To round out the complications, cholera was at near epidemic levels, which the Beatles and their entourage did not know until they were in the country.

Upon arriving early in the month, the musical expedition also discovered that the studio was equally not up to expectations. Located in the Lagos suburb of Apapa, the building was really a ramshackle tin shed, and an under-equipped one at that. Producer George Martin and engineer Geoff Emerick quickly discovered that the control desk was faulty, the microphones second-rate, and there was only a single Studer 8-track on which to record the output of the most popular band on the planet.

The Beatles rented houses near the airport in Ikeja, a full hour's drive from the studio that included some rough roads in both construction and neighborhoods. Paul, Linda, and their three children stayed in one house; John and Ringo shared another; and George crashed with Emerick and Martin.

"It's so glamorous out here," said George. "I don't know how we can ever go back to the way we used to live." He said it in jest, but the truth was that the four Beatles had stayed in much worse conditions during their early club and touring days. The sense of deprivation and danger in Nigeria actually helped them bond again.

They established a routine of recording during the week and playing tourist on the weekends and temporarily joined a local country club where everyone but John and Ringo, who preferred to sleep in, spent most mornings. In the early afternoon, a trio of four-wheel-drive vehicles would pick everyone up for transport to the studio, where recording could last into the early evening and, when the energy was good, until early morning.

The sessions became a reverse of earlier days when John and Yoko were inseparable. Yoko was nowhere to be seen this time, and it was Paul and Linda who seemed to be never apart.

> [Linda McCartney] "I wasn't comfortable taking the kids to many places by myself so we ended up hanging around the studio. A lot. It wasn't very big and there were times when we were all on top of each other. Everyone treated us nice, though, maybe because I made sandwiches and tea and did a lot of the shopping. There were times when I'd feel John just staring at me and I always thought he was thinking about Yoko. Or maybe he was just thinking about how the others felt when he brought Yoko in all the time. He was nice enough, but he didn't talk to me much, or anyone else, except for Ringo. They were pretty tight."

The album's working title of *A Band Apart* was changed almost immediately to *Band on the Run*, given the band had actually come together, albeit in a scary foreign country. Soon McCartney had a working song structure for an opening tune to be called (no surprise) "Band on the Run."

Lennon, feeling lonely and lost, began to fantasize about a reunion with Yoko when he returned to America. He wrote her a note on a napkin that included the first line Paul had been playing with, "*Stuck inside these four walls, sent inside forever,*" and added his own, "*Never seeing no one nice again, like you, Mama, like you.*" The mash-up of lyrics got the song rolling and was followed by an indirect contribution by George based on Paul remembering him complaining in 1969, during a contentious Apple meeting, "*If I ever get out of here, I'm thinking of giving it all away.*"

Even with contributions, McCartney was surely the architect of both the song and the album, at least initially. He told

Linda, who let George Martin know, hoping that Martin would inform the others that he thought all four Beatles should share the writing credit on "Band on the Run." McCartney believed this would encourage a sense of collegiality often missing in their latest sessions.

"I'll have to hear the final version," Lennon told Martin, "and then I'll let you know if I'll accept it."

The Lagos sessions were plagued by an escalating number of troubles. The first came about just after the first week. Ringo, John, and George were all smoking nervously while Paul (also smoking) was laying down a vocal track. In the middle of the work, Paul turned white as a sheet and said he couldn't catch his breath. Linda escorted him outside for fresh air, but the blazing heat made him keel over, and he fainted dead away. Linda began screaming hysterically, convinced that he was having a heart attack. McCartney was packed into one of the four-wheel-drive vehicles and spent the afternoon in the hospital.

Lennon actually showed up and sat by his partner's bed, noting "Now we're even," a reference to the time when McCartney showed up for him in Scotland after the car accident. By the end of the day, the official diagnosis was bronchial spasm from all the smoke, both Paul's and the secondhand variety from his bandmates.

Next up was a confrontation with Nigerian musical star and political activist Fela Kuti. With no proof, and without hearing any of the songs they were writing, Kuti publicly accused the Beatles of being in Lagos to steal African music after John, Paul, and Ringo had visited his club a few days earlier. The accusation was false, but the facts didn't seem to matter in such a volatile political climate, where the poor could still view the Beatles as British colonialists. In the end, Lennon brokered a deal where Kuti played on several of the songs. The Nigerian was paid for his work, which was always considered a bribe by everyone else. Yet his work was so original that he appears on two songs on the album.

One night, toward the end, Linda went home early with the kids because Mary had a fever. George and Ringo left an hour later to get home in time to watch an episode of *Monty Python's Flying Circus*, George's favorite new TV show.

Only John and Paul remained, working on a musical bridge that was stubbornly resisting solution. Finally, they, too, decided to call it a night. The vehicles were all out, and rather than making someone come back to get them, they decided to walk to a nearby taxi stand. It was a bad decision.

They realized they were being followed by a car with a number of men inside. The man in the passenger seat kept calling out, asking if they wanted a lift. They said "no," but the car kept following.

"Nice move, McCartney," Lennon said. "Great night for a walk, it is."

Suddenly, the car pulled ahead, and six men jumped out. At least one of them was holding a small knife, brandishing it like he was ready to use it.

If it did not involve two members of the Beatles, it would have been a garden-variety robbery. The bandits relieved both John and Paul of their watches, a camera, and their wallets. Even as he handed over his valuables, Paul told them: "We don't see you, man…we're not looking at you…we don't know who you are."

At that point, the man with the knife demanded the bag that Paul was carrying. "You don't want this, mate. It's got nothing valuable, nothing you can sell."

That, of course, was not quite the truth. The bag actually contained a notebook full of handwritten and unfinished song lyrics, as well as cassettes for demos of songs to be recorded in the days ahead. To the right person, it might be worth a great deal. In any case, Paul telling him it was of no value only made the man want it more. He went through the contents in front of them. "What is all this?"

"We're the fucking Beatles, you know," said John. "It's our new fucking album." The bandits took a good look at their prey— two men, each with scruffy beards, dressed like a couple of broke travelers. Hardly rock royalty.

The man laughed at the impossibility of Lennon's statement,

that the most famous musicians in the world could actually be standing before them in Nigeria. He motioned to the others, and they all got in the car and took off.

The next day, at the recording studio, it became clear what had been lost. At least six songs were missing in full, the only trace of them residing in the minds of the four different Beatles, with each one having only partial memory of how the tunes and the lyrics went and disagreeing among themselves about even that.

It was an awful loss, but there was little that could be done. The Beatles reconstructed their stolen songs as best they could and tried their hardest to move forward. In the end, despite the obstacles, they completed recording for the majority of the album's basic tracks after a month and a half in Africa.

Everyone felt that flying back to London toward the end of September sounded like a great idea. After the band's return to England, final overdubs and further recording were carried out at the Savile Row studios, which made everyone from Beeching on down very happy.

The album cover's photograph was taken at Osterley Park, in west London, by photographer Clive Arrowsmith. It depicts the four Beatles dressed as convicts caught in a prison searchlight. The low potency of the light that Arrowsmith used meant that everyone had to stand still for two seconds for proper exposure.

No sooner had the photo shoot wrapped than John was back on a plane to America. He stopped in New York with plans to stay with Yoko, but she would only agree to meet him at the airport. She told him that it was not yet time for him to return.

Passers-by who saw the two of them reported that Lennon alternated between begging to be taken back and threatening consequences if he wasn't. "I've done exactly what you want," he pleaded. "But if it's not enough, well, it's never enough for you, is it?"

Yoko got him on a plane to Los Angeles and kissed him goodbye at the gate. The evocative picture made the front page of the *New York Post* with the headline "JohnandYoko Need More Than Love."

Meanwhile, the Apple offices received a strange message, opened first by a secretary who then immediately passed it on to Peter Brown. It was from an anonymous sender, written in letters cut out from a magazine, and it spelled out an attempt at ransom:

ATTENTION BEATLES

WE HAVE YOUR MUSIC. WE WILL GIVE IT TO YOU FOR ONE MILLION BRITISH POUNDS IN CASH.

DO NOT TELL THE POLICE. YOU WILL BE CONTACTED.

Brown admitted that this was outside of his job experience and he passed it to Allen Klein, who stepped in to fill the vacuum. He called Interpol, reported the theft of the lyrics and demos in Nigeria, and showed them the blackmail message.

[Allen Klein] "I thought we could get it all. I wanted to get the tapes and lyrics back so the guys could use them in the new record. I thought it would be one of the greatest stories ever and would sell an extra million copies worldwide. And I wanted to put the sons-of-bitches who stole it all in jail."

Interpol's working theory was that the Nigerian bandits had eventually looked in the wallets, listened to the tapes, and come to realize what they had. Somehow they had made deals in a criminal network that resulted in the ransom note. The Nigerians were one matter, but the main culprits everyone wanted were the people who were trying to score the money.

The four Beatles were summoned to Apple to be informed of the situation. McCartney, Harrison, and Starkey came in person, while Lennon was put on a speakerphone. Already in a dour mood from his encounter with Yoko in New York, Lennon immediately blamed McCartney: "Looks like your little field trip to Africa is the gift that keeps on giving, Paul."

McCartney went off on Lennon with equal venom, but Klein wisely and surreptitiously hit the "mute" button. When Paul was finished, Klein put the line back in play and said, "John, we're getting a lot of static here. You know these damn British phones."

In the aftermath, Klein and Interpol responded, and after some back-and-forth, the two parties arrived at a plan that involved Klein, accompanied by at least one Beatle, carrying a briefcase with the money into a train station in Brussels, Belgium. Assured that there would be decent security, McCartney volunteered. Although he didn't like Lennon blaming him, he did actually feel responsible.

To this day, the idea that Paul McCartney and Allen Klein, two men who had never, ever trusted each other, would agree to be bait in an Interpol sting seems outrageous. And yet, they did, and with little convincing.

Interpol's tactics have never been clearly revealed. It appears, basically, that McCartney needed only to make an appearance at a kiosk in the train station to guarantee authenticity. Having met Klein there and patted him on the back, he walked out the front door into the waiting arms of a security team, who hustled him into a protected car and sent him to a safe house location. Back at the train station, it was Klein who gave a man the briefcase, risking his own life in an exchange with a blackmailer who could have been armed with a knife or a gun.

Folks were more naïve then than they are today. Interpol had arranged for the bills to be all marked and coded, although with cash paid for from an Apple wire transfer. The man to whom Klein gave the money was followed by Interpol agents for days and eventually ended up in Brussels, Belgium, where he gave the money to a British citizen called Winston Fourney.

Fourney turned out to be a confidence man with a rap sheet even more extensive than the Beatles' song catalog. Ironically, he had met a handful of his confederates in prison, not unlike the set-up from *The Hot Rock*. Fourney insisted on his innocence, despite all the evidence to the contrary, forcing a trial, and the testimony of Paul McCartney. During McCartney's testimony, Fourney beamed, as if compelling a Beatle to be in his presence was victory enough. Indeed, it was. After Paul had been excused by the judge and thanked for his testimony, Fourney tendered a confession through his attorney.

Fourney spent fourteen years in prison and died just two years after his release. His associates received lesser sentences. The Nigerians were never identified, although an investigation went on for the rest of the decade.

The one upshot was that the Beatles came back into possession of their stolen creative material after they'd attempted to duplicate it in the Lagos studio. For an entire week, George Martin, Geoff Emerick, Paul McCartney, and George Harrison went back and forth between what was recorded and the demos and lyrics that had preceded it.

> [George Martin] "At first, we were all so relieved. We thought that we could go back to the gold that we had and restore the songs to their rightful state. Song by song, word by word, note by note, we came to realize the opposite. The songs that had been re-constituted in the aftermath of the robbery were stronger. There were a few minor adjustments made, of course, but overall, we stayed with what we had."

Years later, those original demo tapes were pulled out of the Apple vaults, cleaned up, and released for fans as *Band on the Run Naked*, letting listeners hear the first versions and judge for themselves. Even in the aftermath of the crime's resolution, there was still money to be made.

In the end, though, the original *Band on the Run* album was hailed as an example of an honest collaboration between Paul, John, George, and Ringo. When they had recorded in London and in Los Angeles, they were surrounded by inspired, driven teams, making the recording sessions feel like a day job with talented and creative colleagues. Conversely, Lagos, Nigeria, for all its hassle and difficulty, had created the opportunity for the four Beatles to hang out with only each other—there was not much else to do. They blended their talents, voices, and instruments to make an album that's still lauded as the most polished piece of work they put forward since *Everest* back in 1969.

> [John] "I don't want everyone to get all, 'Look, the Beatles like each other again.' It's not that at all. We're professionals; this is what we do for a living. So we've gone and done it again, maybe a little better than the last couple of times, but it doesn't mean a miracle has happened. We just made a record, like we always do, that's all."

Band on the Run maintains another distinction in the intensive discography all Beatles albums have been subjected to—both the band members and the album's producers found it difficult to ascribe a singular songwriting credit to several of the songs because, regardless of their point of origin, they had become group efforts.

It is still generally accepted that Paul and John had four songs each, followed by George and Ringo with three each, and within that breakdown each Beatle had standouts. Paul opened the album with the titular "Band on the Run" and closed it out with the mash-up of "Jet/Mrs. Vandebilt," while John scored with his political "Bring on the Lucie (Freda Peeple)" and his rocker "New York City." The two men each delivered beautiful moments as well, Paul with "Bluebird" and "My Love" and John with the Yoko-inspired pair of "Bless You" and "Out the Blue." George delivered the enormously popular "Give Me Love (Give Me Peace on Earth)" and the well-regarded "Run of the Mill" and "Don't Let Me Wait Too Long." Ringo benefited the most from the band's fragmentation, voicing Harrison and Starkey's "Photograph," Lennon's "I Am the Greatest," and McCartney's "Six O'Clock." It was the first time Ringo had three songs, and standout hits at that.

• • •

John Lennon returned to Los Angeles by way of London from Nigeria, having been deported from Yoko's side once again. He had had his fill of the Beatles and was not in a good mood about his wife, so he showed up at Linda Ronstadt's house.

She was not home. Her own *Don't Cry Now* album had become Ronstadt's most successful to date, selling 300,000 copies in its first year of release. It had also earned her a spot as the opening act on Neil Young's *Time Fades Away* tour, where she would be playing for larger crowds than ever before. Even if she had been home, Ronstadt would have asked Lennon to move out over the upcoming Christmas holidays. She told friends that she liked big-size personalities and strong men, qualities she certainly admired in John Lennon, but she could no longer stomach his paranoia. If he really was being targeted by the government, that was scary enough. If he was not but thought he was, that, too, was more than she bargained for.

Despite this breakup, John Lennon always spoke well of his time with Ronstadt.

> [John] "Linda takes command. She runs the recording studio, and nobody challenges her. She's got strong opinions about everything and, you know what, she's right. She runs her own life that way. Even when her opinion was that it was time to call it quits between us, she was right about that, too."

Lennon found his own Laurel Canyon home locked up as well and quickly phoned Yoko, who confirmed that she had stopped paying the bills. He then rang up his friend Harry Nilsson, who granted Lennon permission to crash on his couch that night. The next day, he went out looking for a place on the beach.

With the year winding down, Lennon had time to take stock. He had been told by the second woman in less than a year that he should leave the home they were living in together. While he never actually admitted it, he was unusually happy to see that *Band on the Run* had become the critical hit that it was. He needed to feel artistic and relevant, particularly given Ronstadt's rising success, and he did.

Paul, meanwhile, retreated to his Scottish farm with Linda and the children. They received matching kimonos from Tokyo, sent by Yoko with the note "*Love, John and Yoko*" although Lennon knew nothing about the gift. In return, the McCartneys sent John and Yoko matching wool sweaters from Scotland. John's was mailed to him care of Elliot Mintz, a Los Angeles disc jockey with whom he had become friends. The sweater was outrageously cheesy, and Lennon gave it to Nilsson, who lost it one night at the Troubadour.

George spent his Christmas alone at Friar Park, and the huge Gothic mansion seemed dark and lonely. Pattie, who had threatened to move out with Eric Clapton, was missing. His own infatuation with Maureen Starkey was still threatening to end a friendship with her husband and George's bandmate, Ringo. Meditation over the changes that had occurred in his life only made matters worse. He turned to cocaine, but even the drug could not cheer him up.

Ringo threw a gala New Year's Eve party at Tittenhurst Park but failed to invite his own wife, Maureen. Asked by party guest Elton John whether this meant he was getting divorced, he merely said, "Would you like another appetizer?" George did show up that night with Pattie, and he used the occasion to tell her he wanted a divorce. For those keeping score of such things, George was now interested in Ringo's wife at the same time that his friend Eric Clapton was putting the moves on his own wife. Seeing George come in the door, the usually gregarious Ringo retreated to his own bedroom and stayed there until his fellow Beatle left the party two hours later.

Lennon heard all about the drama from his new housemates at his Malibu beach house. Relieved to hear that the Beatles could still be fighting with each other while he was over six thousand miles away, he phoned up the only person who might understand his thinking, Yoko Ono, noting that there were still three hours to go before the New Year would be celebrated in Los Angeles.

[John] "It's like the old British royalty, isn't it? Go away for the weekend and swap wives. Well, maybe the only women who get through to rock stars besides the groupies that get disposed of like a Kleenex are the wives of their friends. They're the only ones who get to stick around when the sun comes up."

If John Lennon thought discussing wife swapping and sleeping with groupies was the way to his wife's heart, she quickly disabused him of this notion, hung up, and went to a party being thrown by Andy Warhol. As the final hours of 1973 turned into the first hours of a new year, Lennon got out his book of phone numbers and started calling around. No one, it seemed, was at home, except for Paul McCartney, who was having a late breakfast with his family in Scotland.

They discussed making another record in the next year but only after admitting to themselves and fans that it would be the last one.

"Let's go out on top," said Lennon, slurring his words from his fourth Brandy Alexander of the evening.

"Whatever you say, John," answered McCartney, as he chased Stella, his two-year-old daughter, around the house. "My place or yours?"

CHAPTER SEVEN

LAST WORDS (1974)

TALK OF THE TOWN

Could it really have been ten years?

February 8, 1974, marked the tenth anniversary of the Beatles' U.S. debut on the CBS stage of *The Ed Sullivan Show*. Sullivan had been gone from television for three years already, but New York Mayor Abraham Beame, a Democrat who had been in office a mere nine days, knew an opportunity when he saw one. He declared the anniversary to be "New York Loves The Beatles Day!"

None of the Beatles were keen to be loved in New York at that particular moment, but they did have an album to promote. *Band on the Run* was the #1 album on *Billboard*, but *You Don't Mess Around with Jim* from the late Jim Croce, who had died just months earlier in a plane crash, threatened to knock it from its spot. To make matters more dire, Bob Dylan's *Planet Waves* album would release next week and was expected to be huge.

The Beatles' presence in New York would be a politically tinged PR affair, given that the government of Richard Nixon was, at that very moment, attempting to deport John Lennon and Yoko Ono from the United States, while making Paul McCartney and George Harrison out to be drug abusers undeserving of any visas to visit or work.

With the American political system convulsing with Watergate, however, the Nixon team needed to avoid unnecessary public confrontation. The word at the INS was to quietly let the outsiders in. Paul, George, and Ringo soon managed to qualify for temporary visas. By this point, the three of them had hired the same immigration attorney that John was using, the out-of-the-box thinker Leon Wildes.

Out in California, the FBI was maintaining its regular and costly surveillance of John Lennon's increasingly dissolute lifestyle. Agent Tad Ostroff had the opportunity to observe Lennon up close in a first-class seat on a nonstop flight from Los Angeles to New York. He watched his prey drink too much and almost have mile-high sex with a willing stewardess, stopped only because the woman in question had a jealous coworker. It was all in the report he dutifully made to the new director, Clarence Kelley, and released years later after a Freedom of Information Act request filed by *Rockstar*.

Once on the ground in New York City, at Beame's urging, all four of the Beatles appeared at a news conference that was staged in the same room at JFK Airport as their first meeting with journalists upon their arrival in 1964. The Beatles ended up making almost as much news in 1974 as they had a decade earlier. They sat in the same order they'd sat in all that time ago, and the photographs, when juxtaposed, were telling. The boys of 1964 had become independent men in 1974. They not only looked like they had changed, but they talked like it, too.

The conference began predictably enough, when John, who had long shed any guise of innocence he might have previously maintained, told the news reporters, "Richard Nixon shouldn't be in the White House; he should be in the Big House," using the gangster slang term for prison. Even the typically politically reticent Paul made his position clear: "When it's time to go, pack your bags and get out of town."

When another reporter asked McCartney if he was talking about the embattled American president or the Beatles always teetering on the verge of a breakup, Ringo tried to joke it off.

"We just hope we can hang in longer than he can," Ringo said, lighting another Marlboro.

"Don't put any money on that one," added George.

• • •

In truth, all four of the Beatles had already accepted that they probably had only one final studio album left in them. That's what they had agreed to in the Grand Bargain—at least one studio album a year for five years, which meant, as Ringo summarized, "One More in '74." After that, they would be done with each other, if that was what they wanted.

It was odd for the Beatles to think of their group finally disbanding just as they were given a grand welcome by Beame's New York. For a group of musicians on the brink of ending their collaboration, they presented themselves as a united front to the press people holding out microphones. By then, the Beatles knew from hard experience that airing their dirty laundry in public brought mixed results.

Ironically, "New York Loves The Beatles Day!" became a three-day collection of events and appearances involving radio and TV interviews, a party at Gracie Mansion, and even a night out on Broadway to catch the revival of *Gigi* before it closed after a disappointing run of 103 days.

Only McCartney, Harrison, Starkey, and their spouses attended the Broadway night out. Paul led the charge, wanting to hear the several new songs that had been added to the Lerner and Loewe musical before the show disappeared, possibly for good. By this point, it seemed as though all of New York was obsessed with figuring out where the Beatles might be. Their security team leaked that the band would be attending another Broadway show called *The Iceman Cometh* and then diverted Paul, George, and Ringo to the Uris Theater at the last minute.

[Ringo] "The entire time we were in New York that February felt like it was a Beatles revival anyway, so the idea of going to see a musical revival on Broadway seemed about right. We were in and out of cars a lot during that visit, going in the back doors, hiding in hallways, that kind of thing. We knew from the last time that fans might love us to death, but we were grown men by this time, and the whole Beatlemania thing seemed a bit silly by now."

Lennon chose not to participate in the caper to see *Gigi* because he knew he would be "bored to tears and fall asleep." His real reason was that he had secured an invitation to take Yoko to dinner. They ended up at McSorley's Old Ale House, not for the food but for the secluded table in the back and the management's agreement to steer fans away.

Yoko Ono had attended all but one event with John, which put her in contact with Linda McCartney, Pattie Boyd, and Maureen Starkey. Neither George's marriage nor Ringo's seemed to be in much better shape than John's, but the show went on as if all were happily settled, a contrast to the last decade when everyone acted single and carefree.

Dinner out was strange for both John and Yoko. They had so much to discuss, so many feelings to unearth, so many decisions to make. At the Beatles events, they were always surrounded by other people, and the timing was never right. At McSorley's, though, they talked. Yoko told John in no uncertain terms that it was time for him to sober up, send May Pang packing, and start writing songs like nobody's business. "You're the leader of the Beatles," she said. "It's time to act like it."

This was not what John wanted to hear. He felt that being a Beatle had nearly gotten him killed in Nigeria. Now here they were in New York, the city he loved above all others, and he and Yoko had to skulk about like criminals just to get a beer and a burger. It was insane, and he told her so.

They talked about him coming back and living with her in the Dakota again. "I wanted you to grow up, John," she told him at the very beginning. "Instead, we have grown apart."

Yoko felt that John had not followed what she understood to be the terms of their separation. Rather than taking a short vacation and sleeping with her approved lover, Pang, he had bought a house, parked the Chinese-American assistant in it, and then shacked up with a rock diva in LA's hippie Laurel Canyon. Plus, he was hanging out with a collection of friends who all seemed to be about the next party.

> [John] "I had this whole thing planned out in my mind, I did. Yoko and I would eat some dinner, we'd go back to the Dakota, and we'd make love like it was the old days. So it turned out to be something different than champagne and violins."

The problem was that Lennon had enjoyed his life in Los Angeles after returning from Nigeria. Ono asked him to tell her about his life now, giving him just enough rope to hang himself.

Lennon explained that he was beginning to produce his friend Harry Nilsson's *Pussy Cats* album. Plus, he had rented a Santa Monica beach house that had been built by film producer Louis B. Mayer. It had been a hot spot for movie royalty, including actor Peter Lawford, who continued the tradition by hosting fellow Hollywood luminaries as well as his brothers-in-law, John Kennedy and Robert Kennedy, on many occasions. Marilyn Monroe had been a frequent visitor, which greatly piqued John's interest—so much so that he and Pang had taken the master bedroom because, Lennon believed, "This is where they [JFK and Monroe] did it."

Yoko listened to all of this with an impassive expression, and when it was over, told John, "You are not ready to come home. You have more to learn." She said that it sounded like John was living in some kind of college fraternity, a point with which he could not disagree.

That night, Lennon slept alone in his hotel room, while Ono returned to the Dakota.

• • •

The three days in New York City represented the first real time since Friar Park in 1970 when all four Beatles, their significant others, their three managers, key Apple staffers, and even children were in one place together.

McCartney asked Lee Eastman to rent out Danny's Hideaway for their last evening in the city. At eleven dining rooms and seating for two hundred people, this was no small ask. Still, the restaurant had been the scene of the post-show debauchery with Johnny Carson, Ed McMahon, John, and Paul back in 1968, and it had spawned the memorable collaboration song "Show Up." Even so, under new Apple policy, Eastman had to ring up Allen Klein, who in turn rang up Lord Beeching. Beeching complained that the party could not be expensed as publicity or entertainment, given it would be a secret. "These guys are always looking for a way not to work together," pushed back Klein. "You want to give them another reason, take away their party." Seeing the value in this fractious clan coming together, even for a few hours, Beeching approved the expenditure.

In 1972, *The Tonight Show Starring Johnny Carson* had moved from New York to Burbank, California, so there would be no Johnny or Ed McMahon to reprise their roles. To respect their memory, however, McCartney saw to it that the bar featured the vodka sours and J&B scotch and waters the two entertainers favored.

There was an attempt to control the guest list, but, as had been the case at Friar Park, it soon expanded. Mayor Beame, his staffers, and their friends were in charge of coordination. Actors like Robert De Niro and Liza Minnelli made the scene for about twenty minutes, as did Jacqueline Kennedy Onassis. Local musicians, including members of Elephant's Memory, a band that John liked, also put in an appearance.

Both Paul Simon and Art Garfunkel came separately—they had broken up in 1970, at the same time the Beatles nearly had. Garfunkel lamented his own breakup and asked Harrison what the Beatles' secret was. "We all write songs, even Ringo, and the others make them better," was his response, not realizing how that might have cut Garfunkel to the bone.

When Lennon invoked the challenge of the two Pauls

(McCartney and Simon) to Garfunkel, the singer told him to "put all the personality crap aside and go make music with somebody who brings out the best in you."

Even with all this madness swirling about them, the Beatles had some important conversations with their families and respective entourages that night.

As always, McCartney remained the band's greatest cheerleader. He wanted to plan the Beatles' exit from the stage methodically, as if it was inevitable, rather than let it play out as publicly as the *Savile Row* warfare that had shattered the rock world nearly three years earlier. He wanted them to go out singing.

> [Paul] "It's true. I thought we should shake ourselves up one final time and do a world tour. We had more hits than anyone ever, or it seemed that way. We'd been tight as a band before and we could be again. It would be a great way to say goodbye and thanks. I mean, we'd played the Roundhouse, we'd played at Woodstock, and we'd played at George's concert. We knew what we were doing. The only question was whether we'd agree to do it for more than one night in a row."

Ringo seconded the motion, but George was noncommittal, and John acted like he was just too busy with personal issues to consider such a decision at this time. "I can understand what a burden it must be to produce a Harry Nilsson album, John," said Paul, dripping irony. "Maybe when that's behind you, we can take up the Beatles again."

"Oh, bugger off, Paul," said John.

What seemed different from past years when Paul and John had jousted about the Beatles was that now they did so without the overt anger. "John seemed more ready to admit he said things just to drive Paul mad, and Paul knew not to always take John at his word," observed Ringo. "I just made sure to keep the number for Rory and the Hurricanes in my Rolodex."

As their spouses argued, Yoko and Linda had another of their private get-togethers. Yoko told Linda that she wanted the Beatles to stage a group intervention to rescue her errant husband from the charms of Los Angeles and get him back into a recording studio, where he could sober up and double down on his music. Linda said she would discuss it with Paul, but she wasn't optimistic.

The night was fueled by liquor and pot—the group took turns sneaking behind the restaurant to smoke the weed Paul had brought in from London. The Beatles and their affiliates discussed that two things needed to happen before a final decision about the group could be reached: the immigration case needed to be resolved, and the final studio album needed to be recorded.

Peter Brown observed the discussion ping back and forth from a short distance. "I realized that what I was watching was this ever-so-strange but completely real, extended family," Brown explained to author Hunter Davies, whose untitled follow-up to his 1968 authorized biography was due out within the year. "It became so clear that this group of people, most of them at least, would never, ever be free of themselves, even if the band itself went away."

Hunter Davies would cull his title from that conversation with Brown. *The Beatles: A Life Within* came out that summer.

HAPPY DAYS?

The next day, Lennon parted company with Ono and flew back to Los Angeles, where factotum Harry Nilsson met him at the airport and drove him back to the rented beach house. John told him immediately about Paul's cutting remarks, even though he knew it would only cause trouble later.

Lennon explained that Yoko was insisting that his eleven-year-old son Julian come visit his father in Los Angeles. John had initially resisted, saying, "I'm not exactly living like the Dad of the Year now, am I?" In response, Yoko sent May Pang to London to pick up Julian and fly with him to LA. Once he was there, John was faced with the problem that confronts all divorced fathers who get a few weeks with their children: How would he keep his kid entertained?

Lennon, who most often lived life with the television set on, had recently caught the premiere of the new sitcom *Happy Days*, a show that took a nostalgic look at the 1950s in much of the way the sitcom *That '70s Show* riffed on the 1970s. Filmed on the Paramount lot, the series was a one-camera show in its first season (to be turned into a more conventional three-camera sitcom by its third season). In other words, there were no fans in a studio audience who would turn an appearance by Lennon into an event that would disrupt filming.

Pang set to work scoring John and Julian an invitation to hang out on the set and watch the filming of an episode. On February 27, they arrived with Pang to see several scenes that involved most of the cast, which, at that time, included star Ron Howard, star-in-the-making Henry Winkler, Tom Bosley, Marion Ross, Anson Williams, and Donny Most.

Characterized by crew members as "kind, gentle, and shy," the Beatle did dozens of doodles during the day, partly because everyone loved them, and partly because they seemed to impress Julian. Nearly everyone John met would later use the word "humble" to describe his demeanor. Lennon was still such a fan of '50s music that he wanted to see the show up close and personal.

Producer Garry Marshall knew that a rare and genuine magic had just entered his life. Several episodes of *Happy Days* had already aired. The critics loved them, and so did ABC. But there could always be more viewers. Marshall, no shrinking violet, created a plan to give his show a launch that would get eyeballs across America watching.

[Garry Marshall] "Making a great TV show isn't enough to stay on-the-air. You need people to find it on their TV set, and they have to have heard about it to do that. When I saw we had a Beatle on the set, I told Jerry Paris, our director, to start shooting fast, to get the shots he needed in a single take.

Another series had used a school bus in an episode, and it was still on the Paramount lot. The whole thing came together in minutes."

The "whole thing" was a plan to use Lennon's celebrity to get people talking about the show. The first thing Marshall did was ask two of his actors, Anson Williams and Donny Most, to hang out with the Lennon group while Ron Howard and Henry Winkler shot a scene together in the Cunningham kitchen set. Most was recruited to ask Julian if he had ever been to Disneyland. As it turned out, Julian, who had been in LA a mere three days, had not, but his excitement at hearing about it was hard to miss.

Marshall, a decent actor himself, then approached John as if he had just gotten an idea. They'd already shot their bare minimum of production, he said. It would be possible to suspend shooting for the day and take Julian to Disneyland with the cast and crew. He made it sound just plausible enough that Lennon, Pang, and Nilsson all gave the plan the thumbs up.

"It happened so fast we weren't even sure what was going on," said actor Most, the redhead who played Ralph Malph. "Within ten minutes the bus was outside and we were all getting on."

Marshall had seen Julian's eyes light up like any child's would at the possibility of visiting the Happiest Place on Earth, and Lennon was unable to deny his son the opportunity. Soon, nearly forty-five people, including John, Julian, and the *Happy Days* cast and crew, were on their way to Disneyland in a truly *Magical Mystery Tour* bus, courtesy of Paramount Television.

John regaled the passengers with the story of how he and Paul had used the real *Magical Mystery Tour* bus to lure the Hells Angels out of the Apple offices. He managed to make it sound exciting and dangerous and more fun than most people have in a lifetime.

Marshall, no fool, knew that if a joke killed on the stage but there was no audience to hear it, then it counted for nothing. He needed his series to get some notoriety, so shortly before the bus departed the Paramount lot in Hollywood for Anaheim, he called the *Hollywood Reporter* and *KABC Eyewitness News* and leaked word of the adventure.

By the time Paramount's school bus arrived at the gates of Disneyland, there were already reporters staked out to watch them off-load and be greeted by park officials. Lennon immediately knew that Marshall had played him and confronted the producer. Marshall tried to shrug it off, but Lennon was having none of that.

At that moment, however, Robert McBride, Disney's PR man, showed up with an honorary "key" to the park and presented it to a beaming Julian.

At that point, John was presented with his own choice: hold Marshall's feet to the fire and ruin one of the greatest days in his son's life, or be Julian's hero. Within an hour, John Lennon had spoken to nearly every TV news crew in Los Angeles, flashing the peace sign in every interview and mugging with Garry Marshall, the man Lennon was now calling "Mr. Kite."

• • •

It seemed so simple and pleasant, a harmless PR prank by an over-anxious Hollywood producer. But there was one problem. Among the many people watching Lennon hang out with the *Happy Days* cast and crew at the most recognizable icon of capitalistic excess were radicals from the Weather Underground, Bernardine Dohrn and William Ayers. During the 2008 presidential campaign when the Republican party tried to link their names to Democratic candidate Barack Obama, they first told their story publicly.

[William Ayers] "John Lennon was still the political Beatle to us. Granted, some of the lyrics to his 'Revolution' had turned us off, but his behavior in 1970 and 1971 had placed him firmly left-of-center. When the Beatles tried to play their Nixon protest concert in Miami Beach, we thought that was cool, even though we had stopped believing in elections."

[Bernardine Dohrn] "But then, one night in early 1974, there he was on the evening news, going to Disneyland with a bunch of comedians. Bill and I just looked at each other. What had happened to him? This left-wing radical now looked like any other capitalist tool, no longer committed to the revolution. We felt he could have become a symbol."

The truth of the matter was that by 1974 the best (or the most destructive) years were behind the Weather Underground. Their brand of radicalism had stalled (or dimmed) and was not so active among the revolutionary elite, its rank and file, and even the public and the media. As Vietnam crawled toward its conclusion and even radicals started to get jobs and drop back into society, the organization was burning itself out.

Both Ayers and Dohrn knew that something had to be done that would re-focus the world's energy back on them. They had just finished writing a book they hoped might do the trick: *Prairie Fire: The Politics of Revolutionary Anti-Imperialism*. Within its pages, Ayers and Dohrn advocated the overthrow of the current capitalist system as the only solution to racism, sexism, homophobia, classism, and imperialism.

Still, they all wondered, would it be enough? Like producer Garry Marshall, Dohrn and Ayers felt that the power of the Beatles could be harnessed to their own advantage. They certainly knew that the Weather Underground needed to adjust its tactics and goals to a post-Vietnam world. They needed to seize the world's attention as they had done a few years earlier, and the sooner they could do it, the better.

The Weather Underground leaders had heard through the revolutionary grapevine that the Symbionese Liberation Army was planning something big, like the kidnapping of newspaper heiress Patricia Hearst, and they wanted to strike first.

They would kidnap John Lennon, subject him to "re-education" tactics, and force him to become their mouthpiece to the world. When a living, breathing Beatle laid out the case for radical change, the reasoning went, the world would pay attention. He could start the "prairie fire" of revolution that they so craved.

Dohrn, Ayers, and others began to stalk Lennon. They observed his comings and goings from his Malibu rental home. Among them was the departure of Julian Lennon to his life in England.

> [Julian Lennon] "It's no secret that my dad wasn't much of a dad to me. But that vacation in LA was like it was supposed to be. Dads take their kids to Disneyland. So that was good. If I'd known what it was going to lead to, though, I guess I'd rather have missed out on it."

Once Julian was safely back to the care of his mother, Cynthia, John returned to his party life in Malibu. The Weathermen followed him constantly. Ironically, even though Lennon spotted them several times, he dismissed them as junior FBI agents and ignored them.

The nightclubs they followed him into included the famed Troubadour in Hollywood. Wearing disguises, the Weathermen observed Lennon and Nilsson throwing back Brandy Alexanders like mess possessed. One night, an inebriated Lennon came from the restrooms wearing a sanitary napkin attached to his forehead. Dohrn and Ayers watched as a waitress questioned him as to whether he was leaving a tip on the way out.

"Do you know who I am?" Lennon asked.

"Yes," the waitress shot back. "You're the asshole with a Kotex on your head."

The plan had been for Dohrn and Ayers to pick up Lennon after he left the Troubadour, but now there were too many people around, from bouncers to club owners to fans gathered to watch the stumbling Lennon. If anything, the scene convinced Dohrn and Ayers that Lennon was a worthy target who would benefit from some re-education—they'd just have to wait a little longer to implement their plans.

As it turned out, they didn't have to wait as long as they thought. The evening of March 12, 1974, had been a dark one for John Lennon, now almost a year into his banishment by Yoko Ono. Lennon and Nilsson began throwing down more cocktails and decided to heckle the Smothers Brothers, the controversial political satirists.

"The comments got so ugly and personal that we were about to get pulled off the stage," Tommy Smothers said. "We loved the Beatles and it blew our minds that one of them would try to ruin our show."

As the situation escalated, club security attempted to remove the drunken and enraged rock stars in the audience. The struggle turned physical, and Lennon lost his memorable glasses in the scuffle.

All of this, of course, attracted just as much attention as the Kotex incident, but this time, the Weather Underground was prepared—they had a spotter in the crowd who used a nearby payphone to call Bernardine Dohrn, stationed at another payphone near Lennon's rental house on the beach.

As a taxi dropped off Lennon, Nilsson, and Pang at Lennon's, a coordinated team of five members of the Weather Underground made their move to grab Lennon. Nilsson tried to hold on to his friend but was punched out cold for his bravery, suffering a concussion when his head hit the stone driveway. A car appeared, driven by Ayers, with Dohrn in the passenger seat.

Pang screamed, terrified she might be raped, and was gagged, blindfolded, and thrown into the back seat. The Weather Underground radicals overpowered Lennon as well, tied his hands with duct tape, and threw him in the trunk of the vehicle. Within less than a minute of exiting the taxi, John Lennon, inebriated and vomiting, found himself locked in a dark car trunk without his eyeglasses.

The car sped off, going north on Pacific Coast Highway. Twenty miles away, on a dark, deserted stretch of beach highway outside of Trancas, a member of the rebel group threw May Pang from the car.

It took her over two hours to find her way to an all-night liquor store with a phone. The manager, a volunteer member of the Malibu Sheriff's Department, took care of the frantic Pang and helped her remember the physical descriptions of the assailants as best as possible.

With Pang's assistance, deputies found Harry Nilsson shortly before daylight, still unconscious, in the driveway of the beach house. Within another hour, AP had broken the story.

• • •

Breaking News
APB107
-BULLETIN- (AP)
(LOS ANGELES, CALIFORNIA)—THE RADICAL
WEATHER UNDERGROUND TERRORIST
ORGANIZATION SAYS THAT MUSICIAN JOHN LENNON
IS IN ITS CUSTODY. LENNON, A MEMBER OF THE
POPULAR MUSICAL GROUP THE BEATLES, HAS BEEN
MISSING SINCE TUESDAY.
05:18gAPD 03-15-74
APB108
LENNON-BULLETIN-TAKE 2
FBI DIRECTOR CLARENCE M. KELLEY
CONFIRMS THAT BUREAU AGENTS BELIEVE THE
COMMUNICATION FROM WEATHER UNDERGROUND
LEADER BERNARDINE DOHRN IS AUTHENTIC.

• • •

After a three-day search that involved coordinated investigations by police from Los Angeles to San Francisco and all points in between, the car into whose trunk John Lennon had been thrown was discovered by officers in a Medford parking lot in southern Oregon. This fact of geography caused Lieutenant Samuel R. Forster, the lead LAPD detective assigned to the case, to designate that John Lennon was in the wind. The investigation was officially handed off to the FBI, as the evidence had already crossed state lines.

From the perspective of today's scandal and celebrity-saturated culture, it is hard to comprehend the impact the news of Lennon's kidnapping had on the general public when the story first broke on March 15, 1974. One of the world's greatest celebrities had just been taken hostage by a revolutionary group most Americans knew sought to destroy the world as they knew it. Against the backdrop of the daily implosions of the Nixon Administration, the Lennon kidnapping mesmerized the country.

"The news just went nuclear," shouted New York journalist Geraldo Rivera when he arrived in Los Angeles, determined, he told his viewers, to "find John Ono Lennon and bring him home."

The Weather Underground's kidnapping of John Lennon became, after Watergate, the greatest media event of the 1970s. Before it was over, Lennon's face would appear four times on the cover of *Time* alone.

News coverage grew more hysterical by the day. There seemed to be no limits around who John Lennon was and what he represented, what the crime meant, and what it symbolized for Americans battered by war and scandal.

Less than a day after Lennon had been abducted, Robert W. Morgan at radio station KMPC received a call. A woman's voice informed him that John Lennon had become a "prisoner of war." She made no ransom demand but directed Morgan to broadcast the news immediately. More news would be forthcoming, the woman said, and then she hung up. Morgan told the FBI his belief that it was Bernardine Dohrn who'd been on the other end of the line.

After taking credit for the Lennon kidnapping, the Weather Underground went silent. As Apple's first order of business, security details were hired for Paul McCartney, George Harrison, Richard

Starkey, and Yoko Ono. Never again would a Beatle or a family member be without protection.

PR man Derek Taylor was called back from vacation in France. He locked all the marijuana and alcohol in his safe, and then he got to work. The first thing he did was craft a statement that had none of the tongue-in-cheek nuance he was known for.

> [Apple] "Apple joins with Beatles fans worldwide in condemning the illegal kidnapping of John Lennon in Los Angeles. We urge law enforcement officials in the United States to treat this as a serious crime and act immediately to find and free our John. We also urge any individual who has information that could free John and bring the perpetrators to justice to call police immediately."

Each of the individual Beatles found reporters on their doorsteps even before the security details could arrive. All of them were, to say the least, freaked out, not only for their comrade but for themselves, not knowing if this was part of a larger plan.

McCartney, whom the press tracked down in a London studio where he was producing a Badfinger song, was so guarded in his first remarks that he was forced to amend his statement that same day. "John is our great friend," he said with the proper sense of gravity. "We'll do anything to bring him home safely."

Harrison viewed the event in his stereotypical cosmic perspective. "The universe has many dark forces," he told BBC, "but John is a being of light. The light always finds a way."

Starkey's response was, perhaps, the most compelling. He stared into the camera's lens and spoke directly to his friend: "John, we all love you, and we will find you. If you see this, just remember that. We won't give up until we find you." Starkey then went silent and went back into his home, knowing that if the short sound bite was all reporters had on film, the news stations would play it over and over, increasing Lennon's chance of actually seeing it.

Yoko went into hiding in the Dakota, distraught as one might expect, especially given that nearly two months earlier she'd turned down John's plea to return to New York, and to her. Instead, she'd sent him back to Los Angeles, and now he was missing altogether. She blamed herself.

Yoko's new personal assistant rang Paul with her new number, and Paul called her back immediately. "John's thinking of you right now, and he's okay," Paul said, trying to sound reassuring. "You did nothing to cause this. He'll be coming home soon, and he's going to want to be with you." Their conversation was cut short when the FBI arrived to interview Ono for their investigation.

This, of course, created a terrible problem. Yoko knew, more than almost anyone, how deeply the FBI, an instrument of the Nixon government, had been involved in surveillance and harassment of her husband. All of the Beatles, in fact, had come to see the FBI as the enemy. Now they were being told to work with them to find John Lennon.

> [Yoko] "I became sick to my stomach when I thought about this. I could not trust these people to keep my husband alive. I pretended that I did not know what evil things they had done to us because I did not want them to know what I knew. It was a very terrible thing that happened."

The arrival of the FBI team, however, sent Yoko into action. She checked into a room at the Plaza Hotel under another name and had her new security detail make certain she was not followed. In the Plaza suite, she began to collect call everyone at Apple, dispensing the insight that John was in terrible danger, but not just from the Weather Underground.

Allen Klein, with his aggressive New York instincts, also understood that in a takedown of the Weather Underground, the FBI could "accidentally" see that John Lennon was killed as collateral damage. Klein had heard from his own sources of the FBI's nefarious Squad 47, formed specifically to break up the Weather Underground by any means necessary. They were said to regularly violate civil rights by tapping phones and opening mail without warrants, but they were also conducting black-bag break-ins that were not sanctioned by the Bureau.

Klein told Yoko that he would put together a private team of ex-agents and military to find Lennon before the FBI did. He had made key contacts during the short period the year before, when blackmailer Winston Fourney had held the tapes from the Nigerian *Band on the Run* sessions. The most important was former Marine Corps special operative Connor McNary, a man Klein had grown to trust.

"Listen up, Connor," Klein told him on the phone. "John Lennon's gone missing and I need you to drop what you're doing and come help us find him." To his unending credit, McNary packed his bags and got a flight to New York that same day.

Klein's next call was to Lord Beeching. "I've found help, but it won't be cheap," he said. "I need a line of credit now, a big one, no strings, and if it doesn't happen within an hour of this call, you're going down in history as the man who let John Lennon die."

Beeching took a long moment to consider this demand. Then he did as instructed, with no complaint or evasion.

To the world at large, it was starting to seem as though John Lennon had simply disappeared. The longer the Weather Underground Organization stayed silent, the more hysterical the press coverage became. Newscasters openly discussed that Lennon might already be dead. A mutilated body found on the side of the road in Dearborn, Michigan, earned twenty-four hours in the news cycle, despite being three inches shorter than Lennon, before the local coroner ruled that the body was not his.

Although no one knew it, Lennon was alive, if not well. Physically, the manhandling of the kidnapping and the transit in the car trunk had covered his body with cuts and bruises. His right shoulder was dislocated in the struggle and had to be popped into place by an inexperienced Weatherman who claimed medical experience only so he could meet the rock star but ended up causing Lennon excruciating pain.

Dohrn, Ayers, and the rest of their fellow revolutionaries had acted before they had a real plan. No one considered how complicated it might be to have one of the world's most famous faces in their care and to keep a lid on the situation so nobody found them out.

Seeing the ad hoc nature of what was happening, John Lennon tried to bargain for his freedom. Ironically, only Lord Beeching and Yoko Ono knew exactly what his total net worth was, but he promised it all to the Weather Underground. "You'll be the scariest kind of revolutionaries," he reasoned, "the kind with money."

The kidnappers briefly debated asking for ransom money but firmly rejected the idea. Even though the Weather Underground routinely laundered money from supporters to members, something of this scale, with the eyes of the world on alert, seemed foolish and likely to end up with the group broken and in prison. No, the reasoning went, Lennon was theirs and they were going to keep him.

As Lennon was shuttled about the West Coast, Dohrn and Ayers found that even fellow Weather Underground members were hesitant to help them. The entire nation seemed to be following the case with intense interest. Every local police department that had suspicions about undercover revolutionaries in their midst used the case as an excuse to check them out. Soon the FBI had over two thousand alleged sightings.

As a result, in the first two weeks, John Lennon was transported in three different vehicles to five different locations. He was placed in handcuffs, and his body was chained to everything from heating furnaces to steel beams. Because of his celebrity, all of the Weather Underground co-conspirators along the road seemed to want to talk to him, causing Bernardine Dohrn to decree that he was not allowed to speak at all, and that, if he did, they would crush one of his fingers with a hammer for each instance of disobedience.

At one point, Lennon tried to talk to his captors, to strike a deal. He received a hard physical beating for his attempt and was not fed again for two days. During this time, Lennon was locked in a coat closet, where he was in earshot of the news coverage.

Even in the complete darkness, he could still hear Ringo say through the television: "We won't give up until we find you."

It gave him hope.

ON THE ROAD TO NAINITAL

A nineteen-year-old Steve Jobs was already in India when thirty-two-year-old George Harrison landed in New Delhi, seeking refuge from the rising hysteria over the Lennon kidnapping. Jobs had quit his job at the Atari game company and had also come to India searching for enlightenment and a guru. He arrived in New Delhi weeks before Harrison but had fallen sick with dysentery almost immediately. With a fever spiking for days at a time, he claimed to have dropped from 160 pounds to 120 in just three weeks. He knew he had to get out of the city.

Fate decreed that Harrison would first meet Jobs near the Ganges River at Haridwar, a town in western India where a festival known as the *Kumbh Mela* was underway. It was a time of madness, as more than ten million spiritual seekers descended upon a town of one hundred thousand. The skinny, sickly white kid in the throng stuck out like a sore thumb. Harrison knew he was in trouble the minute he saw him and immediately bought Jobs a giant bottle of certified filtered water.

"There's a hole in me and I have to fill it," Jobs told the Beatle as he drained the bottle. "That's why I'm here. 'Fixing a hole.'"

George confessed later to being put off by Jobs's quoting the Beatles back to him, but it was apparent to him that the last thing this malnourished and dehydrated American fan should do was to stay in Haridwar. Overlooking the minor annoyance, George bought himself and Jobs a couple of train tickets, and they began a journey to get anywhere but where they were.

As the miles rolled by, Harrison realized that Jobs knew more about Apple Records than he did.

[George] "I had to confess to him that I had very little to do with Apple originally because I was actually here in India when it started. It was John and Paul's madness—their egos running away with themselves. There were a lot of ideas, but when it came down to it, the only thing we could do successfully was write songs, make records, and be Beatles. That's what I thought, but this kid, barely out of high school, he had other ideas."

Jobs knew the players at Apple and the company's history like he had lived the events himself. Even more astonishing than his knowledge was the fact that this nineteen-year-old nobody had opinions on Apple's past—and future—that he was not afraid to share with the Beatle.

[Steve Jobs] "I remember telling him that I thought he'd gotten screwed in the Grand Bargain, that if I were him, I'd have settled for nothing less than full parity with Lennon and McCartney. Everybody gets the same amount of songs on an album. No exceptions. But I also told him that ultimately it wouldn't matter because music in the future was going to transcend albums, that Beatles fans were going to make their own even, and that his hits would rise to the top."

Harrison had never met anyone like the "enthusiastically detached" Jobs. The young man from California said he believed in destiny and karma (and he passionately loved Lennon's "Instant Karma!") and was convinced that he had been meant to meet Harrison, even if the reason was not yet apparent.

"Do you still take acid?" he asked. Jobs had brought two tabs of LSD into India, smuggled inside a Band-Aid travel kit. He had been saving them, he told George, for a moment that would reveal itself. He felt that moment had been revealed.

After one particularly bad trip in San Francisco during the Summer of Love, Harrison had avoided LSD altogether, with the single exception of the night of the California primary debate where all the Beatles tripped with Hunter Thompson. From what he could remember, that had worked out.

Still, he told Jobs that he would pass but would be happy to guide the young man on his own trip as his travel companion. Jobs took his hit of blotter acid, and once again the two got on a train together with no destination in mind.

They found themselves having an animated conversation mid-journey about what it meant that the Beatles had picked a green apple as the icon they wanted the world to know them by. Jobs was fascinated by the apple, and the way he talked about it made Harrison marvel and laugh at the same time. "It's naughty like the Garden of Eden, but it's got crunch and taste, and everybody has eaten one and feels good about that association. It's almost primal…"

Apple signaled friendliness to the young genius. He said it didn't sound like any company that had come before it, but still it felt as American as apple pie.

After a few minutes of this, Harrison stuck out his hand: "If this is going to work, I guess I'm going to have to take that other tab." George always insisted that he knew, as he placed the blot on his tongue, that he was making the right choice to drop acid that day and that he also knew he'd never do it again, which turned out to be true. On that train with Steve Jobs was the last time George Harrison would ever dose.

Now that Harrison was with Jobs on the same psychedelic astral plain, the two continued to talk about religion, music, the potential of the human mind, and the future.

> [George] "He started talking about this vision he had, that the way we were hanging out, that people in the future could do that with friends who weren't even there with them or even people they'd never even met. We were all going to have little machines in our homes, little computers, and they would wake us up, talk to us, sing to us, and make our lives wonderful and wire us all up together somehow. I never used this phrase

much, but I was quite high when he laid this on me, and all I could say was, 'far out, man.'"

Searching for a real apple, they exited the train at the next stop to find a local market where they could score a couple of pieces of fruit to eat now and a few others they could take with them to eat at the foot of the Himalayas.

While absorbed in the Zen of Apple, they missed the train they'd intended to take and instead were forced to travel by bus to Nainital, a small village surrounded by the great snowy range that forms the spine of the Himalayas. George explained that the lake was one of the Shakti Peeths, or religious sites where parts of the charred body of *Sati* fell to Earth.

While that might have been hard for the average Westerner to relate to, Steve Jobs understood immediately. Jobs loved the mythology of the place and even argued with Harrison that a thousand years from now, people would still be talking about the Beatles as legendary artists in much the same language of respect. He also said that he himself might someday be in that same historical class of legends, and he wasn't kidding.

They rented a small room with a couple of mattresses on the floor from a family who promised to help Jobs recuperate from his illness by feeding him a strict vegetarian diet. Harrison went to town to look for any news he could find from America on the fate of John Lennon.

He returned the next day with a week-old newspaper and a young Hindu holy man. When Jobs asked who the man was, Harrison said he was "karma." The man produced a bar of soap and a straight razor, which he proposed to use to shave Steve Jobs's head, a process that would, he asserted, "save his health" from his bout with dysentery. As the man went about his work, Harrison read the front-page article from the *New York Times* about the search for John Lennon.

Much had happened while Harrison was abroad. For starters, the Weather Underground had gone public in a big way, and there was definitive proof that John Lennon was alive. A photo had been released of Lennon in captivity, sitting in a kitchen chair with a white sheet hanging in the background to prevent the gathering of any clues regarding the location. Robert W. Morgan, the disc jockey in Los Angeles, had received a second "Declaration" from the radicals who had taken Lennon. The statement demanded that the Beatles donate $50 million worth of food to create and sustain "The People's Food Bank" in Chicago. Deeper into the article, the FBI was quoted as saying that the Lennon investigation was "ongoing" and "subject to resolution" at any moment. George closed the paper, folding it carefully. "They haven't a clue," he said.

All in all, it was a depressing state of events. Both Harrison and Jobs decided that the only thing they could do at that time was to meditate on the situation. If the Universe was trying to tell them something, perhaps they might be able to hear it.

> [Steve Jobs] "I started to think obsessively about John Lennon. I thought, here's this famous person, only he's disappeared and nobody can find him. But there's got to be plenty of data about what's happened to him, and it's just that we're not asking the right people the right questions. And I started to wonder if there was something that I could do to put these people together."

By the next morning, George Harrison's meditation had convinced him—or, he had convinced himself—that he needed to accept whatever version of reality was revealing itself to him. John Lennon would either live or he would die. That outcome could not be controlled. The only thing Harrison could control was his own response to whatever came to pass.

Steve Jobs, however, had come to another conclusion. He was going to create a self-sustaining network of like-minded individuals who wanted to find John Lennon. Jobs reasoned that if Lennon had gone off the grid, voluntarily or involuntarily, with radicals like the ones from the Weather Underground or the Symbionese Liberation Army, they would have to rely on a network of other radicals to hide them from law enforcement authorities. Those other radicals were already living in communes across America. Members of one commune often knew members of others.

Jobs had experience with a commune he had spent time at while attending Reed College up in Portland, a place called All One Farm, run by a man named Robert Friedland, who'd been arrested in Oregon and served time for possession of twenty-four thousand tablets of LSD valued at more than $125,000 before meeting Jobs.

The connections were too obvious, Jobs claimed, to ignore. All One Farm was a 220-acre *apple* farm. Jobs had even worked at the commune pruning Gravenstein apple trees. In fact, for a period of time, he had run the orchard the commune operated to support an organic cider business. Jobs had literally brought the neglected orchard back to life by getting a crew of monks and disciples from the Hare Krishna temple to do backbreaking work for days on end.

By then, Harrison was well versed in Jobs's fascination with apples and acid but wondered what this might have to do with finding Lennon alive before the FBI could find him and shoot him as collateral damage.

Steve Jobs explained that everything was cosmically linked. Lennon and Ono had just finished primal scream therapy with Doctor Arthur Janov, right? So had Robert Friedland, the guru behind All One Farm, and Jobs knew this because he, too, had done the therapy. He listened to "Mother," Lennon's painful song the Beatles had included on the *And the Band Plays On* album. Jobs had his own father issues, given that his Syrian father had given him up for adoption, but he maintained no interest in reconnecting with him.

Jobs would contact Friedland and through him reach out to his contacts from primal scream and All One Farm. He would ask the people he contacted to contact their own circle of friends (Jobs kept calling it a "network"), and then they would contact their circle of friends.

They would state they were looking for anonymous information only, and anyone who knew anything could call in to a phone number Apple would set up and monitor closely to make sure it was not bugged by any branch of the United States government.

Eventually, someone who knew where John Lennon was would want to help him. Anyone in Lennon's network would likely feel uncomfortable passing on information to Nixon's venal FBI. But Apple Records and the Beatles? That was something entirely different.

This "social network," said Jobs, would find John Lennon faster than any wiretap the FBI could set up. Harrison called Yoko long-distance from the British Consulate in New Delhi and told her he had met a man who had a plan to locate her husband and was returning with him immediately. With the help of the British Embassy, he and Jobs then boarded a return plane to New York to put the young man's bold plan into action.

THE RE-EDUCATION OF JOHN ONO LENNON

It was late spring, May 14, and John Lennon still had not been found. The days were getting longer and warmer, and he had now been missing sixty-two days, according to the sheet of paper tacked to the wall of a large suite in New York's Plaza Hotel.

The suite had been turned into the headquarters for the search to find John Lennon. Both Yoko Ono and Paul McCartney had desks pushed into the middle of the room, one facing the other so they could talk without getting up from their phones. Both had stopped their own lives to devote maximum effort to an intensive search, living on coffee and cigarettes and working 24/7, united in a common purpose. They felt it was a race against the clock. Only if they found John before the FBI could his safety and his life be guaranteed.

"I felt like I'd quit being a Beatle and gone to work for the coppers," said Paul, not really exaggerating.

This was a reasonable feeling, given the suite had become the hub where private investigators and former military intelligence operatives, financed by Apple and managed by Allen Klein, were at work. The leader of this group was former Marine operative Connor McNary. The entire operation—the team of retired military and police and all the Apple employees—quickly became known as "The Core," a play on both Marine Corps and Apple Corps.

"Me and my men don't really agree with John Lennon's politics, but we believe in America, and in America, we don't let people take away the freedom of our citizens without a fight," explained McNary in his job interview with Ono and McCartney. "Besides, I loved that song of his, 'Let It Be.'" Yoko and Paul shared a smile; the song was Paul's from start to finish, but neither corrected McNary, given the stakes of the moment.

Based on leaks out of law enforcement, the Core began tentatively operating on the assumption that John Lennon was somewhere in the western United States, most likely San Francisco or Los Angeles. Yet there was only supposition and wishful thinking to back up that belief.

The *Washington Post*, feeling confident and bold after their Watergate coverage looked as though it would drive Nixon from office, was about to write a major piece about the Lennon search. In it, Watergate icons Bob Woodward and Carl Bernstein would report that the FBI investigation and the Apple-sponsored search were no longer involved with one another, each ascribing the worst possible motives to the other.

In the article, an FBI spokesman outrageously claimed that the organization had not ruled out the possibility that John Lennon had participated in his own kidnapping as a political stunt. In addition to being a leader in the revolutionary left-wing movement, the logic went, he was PR conscious, having staged "Bed-Ins" for Peace; he was known to be friendly with radicals like Jerry Rubin and Abbie Hoffman; and he had performed at leftist charity concerts.

With good reason, then, Apple deeply distrusted the FBI. Their team of investigators had concluded almost immediately that the FBI had a large surveillance file on John Lennon that had been years in the making (and selectively leaked to the press from the day of his kidnapping).

Meanwhile, the FBI's famous Squad 47 had been covertly tasked with making the Lennon case its highest priority, but there was never any public confirmation, given that only a very few insiders even knew the group existed. They broke the law routinely and none of it was being reported.

This was the situation when George Harrison returned from India with Steve Jobs and showed up at the Plaza suite. He introduced the nineteen-year-old as a "living computer" who had an idea that just might work if they gave it a chance. Jobs spoke passionately about his vision.

> [Steve Jobs] "There is at least one person, and maybe a dozen, who know where John Lennon is right now, today. Your problem is you don't know how to find any of them, but I do. We have something the FBI will never have. You represent the Beatles. They represent Nixon. Who do you think people who know where John Lennon is want to talk to? We're going to set up phones right here in the second bedroom. And we're going to make sure that the entire counter-culture of this country knows that when they call us, they can be anonymous, and they're helping John, not the Man. We're going to build a social network from the ground up. We're going to find the patterns, connect the dots. And, one day soon, the answer's going to reveal itself to us. When that happens, you guys be ready to go get him."

Paul and Yoko were initially skeptical but allowed Jobs to test his theories. Once new phones were installed, Jobs recruited a half dozen friendly young people, known as the "Jobbers," to begin to make the "cold" calls. That meant calling everyone anyone knew to be living at a commune or an alternative living arrangement, chatting them up, getting more names to call from each of them, calling the new people, and getting new names. With every call, the private, confidential call-in number for Apple's effort would be given out, "just in case."

The information these Jobbers obtained was transferred to maps and boards, and day by day, what first appeared to be chaos began to very slowly take on shape and purpose.

The kidnapping story itself kept moving and morphing in unexpected ways. There was no appetite to liquidate Apple to create a $50 million fund to comply with the Weather Underground's earlier demand to create and fund a substantial food bank. Even Yoko agreed with the professionals that paying such a bribe would fail to obtain John's release but would trigger new demands. They told the Weather Underground through a public statement that they would be willing to discuss a significant increase in charitable giving from Apple but only after Lennon was home safely.

Less than two days after the food bank response, a film canister was deposited at the front desk of KMPC, again for disc jockey Morgan. He immediately called the FBI. Soon, the entire world was watching John Lennon read a prepared statement.

> [John] "The Weather Underground rejects as insufficient the response made by Apple. We condemn this capitalistic cop-out made to protect their almighty dollars. The people are going to rise up, and this is the beginning. Start the food banks now."

In the statement, Lennon had used the word "we" when referring to the Weather Underground. It became an immediate guessing game. Had John Lennon joined the group that took him? Or, as the FBI suspected, had he been with them all along? Lennon had white gauze wrapped around the little finger of his left hand. It looked like he had been hurt. Was the Weather Underground using physical force to pressure Lennon into speaking on their behalf?

Richard Starkey called in from Los Angeles with a suggestion. Apple, he thought, should ignore the specifics but donate to an existing food bank, though not at the level that the Weather Underground demanded. Everyone agreed that it would change the course of the conversation, and they made an immediate donation of $250,000 to the Chicago Food Cooperative and stated that they would match the donation when John Lennon was released safely.

Then came a wild card that neither Bernardine Dohrn nor William Ayers had expected. Because their kidnapping of the Beatle had generated such intense public interest, the East Coast chapters of the Weather Underground decided they had to act fast to make it seem to Americans that the end of the old order really was near.

The eastern Weather Underground bombed the U.S. State Department. No one was killed, but two security guards were seriously injured, and a great deal of damage was done, impacting over a dozen offices on three separate floors.

Then, once again, a film of John Lennon surfaced. He read another statement, this time supporting the bombing as a protest against Richard Nixon and the still raging Vietnam War.

> [John] "The U.S. State Department has been bombed because the government continues to wage war against Vietnam and Cambodia. The government that divides us against each other through racism also tries to divide us from the people in the world who are liberating themselves. We cannot allow the government to turn to war again, in Indochina or the Mideast, to paper over the crisis of Imperialism…"

Lennon's statement went on for over ten minutes. It was apparent to anyone who'd listened to his past interviews and news conferences, or had heard him speak at all, that these were not words he'd chosen of his own volition. When the film was studied by the Apple team, the consensus was that the Weather Underground had written the statement and compelled Lennon to read it. It was also duly noted that the little finger on his other hand was now bandaged.

With Richard Nixon on his way to a showdown in the U.S. Supreme Court over the Watergate tapes, the Administration decided to double down on Lennon, hoping that his case would provide distraction to the masses.

The United States Federal Bureau of Investigation placed John Lennon on its "Ten Most Wanted" list. In the last gasps of the Nixon Administration, the FBI suggested, again, that Lennon was not kidnapped but rather had staged his own disappearance to commit himself to revolution. This, despite all journalistic analysis that Lennon was reading someone else's words and looked as if he had been compelled to do so by physical torture of some kind.

Nixon himself appeared in the White House Briefing Room to make the case to reporters.

> [President Richard Nixon] "Today I have advised FBI Director Kelley to take the possibility of the involvement of John Lennon with the Weather Underground very seriously. Rather than being aggressive in dealing with radicals, America has become increasingly distracted by partisan politics, and this must end. Right-thinking Americans know that it is more necessary to clamp down on domestic terrorism than it is to continue this endless debate about a small-time burglary."

Trying to use John Lennon as a distraction to his own problems was a daring gambit, fraught with danger, but Nixon, by this time, had very little to lose.

Worse than being targeted by a U.S. president thrashing about in survival mode was the reality that days continued to slip by with no breaks in the case. New strategy or tactics needed to be tried.

While newspapers continued their shrill coverage, Harrison approached Ono and McCartney a second time. Jobs had another idea, he said, a good one, but it could only be implemented if Yoko agreed. It was "a bit sensitive."

"Steve wants to try something. He wants to call Linda Ronstadt and Elton John. They're both in the middle of national tours," George explained. "He wants to ask both of them to give out our number each night at their concerts. They can talk about how important it is to find John and ask the audience to help."

There it was. Was Yoko willing to reach out to the woman who had, however briefly, been the object of John's infatuation? To her unending credit, she was.

"They both have different audiences," she said. "We need to get the word out fast. She can help."

And that was that. Effective immediately, two major rock acts playing to sold-out crowds were talking about the Lennon kidnapping. Ronstadt, who, like Ono, blamed herself for throwing Lennon out of her life, took a moment in each concert to asked the audience to pray for John's safety and to call in any information they had to the Apple "Save John" hotline.

The emerging database quickly spread across each and every wall in the suite. A pattern began to appear.

• • •

John Lennon had not had it easy. He refused to read both of the written statements given to him by Dohrn. In each case, a man who referred to himself as "The Hammer" paid him a visit. Lennon had never met this man, and his real identity was never revealed to him. Using a small ballpeen hammer, the man had first broken Lennon's left little finger, and then his right, with one smartly executed smash to each knuckle.

Lennon continued to be moved among various underground safe houses throughout the West Coast, subjected to classic sleep deprivation and nonstop indoctrination. Both Dohrn and Ayers spent time with him, preaching the ideology of the Weatherman movement. They allowed Lennon to speak after three weeks of silence but only about their revolutionary issues. He acted like a good student.

At one point, he spent two weeks locked in a small toolshed in the Cascades while Dohrn and Ayers were preparing for an East Coast and West Coast summit of the Weather Underground. The man who watched over him never gave his name, either, but did want to know stories about the Beatles. It turned out that he had seen the Beatles in St. Louis when he was just fourteen years old.

Lennon obliged with insider tales. It felt good to talk, to be sure, and there was the sheer relief of being allowed to remember that he had another life waiting for him, if only he could escape to claim it. More than any of that, however, was the fact that he knew in his bones that if he could win the man over, he could escape.

When it was time to move him again, Dohrn and Ayers were practically giddy. They reported the news that Articles of Impeachment had been brought against Richard Nixon by the House Judiciary Committee. The president's attempt to use the INS to deport Lennon and the FBI to stop the Beatles from playing a protest concert outside the Republican National Convention had actually been incorporated into the case made by the House Judiciary Committee.

To their way of thinking, on the one side, there was Nixon and his corrupt establishment. On the other was Nixon's victim, John Lennon, a man who was now seen as a committed member of the Weather Underground. In their minds, the revolution was near, and from what they saw each night on TV, this one would indeed be televised.

These powerful news narratives played out in the summer of 1974. Nixon and Lennon had a quantum entanglement with each other, making for some strange bedfellows. Comedian George Carlin tried to dissect the situation in his stand-up act.

> [George Carlin] "The people who think Nixon fucked over all of us think that Lennon is getting fucked, only not by Nixon but by the people who most want to fuck over Nixon. Then the people who think Nixon is getting fucked over by, oh, I don't know, everybody else, they tend to think that Lennon is one of the guys trying to fuck him over, him being Nixon. But Lennon can't fuck over the Big Guy in Washington because he's tied up in some dark closet being fucked over by the guys who have been trying to fuck over Nixon since they were in

college. All I know is I'm missing John Lennon way more than I'm going to miss Nixon."

As far as the strangeness of bedfellows went, there was also a summit meeting between the Weather Underground and the leaders of the Symbionese Liberation Army. The SLA offered to "protect" John Lennon, but Ayers rejected their plan, believing that they simply wanted to take Lennon from them and make him their own hostage. In spring, the SLA had tried to kidnap newspaper heiress Patty Hearst, but their attempt was foiled—after the Lennon kidnapping, her parents posted round-the-clock security guards at her home in Berkeley.

The offer from the SLA, while rejected, addressed an element of true need. The Weather Underground had kept Lennon hidden through extraordinary measures and some luck. The measures could not continue forever, and luck, as it so often happened, could run out at any moment.

In the beginning, the FBI had the edge over the Apple effort. By mid-summer, however, Steve Jobs's social network program was starting to bear fruit. He attributed this to refining what he called his "search criteria." Jobs and his team of young acolytes believed that all data was powerful and that seemingly unrelated data could yield relationships and information that would break the case.

"We get lots of very specific leads, but they could be polluted by disinformation from the FBI and fans who want to feel important," he said. "We're now assigning values of one to ten for every person who calls, ten being the most reliable. Now we only follow good sources to see where they take us even if they have less specificity than others who are not reliable."

Leads were coming to the Apple command center at the Plaza Hotel. Good leads. They would be looked over by Jobs and the others, and the most promising ones were passed to the Allen Klein-directed paramilitary unit for investigation and, when the time came, action.

At a small gathering north of San Francisco, in Santa Rosa,

Dohrn and Ayers spoke to the loyal few. "If we want to keep him, we have to stop moving him," Dohrn said. "We need to find the right location, one that can be both hidden and protected, and we need to go there now."

The right location turned out to be a "safe house" in the Queen Anne district of Seattle, a neighborhood built on the town's highest hill. The Weathermen referred to the house as "The Castle." In reality, it was a Victorian home that Weatherman David Bronk had inherited from his parents after they were killed in a 1967 car crash. "We can see in all directions from here," said Ayers. "If they come at us, they'll be sorry they did."

By the time he was moved to Seattle, Lennon had been accepted by his captors, who believed he had been successfully converted to their revolutionary ideology. They couldn't be blamed for thinking so. Lennon knew that his privileges were tied to his acceptance within the group, and he knew that he could only escape after he had gained that status. He asked questions, talked like a wild revolutionary, and acted like he had learned his lesson. Now, although he was still always under guard, he was allowed to sleep on a couch and take meals with the others.

On a weekly basis, they would write a new diatribe for Lennon to read on camera. With his long hair and beard, the wild rhetoric seemed close to the old days of Bed-Ins and Peace concerts.

> [Yoko] "I would come into the office area, late at night, many nights, and watch the films of John. I could tell that he was just acting, saying whatever they want him to say, but still I took comfort to see him. It meant he was alive, and it was just a matter of time until we would find him."

On August 7, Philippe Petit crossed between the Twin Towers of the World Trade Center in New York City in the most daring act of high-wire walking the world has seen. While Yoko and Paul were as transfixed by the local TV coverage as anyone, Jobs was staring at his boards full of lists and connections. He interrupted them, barely noticing what was on the television.

"He's in Seattle. Somewhere on a hill."

Interest in Petit's crossing was abandoned immediately.

As it turned out, the fourteen-year-old Beatles fan who grew to become a member of the Weather Underground and was put in charge of watching Lennon on a few occasions had a name: Philip Michaels. Michaels simply could not keep the secret about having a personal relationship (although guard to prisoner) with a Beatle. He told a girl he was trying to impress but swore her to secrecy. She told a friend and asked for the same vow. That friend called the Apple hotline.

McNary, the leader of the Core, had his team on a plane to Washington State within two hours. For the next forty-eight hours, the Apple team quietly scouted Seattle, careful not to draw attention to themselves. There was a brief discussion about bringing in the FBI now, given that they had the upper hand. The idea was rejected. If John was going to be rescued, it was going to be by people who wanted him to come home alive.

At the same time, the nation was watching the final collapse of the Nixon Administration. On August 8, Nixon announced he would resign the next day. The media focus proved to be excellent for the Apple effort, diverting everyone's attention, including the Weathermen who were holding John.

What happened on August 9 was the greatest juxtaposition of news stories in modern history, even eclipsing the 1981 Ronald Reagan inauguration during which the Iranian hostages were released at the exact instant that Reagan took the oath of office.

Similarly, at the same time the Nixon staff packed the president's bags, a confrontation in Seattle became inevitable. The Core had located the house on the hill and had it in stakeout mode. Somehow, the FBI had gotten wind of the operation. To this day, it is believed that someone in the Apple offices had given them the information, but no one has ever been named. In any case, when federal agents showed up that night, they told McNary and his men to stand down, an order they ignored.

Soon the Seattle Police Department was on the scene. They

placed the house under a three-block quarantine. Even as people were being evacuated, it was obvious to law enforcement and civilians alike that immediate action was needed in the house itself. The FBI, the SPD, and the Core sorted out their jurisdiction under extremely heated conditions. It had to go quickly. With three square blocks in lockdown, people would talk, and the people in the zone would see what was happening on the TV news.

As this was going on, Paul McCartney, Yoko Ono, and Allen Klein were on a plane about to land in Seattle.

In the stress of the moment, the groups struck a highly unusual truce. McNary told the FBI that there was no way he would let them go it alone. The FBI told McNary there was no way they would turn over public safety to a group of vigilantes.

The compromise involved letting the Seattle police enforce the quarantine zone while the FBI maintained tactical control around the house. The FBI and the Core would each send a team of two to the house itself. The Core's team would use its two members who were retired FBI and thus familiar with strategy and tactics. Each team would need approval from the other.

While the terms were being hashed out, a couple emerged from the home in running gear and began to stretch. As they proceeded to go for a jog, an FBI car cruised behind. The moment the couple rounded the corner, they were confronted by four FBI agents leaping directly from a parked sedan. "We're the FBI!" shouted one of them.

Without a word, William Ayers raised his hands. Bernardine Dohrn, however, turned and ran, only to be confronted by two FBI agents, one with a shotgun pointed at her chest. "Fucking pigs," she said as she surrendered.

At this point, a decision was made to move on the house immediately, and the FBI team and the Core team (led by McNary) assumed their positions. The FBI took the second floor, and the Core took the ground floor.

Using hand signals, McNary and his backup, Alberto Sanchez, entered the house from the back door. In the kitchen, they came face-to-face with the house's owner, Weatherman David Bronk.

"Freeze!" ordered McNary. Bronk stopped in his tracks and was taken into custody by Sanchez.

McNary looked past Bronk and saw the back of the head of a man who was watching television coverage of Nixon's final day in office. He remembers the image on the screen being the now-famous one of ex-president Nixon waving from the steps of the Marine One helicopter.

"Freeze or I'll blow your fucking head off!" screamed McNary at the man on the couch. With his gun drawn, he moved around to confront him. He saw John Lennon, one hand handcuffed to a heavily weighted barbell, looking back at him. McNary, not knowing what shape Lennon was in, did not lower his weapon.

"You're safe now, John. I'm getting you out of here."

Lennon pushed up the black plastic-framed glasses they had given him to replace his broken wire-rimmed ones months ago.

"What took you so long?"

• • •

"Where were you on August ninth?" is still a valid question for most Americans who were alive at the time. They remember the smallest details of what they were doing when they heard the news that Richard Nixon was gone and John Lennon had been found.

Lennon was reportedly confused as he was taken from the house by McNary and Sanchez. He was not sure if he was being kidnapped again, given that the two men escorting him out wore no badges. Soon McNary and the FBI were arguing about what to do with him. The FBI was taking him into their custody for questioning, they said, come hell or high water.

Fortunately, the media had arrived by this time as well, along with Paul, Yoko, Klein, and a group of legal talent that would accompany Lennon to the Seattle FBI office.

Images were soon beamed around the world of John Lennon and Yoko Ono in a tearful and emotional embrace.

"You found me, Mama," he said to her.

Yoko, practical even then, used the close embrace to whisper into his ear: "Don't say anything to them. Only talk to lawyers."

John nodded, and after he and Yoko broke apart, he received a bracing welcome from Paul McCartney.

"Are you all right, mate?" asked Paul.

"They broke me two tiny fingers," answered John. "Might play even worse than before."

On that note, with network and local TV cameras rolling, Lennon, Ono, McCartney, Klein, the lawyers, Jobs, plus McNary and his team, and the FBI, all got into their respective cars and headed away in a procession.

One man, standing with a group in the street with his friends, was heard to call out as Lennon's car passed by: "You found your way back home, John!" Again, as had happened so often, Lennon found McCartney's lyrics quoted back to him as if they were his own.

From inside the car, Lennon flashed the peace sign at the crowd. As the images and the breaking news about Nixon's fall and Lennon's rescue spread across the nation, there were concurrent reports from coast to coast of people dancing in the streets.

FAMOUS LAST WORDS

With the world watching, the FBI chose not to arrest John Lennon, even though he was on their "Ten Most Wanted" list. Instead, they released him into a legal limbo, referring to him as a "person of interest" in multiple Weather Underground crimes, including several that happened even before his kidnapping.

Lennon never went back to Los Angeles or his home on the beach, calling them both "cursed and unlucky." Instead, he returned with Ono to New York and moved back into the Dakota, which greatly increased its security measures as a result of his kidnapping.

"John had nightmares every night," Yoko said. "We did not speak when he woke up, and I would just hold him close to me."

After a few weeks, Lennon confided in Ono that in order to survive the ordeal, he had gone inside his head and written music. He had a collection of new songs, formed from his experience, that included revisions to the newly emergent "Mind Games," "Whatever Gets You Thru the Night," "#9 Dream," and "Nobody Loves You (When You're Down and Out)."

The songs were so vivid in his memory that he sat down and recorded a demo of each in a single day. It pained him terribly to play the guitar without the use of his two little fingers, and he was not sure he had done them justice. On three of the tracks, he chose to pick them out on a piano instead.

Yoko listened attentively to all of them and felt differently. "They're beautiful. What do you want to do with them?"

This was another way of asking the big question. After six months in cruel captivity, what did John Lennon think of the Beatles?

"You're telling me that Paul moved to New York just to help you?" he asked.

"He was very worried about you. I think he loves you."

Lennon thought for a moment. "Well, since I can't play the guitar worth shit anymore, I'm going to need all of them, so what the hell?"

Yoko immediately rang up Paul, who had returned to London to "pay some bills and see some friends" and told him that John would be ready to record again after he'd had a week or so to get his head together.

"Are you sure?" he asked. "Sounds a bit on the early side, don't you think?"

Indeed, she did not think so. Yoko and Paul had worked side by side for six months. At this point, she knew him as well as her husband. They spoke directly to each other and had both come to appreciate the openness in their new relationship. "John needs this. Get everyone. Come now."

Exhausted as he was by his stay in New York City, McCartney made plans to return. There was talk of recording at the high-profile

Record Plant on 44th Street, where fans would often wait outside to catch a glimpse of their favorite artists. But the Record Plant would not do for these recording sessions, particularly after what had happened to Lennon. After some debating, the band decided to move to the boondocks of 48th Street and 9th Avenue, where a new and relatively unknown studio known as the Hit Factory was available and discreet.

Lennon had not spoken to the press due to his own reticence and the advice of his lawyers, but he did release a statement.

> [John] "Yoko and I send our love to our fans who have given me the greatest gift, the freedom of being alone together with the woman I love. It looks like all that time away has squeezed one last album out of the Beatles. I have some songs that I wrote in my own head during those days, and Paul, George, and Ringo have all agreed to come to the greatest city on Earth and help me get them out of my head and onto an album. Love, John."

With that, the four Beatles showed up at the Hit Factory and prepared to make more history. The security presence outside the recording studio was fierce.

> [Paul] "I think we all figured that John had traveled more than enough in the past year. We decided to come to him, assuming we could all get visas extended, which, after Nixon's resignation, we miraculously did. So we took our Apple to the Big Apple and got to work."

Soon enough, all four of the musicians had resolved to make their time together count. No walking out or walking away. They were determined to do the job like the professionals they were, and as a result, the work turned fun again. Linda McCartney was allowed to document the sessions in photographs, many of which showed the Beatles laughing together—in stark contrast to the glum images from earlier albums. Yoko participated, too, and contributed a vocal riff on McCartney's "Junior's Farm" that fans came to regard as a key part of the song's sound.

If McCartney had been ascendant in their previous effort *Band on the Run*, then *Last Words* was Lennon's turn, featuring his collection of deeply personal songs.

Most surprising to McCartney was Lennon's "Whatever Gets You Thru the Night." In Nigeria, during a tense moment, Paul had challenged John to "write one fucking happy song once in a while." The fact that he had done it while wondering if he would live long enough to record it was mind-blowing.

Lennon's "Mind Games," a melody he'd composed years before under the title "I Promise," now came with an entirely different meaning. During the long days and nights of silence, John had to rely on mind games to get him through the night. They had manifested themselves in song.

McCartney came to the sessions with some power rockers in the form of "Nineteen Hundred and Eighty-Five" and "Junior's Farm." He even brought "Let Me Roll It," a song that sounded like it came from Lennon, which he had written for his partner during one of the long nights of waiting in New York.

Harrison placed three songs on the album: "The Ballad of Sir Frankie Crisp," "Dark Horse," and "The King Is Dead." The lyrics were universal enough in "The King Is Dead" that it was widely interpreted to be about Elvis Presley, Richard Nixon, and the Beatles. Harrison gave one of his song positions to Lennon, not wanting to cause trouble after the ordeal of last year.

Starkey actually wrote the upbeat "Oh My My" and delivered a fine performance on a song written for him by Lennon: "(It's All Down To) Goodnight Vienna."

Last Words ends with McCartney's own final statement—the bittersweet "Picasso's Last Words," which took its title from the death of Pablo Picasso the year before and was inspired by a dinner that McCartney had with actor Dustin Hoffman during his time in New York, who challenged the composer to write a song based on any article from the most recent issue of *Time* magazine.

McCartney did, on the spot, forever earning Hoffman's admiration. In some ways, when the album first came out, this final song felt like the saddest thing ever recorded by the Beatles, and yet fans couldn't help but fall in love with it.

That Lennon let McCartney take this final studio bow has been seen by virtually all observers as a grudging acknowledgment of his lifelong partner's influence on him. It wasn't.

Lennon had gone back to work too early, clearly suffering from what we now call PTSD and had fallen into deep depression. With the songs now cleared from his head, he retreated to his apartment in the Dakota and resumed his tortured isolation.

CHAPTER EIGHT

LIVE FROM NEW YORK (1975)

SILENT RECKONING

John had briefly come back to life in the fall of 1974 to record the *Last Words* album. Yet like a man who comes out of a coma for a day, then slips back into his quiet state once his contribution had been made, Lennon faded away.

John and Yoko once again hunkered down in their now-beloved residence in the Dakota Building. John refused prescription medication, shunned marijuana and alcohol, and dismissed outright the idea of stronger drugs. "My head got scrambled and I don't need anything to cover that up," he said to his wife. "I need to do this by myself."

The world outside had become a dangerous place. Even when they went out for a small errand, the Lennons were never without security. No more did they sign autographs or interact with fans outside the building. Even when they had a car, the driver was instructed to go directly into the parking garage entrance on the back side of the building and under no circumstances drop them at the front curb where fans were known to gather.

According to Yoko, John would stand in the window, often using binoculars, watching the park and the people walking through it. She described the action as "trance-like," but it seemed to calm him down. Without questioning him, she would continue to work around the apartment and would join him at the window from time to time. After weeks of looking out over a Central Park that was now covered in snow, John spoke to Yoko when she'd come to join him.

"You realize that we could be here just enjoying the view, and suddenly men with guns could come through that door, throw me in handcuffs, and take me away?" He was speaking about the legal jeopardy the FBI had placed him in.

Yoko agreed that this could happen. "We have to work harder at enjoying the view."

"I loved that she said that," John told countless interviewers in later years. "She knew me as a man who always spoke his mind, and she knew I'd speak again, and probably too much. So she gave me my space and she gave me my moment of silence." Even now Lennon talks about this period with an uncharacteristic reserve.

For her part, Yoko never pried—she knew that John would share what he could, when he could. It took months for him to confide all his feelings, and, by his own account, he "held nothing back."

Over the Christmas holidays, Lennon had outpatient surgery at Mount Sinai to re-set his fingers. The surgery, performed by an elite team of surgeons, was considered a success. He got most of the use of his fingers back but for the rest of his life would have trouble playing certain chords with his left hand.

As he recovered at home, lost in contemplation, Yoko was as busy as ever running the new team of lawyers with the same bravado and competence that she had exhibited during the nation-wide manhunt for her husband.

> [Yoko] "It had so many moving parts, you know, all the gov-ernment agencies, investigators, Apple, press people and, of course, Paul. When John came home, everybody acted like it's all over, everybody go home. But, of course, it wasn't over. John was in just as much jeopardy, I think, after he came home as he was when he was a prisoner."

On the day that John Lennon was rescued and Richard Nixon was sent packing, Vice President Gerald Ford ascended to the office of president of the United States. He knew the country was in a terrible state, and when he addressed the nation, he told citizens that "our long national nightmare is over."

Except it was not.

As it turned out, separate federal grand juries on two sides of the continent were considering what to do about the most unlikely pair—Richard Nixon and John Lennon.

In Seattle, in the Western District of the United States District Court, grand jurors were debating whether to add John Lennon to the conspiracy counts that included the Weathermen, who had already been charged in the bombing of the U.S. State Department, in addition to other crimes.

Lennon, in speaking privately to his lawyers, was clear on the point of his innocence.

> [John] "I think people that really know me can figure it out. They had a ballpeen hammer, man, and they were going to crush my hands one finger at a time. I made it through two of them, then I said whatever they wanted. But I never had any-thing to do with any bomb. That's just madness. End of story."

Besides Lennon's predicament, now that Nixon had left office, the grand jury that had named him an unindicted co-conspirator in the Watergate crimes was considering indicting him outright, which would allow federal prosecutors to put the ex-president on trial.

Every day that President Ford entered the Oval Office during the fall of 1974, he was confronted by international problems, a failing national economy, and an electorate that had lost faith in government. The last thing he needed on his desk was a briefing about either Nixon or Lennon being on trial. As the new year began, it became more and more obvious that one (or both) of those shoes was going to drop soon.

Ford knew from close-up experience that Nixon probably deserved to be in jail, though he also believed that for Nixon, a man of enormous pride and ego, being driven from office was a huge punishment in itself.

The case of John Lennon, however, bothered him greatly. His own children were lobbying him to do something.

"Is John Lennon a petty criminal, or is he an artist whose fame, and, yes, his political opinions, placed him in a situation I'd wish on no man?" Ford asked his advisors. "Was he under such emotional duress that he started to believe he was part of this Weather Underground?"

The answer to Ford's unexpectedly astute analysis was that it was not the job of the president or the U.S. government to make that determination. The question could only be answered in court.

Ford persisted. "Are we saying that the only way I can help this man," he asked, "is to let a jury put the matter to rest one way or the other?"

To Ford, it seemed especially cruel to free Lennon after he'd endured a horrific political kidnapping where his life was in danger every day, only to put him on trial and threaten again to rob him of his freedom.

At the end of this discussion, Ford was frustrated. To get involved in Lennon's criminal case or the Beatles' immigration status would be perceived as a completely political act. This was hugely ironic, of course, because helping Lennon and the Beatles would align Ford on the side of revolutionary criminals and outside agitators. Helping Nixon would align him with the hard right wing that always felt the Watergate charges had been trumped up.

The system had created a situation that could only be solved by that same system playing itself out, a catch-22 that drove Gerald Ford mad. Management consultants had begun using the phrase "outside the box" to refer to novel or creative problem-solving, but whether the solution to this particular problem was inside or outside of the box, Ford had not yet conceived it.

Then President Ford got another briefing, shortly before Christmas. This one made it clear that because of the likely illegal FBI overreach from its COINTELPRO (Counter Intelligence

Program) activities, the Department of Justice was considering dropping charges against the Weather Underground. The DOJ cited a recent decision by the Supreme Court that barred electronic surveillance without a court order. This decision would hamper prosecution of the WUO cases and force the government to potentially reveal foreign intelligence secrets that the court has given orders to disclose.

Ford went to bed angry, his head spinning. He woke up the next day, summoned his top advisors to the Oval Office, and, after hearing all their objections to his plan, decided to go ahead anyway.

On the first day of the new year, January 1, 1975, Ford addressed the nation from the Oval Office.

> [President Gerald Ford] "The nation has unfinished business. I have been advised to ignore some of it and allow the legal system to resolve this business, but my conscience tells me that is something I cannot do. The Vietnam War will soon be firmly in the past, but not the victims of it. Richard Nixon will soon be in the history books alone and not in the newspapers. Even a young man named John Lennon waits to hear what a country he wants to embrace will finally make of him. Today, in the spirit of healing, I intend to use the powers granted me as President to write an end to these stories."

With that, President Gerald R. Ford affixed his signature to the collection of documents that had been drawn up in short order by White House lawyers. Known formally as the "Presidential Action for National Reconciliation," they came to be referred to by average Americans as "Ford's Olly Olly Income Free," referring to the phrase shouted at the end of a game of Hide and Seek when players can come out of hiding without losing the game.

The first documents pardoned all Vietnam War draft resisters, granting them full, free, and absolute amnesty for all offenses against the United States which they might have committed.

The next set of papers pardoned Richard Nixon for any crimes he might have committed while holding the presidency. Those papers became the most controversial act of Ford's presidency.

He also pardoned John Lennon for any crimes he might have committed during the period of his kidnapping by the Weather Underground in 1974. For good measure, Ford granted John Lennon and Yoko Ono permanent green card status and removed work visa obstacles that had been put in place to harass George Harrison, Paul McCartney, and Richard Starkey.

In his terse seventeen-minute speech, buttressed by affixing his signature to the legal documents, Ford settled much of the country's emotional business. There was something in it for everyone, and that may have been part of its genius.

Ford knew that no single news cycle could deal with these three stories effectively at the same time. Rooting values were scrambled, alliances revised, and across the nation, people were traveling to get home from the holidays and preparing to go back to work. One week later, even the shouts of protest over the bold action had faded.

At his children's urging, Ford invited all of the Beatles to the White House in mid-February, and all of them came. John and Paul brought their spouses, while George and Ringo showed up alone.

"I want to thank the Beatles for believing in America," said Ford before the White House press corps, "and I want them to know that America believes in the Beatles."

After the public meeting before the press, President Ford, his wife, Betty, and their children, Jack, Steven, and Susan, all retired to the Old Family Dining Room on the State Floor for an early lunch. As they were walking inside together, Betty Ford took John aside.

"Mister Lennon, I want you to know how sorry we are," she said and then hugged him. "The America I love welcomes artists like you and your friends."

Lennon caught Yoko's eye from the hug and winked. Then he smiled at Mrs. Ford. "Call me John," he said. "That way I won't feel so guilty eating all your food." He had seen the menu for the lunch that included freshly baked bread, crab soup, and lean pork chops simmered in red wine.

The lunch itself was a cordial affair, and the Ford children, to their delight, were seated amongst the Beatles. Jack, the middle son, made the White House press team panic after he admitted to the table that he smoked pot. There were no reporters in the room, and the president and the First Lady pretended not to hear.

Looking to change the subject, Jack, who knew the discography of the Beatles down to which song was on which side of which album, asked the captive audience sitting at his father's table when the next album might come out.

"We don't want to disappoint anyone," said Paul. "We named the last one *Last Words*, you know."

"Whatever you do," said President Ford with a broad smile, "don't make any announcements for a while. I don't want anyone to think I had anything to do with it."

Indeed, America had a new president, the Vietnam War was nearly over, and the feeling that the Beatles had finished their own jobs somehow seemed palpable. Although John Lennon and Paul McCartney had implied with the release of the last three albums that each would be their last together, a nearly universal recognition that *Last Words* really was the Beatles' final album was emerging.

Even so, there was something unfinished about that scenario, too. "We don't mean to be all grandiose," explained George to reporters. "It's just that shutting the studio doors and taking a taxi home seems a little anticlimactic, considering how much we've fought over all this."

THE BEATLES IN CENTRAL PARK

The good (and bad) news in all of this was that with the Beatles out of legal jeopardy and in the good graces of the U.S. government, Paramount Pictures finally decided to release *Murder on the Orient*

Express at Christmas where it opened with a bang and chugged along into 1975. The film had been produced in 1973 with an all-star cast that made the Beatles look like bit players in their own film.

Some critics felt the film's train setting was a desperate call-back to *A Hard Day's Night,* and others, including a young Roger Ebert, thought the Beatles were a distraction in their own film.

[Roger Ebert] "Having all four of the Beatles peppered about the ensemble cast is the film's greatest distraction. I felt the same way about *Stanley Kubrick Presents J.R.R. Tolkien's The Lord of the Rings Starring The Beatles,* although it was easier to embrace because they were the film there. In this vehicle (literally, the train), my mind constantly wandered to what actor would have been cast in their roles had they decided to pass on the project. Even so, *Murder on the Orient Express* provides a good time, high style, and is a loving salute to an earlier period of filmmaking."

The leading role of Hercule Poirot had gone to Paul McCartney, a piece of casting that even McCartney felt undermined the credibility of the entire film. Director Sidney Lumet favored John Lennon for the part, but given that the majority of the film was to be shot outside of the United States, Lennon was deemed an impractical choice. He instead took the part of secretary and translator Hector McQueen. All of his scenes were shot on a Hollywood sound stage, where minimal sets were re-created and actors were flown in. It is estimated that Lennon's inclusion cost the production over $200,000 in additional expenses.

Ringo, as had come to be the norm, was a standout in a part that might have ordinarily amounted to very little. He played Beddoes, the English manservant to an enigmatic American businessman. George played Hungarian diplomat Count Rudolf Andrenyi, a part that would otherwise have gone to a young Michael York.

Budgeted at just under $2 million, *Murder on the Orient Express* was a great success at the box office, earning $49 million in North America alone. Financed by EMI Films, it was the first movie completely funded by a British company to make the top of the weekly United States box office charts in *Daily Variety*.

By the time of the film's release, given Lennon's recent globally publicized ordeal, it was jarring for audiences to see him playing what had been re-written as a comic role the year before. His performance now came across as a two-hour wink at the camera.

Murder on the Orient Express threatened to keep Lennon in the Beatles just a while longer, in much of the same way *Lord of the Rings* became his reason for sticking it out back in 1970 when it was filmed, and in 1971 when it was released. It was one thing to go out on the creative artistry of *Last Words*. It was another matter entirely for *Murder on the Orient Express* to go down in history as the Beatles' conclusive artistic expression.

• • •

Even though they had managed to make it to 1975, the Beatles still had not toured together since 1966—almost a decade now.

What the Beatles had seemingly excelled at was the surprise concert venue. They had shown up at the Roundhouse in 1969 to test out their *Get Back* material and ended up making a classic live album. That same summer they had turned up at Woodstock, seemingly out of thin air. Then there was the group appearance at George's *The Concert for Bangladesh*, another one-off that made an indelible impression on fans.

Now President Ford had settled the family business, as it were, by making America a free zone for the Beatles, especially John Lennon, the group's most recalcitrant member. There were no more obstacles about locations or access. John, Paul, George, and Ringo were, more than ever before, the masters of their own destinies.

Suddenly, the unthinkable became thinkable. Paul had wanted to perform live again during the bad old days of *Get Back* and *Everest*, telling his mates, "Let's get back to square one and remember what we're all about." John said then that he was daft and vetoed the plan in no uncertain terms.

After waiting six months since John's release, and with Yoko's blessing, Paul and Linda planned a surprise visit to the Dakota. At first, John was angry, refusing to come out of his bedroom to greet them. Paul reminded him through the bedroom door of Ed McMahon's assessment that the person being showed up for would always act like it was an imposition, but the important thing was to show up anyway. It was a moot point soon enough, as Yoko invited Linda into the kitchen for tea.

At this point in their history, John and Paul had come to respect their long-standing friendship, even if they were not always friendly. The one thing that always cut through the tension between them was music, so, after a brief bickering, they broke out their guitars. John showed Paul how the surgery had given him back the ability to play most of the chords he used to play and how he'd gotten around the ones he still couldn't manage.

In the kitchen, Yoko and Linda drank tea and made dinner. Linda was in the midst of embracing a vegetarian diet and wanted to share a new recipe for a vegetable soup.

As they chopped onions, carrots, and leeks, Yoko dropped a bombshell. She had recently discovered that as early as 1973, New York City officials had funded a feasibility study for a live Beatles concert in Central Park. Everybody was ready. The Beatles only had to say yes.

"Does Paul know this?" asked Linda.

Yoko smiled. "He told me about it last week. He's talking to John now." The idea that Yoko Ono and Paul McCartney had shared a secret with each other before their own spouses was mind-blowing. Yet Yoko and Paul had stepped up to take an active role in Apple, and their relationship had been bolstered by their six months of working together when they were looking for John.

The truth was that New York City in 1975 was a city teetering on bankruptcy. Central Park, an oasis that functions as the city's "green lung," was in a state of deterioration, even though it had been designated a National Historic Landmark in 1962. Still, the city lacked the financial resources to spend the estimated $3 million that would be needed to restore the park. A Beatles concert would give the band a send-off worthy of their historical importance, would provide a chance to say goodbye to their fans, and would jump-start a much-needed campaign to raise renovation funds.

McCartney waited until Lennon had strummed a closing chord before suggesting the two smoke a joint before dinner. Even though Lennon was now drug-free, he stood with McCartney at the window, watching his friend toke while looking out over Central Park in the late afternoon light. John explained how he had spent months in near total silence, standing in this very spot looking out over the same view. When he was in captivity, he retreated inside his own head, far deeper than he had ever been before.

"I've never told anybody this, not even Yoko," he said. "I had a vision one day, looking out over the park. I saw a million people out there and a stage that was built just for the Beatles."

Paul was flabbergasted. He had all the arguments planned out in his head, ready to pitch to his challenging partner. Only now his partner was pitching to him. He ventured cautiously: "That would be bigger than Woodstock."

"Only with working toilets and good food." Lennon still had his sense of humor.

Over Linda's meal, both couples joined in discussing the possibility of a Central Park blowout concert. The one thing they knew was that if the Beatles did not take advantage of the city's openness, another group surely would. Already there was talk that a Simon & Garfunkel reunion was the backup if the Beatles said no.

"The only thing I want to hear from them is *the sound of silence*," said Lennon, working in their hit song effortlessly. "Somebody needs to go there and rock it out, and it might as well be us."

McCartney still couldn't believe what he was hearing. He had spent the better part of eight years fighting with this man about the Beatles and running into constant obstacles. His partner had never before seemed so at peace about issues involving the Beatles—or anything else, for that matter.

• • •

The Apple PR machine ran with the good-news-bad-news nature of the announcement: the Beatles really, really meant that they would never record in the studio again, but they had agreed to play one final live blowout concert in order to say goodbye to fans in a more personal way. The Michael Doret-designed posters began to show up all over New York City with a date of July 19 fixed for what promised (and threatened) to be the largest gathering of people ever assembled in New York's Central Park.

While backing musicians would achieve some of the musical effects from the Beatles' more studio-oriented songs, there would be no special guests. No Eric Clapton, no Elton John, no Badfinger or anyone of that status. Four men in their early to mid-thirties would take the stage that night—John Lennon, Paul McCartney, George Harrison, and Richard Starkey—and they would rock the house down.

Both planning and rehearsal for the concert were held secretly at Players Theater in Manhattan and took about three weeks in total. While so many other rehearsals and recordings involving the Beatles had been marred by tensions and resentments, these sessions were remarkably trouble free.

> [Ringo] "It was like getting ready for a school graduation. It's going to be a big deal and everybody's coming, but you know after it's all over, it's really all over. Everyone is going to move on with their lives. Since this is it, and you're going to remember it forever, you want it to be a good memory."

The group formed an early consensus that the concert should adhere to the same rules about equality that had guided the 1970s albums, but that was abandoned in order to concentrate on putting together the best concert possible.

"We knew we'd be playing a lot of songs that night," said George. "We knew everybody would have plenty to do. So we decided to try to make it more about the music and less about us." George was being kind. The concession was his to make, and he made it, not wanting to be seen as the spiritual Beatle who also counted songs to get his fair share.

The musical arrangements for the concert were written by George Martin. Even though other producers had been involved in Beatles material over the past few years, the band decided that, as Lennon put it, "we should dance with Georgie-boy since he brought us to the party."

• • •

The concert, billed as "Live From New York: The Beatles!," was to take place on the Great Lawn, the central open space of Central Park. The first spectators, many carrying chairs or picnic blankets, began arriving a full week before the event and were chased away by New York police every night. As a consequence, the Saturday morning of July 19 saw over hundred thousand people show up at dawn to claim a space.

Throughout the rest of the day, a huge projection screen featured a photo from the Apollo-Soyuz linkup in space that happened two days earlier, when the American and Soviet commanders exchanged a much-ballyhooed handshake as a gesture of detente between the two superpowers. The Beatles decided to make it part of their own mythology, fusing a bit of "Back in the U.S.S.R." with "Give Peace a Chance."

"I thought it was great," said Ringo, who had gotten divorced from his wife, Maureen, on the day of the handshake. "One door closing, one door opening, that kind of thing, so let's party."

As the time drew increasingly closer, everyone knew that Central Park was packed to the breaking point. No measurement of crowd size has ever pleased everyone, but computer programs in the 2000s have fixed the number, based on photos from the night, at between seven hundred thousand and nine hundred thousand.

Within that crowd, the concert was heavy on celebrities, with everyone from Bob Dylan to all of President Ford's children, and film and TV stars like Dustin Hoffman, Steven Spielberg, Jack Nicholson, Lynda Carter, John Travolta, Gabe Kaplan, Mary Tyler Moore, Robert Redford, Warren Beatty, and even Woody Allen. What everyone had in common was a profound sense of history—if this was actually the last time the Beatles would ever play together, then they would be there to see it.

At twilight, Mayor Abraham Beame was supposed to walk on stage and announce the Beatles, but a substitution was made at the last minute. The crowd was astonished when newly re-crowned heavyweight boxing champion Muhammad Ali strode onto the stage and up to the center microphone. Ali had famously met all four of the Beatles in 1964 when he was training in Miami for the fight with Sonny Liston that would make Ali heavyweight champion. Now, over a decade later, Ali had just regained his championship by defeating George Foreman in the famous "Rumble in the Jungle" and was a few months away from a third brutal fight with Joe Frazier, the "Thrilla in Manila." Ali knew that introducing the Beatles would be good publicity and opened up with a bit of poetry.

> [Muhammad Ali] "We met in '64 when boxing was just a snore. I kayoed the Big Bear when their songs were all over the air. We both go up and down, we both say what we want. The Man said I had to go to Nam, and they had to fight Uncle Sam. You ain't never gonna have another night like this, and you gonna be telling the kids about the show you could not miss."

The crowd, knowing that the time had come, let loose with an awesome roar. Allen Klein, standing backstage with all four of the Beatles, yelled to them, "You fucking earned every fucking decibel."

"At least that's what Klein claims he said," McCartney has always clarified in interviews. "None of us could hear him."

By prearrangement, Klein grabbed the backstage microphone and screamed into it. "Ladies and Gentlemen," he yelled like a ring announcer, "live from New York, it's the Beatles!"

On stage that night in Central Park, Muhammad Ali raised the arm of each Beatle, one by one, as the symbol of victory, and then left the stage. The audience was wild. Observers claim, with only a bit of hyperbole, that the ruckus could be heard in Queens.

In the electric present, the party got started with McCartney's smash hit "Band on the Run." The song was great when McCartney played his first version to everyone in Nigeria. Tonight, after everyone's input, and after being practiced repeatedly in preparation, it was tight, powerful, and fun.

After the opening song, McCartney, who had been nominated by his fellow Beatles, was supposed to be the first to speak. "I want to hear what you have to say first," said Lennon when the decision was made. "Then I'll set the record straight." He said it in jest, but it also sounded vaguely like a threat.

As a result, Paul wrote some words and committed them to memory. When he found himself looking out at this massive outdoor audience that spilled across the night landscape, he was overwhelmed. He looked over first at Lennon, Harrison, and Starkey.

"We never expected this, did we?"

McCartney pivoted back to the crowd. "We love New York City going back the first time we came here to do *The Ed Sullivan Show*, and we love that you've all stuck with us over the years, and now you've come out here tonight to do a bit of celebration with us. John's even written a rocker for you."

McCartney teed up the perfect segue to John Lennon's "New York City," a song he had written with a revolutionary slant years before, and played it this evening with a revised set of lyrics about John's love for the city as his new home.

When it was over, John peered out over the crowd, standing

packed together for as far as the eye could see. "One of the reasons we love New York City," he continued, appreciating the vast scale of what was being attempted, "is that they always do these nice little neighborhood concerts to bring the locals out."

Then came Harrison with "My Sweet Lord," a song which, if the audience wasn't already on its feet, would have gotten them there fast.

"We were afraid it was going to be all Beatlemania again," said George, unable to suppress his urge to come across as judgmental when he didn't intend to. "People were screaming so loud that we couldn't hear ourselves play, and then everybody just might as well go home. But you actually let us play."

Before launching his own song, Ringo offered his own words. "Fate put me in the Beatles," he told the audience, peering out from behind his drum set. "It's all gone too fast for me. It wasn't perfect. We all quit the band at least once. But here we are. Rock on. Peace and love."

The song chosen by Ringo, "It Don't Come Easy," was a song that he'd co-written with George. The entire group was warmed up now. Both Paul and John had spoken without incident, and they were now ready to play. This was no friendly "With a Little Help from My Friends" but instead the truth that nothing comes without struggle, not even the legendary group, the Beatles.

"Band on the Run," "New York City," "My Sweet Lord," and "It Don't Come Easy." Many critics consider this to be the strongest opening set in concert history. Not a single song in that run would have been a Beatles song if the group had actually broken up in the dog days of 1969 and 1970.

As the night continued, the Beatles played their share of cuts from across their lengthy careers as bandmates. Long before the concept of the "mash-up" became popular, the Beatles strung together bits and pieces of many of their classic songs in bold new ways, as if to fit in as many moments as possible before they left the stage.

To conclude the performance, McCartney sat at a piano by

himself and played "The Long and Winding Road," then got up, hugged his lifelong friend Lennon, and offered him the piano seat. Lennon graciously accepted, and as McCartney strapped on his bass, Lennon settled in and played "Imagine." When Lennon finished, the Beatles left the stage to thunderous applause that continued full-throttle for fourteen minutes before the entire band re-appeared and played their first of two encores, "Sgt. Pepper's Lonely Hearts Club Band," a song that gave vocals to both Lennon and McCartney. Then came the last song of the night.

At the beginning of the song, Lennon told the audience: "You know the words...let's hear 'em!" It's fair to say that everyone— including that sober segment of the crowd—was floating higher than the penthouses ringing the park. Men, women, and children smiled and clapped as they sang along, but many also sobbed. Something that they desperately wanted to stay a part of their lives was actually ending.

Because of those stakes, the Beatles' performance in Central Park was so much more than a concert. Three babies were born in the park that evening: two to mothers who could not be evacuated through the crowds, and one to a young woman who simply refused to leave, insisting there was no better place for her child to make his earthly debut. (She named the boy John-Paul.) Over two dozen fans were hospitalized from drug overdoses that night, although New York police and city officials shrugged it off as statistically inevitable with so many people gathered in one place.

A public opinion survey conducted in 1998 concluded that as many as four million Americans claimed to have actually attended the Beatles' Central Park performance, an obvious impossibility given that the highest estimates have never placed the number at more than one million people.

However many actually attended, one of them was writer/producer Lorne Michaels, who was just months away from debuting a sketch comedy series on NBC, *Saturday Night Live*. Michaels liked the way the phrase sounded when Allen Klein shouted, "Live from New York, it's the Beatles!" and adopted it for his show, which always begins with "Live from New York, it's Saturday Night!" Klein actually had Apple lawyers draft a request for royalties from NBC but never sent the document.

Another soon-to-be-famous attendee was a young rocker from New Jersey named Bruce Springsteen, who often reminds fans at his own concerts: "By the time I went home that night, I knew that something extraordinary had just happened to the world, and I was in the studio recording my feelings the very next day." Those feelings became "Twilight of the Gods," the classic Springsteen song that is distinguished by its last-minute addition to the *Born to Run* album, released just thirty-eight days after the Concert in Central Park.

"It's an elegy," explained Springsteen, "and it had to be there, even though it was unexpected and inconvenient." Mournful, melancholy, and plaintive, "Twilight of the Gods" plays as a poetic lament for the dead, even as it rejoices in the spirit they embodied.

Rockstar's Booth Hill famously chided Springsteen in his review: "The New Jersey upstart wants to bury the Beatles so he can present himself as the new incarnation of rock and roll." If that was true, then it certainly worked. Bruce Springsteen appeared on the covers of both *Newsweek* ("Making of a Rock Star") and *Time* ("Rock's New Sensation") in the same week of October 1975.

The Beatles never took any offense anyway. "Getting all over Bruce, that's rubbish," said John Lennon. "The Beatles said goodbye. That's a death like anything else, and he wrote a song about it. Like we all do when we find something that makes us stop and think. I just wish I'd written the song first."

• • •

The double concert album remains the most successful live album of all time, having continued to sell at a healthy rate every year since it was recorded, now estimated to have sold more than thirty million copies worldwide in over four decades.

The legacy of the concert can be seen every day by visitors to

Central Park. Nearly all go to view the statues of John Lennon, Paul McCartney, George Harrison, and Richard Starkey. People always pose for pictures, either hiding between the Beatles or kissing their favorites. The Beatles stand frozen in time here, not as very young men in matching suits but as grown men in their thirties, all with different tastes and styles. Yet, as the sculpture makes clear, all of their disparate parts come together as a whole, forming a group for the ages.

The plaque at the side of the sculpture memorializes the 1975 concert with these words: "The Beatles Say Goodbye in Central Park, July 19, 1975."

The soundtrack and subsequent documentary film raised $1.7 million for the Central Park restoration fund, a donation that kick-started private giving and public funding.

When it was released on April 4, 1976, the documentary film *Live from New York: The Beatles in Central Park* became a must-see piece of filmmaking, keeping company with the likes of *Woodstock*, *The Last Waltz*, the Beatles' very own *Get Back—Live at the Roundhouse*, and *The Concert for Bangladesh*, these being some of the greatest concert film documentaries of all time. As the box office totals for the goodbye to the Beatles continued to mount, the film threatened to overtake *Rocky*, eventually settling for the year's second place slot with $97 million in domestic receipts.

Live from New York was more than a simple concert film. It captured the profound sense of loss about the event but wove it into a shared hope for the future. Directed by documentarian D.A. Pennebaker, the film had everything: size, execution, and emotion. Both the Beatles and UA liked what they saw. The film gave the audience an intimate night with the band as opposed to the unnerving bickering that marked the *Get Back—Live at the Roundhouse* film.

All four Beatles actually watched the final cut together with a nervous Pennebaker. At the end, when no one spoke, Ringo stepped in: "Says a proper goodbye, if you ask me."

Live from New York: The Beatles in Central Park ends when one of the seven crews shooting film that day catches John Lennon and Paul McCartney exiting the stage into the nearby wings after the last note's been played. Harrison and Starkey have exited to the other side.

"Fucking hell, that was great," said John Lennon to his partner.

Paul McCartney's reaction was captured perfectly by the cameras. He spontaneously grabbed Lennon by the arm and dragged him out to the stage area to make one final wave. Just the two of them.

• • •

"Beatles Let It Be"

"At the End of the Long and Winding Road".

"They Don't Believe in Beatles"

Headline writers had a field day describing the creative triumph of the Central Park Concert. In reality, most journalists who thought about the career arc of the Beatles still didn't believe it was really over.

"We gave them a slow dissolve," said Ringo, using the lingo of his new passion, filmmaking. "It could have been a hard cut in 1969, but we coaxed another five years or so out of it all. Let's just leave it at that for now. Peace and love, fan-people."

It had been an eventful time to be sure, one which placed the Beatles squarely in the middle of the political turmoil of the late '60s and early '70s, giving them so much more to feel and experience and write about.

Still, after the concert, they were a spent force. The energy required to keep the group together and to keep their old friendships current was simply not there. All members of the band needed to find new lives and live them as hard as they could. They would stay in touch, but they were men looking to the future.

George summed up the feelings they all had by that point: "We all need to get busy not being Beatles."

John, Paul, George, and Ringo all seemed to shed their Beatles personas almost instantly and fully retreat into their own private lives.

Lennon and Ono began packing up the Dakota apartment, despite the public display of love for New York shown just that summer in Central Park. Sean Ono Lennon was born on John's own birthday, October 9. Less than a month later, the Lennons moved their new family to London, wanting to get out of the American limelight. *"People ring me up now and say, 'John, you're so hard to find,'"* he wrote Harry Nilsson in a postcard. *"And I tell them not hard enough, 'You just found me.'"*

After a short vacation, Paul started to audition musicians to be a part of a group that he named Wings. His ultimate goal was to do the one thing the Beatles had kept from him for a decade now—go on tour. "It's not meant to be the end of the Beatles," he insisted to rock journalists. "If the 'Big Band' comes calling again, I'll still be able to play the chords."

The day after the concert, Ringo was on a plane to New Mexico to join the production of the science fiction film *The Man Who Fell to Earth* starring fellow musician David Bowie. Ringo played the role of patent attorney Oliver Farnsworth, a part given to him after the Central Park Concert buzz at the expense of actor Buck Henry, and a part that had certain similarities to his gadget enthusiast "Q" persona in the Bond franchise. "I don't mind being typecast," he said. "So long as I always get to play myself."

George also couldn't wait to leave New York and immediately retreated to Friar Park, intending to spend the fall gardening. He had become fast friends with Monty Python troupe member Eric Idle, and the two began to hatch plans to make a series of comedy films together. Soon George had fallen for Apple assistant Olivia Trinidad, and there was talk of marriage.

Throughout all of this, the fans still debated the likelihood of a reunion, as well as the relative strength of the 1960s albums versus the 1970s albums versus the potential of new solo albums. They knew that there was one more Beatles album to hope for. Since *Everest* and then *And the Band Plays On*, it had been the continual game. Would this current album be the last? Would there ever be another one? There always was. Hope was alive with the Beatles.

• • •

As the 1970s came to a close, no one could deny that the Beatles, actively playing together or not, were now presiding over an Apple that was one of the most profitable companies in the entire world of music. Rather than closing down the shop at the turn of the previous decade, Apple had reinvented itself, growing from a counter-culture experiment to an active media company. Its recording artists were no longer limited to the Beatles and included other names like Peter Frampton and Blondie.

The changes went all the way to the top. Lord Beeching, Allen Klein, and Lee Eastman were all gone from day-to-day responsibilities after Apple poached Atlantic executive Jerry L. Greenberg to run the company in 1977. He referred to the Beatles as "The Founders" and dedicated himself to working tirelessly to make it clear to artists, distributors, and fans that Apple was far more than a vehicle for the most classic rock band of all time.

> [Jerry Greenberg] "Apple has survived the loss of its greatest act, the Beatles. We have done it by becoming a full-service company that can stand head-to-head with Atlantic, Decca, Warner, EMI, Capitol, you name it. The Founders of this company were and are great visionaries. We do not see Apple only as a recording label. We see Apple as the gateway to the future. Whatever happens in the media, today or tomorrow, we intend to be a part of it."

Laboring away in the newly created offshoot department of Apple Computers was Steve Jobs. Having learned its lesson with Magic Alex, Apple management had Jobs draw up specific goals and stick to them. Each benchmark brought new funding for Jobs's division, which was making fast progress in the world of personal computing, and he was happy to lay out his plan.

> [Steve Jobs] "Music will be a cornerstone of the personal computing experience in the future. Because of new technology that will be transforming the world, selling vinyl records will soon be part of the past, but the Beatles never will be. My goal with the Apple Computer division is to create the digital vehicle that will deepen the user experience. There are so many ways that the Beatles should be a part of that."

• • •

At Christmas 1978, John Lennon called Paul McCartney from Tittenhurst Park in London with what Paul assumed would be the obligatory holiday greeting. He got more than he bargained for. "Yoko and I have been talking about something," said John.

Paul prepared for the worst, expecting John's analysis of the state of their long-delayed freedom. "I heard you were going to take the Wing-Dings on a U.S. tour," John continued.

McCartney confirmed that this was true. Wings—as the band actually called itself—was scheduled to rehearse next month and go on tour the next spring. "You'll have to come and hear us," he told John. "Sit in, if you want."

"What if the Beatles wanted to take those dates instead? Are you locked in with these other guys?" asked John.

"Are you saying you'd go on tour with the Beatles?" responded Paul, not sure if he was hearing this correctly.

"Are you going to say 'I told you so' and act like Sir Paul?"

"No, I can hold off on that, I suppose." Still, McCartney wanted to know if John thought they would be attacked as hypocrites for changing their minds.

"I've not changed my mind, but I can't bake any more bread here, and me and Yoko, we think Sean needs to grow up in

America." Lennon was more worried about George Harrison than irritated fans. "We'll have to talk to George. You know how he can be, but I think Richie would be on board right away."

McCartney could have been knocked over with a feather, hearing John Lennon tell him he wanted to try touring again. He was not, however, about to let his partner know that right away. "Let me think about it," he said.

Ringo was in immediately, as predicted, while George took a week of daily gardening to center his mind and then emerged with his terms: there would be no more than a month of rehearsal and no more than three months of being on the road.

They had not toured since 1966 as a group, focusing instead on the single appearances culminating in Central Park, and so decided to give the tour a name befitting of their history: "The Beatles Encore." The biggest difference from their tours in the '60s was that now they would not travel as four young men sharing hotel suites. Those days were over.

"Yoko says Sean can travel by the spring," said John.

"Linda and I will probably drag along Heather, Mary, and Stella," added Paul. "Where we go, they go."

"You can both do what you want," said Ringo, "but I'm not sharing a room with George just because you're bringing all those mouths to feed and spending all the profits."

As it turned out, the 1979 *Encore* tour turned into a family affair. The Lennons and the McCartneys traveled as units, and Lennon even invited his now teenaged son Julian to join in for a month when he was out of school. Ringo brought along his girlfriend, Nancy Andrews, for most of the tour, and his three children, Zak, Jason, and Lee, all under ten years old. George and Olivia traveled together and, a month into the tour, got married in front of his fellow Beatles, the spouses, loads of children, and the entire crew.

The Beatles had turned a corner. The band no longer needed to stay together to avoid catastrophic financial loss for Apple Records, the company the Beatles had founded. Over the past few years, the now mature men, and the women who loved them, had been through so much, not much of which had been easy. Now the Beatles were a group that existed because John, Paul, George, and Ringo had realized something profound.

They really had taken a sad song and made it better.

AND IN THE END

During the final days of the classic 2013–2014 "History of the Beatles" tour, John Lennon, Paul McCartney, Richard Starkey, and Eric Clapton sat down with *Rockstar's* founder Booth Hill for an interview that was tied to the fiftieth anniversary of the appearance of the Beatles on *The Ed Sullivan Show.*

The interview took place over January 9–11, 2014, in Chicago, Illinois, and spanned over six hours of conversation. That interview is excerpted here. To note, this is not a complete transcript.

• • •

BOOTH HILL: Did you ever imagine that the Beatles could make it as a band that has lasted over five decades?

JOHN: We didn't make it that long. George died on us. (To Clapton) No offense. (To Hill) We started as the Silver Beatles. We became the Beatles. I suppose now we're the Golden Beatles.

BOOTH HILL: But are you surprised?

JOHN: No one's more surprised than I am that the Beatles made it. Maybe Yoko.

BOOTH HILL: You brought up George. Should we talk about him? He's been gone twelve years.

PAUL: Love to George.

JOHN: Love to George.

RINGO: Peace and love to George.

ERIC: I remember George asking me to come over when he knew his time was running out. He told me that "spiritual wisdom means not wasting the gifts of the Universe, even if it's the three of them." He loved them back.

JOHN: We were going to hang it up, again, but maybe then for real. We'd already gone three decades more than anybody thought we would.

PAUL: Even then, that would have been complicated. Contracts, taxes, families, fans, and such.

JOHN: You've been saying that since 1969.

PAUL: But it's always been true, Johnny.

JOHN: You see how he can be such a right bastard?

PAUL: It's hard to live up to your high standards of civility. (To Hill) He's a paragon, he is.

JOHN: George is gone, but the truth of the matter is that what we're all doing is cascading toward death from the moment we're born.

RINGO: Cheerful.

JOHN: It's undeniable. You can try to trick it up by acting young and crazy or you can do the old nip-and-tuck and try not to show the truth, mostly to yourself. Everybody gets confronted by the certainty that portions of our life are in the rearview mirror and we can't really get them back even if we wanted to. It's the old existential crisis—and it's just natural. It happened to George. It'll happen to me. And it'll happen to all of you.

BOOTH HILL: Let's talk the "Freedom" tour you did after George passed. That was 2002.

RINGO: The Stones hadn't played for three years. Georgie knew if we could get back out there, we might be the longest playing rock and roll act in history. He wanted that for us.

PAUL: There he was, so weak, and he motions us to lean in close, like he's got this big, important thing to say. He says, "After all the three of you have done to kill the group, it's not fair if you blame it all on me just because I have cancer."

BOOTH HILL: Funny, in a dark way.

JOHN: That was George. He wanted us to man up. Eric was his idea.

ERIC: I didn't want to do it. I mean, who would? Under those circumstances?

BOOTH HILL: What made you do it then?

ERIC: I had to. If these guys wanted me to do it for George, that was that.

JOHN: Eric made me bloody say it. "You have to say it, John." So I said, "Yeah, okay, let's do it." He said, "No. You have to say it. 'Yes, Eric, I want you to do it.'" I'm just glad he didn't make me get on my knees for him.

BOOTH HILL: So you did the tour, and then the Stones came out of retirement a year later to take the record back. Since then both bands have stayed at it, refusing to quit.

RINGO: Fucking juvenile, isn't it? (Laughs)

JOHN: It was like we were both daring the other to retire first. Neither band would back down.

BOOTH HILL: Mick Jagger said, "We're just playing chicken. We finish a tour and say 'never again' and then the boys do another one and we can't let that stand and so out we go again."

RINGO: If they would just quit, we promise to quit, too. Lay down your arms, gents, and let's give peace a chance.

BOOTH HILL: What's the process for keeping the band together?

PAUL: Play, quit, repeat. That's been the secret.

RINGO: Just when you thought we might never play again, we did. Then one or even a few of us would say something bitchy about the others in the papers, offense would be taken, people would speculate, and the cycle would repeat.

BOOTH HILL: That sounds a bit like the Eagles.

PAUL: Maybe.

JOHN: They're still playing together? Didn't know that. What a fucking shame.

RINGO: We all quit. We just never all quit for good at the same time.

BOOTH HILL: Your concert tours have always been sold-out affairs with fans that span generations. How do you explain that, even today?

JOHN: All the Baby Boomers got old at the same time we did. Then they dragged Timmy and Suzy to our concerts.

PAUL: There's no age limit on being ready to rock.

ERIC: They're just being modest. The truth is, the question has never been what to put in but what to leave out. These two men, plus George and Ringo, have kept up a steady stream of material, and they've always adapted to the times and experimented with the form. Even their classics have been reinvented. On this tour, we have a centerpiece section with Paul and John on acoustic guitars playing these beautifully re-worked versions of the early material, like "I Want to Hold Your Hand" and "I Saw Her Standing There" and "Please Please Me."

PAUL: We wanted Eric to get his own stool, but he wouldn't do it.

ERIC: That wouldn't have been right.

RINGO: They got that from you, Clapper. You turned your "Layla" into a completely different song and in that first tour after George's death, you did the same with "While My Guitar Gently Weeps."

ERIC: Just for the record, that was a tribute to George, not because I thought I could do it better. They'll be playing it George's way forever.

BOOTH HILL: Let's talk about the current tour, "The History of the Beatles."

JOHN: I hate that name. Sounds so fucking pretentious.

BOOTH HILL: Then why'd you do it?

PAUL: It was a part of a grand scheme for Apple. It gave them a tour identity, and gave us a creative chance to look into all the corners of our catalog, and everybody got a new compilation, maybe even a documentary film.

RINGO: Right. Because we've never done any of those before.

ERIC: I was excited to do it. I was not on that journey from the Cavern Club to being global artists. I mean, the Beatles brand is rivaled only by Coca-Cola and Muhammad Ali.

PAUL: Eric had the detachment we needed to sort out the old wheat from the chaff, as it were.

RINGO: Chaff. Anybody here know what that actually is?

JOHN: It's the part of the grain that gets thrown away. I read that on my little Kindle.

RINGO: Aren't you the wise man? I stand corrected, I do.

JOHN: We've had our share of chaff. Right, Eric?

PAUL: Now, John, don't go putting Eric on the spot.

ERIC: I wasn't a fan of "Honey Pie" and I never cared for "Cold Turkey." But I chaffed up my share before I joined the boys.

BOOTH HILL: Let's move on then.

RINGO: Dear God, yes.

BOOTH HILL: The tour started July 6, 2013, in Louisville, Kentucky, and when it's done will conclude in Liverpool, England, next month. Will this be your last tour?

JOHN: Depends.

BOOTH HILL: On what?

PAUL: The Stones are playing that same night in Rio as we are in Liverpool and have said they're wrapping up, too. We've both agreed to declare a truce in the tour war, and put the Beatles and the Stones in the history books together.

JOHN: It's all lovey-dovey now. But that Jagger, he's a sneaky one. We've got to keep our eyes on him, Paul.

BOOTH HILL: I want to read you a section of a review from our music critic Coleman Birdwell at *Rockstar*. "The Beatles never liked open-air stadiums but as they aged and so did their audience, the reasons for the breakup between rock group and fans in large venues largely disappeared. The fans agreed to let them play and be heard, and the Beatles agreed to show up in a handful of stadiums as part of any tour." Thoughts?

PAUL: Guilty.

RINGO: Fish and fowl. In the smaller venues, people can actually see the twinkle in our eyes, but in those stadium gigs, folks just have to take our word for it.

JOHN: We're just a bunch of twinklers at heart.

ERIC: I just leave the twinkling up to them.

PAUL: Back in '66, we stopped playing these big shows because it was just madness. But once our fans got too long in the tooth to scream every second, we gave it another shot. The demand for tickets is so strong that we just do it. Why not?

BOOTH HILL: Because you were famously opposed to touring?

JOHN: I changed my mind. I realized that I wanted to get out there and play for people, like a proper rock and roller. Then I thought, do I want to do that with a new band when I can do it with the Beatles?

BOOTH HILL: By my count, last night you did three distinct sets and two encores for a total of twenty-seven songs. That's quite a work ethic.

JOHN: All for you, my lovely.

PAUL: If this is the last tour, we want everyone to get their money's worth.

RINGO: Look, it's been fifty years for fans and more for us. If this is goodbye, then we have to do it as right as we can.

BOOTH HILL: The last album was your double LP, *The Road Taken*, another tour album. Is there any part of this that has to do with not wanting to come up with original material?

PAUL: We may do another studio album.

JOHN: Or we might not.

RINGO: What they said.

BOOTH HILL: By my count, you have broken up and re-grouped five distinct times.

JOHN: That many? Really?

BOOTH HILL: After the Concert in Central Park in 1975, but then you got back together in 1981, 1992, 2002, and now.

PAUL: Not to get technical, but we never actually said we were broken up after the first time.

BOOTH HILL: But you stopped playing together for years at a time in between.

JOHN: Mental hiatus.

BOOTH HILL: What are your favorite songs that have been done since the 1975 breakup?

JOHN: Is this a trick question? We can't include anything done before Central Park?

BOOTH HILL: Well, if you want…

JOHN: "Instant Karma!," "Blasted (By the Light)," "Enemies List."

PAUL: "Show Up," "Band on the Run," "Maybe I'm Amazed." Post-Central Park, probably "Beautiful Night."

JOHN: Thank you, thank you, thank you.

PAUL: For what?

JOHN: For not including "Silly Love Songs" or "With a Little Luck."

PAUL: Right. (To Hill) Those too.

RINGO: I like everything they did, and Georgie, too. From the ones I performed, though…"Photograph," "Uncle Albert," "It Don't Come Easy."

BOOTH HILL: John, you had two very strong turns last night with "Instant Karma!" from the *And the Band Played On* album and "Imagine" from *Imagine Another Day*. But in your introduction—

JOHN: —I know. I said, "God knows what album this is on." It's not Alzheimer's. We've recorded 453 songs more or less together and 21 studio albums. You try remembering them all.

ERIC: It's an insanely deep catalog. I only know how to play about a third of them.

RINGO: Me, too.

BOOTH HILL: Back to that review. "What Lennon still can't quite bring himself to do is ask the crowd 'How're you doing tonight?' and sound like he means it—his words sound like they've been marinated in irony, suggesting that there is a corner of Lennon's soul that was never touched by show biz."

JOHN: Everyone knows when I say things like that that it's not really me saying it. So what's the point? Last night, when we put in "Eight Days a Week" because of some fan poll, they wanted me to say we didn't know the results until they appeared on screen. I just couldn't.

BOOTH HILL: You tried. You said, "It's a surprise for us," but you added, "If you believe that…"

RINGO: Next time, I'll do it. Everyone knows I don't mean what I say.

BOOTH HILL: Paul, you were described as the "gracious host." The review went on to say "McCartney has utter commitment to his job: he clearly works the stage more than his bandmates, like he's doing wind sprints to qualify for an Olympic squad."

JOHN: I think they confused him with Jagger again.

RINGO: I can't work the stage because I'm behind my drum kit and they won't let me out. Now that George is gone, I'm the quiet Beatle.

PAUL: Everybody in the Beatles has their own part to play. If John wanted to get up and jump around more, I'd let him.

BOOTH HILL: Why don't you, John?

JOHN: I'm enjoying the view of Paul doing it.

BOOTH HILL: Eric, the review said you were "lighter and brighter" than your persona when you first took over for George Harrison.

ERIC: At first, I never spoke because I didn't want to invite any comparison. After a while, I've been accepted by the fans. They know that George is gone and if I could bring him back that I'd do it and be on my way. So I talk a little more and that makes me brighter. It's all relative.

BOOTH HILL: And Ringo, the review further said, "Drummer Ringo Starr was indispensable, as always. If McCartney is the people pleaser, Clapton the consummate professional, and Lennon the compelling artist, it is Starr who is the life of the party. His smile, as much as his blistering drums, tells everyone that there is a party going on." Is that how you see yourself? The life of the party?

RINGO: The fans see me that way. It goes back to the bad old days when I was pretty heavily into the whole drinking scene. Now I'm sober, so it's an act. I'm the Dean Martin of rock and roll. Sorry, kids, old reference. I'm really the Chris Martin of rock and roll.

BOOTH HILL: John, I know we said we weren't going to talk about 1974, but can we talk about how it changed or affected the idea of the Beatles as a group?

JOHN: The Beatles nearly met their Maker a few times, but this was worse. I'm the one who goes over the security plans at the concerts now.

BOOTH HILL: You used to say you loved New York because you could go anywhere and people would just leave you alone.

JOHN: We came back to America in '80, I think it was. But we never took chances when we got back into the Dakota. None of that stopping to sign autographs outside, that kind of thing. You know they arrested somebody with a gun outside the Dakota, waiting for me to sign an album or something, I think it was December that year. It only takes one asshole. If this is what you want to talk about now, then I'm done.

BOOTH HILL: Understood. Let's talk about Apple. Over the years, you've turned Apple Media into a top ten company in the Fortune 500. How do you explain that?

PAUL: Steve Jobs was a genius. The best discovery George ever made besides "Here Comes the Sun." He's been gone almost five years now.

JOHN: Love to Steve.

RINGO: Peace and love to Steve.

PAUL: Love to Steve. He had a vision.

JOHN: Christ, we're back to 1974 again. Steve Jobs made it possible for Paul and Yoko to find me. Then he created personal computing. He changed music. He made me a billion dollars.

PAUL: The truth is that the Apple that the Beatles created in 1968 was all about taxes. We turned it into a counter-culture thing, and that was a disaster. Had we broken up in 1970, it would be a distant memory, I suppose. The Beatles stayed together and we stumbled across Steve Jobs. That made all the difference.

RINGO: Amen to that.

BOOTH HILL: You're all quite fun together and I know that has been a source of your popularity going back to even before you came to America in 1964. I want to ask a final question now, and I'd like your answers to be as honest as you can make them.

JOHN: No pressure there.

BOOTH HILL: The question is as simple as I can make it and as complicated as your answers may be. What do you think explains the group's longevity more than anything else?

ERIC: Let me talk for a moment so they can get their own thoughts together. I'm not a Beatle in any way that allows me to answer that question. As a fan, I always go back to the music. But I know what George said to me. He said that they managed to stay together only because they loosened up the reins on the group and let them all express themselves as individuals. Once he knew they could all do this, he found it easier to see the benefits of working with these incredible musicians because they were also his incredible friends. With that, I'm leaving because I have a date with my wife.

JOHN: What are you doing on this date, Eric?

ERIC: Eating.

JOHN: Just checking.

BOOTH HILL: Okay, all right then. It's down to the three of you, the surviving original Beatles. Ringo, can we start with you?

RINGO: If I'm being completely honest which, as I've said, is not exactly my thing in interviews, the Beatles remained together because these two gentlemen sitting with me decided that we could. That's it. Period. But the biggest danger was in, I guess it was 1969 or 1970, and I think you'd almost have to credit the *Lord of the Rings* movie. We had to pull together to make it. Then we had to shut up to publicize it. That gave us enough time to work out some of the other details. I guess, finally, it's because we had no other visible skills besides being Beatles, so that was our only option.

PAUL: Even though it was John's group, I mean, he started it, I guess I always loved it more than John. I never wanted to give it up. For me, I always go back to when the two of us went to the U.S. in 1968 and did *The Tonight Show*. It could have gone bad, it almost did, but instead when John got stubborn and demanded Johnny Carson had to be there, out of that chaos it turned into magic. That's where big old square Ed told me that the secret was to show up for each other. I thought it was probably just silly happy talk but told myself I'd give it a try. I went to Scotland for John and Yoko's car crash and I think he appreciated it. (To Lennon) Did you? I guess I've never really asked.

JOHN: Don't make me get all weepy and everything, Paul. But, all right, I was happy to see you because I was on painkillers. And I guess we wouldn't have done Woodstock if you hadn't made the scene.

PAUL: Then we each went to each other's weddings. (To Lennon) You showed up and I didn't think you would.

JOHN: I didn't think I would.

PAUL: So I threw the caution to the wind and showed up at yours.

BOOTH HILL: Which reminds me…John, in some of your more impassioned interviews, you said that Paul and Linda just followed what you and Yoko did and did it later themselves.

JOHN: Did we say that?

BOOTH HILL: Often. But Linda and Paul got married, and then you and Yoko got married a week later.

JOHN: That's how it seemed to me. Maybe I wasn't in my right mind. Or maybe I was then and I'm not now. It's impossible to say.

BOOTH HILL: You wrote a song together about showing up.

PAUL: That's mostly John's song.

JOHN: Don't say that. Everyone will think I was an old softie. Paul put some sugar on it, and that's why it works, I think.

BOOTH HILL: So, Paul, showing up. That's it?

PAUL: No, no, no. A thousand other tiny things. But going back to Linda and Yoko. I think that gets overlooked. Both of them were very strong women…

RINGO: Peace and love to Linda.

JOHN: Love to Linda.

PAUL: So both of the ladies were outsiders to the Beatles. I resented Yoko first and John resented Linda later. And, if they wanted to, they could have torn us apart because we were so into them. We put them above the group. I don't remember now how it happened, but they both decided together to not be threatened by the Beatles and to let the Beatles be. Then the Beatles were free to let them into our world a bit more. The same was true for Richie's women and George's, but their situations were more complicated.

RINGO: Like all the divorces maybe?

PAUL: Not to slag anyone off, but I suppose the Grand Bargain laid out the road map for staying together.

JOHN: My head was very anti-Beatles for a few years. But that didn't mean I was anti-Apple. So when Beeching got on his soapbox, I didn't think he was crazy. I didn't want to tour, but the idea of one album a year seemed practical. It doesn't take a year to make an album, especially when you don't have to write it all yourself, so that left each of us with enough time for a private life.

BOOTH HILL: You mentioned Lord Beeching. What part did the management compromise play?

JOHN: Paul wanted his father-in-law which, sorry, Paul, seemed like something only a selfish prick would want. But then I wanted Allen Klein, who was a selfish prick himself, and so was I.

PAUL: If we'd stuck to those positions, there would have been no way out. The Beatles would have been finished.

RINGO: I never liked any of them. I liked the fact that Klein wasn't related to Paul—that was his big strength. Beeching was the tie-breaker.

PAUL: We figured if he could fix Britain's railroads then he could fix the Beatles.

JOHN: Except he never really fixed the railroads. But he was so square, the way he talked, the way he looked, you just figured that he must know something about money, since he would never have gotten where he did on looks.

BOOTH HILL: The argument still gets made that if the Beatles had split in 1970 that they would have gotten out at the top of their game and would be a mythical rock story today. By playing on, that theory goes, the Beatles were revealed to be merely human.

JOHN: But we are human, aren't we? That's just the truth. We didn't want to hide it, or make something of it that it wasn't. We were, we still are, just a rock and roll band, although we're a good one, better than most.

PAUL: If that had happened, that we broke up at the end of the '60s, we would have lived over four decades as a myth. That's not living. Living is living. This is better.

BOOTH HILL: What role has friendship played?

RINGO: Who said we were friends? (Laughter)

THE SOURCES OF SPECULATION

Alternative history is about what *might* have happened. So, yes, this book is full of speculation.

In what follows, the goal is to explain the moments of Beatles trivia that you may not be aware of that are included in the book and to discuss the plausibility of the larger story points.

ALBUM TITLES

Album titles changed frequently under the Beatles, and the narrative uses this fact to give a sense that the alternate history in this book unfolds not just after they broke up, but before as well. In three distinct cases, the working titles of the real timeline became the actual titles in my alternative story.

The White Album began as *A Doll's House*.

Abbey Road began as *Everest*.

Let It Be began as *Get Back*.

In other cases, the assumption has been that certain titles and songs created in our actual reality might have been adapted into a universe where the Beatles stayed together. That explains *Band on the Run* as an eventual Beatles title in both the real and the imagined universes.

SONGS AND SOLO ALBUMS

It is impossible to assemble consensus albums constructed out of the Beatles' solo albums we're familiar with as well as songs that never were from our alternate world. This book takes a crack at it in service of the larger storyline, but the permutations have almost infinite interpretations by fans. Readers won't agree with all of the choices here, nor should they.

The subject of what songs might have appeared on solo albums put out by individual Beatles in a world where the group itself stayed together is a valid one. This book simply avoids it to spend more time and space on the characters and their lives as members of the Beatles and because even fewer people would agree on these choices than they would about potential songs on the Beatles albums. Please assume that significant solo work was recorded even in this alternative timeline as is alluded to multiple times throughout the book.

THE LORD OF THE RINGS

The actual truth of the matter is that, yes, there was talk in Hollywood about having the Beatles star in a *The Lord of the Rings* movie that could be directed by Stanley Kubrick. Additionally, it was John Lennon who first seemed to have become attached to the idea.

There are multiple sources for this. The greatest is Paul McCartney himself, who has confirmed it as fact on several occasions, going back to a conversation with Peter Jackson in 2002, when Jackson's film version was first being talked about.

There is also a reference to the film in Steven Bach's *Final Cut: Art, Money, and Ego in the Making of Heaven's Gate, the Film that Sank United Artists*

THE *TONIGHT SHOW* APPEARANCE

John Lennon and Paul McCartney actually did go to New York, as described in this novel, to promote their new company, Apple Records. They did appear on *The Tonight Show Starring Johnny Carson* but were subjected to the cluelessness of guest host Joe Garagiola, magnified by the probable alcohol-inspired abusiveness of Tallulah Bankhead. Bottom line, it was not a fun night. The change in this alternate history is Johnny's coming back to the city to do the special show and demanding as his condition that the Beatles play a song or two. This could easily have happened.

Johnny Carson and Ed McMahon did, in fact, often retreat to Danny's Hideaway for drinks after recording their show. The advice of McMahon to McCartney about "showing up" is purely my invention in the service of the book's narrative.

HELLS ANGELS

Crazy as it seems, George Harrison honestly did invite the Hells Angels to come visit Apple at Christmastime. They came, as described, accompanied by both the Pleasure Crew and Ken Kesey.

Harrison wasn't even in London when they showed up, leaving the hosting duties to his bandmates. John and Yoko had the most direct and potentially dangerous confrontation with them. The Lennons had shown up dressed as Father and Mother Christmas for the holiday party and ended up on the receiving end of a Hells Angels rampage over not being served turkey when they wanted it.

In the real life of our history's timeline, the Angels, the Pleasure Crew, and Kesey all stayed through the holidays and into the New Year, trashing the Apple offices as only they could. It was up to Harrison, when he returned from his own vacation to New York, to tell them it was time to leave. They wanted to know if George didn't like them. "Yin and Yang, yes and no," was his answer. They accepted and moved on.

Getting the *Magical Mystery Tour* bus out of mothballs and

using it to lure the Hells Angels out of Apple is a creative invention, nothing more.

PLAYING AT WOODSTOCK

The Beatles were certainly invited to play at Woodstock. That seems to be an established fact, but not much else beyond it has been. There have been three theories about this:

The first is that John could not get a visa to come to the U.S. because of his drug arrests. This seems more than possible, given the trouble he encountered when he did move here later.

Secondly, other than their rooftop concert in January 1969, the Beatles had not played a show together since 1966. They might have been intimidated.

The final theory is that John Lennon did agree to play only if Yoko was allowed on the same stage with the Beatles and the Plastic Ono Band also got an invite. It doesn't appear that such an invitation was made, and it seems unlikely the Beatles would have welcomed this attachment.

For his part, Ringo has claimed that none of these theories hold water. He says that the Beatles didn't go to Woodstock because they were "busy doing other things." He makes the point that it was hardly like they had a plane standing by.

There may be another possibility. During the research phase for any book or film project that is based on historical facts, it can be instructive to look at the timeline to see the relationships between news and professional and personal events. In reality, John and Yoko had their car accident just a couple of weeks before Woodstock. They were shook up and, again, not likely in the mood for Woodstock.

Could Paul McCartney, by showing up at the hospital and helping out, have changed that mood? That's why they call this work alternate history.

NIXON'S HARASSMENT

There are mountains of emerging information about this topic, based on released documents from the FBI. John Lennon and Yoko Ono spoke often about the reality of their harassment by the agency. Finally, all aspects of their INS immigration action are now on the table.

Books have been written and documentaries filmed about the unsavory focus of the Nixon Administration on John Lennon. If the Beatles were still a force, they would likely have been tarred by the same brush.

The Nixon Administration had indeed created an "enemies list," and John Lennon was on at least one version of it. Our alternate history only adds the names of Paul McCartney, George Harrison, and Richard Starkey because they, too, would almost certainly have been included had the Beatles continued as a musical force during those dark days.

In real life, George Harrison actually did go to the White House when Gerald Ford assumed the presidency after Nixon's resignation. If the Beatles had still been recording, it would have been a group invitation.

RECORDING IN NIGERIA

Paul McCartney did take his band, Wings, to Lagos, Nigeria, in 1973 to record *Band on the Run*. He was also robbed at knifepoint one night with his wife Linda and lost all of the demos and lyrics the band had worked on so far.

The invention in this book is that the Beatles, not Wings, had taken the trip to Nigeria.

LIFE IN LOS ANGELES

John Lennon called it his "Lost Weekend." By any name, the eighteen-month banishment to LA by his wife really happened. So did his awful behavior in the club circuit where he did, in fact, harass the Smothers Brothers and put a Kotex on his head. It got that bad.

He did not live in Laurel Canyon, nor did he date Linda Ronstadt. That part is an invention of this literary work. However, if the Beatles had gone to Los Angeles during the 1972 election period, much would have changed as a result. They would have met other people, and some of those people might have been part of the Laurel Canyon scene. As it was in our timeline, some of those people, notably James Taylor, did record for Apple, and others, like Crosby, Stills, Nash & Young, almost did.

And, yes, John Lennon and his son Julian did spend the day on the set of *Happy Days*. There are pictures to prove it. All the nice things the cast and crew said about John Lennon in this book were as described, including the much-appreciated doodles he did for everyone. If you want a nice memory of John Lennon, imagine him with Julian on the set of *Happy Days* having a great time.

STEVE JOBS

Steve Jobs did not meet George Harrison in India. On the other hand, Jobs was in India on his life-altering trip as described by Walter Isaacson in his biography, *Steve Jobs*, at the same time as the Lennon kidnapping happens in our alternative timeline.

It could have happened, had George gone to India when John was taken, and that license is what makes alternate history work.

KIDNAPPED

The Lennon kidnapping of this book is based, loosely, on the massively publicized celebrity kidnapping of Patricia Hearst by the Symbionese Liberation Army that took place in 1974. Like John Lennon in this book, Hearst was simply going about her life when she was plucked from it and thrust into a radical politics drama that captivated the entire world.

The Lennon kidnapping is also informed by research into the

path of the Weather Underground by this point in time. Leaders of the group—like Bernardine Dohrn and William Ayers—were desperate and looking for a big play, something to stoke the fires of revolution that they saw burning down into barely glimmering embers. Ayers went on to become Barack Obama's friend and their relationship was used to try to block his march to the presidency because of his friend's radical past.

CONCERT IN CENTRAL PARK

Simon and Garfunkel are best remembered for their big Central Park Concert in 1981. Others preceded it, but it was the biggest and most widely publicized concert.

It is true, also, that there was interest from the city of New York to stage a concert in Central Park throughout the 1970s. Numerous mentions of a feasibility study are in the literature.

ACKNOWLEDGMENTS

There would be no book, of course, without George Harrison, John Lennon, Paul McCartney, and Richard Starkey. Thank you.

My older brother, Alan Zabel, brought the *Sgt. Pepper's Lonely Hearts Club Band* album back home to Oregon from MIT and changed my life. My college friends, Karta Purkh Singh Khalsa, Ralph Kolby, and Taylor Welsh, continued my Beatles education.

Special thanks for early encouragement to Lauren Zabel, Jonathan Zabel, Eric Estrin, Rick Porras, Evan Kent, Steve Elzer, Howard Karel, Daniaile Jarry, Randall Klein, and Don Most.

Diversion Books editor Lia Ottaviano gave my original manuscript a fresh read, fired back some great comments, and helped to build the book more solidly. Sheelonee Banerjee gave it a fine edit that found and fixed all the inconsistencies. Sarah Masterson Hally produced a beautiful looking novel from this work.

Our graphics team includes Diversion's talented cover artist, Scotland's Kit Foster, and my brilliant Los Angeles friend and Movie Smackdown partner, Lynda Karr (who created a collection of albums that never were), with other graphics contributions used in our promotion campaign from Ireland's Georgina Flood, Argentina's Pablo Lobato, Miami's PhoJoe, and USC's Nate Gualtieri.

The book's personal rock star is Brian Bringelson, who took the book's storyline about showing up and turned it into "Show Up," performing, singing, and arranging his terrific version with his band, Anchor & Bear, with Katy Pearson and Eric White. Directing and editing, Jared Zabel turned the performance into an evocative 1971 music video that shows the Beatles still having fun together. Thanks and appreciation to Kc Staples for mixing this song and letting us shoot at his amazing vintage studio. Final thanks to Edward Kaspar, Anthony Abbas, Clinton Staples, Theo Kokiousis, and Danny Carter for being a part of the shoot.

Beatles fans, of course, get the final shout-out. Without their persistent love and interest over the years, there would be no reason to have written the book in the first place.

CNN correspondent-turned-screenwriter **BRYCE ZABEL** has created five primetime network television series (i.e., *Dark Skies, The Crow*) and written and produced on a dozen TV writing staffs (i.e., *Lois and Clark, L.A. Law, Steven Spielberg Presents Taken*).

Bryce is a produced feature writer in both live-action (*Mortal Kombat: Annihilation*) and animation (*Atlantis: The Lost Empire*). His latest big-budget feature film is *The Last Battle*, based on a *New York Times* bestseller, being produced with Europe's STUDIOCANAL in the spring of 2018.

Bryce and his wife, writer/producer Jackie Zabel, won the Writers Guild of America (WGA) Award for writing *Pandemic*, his third four-hour Hallmark mini-series (the first two being *The Poseidon Adventure* and *Blackbeard*). Bryce and Jackie's Stellar Productions has produced for nearly all major Hollywood networks and studios.

Bryce served as the elected chairman/CEO of the Academy of Television Arts & Sciences (now, The Television Academy), the first writer in that position since Rod Serling. He has taught graduate-level screenwriting at the USC School of Cinematic Arts. Bryce's debut novel, *Surrounded by Enemies: What if Kennedy Survived Dallas?*, won the coveted Sidewise Award for Alternate History.

For more information and additional material,
please visit **www.WhatIfBeatles.com**.

Printed in the USA
CPSIA information can be obtained
at www.ICGtesting.com
JSHW031708140824
68134JS00038B/3578